MW01404692

Beach Bliss

ALSO BY JOANNE DEMAIO

The Seaside Saga

Blue Jeans and Coffee Beans
The Denim Blue Sea
Beach Blues
Beach Breeze
The Beach Inn
Beach Bliss
Castaway Cottage
Night Beach
Little Beach Bungalow
Every Summer
–And More Seaside Saga Books–

Summer Standalone Novels

True Blend
Whole Latte Life

Winter Novels

Eighteen Winters
First Flurries
Cardinal Cabin
Snow Deer and Cocoa Cheer
Snowflakes and Coffee Cakes

beach bliss

A NOVEL

JOANNE DEMAIO

This is a work of fiction. Names, characters, places, and incidents are either the product of the author's imagination or are used fictitiously. Any resemblance to actual persons, living or dead, events, or locales is entirely coincidental.

No part of this book may be reproduced, or stored in a retrieval system, or transmitted in any form or by any means, electronic, mechanical, photocopying, recording, or otherwise, now known or hereinafter invented, without express written permission of the copyright owner.

Copyright © 2018 Joanne DeMaio
All rights reserved.

ISBN: 1984227114
ISBN-13: 9781984227119

Joannedemaio.com

To Sound View

A Connecticut beach where
nostalgic memories spin their own stories.

one

BEYOND THE DUNE GRASS, LONG Island Sound sparkles beneath the summer sunshine. It's a sight that never escapes Elsa's attention. Standing on the sloping lawn, she takes in that sweeping view of blue. All the while, there's more. There's the morning dew, dampening her sandal-clad feet. And there's the sea breeze, skimming her face. Just a few short years ago, she could never have imagined being in this place in life. Yet here she is, about to open her newly renovated beach inn at Stony Point. Oh, if she'd only logged her journey.

But with a glance at the Mason jar in her hand, she realizes she has. This particular glass jar is filled with beach sand, and seashells, and a piece of driftwood tucked beside a dried hydrangea blossom. The flower petals have faded to a pale blue and tan. Elsa pauses, and in that moment, every bit of the evening she created this memory jar comes to her. It was at twilight, almost a year ago now, on the day her son was buried. The only way she found peace then was to walk the beach and drop into that jar little seaside things reminding her of Salvatore's life. Flowers … the same blue color he loved. Driftwood … the same worn wood as his cherished rowboat.

And like the turning tide, peace gradually swept back into her days. As it has, she's filled even more jars with tokens and keepsakes to chart her memories, much like a diary.

"Some people say to keep diaries," Elsa says now, lifting the glass jar. "But I say to keep happiness jars."

"*Cut.* Cut, cut, cut, Elsa."

"What?" She looks to Jason standing with the camera crew filming this segment for his new cottage-renovation show. With his hand to his chin, Jason's shaking his head. "What's wrong this time?" she asks him.

"Where's the smile?"

"Didn't I smile?"

"No. We want a big smile for the audience. This clip is for the pilot episode, so it needs a lot of enthusiasm." Jason turns to a producer beside him, who nods in agreement.

Elsa eyes them both. "I *know* I smiled."

"Just give us a little more." As he says it, Jason steps back, arms crossed in front of him.

The producer, Trent, motions to the cameraman, and Elsa takes her position again. The long silver blouse she wears over black leggings flutters in the breeze. On cue, she says her opening line for the third time, or maybe the fourth. "Some people say to keep diaries." Here, she leaves a dramatic pause while stealing a calming glance over at the distant blue water. "But I say to keep jars. Oh! Oh, shoot. I left out a word. *Happiness* jars."

Jason shakes his head and turns up his hands. Once he resettles into his staid stance, sunglasses on, Elsa tries again.

And once more.

Then again.

But each time, there's something wrong. First, a falling wisp of hair bothers her eye, making her blink funny. So an assistant rushes in, pats down the wisp and powders her nose before Elsa tries again. Next, she has a frog in her throat, and *happiness jars* comes out all croaky.

Finally, she pulls it off. Comfortable on the grounds of her renovated beach inn, her entire talk sounds casual and effortless, with just the right smile. The cameraman tapes her standing beside a table covered with white linens and anchored with a big white lantern at each end. Empty Mason jars wait to be filled with displayed shells and stones there. Elsa explains how every guest in her seaside inn will receive their own happiness jar to decorate with trinkets from their beach stay.

"The glass jars will brim with sea glass and stories. Seashells and summer memories."

Then? Well, then she sneezes.

When Elsa slumps with disappointment, Jason does, too. The local public television station's camera crew finished filming the Ocean Star Inn's renovation days ago, and the taping went so smoothly, he should've known. There had to be a snag coming, or some problem—especially with the network's looming deadline. Nothing ever goes off without a hitch. Not in his life.

Today, Elsa's the hitch.

And he gets it. It's not easy standing in front of that camera and talking to a lens. He just wrapped up his own months' worth of scenes: being recorded in the new inn's gutted kitchen; on the scaffolding of each level of the grand turret; doing extensive demo work. As the show's host, Jason explained shingle options and the purpose of wide roof overhangs. While the renovated structure seemingly rose from the sand, he shared the old cottage's history, too. Before it was a shingled seaside inn, it was known simply as Foley's, a small market and hangout spot for the Stony Point vacationers.

Proof enough that, in architecture, the best-designed buildings outlast their original use.

Now, this Friday morning, it's Elsa's turn to be filmed in a special segment for the pilot episode: showing viewers how to make their own happiness jars. Unfortunately, she's struggled with the offshore breeze blowing wisps of her brown hair across her face. And her fingers have toyed with her silver coin necklace. And she's discreetly, but repeatedly, cleared her throat. All little things, but enough to kill a scene. When she almost nails it, of course her sneeze undermines the whole take.

"Bless you," Jason tells her. "But it *was* sounding kind of clinical, Elsa."

"Well, that's because it's coming from index cards ... and not from my heart!"

Which prompts Jason to walk to her, gently lift the index card notes off the table and rip them in half. "Take seven," he says when he moves beside the cameraman again, then crosses his arms over his chest.

"You're distracting me now." When Elsa squints over at him, she gives him an order with a stamp of her jeweled sandal. "Stop looking at me like that."

"Like *what?*" Jason asks.

"I don't know. Like I'm hopeless." Elsa sets down her cherished happiness jar, her fingers brushing the glass, her silver bangles jangling. "Maybe we should try this tomorrow. I'm tired now."

"No, no." Jason walks to her again. "The lighting won't be the same. It's perfect today—not too hot for the middle of June."

Trent steps in, explaining how they want a crystal-blue sky behind her.

As he talks, Elsa swats at a bug hovering close to her arm. "What *is* that?"

"A dragonfly!" Jason says. "And dragonflies are very atmospheric, actually. Leave it alone." Meanwhile, Elsa's distress gets him to pull his cell phone from his pocket. In two seconds flat, he's texting Nick, asking for backup. Assuming he's around on guard duty, Nick should be able to help. After a few lines of explanation, Jason types in, *Bring me the works. 10-33.*

In no time, Nick answers with his own text. *10-33? Emergency situation? Seriously, I'm on it.*

Jason only hopes he's fast. Especially when he's returning his phone to his pocket and notices a new minor catastrophe. As Elsa regroups and prepares for another take, she backs straight into the table, bumping it and spilling sand everywhere.

Lord knows, Elsa's patience with this segment is wearing thin. But during the past several months? She's had the patience of a saint as her inn's walls came down. As hammers nailed up framing; as that imposing turret took shape; as custom floor-to-ceiling windows went in and cedar shingles were hung; as deck railings were installed and a rock wall built.

So Jason hurries over and neatens the simple bowl of sand intended to fill happiness jars. He brushes several grains off the table while advising Elsa to be more careful. "We're on a tight schedule, and budget."

"Oh, *basta*! *Basta!*" She steps back and eyes Jason. "Enough! Just like I used to say to my son."

"Sal."

Elsa nods.

Okay, so she's tense, and he's tense. But it's up to Jason to settle things down—he is the show's host, after all. So he brings in the magic words, words she cannot deny. "And *Sal* would want this scene to be perfect, too. No? With the beach inn he loved being the premiere episode of a cottage-renovation show? He deserves—"

"Only the best," Elsa quietly finishes.

"Exactly. So when you're looking into the camera, you're not talking to me. Or the crew. Talk like you would to your son, okay?"

Before Elsa even has a chance to agree, she's distracted by Nick arriving with a familiar white paper bag in one hand, take-out coffee tray in the other.

"Time out?" Jason asks the producer and cameraman, who motion for him to take five. So he does, grabbing the bag from Nick with a quick thanks, then leading Elsa to the bistro table set up on the far side of her inn.

"You're right, you know," Elsa says as she sits.

"You're hungry, then?"

"No. No, I mean about Sal. If I look out at that water view, I can just imagine my son watching over me … whispering *Sorridi, Ma*, as he does."

Jason glances at her while he lifts out the two wrapped egg sandwiches and a paper envelope stuffed with home fries, but he doesn't say anything. Because if there's one thing he knows all about, it's hearing voices in the sea breeze, in the rustling dune grass. He also notices Elsa pressing napkins open on the table before unfolding the sandwich wrappings, too.

"And I guess I *am* starved with all this work," she says while lifting the top of her croissant roll and examining the cheese melted over her egg.

"Here." Jason slides a few ketchup packets her way, then rips one open with his teeth. "If we could finish this filming today," he says while swirling the ketchup on his egg concoction, then pressing the roll down, "it would really help. The episode is ready to go into final edits."

Elsa raises her sandwich, takes a big bite and nods as her eyes flutter closed. But it's clear that her thoughts are firing as she raises a finger while chewing. "I *am* doing the best I can, Jason."

"I know you are. But with the budget exhausted, this might be our last day with the film crew. If things don't work out, your happiness jars won't make the cut."

"And I told you I only have a couple hours free." She checks her silver mesh watch, then snags a mouthful of home fries. "I have an appointment at the jewelers to custom-order Celia's star necklace." Elsa pats a napkin to her mouth, then picks up her sandwich again. "I really don't have any more time today."

"Hang on." Jason watches as she manages a big bite of cheesy egg, then sips her coffee. "Elsa, the film crew's waiting. Just give it one more go?" He clasps her hand on the tabletop. "I have a feeling you'll get it this time, with a little egg sandwich in you."

He's not sure what does it then, the food or his wink—which she waves off in a huff. But she nods and manages a reluctant "Okay" around another bite of her convenience-store specialty sandwich. The miracle sandwich that always seems to do the trick.

After sliding open one of the trailer-office windows, Cliff Raines sits at his metal tanker desk. It's utilitarian with those squeaking drawers and worn leather blotter—a far cry from the stately courthouses where he used to preside as judge. But this workspace suits his life now. Here at the beach, the damp salt air gets at everything, so he needs a desk that can stand up to a beating.

And to these darn beach doughnuts the kids got him hooked on. Cliff pulls one from a bag and takes a bite—unfortunately before spreading out his napkin. Grains of sugar drop on his desk, so he slides over the trash can and sweeps the sugar into it. Don't need ants marching across his paperwork.

Of course, Elsa's been telling him this trailer isn't suitable for a beach commissioner, but she doesn't really get it. The beach is all about sand and salt, sea spray and grit and nature's coastal elements. So his modular trailer feels like a fortress with its scuffed metal stairs leading to a steel-door entrance. Not to mention that the trailer's clean lines, flat roof and hardy metal features could pass for that mid-century modern style that's all the rage.

Heck, nobody but Elsa and Jason even *knows* that he also lives in his official office headquarters. That's a fact Cliff hides from the rest of the beach community—and a nosy beach community at that. Folks have already been hounding him for the next issue of the Stony Point newsletter. So he pulls up the draft on his computer screen and skims it, typing a few changes to the opening.

Greetings from Stony Point Beach! With June here, another summer season is upon us.

"Darn," he says then, when his fingers stick to a key. And

it's painfully obvious why they're sticking. It's that doughnut on the napkin, the doughnut he lifts and leans to the side to bite into, hearing the sugar grains drop into the trash can as he does. So he stuffs the last of the sweet morsel into his mouth, brushes his hands over the trash, then gets up. If he doesn't wash the doughnut crumbs from his fingers, he'll be fighting a sticky keyboard all morning.

If nothing else, this gives him a good excuse to put on a record while he works on the newsletter. Nothing like a musical interlude to get the noggin firing. So behind the accordion-style door separating his discreet living quarters from the office, he washes his hands in the kitchenette sink. Then, and only then, he reaches for one of his prized possessions—a Dean Martin album. It's the same one his parents danced to on an old cottage deck of his childhood. Gently, he sets the album on the record player's turntable and drops the needle in place.

"Better," Cliff says to himself when he returns to his desk, hearing the crooner's warbling voice fill the trailer. It'd be nice to bring some of Dino's swagger to his newsletter writing, to give some 'tude to the dull updated ordinances on fence installations, golf cart speed limits and food restrictions on the beach. Finally, he sets his dancing hands over the keyboard and concludes that section with his infamous *The rules are the rules.*

When he moves on to writing the next section, his phone rings.

"I'll be late for guard duty," Nick informs him when he answers. "Have to help out Jason."

"Jason? You work for me, Nicholas. You're on my payroll, don't forget."

"I'll just be a few minutes."

"Who's guarding the trestle when you're gone? Fridays are busy, heading into the weekend."

"I'll put up that dummy video surveillance sign. No one will know the difference," Nick adds before clicking off.

Cliff is very much aware that Jason Barlow—resident coastal architect—is running the show around here lately. He's wrapping up filming for the pilot episode of a new CT-TV program on cottage renovations. But Cliff couldn't be more pleased that the first episode is of Elsa's beach inn restoration. It means she's sticking around this little Connecticut beach town, for good.

With that, he inserts a photograph from last fall into the newsletter. It's a shot of Jason sitting in the notorious Foley's hangout room and signing his official TV contract. The whole gang gathers round the booth where Jason sits, pen in hand. The jukebox glows in the background; twinkly lights line the rusted sliding windows.

So much has happened since that October night.

But Cliff begins his beach news with this: an announcement. Jason's premiere episode will air first to the Stony Point community, right on the movie screen on the beach. *B.Y.O.S. Bring your own sand chair!* he adds.

Then, the question is, what should go next? His scuffed domino leans against the stapler. That domino's been a good-luck talisman ever since he picked it up last summer in the Maritime Market parking lot. So he joggles the domino in his hand while skimming sticky notes plastered to the edge of his computer screen. Would Nick's college graduation announcement be a suitable lead-in? Or maybe the Ocean Star Inn's grand opening details?

Still toying with the domino, Cliff pushes back in his chair.

From behind him, Dean Martin sings of a girl and a boy, and memories of joy. Dean's mention of moonbeams and dreams, then, has Cliff think of a sweet lullaby being sung to a baby. A precious little baby. A new one in particular, beloved by everyone here at Stony Point.

That's it. It's time for the very special birth announcement of a baby who deserves every misty moonbeam that drops into its life, a life that everyone hopes is the stuff of dreams.

A heartfelt congratulations, Cliff types, *goes out to our resident innkeeper, Elsa DeLuca, on the arrival of her grandchild! Proud mother Celia Gray has been very busy wheeling the newborn along the boardwalk while enjoying seaside strolls in the sweet salt air. You might see Celia at times, strumming a lullaby on her guitar beneath the boardwalk's shade pavilion. And we're sure that the baby's father, the late Salvatore DeLuca, is smiling down on his child, little …*

Before he can type the baby's name, Cliff gets choked up thinking of Sal and his ready smile, something Sal so often encouraged others to do. To simply smile. *Sorridi.*

And so Cliff does. He makes *himself* smile while shaking his head in bittersweet happiness before finishing the long-awaited birth announcement for all to read.

two

THE NICE THING ABOUT SITTING in the Dockside Diner is that Maris can feel like she's in a boat out at sea. From the fishing net dotted with starfish and seashells draped along the far wall, to the miniature glass fishing globes hanging in the booth-side windows, to the sparkling harbor beyond the shops across the street, she might as well be hoisting a mast on one of those harbor sailboats.

"And how are things coming with the book?" Eva, her sister, asks. Sitting across from Maris, she sips coffee and digs into her scrambled eggs.

It's just that sort of easy chatter that Maris relishes now. Having left her denim design career behind last year in an attempt to focus on her family, Maris' weekly catch-ups with Eva are about far more than coffee. They're about making time and being present with those you love, something her cousin Sal was all for. So for the past several months—while sipping java on the boardwalk, or on Eva's kitchen window seat, or right here at the diner—Maris' life took new shape. Because her long-lost sister is in Stony Point; as is her aunt, Elsa; and of course, her husband, Jason.

Even a new career is here, too.

Considering her sister's book question, Maris spreads jam on her whole-wheat toast. Kyle's diner has the best around, homemade and fluffy as a cloud. "The writing ... It's going okay, but slow. I can't rush the process, and am really stuck on one particular chapter. I could use a male perspective, but Jason's too close to the story to judge it."

"Well, Matt's working so much overtime on the force. But he'd do it, I'm sure. Want me to ask him?"

"That's nice of you to offer. But I don't want to impose on your husband. And anyway, the distractions lately don't help, either. Especially with Jason and his show. I've actually been holing myself up, working in Neil's old shack. I love having another little office set up in there."

"I still can't believe Jason had a tugboat tow his brother's shack off that hidden beach!"

"That's my guy, very supportive of my writing venture." Maris thinks of her cherished time in that salvaged fishing shack, which Jason moved beside their barn studio at home. Whenever she sees the shack's silver shingles covered with old lobster buoys, it brings pure writing inspiration. A creative hideaway ... in her own backyard!

But it's when she's inside the shack that she feels the presence of Jason's late brother, all while surrounded by Neil's salt-coated leather journals; by his old baskets and jars filled with dusty shells and faded sea glass. His brief life seems idled, right inside those weathered walls.

"I try to summon Neil," Maris explains. "Because it's still his novel, after all, and I want to honor his vision. So I light his hurricane lanterns and it's very atmospheric—*when* I get a quiet hour or two to write."

"Oh, I hear you, sister," Eva tells her while adding a shake of salt to her hash browns. "I've been busy with cottage rentals, though there *are* less this year. Folks seem to be bypassing our little beach lately. Then I've got Taylor's sweet-sixteen party next week at Elsa's inn."

"Nice. Elsa loves to practice with events like that, before the grand opening."

"It'll be a beach party," Eva adds. "Tay invited a few friends and they're bringing bathing suits, plus having a sleepover, since school will be out for the summer then."

Maris looks over as Kyle approaches from the kitchen. He's carrying a carafe of hot coffee and stops at their table.

"Now that's service," Maris says. "Food delivered by the chef himself."

Kyle simply nods as he tops off their mugs. He's wearing his long chef apron over black pants and a black tee. But he's unusually quiet. No chit-chat, no trivia, no fun fact to jump-start their Friday.

"Everything okay?" Eva asks. "You all ready for the big moving day tomorrow?"

"Lauren actually started today. We've been living with her parents so the kids could finish the school year in Eastfield. Now Lauren and her dad are moving as many boxes as possible to our new house this morning." He pulls his cell phone out of his pocket and flicks to a photograph of his daughter, Hailey, sitting in a carton with a plush stuffed cat.

"Aw, she's so cute, Kyle." Eva passes the phone to Maris. "Maybe you'll get her a *real* cat once you're settled."

"Whenever that'll be." Kyle reaches for a napkin and swipes his forehead.

Giving him a warm smile, Eva pats Kyle's arm and says,

"It'll be okay, you'll see."

"Appreciate that, Eva," Kyle says while checking his watch.

"Don't forget," Maris reminds him. "We'll all be there tomorrow to help you move in. The whole gang."

"Great. But hey, I've really got to get out of here and give Lauren a hand." He turns toward the kitchen. "Yo, Jerry. You ready to cover for me?"

"You're the boss now, kid," Jerry shouts from the stove as he looks out past his order carousel. "When you bought this place from me, you became Captain."

"Oh, boy. Tension's mounting for poor Kyle," Maris says when he hurries back to the kitchen, right as her cell phone rings. She slides it closer on the table. "It's Jason," she tells Eva while lifting the phone. "Hey, babe. How'd filming go at the inn?"

"Tedious," Jason tells her. "I'm not sure Elsa is on speaking terms with me."

"But you're her favorite nephew-in-law," Maris insists, giving a shrug to Eva—whose husband is *also* Elsa's nephew-in-law.

"Maybe," Jason says. "We finished up, but it wasn't easy today. Elsa was a little tense … until an egg sandwich calmed her down."

"Is she there? Let me talk to her."

"She had to leave for an appointment at that jewelers in town," Jason explains. "Wants to order a star necklace for Celia."

"What!"

"What happened?" Eva asks, her sister-radar ever tuned to Maris' conversation.

"Now I'm miffed," Maris says into her phone.

"What's *wrong*?" Eva whispers across the table. When she leans close to eavesdrop on the conversation, her blonde-streaked auburn hair falls forward.

"It's Elsa," Maris quickly whispers back. "She's buying Celia's star necklace … alone. And she's so distracted, she'll never pick out the right one!"

Eva raises an eyebrow, and Maris nods. Because, oh yes, she already knows what Eva's next question will be.

"You game?" Eva asks.

Maris quickly ends her call with Jason, slips on her knit shrug over her tank top, grabs her car keys and stands. "Let's go."

Emerald cut. Round. Oval. Baguette. Sitting on a stool in the local jewelry store, Elsa is surrounded by gems of every cut, size and shape. Precious stones of every brilliance and luster.

But none are as precious as her new grandchild.

Which is why Elsa keeps flipping pages and pages of catalogs at the counter. It's the gold stars in particular that she's seeking, wondering if she should match her own—because none in the catalog seem good enough, brilliant enough, special enough.

"We can make something custom, if nothing in the catalog catches your eye," the jeweler explains. "Will any of those work for you?" he asks with a nod to the pages.

"No. Nothing yet, Mr. Russo."

"I have one more catalog in the back that we can check."

Meanwhile, stars, stars glimmer all around her. White gold and yellow. Polished and brushed. And seeing these stars, constellations of them on the glossy pages, has Elsa think of fate. And destiny. After all, it's been said that what's written in the stars is destined to be.

Heaven knows, her life has had many fated celestial moments these past few years. If she had to pinpoint when it began, it would be with the arrival of a wedding invitation to Jason and Maris' wedding two summers ago, while Elsa still lived in Milan.

That one piece of paper led to an emotional reunion with both Maris and Eva, the two nieces she hadn't seen in thirty years.

Which led to Elsa uprooting her life and starting it over here, on the Connecticut shoreline, at Stony Point Beach.

A decision that lured her son here from his Wall Street career in New York City, for his final seaside summer.

Her son, Sal, who then fell in love with Elsa's new beach friend, Celia.

Who just last month gave birth to Elsa's only grandchild.

Oh, what a winding, sad, beautiful constellation of moments.

And this moment today is just like so many, many years ago, when it was the first time she picked out star pendants for herself and her very young nieces. After her sister, June, had died, it seemed the only way to keep her scattered family connected across the ocean—connected symbolically by stars on gold chains. A little family constellation.

"Mrs. DeLuca?" the jeweler asks now.

Elsa looks up just as this Mr. Russo hands her his last catalog, opened to the star pendants. With a quick glance at a smooth, simple star, she makes a sudden decision.

"Oh! I think I like that one!"

"Wait just a minute, Aunt Elsa!"

The voice is familiar, unmistakably so. Elsa spins around to see her two nieces, Maris and Eva, rushing across the store in a beeline straight to her. "What *ever* are you doing here?" Elsa asks them.

"Remember?" Maris asks while waggling a finger. "There are no secrets at Stony Point."

"It was Jason, wasn't it?" Elsa puts her hands on her hips. "You talked to Jason."

Eva comes up right beside her and turns the catalog for a better look. "What are you doing picking out star necklaces by yourself?"

"You're all so busy!" Elsa explains, turning the catalog back.

Then it happens. These two sisters do what they so often do—as though on cue. Maris and Eva say the exact same thing. "We are *never* too busy for you!"

"What pendant did you pick?" Maris asks while coming up on the other side of Elsa's stool at the counter and pulling the catalog closer.

"That one." Elsa points to her star choice. "Something different from ours."

"What?" Eva demands.

"Different?" Maris lifts the catalog and scrutinizes the picture, then sets it down. "Are you sure you want to do that?"

Elsa looks at the catalog page, at the small stack of catalogs she just thumbed through, at Eva first, then Maris. And when she finally shakes her head no, it's with tear-filled eyes.

Which is all it takes for both her nieces to instantly wrap their arms around her, and whisper assurances, and find two more stools to pull up to the counter so they can sit beside her.

"Elsa. When you bought our beautiful star necklaces decades ago," Eva says, lifting her own etched-star pendant from the braided chain around her neck, "they were identical. Yours, Maris', mine and even our mother's, though she never had the chance to wear it."

"June." Elsa reaches over and touches Eva's necklace.

"Yes," Eva says. "It's what makes them special. We know we're all linked, wearing the *same* gold stars. So you need to copy ours."

"Now *that* we can do," the jeweler says as he examines Eva's necklace first, then starts noting details on an order form. "This pendant *can* be replicated for you, and inscribed."

"Wait." Elsa reaches out to stop the jeweler from writing. When he does, she turns to her nieces. "You're *sure* you two are okay with this?"

"Yes!" Maris and Eva state together.

"Now there are six of us connected," Maris nearly whispers, the moment is so special.

"Including June's spirit," Elsa adds.

Eva nods beside her. "And we can *always* lean on each other."

"Okay." Elsa hugs her nieces, then turns to the jeweler. "And when could they be ready?" she asks. "I need two necklaces. Exactly alike."

"Two?" Mr. Russo confirms. "I thought it was only one, for the mother of your grandchild."

Elsa smiles warmly. "Oh, no. Two, please. One for my *granddaughter*, and one for her mother."

"Wonderful!" The jeweler adds a second note to the order. "Two it is, then. It'll be a few weeks, give or take."

"That's fine," Elsa explains. "At least I'll have them in time for the baby's christening."

"So one pendant is to be inscribed *Celia*," the jeweler

clarifies. "And the other? For your granddaughter?" He pauses, pen poised over the order form.

When Elsa hesitates, the jeweler looks up from his paperwork at the same time that Maris clasps her hand. They have no way of knowing that Elsa is remembering how Celia quietly told her the baby's name in the hospital, right after giving birth. Celia was exhausted and happy at once—her hair damp with perspiration, her face pale. *Aria*, Celia had said while lying in bed with the baby in her arms. *Italian for air, because, well … the sea air.* She'd paused then, inhaled a long breath, and continued. *It cures what ails you. And little Aria is just the cure I need in my life. Oh, Elsa I feel nothing but love now, and peace, with Sal's baby in my arms.*

"Aria," Elsa whispers.

"Aria? A very lovely name."

"Yes," Elsa explains. "She's named for what her father loved most in his brief life … *Aria di mare.* It's Italian, of course, for the sea air."

In the barn studio behind his home, tracing paper and a few sketches cover Jason's drafting table. He adjusts the angle of the swing-arm lamp over the table, just as a breeze comes in through the open slider. The warm salt air rustles the leaves on the tall maple tree outside.

Almost summer, he hears in its whisper.

"No shit, Neil." Jason pulls a finished blueprint from his rolling bin of plans and opens it over the loose papers in front of him. "As usual, I'm swamped trying to beat that damn Hammer Law." It's an added pressure come every June, that local ordinance preventing construction during the summer months. But it's the only way to keep the seaside community tranquil for the vacationers.

Problem is, Jason's been working on a cottage on Bayside Road, not too far from Kyle's new digs. If his contractor could just meet the Hammer Law deadline and finish up the dual peaks added to the second level, this job would be done before summer sets in.

It's sometimes hard to believe that another summer *is* here—the tenth since Jason's brother died. But with all that's happened in the past year, he's at least relieved to feel his brother's presence again, to hear his voice. Whether it's Neil's spirit or merely Jason's memories hovering about, he'll take it, either way.

"After last summer—losing Sal this time ..." Jason pauses, remembering his cousin who'd been like a brother to him. "Well, I didn't know if I could pull off another one here, again."

With that, all is silent. The breeze subsides; the birds outside quiet. It's a moment Jason would like to bottle on this June day beneath a clear sky. Serenity, or peace—he can't get enough of it lately. Upstairs, in Maris' loft, Madison lies on the floor with her muzzle beneath the second-level railing. It's the German shepherd's way of keeping an eye on him while he works. Even the dog is still now, except for her tall ears following any sound Jason makes.

"You there, Neil?" Jason's hand goes to his father's Vietnam dog tags hanging on his neck, and he slides them back and forth along the silver chain.

Always here when you need me, Jason barely makes out as he joggles the dog tags in his hand.

So he rolls up the final print on the Bayside job, glad that his client is satisfied with the outcome—changing the hip roof to a gable to accommodate the new peaks on the bungalow, all of it polished off with yellow-hued cedar shingles and wide white trim. He gathers together his pens and markers, ready to finish up the workday.

What's next? he hears his brother ask right as he drops those writing utensils clattering onto a tray.

So Jason stands and stretches, feeling stiff from sitting a few hours this Friday afternoon. Two or three knee bends help loosen his muscles, which probably would've felt better if he'd removed his prosthetic limb before settling in at his drafting table. At the prospect of sudden activity, Madison jumps up and rushes to him, her collar jangling as she hurries down the stairs.

Running his knuckle along the scar on his jaw, Jason repeats his brother's question. "What's next? Finding another cottage reno for Trent, over at CT-TV. Got a pile of submissions he's feeling good about." Jason heads to his big L-shaped desk, where the submissions are neatly stacked. "Can't go wrong thinking positively," he adds while paging through the first five or six in the pile.

Now there's a change. Then what? The wood-planked floor creaks right as Jason hears the question.

Before he answers, the screen door slides open and Maris walks in. Her brown hair is down; she wears a simple black tank over faded denim board shorts. As always, her star necklace glimmers around her neck. And before she can take even two steps, Madison runs to her and prances around her feet.

"Time for a walk on the beach with my beautiful wife,"

Jason says as though talking to Maris. But he also throws a glance at the framed photograph of Neil above a display of masonry tools on the far wall.

"And afterward, dinner at The Clam Shack, babe?" Maris calls back while lifting Madison's leather leash off a wall hook.

There it is again, that idea of peace. Serenity. Sitting outside on one of the seafood joint's stone tables at the mouth of the Connecticut River, his wife by his side? Jason can't think of a better Friday dinner. Bliss.

So he walks across the rough-hewn floor, gives his wife a quick kiss, touches her face, then leads her outside, before sliding the door closed behind them.

Later, bro, he hears, getting Jason to glance over his shoulder as he leaves with Maris and the dog. Together they cross the yard, headed in the vague direction of the beach for a leisurely, late-afternoon seaside walk.

three

IT FEELS LIKE HE'S VISITING. Like he's a guest in someone else's cottage on the bay. Walking through the living room late Saturday morning, and hearing chatting voices in the kitchen, yes, Kyle gets that niggling feeling he's a little late to someone's party.

Not like he's walking through his own house. His very own year-round home at Stony Point.

In the kitchen, all the lights are on, and boxes—some opened, some still sealed—line the countertops. Kyle's wife and her friends bustle about, inspecting cabinets and pulling coffee cups and plates and utensils out of the boxes. Wearing leggings, long tees, sneakers and bandanas, there's no mistaking that the women are ready to dig in and get everything unpacked. Even Elsa is helping, wiping out empty drawers, asking Lauren where she wants to stack dishes and silverware.

"Guess the gang's all here," Kyle says from the kitchen doorway. Everyone—Maris and her sister, Eva; their aunt, Elsa; and Lauren—pauses and turns to him. "Jason's backing in the truck," Kyle adds. "Shouldn't take too long moving the furniture in, with lots of helping hands."

Lauren walks over, kisses his cheek and prods him toward the back door. "We've got the kitchen covered, hon. It's the most important room."

"So we can get everybody fed later," Eva tells him as she pulls open the flaps of another carton.

Okay, so they've obviously got this under control. Kyle heads outside just as Cliff and Nick are pulling into the driveway in Cliff's car stuffed with a hand truck, moving straps and furniture sliders. At the same time, Matt's opening the rear of the moving van. The interior is jam-packed, right to the brim. Chairs and mattresses and end tables and mirrors are finagled in every which way.

"*Gesù, Santa Maria,*" Jason says. He stands there in his cargo shorts, tee and work boots, while carefully eyeing the furniture stash. "How much stuff do you own?"

Kyle walks up beside him and considers the household inventory crammed into the truck. "Hey. You let me know what your house looks like when you have kids, and your cozy family of two grows to four. Or five."

"Five?" Jason asks, still mesmerized by the truck's contents.

"What are you waiting for, anyway?" Kyle gives him a shove. "Clock's ticking, guy."

"A lot of clocks are ticking. We're busy, Kyle. Maris is finishing Neil's book, and I'm getting my show off the ground."

Matt joins them, squinting at the dressers and stools and chests of drawers. "Fair warning, fellas. Just keep your women away from little Aria."

"No kidding," Kyle agrees. Behind him, he hears the thud of car doors closing as Nick and Cliff head their way.

"Keep Maris away from Aria?" Jason asks with a glance. "Why?"

"Something comes over them, some baby fever." Matt looks over his shoulder toward the kitchen window. "Eva's ready to try for another kid, even with Tay being sixteen. It's like my wife's put in a trance whenever she's around Celia's *bambina*."

Jason looks toward the kitchen, too. "That can't be true. Just by holding a baby?"

"No. No, guy. You got it all wrong." Matt turns to face Jason and musses his dark hair. "It's that baby *shampoo* smell that does it. It's like an elixir, I'm telling you. Eva's eyes glaze over and she talks baby talk, all *cootchie-cootchie-coo*."

"No shit."

"It's true," Kyle assures Jason. "Hell, Lauren's ready to *give up* her long-awaited art studio for a nursery, *every* time she's near that baby."

"Seriously?" Nick asks as he climbs into the back of the van. "At this stage of the game?"

"Well," Cliff says as he catches the tail end of their baby banter. "That Aria *is* a cutie."

"Good thing they're not around today," Jason adds, keeping a cautious eye on that kitchen window. "Maris says Celia's visiting her father in Addison, with Aria. So hopefully the women won't be getting any ideas."

"No more kids for me." Kyle does it then, too. He joins their furtive gazes toward the kitchen, where the women are all gathered. It's as though the men all fear that their wives might cast some spell, or use their female wiles, to get just what they want.

A baby.

And it scares them.

"Can only stretch the dollar so far, and this house is *it*, I'm telling you." Kyle walks toward the truck while pulling on a pair of canvas moving gloves, calling over his shoulder, "Let's get this done now. No pizza, no brews, till this sucker's empty."

Problem is, Kyle never fully realized the appeal of living at the sea's edge. Even here, at the farthest, most remote spot in Stony Point. But Back Bay is just across the street. Small waves ripple beneath the morning sun; seagulls soar over the water; a slight mist rises from it.

Which is fine and dandy. Lord knows he's paying the tax dollars for that sweet view of blue, though the train tracks running practically through his backyard kept the house within the Bradford budget.

But by early afternoon, you'd think the other guys have never *seen* water before. After several heavy furniture pieces are unloaded off the truck, then wheeled and hoisted inside, it's obvious that his moving crew is shrinking. One by one, starting with Nick, they walk outside—winded after maneuvering some hulking table or mattress through doorways—and turn toward the water while taking a deep breath of salt air. Which entices them closer with some unseen call that they heed. Gloves are pulled off and tucked in back pockets, hands dragged through hair, arms stretched as they cross the street and step foot on the little beach on the bay.

Until Kyle heads them off like a cowboy corralling cattle. "Vacate the beach, all of you," he orders with his arms outstretched, sweeping the guys in the direction of his house. "We need to finish this move, pronto."

They all oblige, until an approaching train is spotted on the sloping bank of land running along the coastline. The train chugs along, just a blur on the distant tracks. It won't be long before it'll be passing by beyond his house … and don't the guys know it. This time it's Matt leading the pack across the yard to get a closer view.

"See if we can get the conductor to blow the whistle!" Matt calls out.

"How?" Cliff asks, watching the train as they all meander toward the tracks.

"Seriously?" Jason elbows Cliff, then crooks his arm, makes a fist and motions as though tugging the pull cord of a steam train whistle. "Give him the sign, like you're sounding the whistle. The conductor will get the message."

The men line up, with Kyle bringing up the rear after giving a longing glance back to the three-quarter-filled moving van. But if there's one thing he's learned with this gang, it's this: If you can't beat 'em, join 'em.

So Kyle shoulders past Jason and Cliff to be first in line as the train approaches. And yup, there they are, a bunch of grown men—standing side by side blowing faux train horns.

And it works.

The conductor gives a few blasts of the whistle. The sound echoes long after the train chugs by as the guys laugh and turn to get back to hoisting furniture.

Except as they're walking, Jason veers off with Matt. "Want to show him my latest reno at your neighbor's house," Jason tells Kyle. "You guys keep unloading. We'll be right back."

"That remodel done yet?" Cliff asks, turning off behind Jason and Matt. "I've been watching the progress on it. What a nice bungalow, with those new cedar shingles."

"Just have to finish some work on the peaks, preferably *before* your Hammer Law takes effect." Jason motions for Cliff to follow. "Come on. I'll show you, too."

"I'd like to find me a sweet little bungalow. They make those in tiny houses?" Nick asks. "That's about all I could swing right now, if I park it on my parents' property. My student loans are killing me." He trots a few steps to keep up with the rest of them, all headed down the sandy street.

The sight dumbfounds Kyle. At this pace, they'll never get the moving van unloaded—and it's already the afternoon! He stands in his front yard and tosses up his hands, then decides to check on the kitchen progress. But after hearing, in only minutes' time, talk of crib types for Aria; and details of Taylor's sweet-sixteen party; and questions to Maris asking if she put any of them in her book; and critiques of the color Lauren painted the kitchen, well, Kyle doubts this house will ever get moved in to … at all!

Every dreamed vision of his home sweet home is quickly fading. By the time the guys return from checking out the neighbor's reno, Kyle's impatiently waiting in the back of the moving van. He lifted a blanket off a chair and sits, chin in his hand, silently cursing the very same distractions along Back Bay that enticed him to buy this house. Now, they're preventing him from moving in.

"Hey, man," Jason says as he steps into the truck. "Where's your kids today?"

"Good question, because I could use some moving help. They'd probably get this truck emptied out quicker than you clowns."

"Eh, we just took a break." Jason motions for Kyle to help him lift an upholstered chair. "Taylor watching the kids, then?"

"No. They're at Lauren's parents' house. And I promised Evan and Hailey they could sleep here tonight, a promise that I obviously *won't* be able to keep."

"Okay." Nick climbs aboard the truck. "For the kids, then. Let's get this done."

"Once and for all," Cliff agrees while hoisting a carton.

"Like Sal would say, *Andiamo!*" Jason insists. "Let's go."

~

Now this is more like it. Finally, his home will take shape. Kyle helps carry a living room chair across the yard. "You got it? Watch out for that shrub," he tells Jason.

"I'm good. Where's Matt, anyway?" Jason asks as they set down the chair near the front stoop.

Just as they reach the door, Matt holds it open for them from the inside. "Amazing," he tells them, holding a bottled water in his other hand.

"What is?" Jason looks past him into the house.

"The women went on for five minutes … *five minutes* … about where Lauren got a dishtowel. Five minutes," Matt says again after swigging his water, "on a towel."

"Listen, guys. You two got this chair?" Kyle heads to the truck. "Because we have to focus. Let's line up the rest of my stuff on the lawn. If we can get everything off the truck first, we can delegate where it all goes."

Jason, still standing at the chair outside the door, argues. "No, Kyle. That just doubles the work. We'll keep bringing it in piece by piece." With that, he lifts the chair himself and maneuvers through the door past Matt.

Kyle's not sure which way to turn at this point. Until Nick

calls him to the moving van.

"Let's put this hutch on a dolly," Nick tells him. "It's pretty heavy."

"Nah." Kyle walks onto the rear of the truck. "The two of us can manage. Just take it slow, and bend from the knees when you lift. On three." Kyle bends and grips the mahogany hutch. "One. Two."

After a quiet second, Nick chimes in from his bent, but idled, position. "Let's go, Bradford. Three, already."

"Hang on," Kyle mutters. "Shit."

"Come on, you wuss." Nick gives the heavy piece of furniture a nudge.

But Kyle sets down the hutch. "I can't move, man." As he says it, beads of sweat form on his forehead.

"What are you talking about?" Nick sets down his side of the hutch, too.

"Cannot move a muscle, I swear." Kyle stands partially bent at the waist. "It's like I'm stuck."

"Hey, you don't look so good. A little pale." Nick cautiously steps closer. "You having a heart attack or something?"

"No." Kyle sets both his hands on his lower back and realizes that trying to straighten is like trying to move a mountain. "More like a muscle spasm."

That's all it takes. Like it's some sort of herd instinct, the guys suddenly circle around him as Kyle presses his hand into his back, drops his head and simply groans.

~

Fifteen minutes later, Jason hears what's going on before he sees it. He and Matt decided to keep unloading the truck as

Cliff and Nick settled down Kyle. So while carrying two lamps, Jason shoulders open the back door into the kitchen and hears Nick's voice giving orders.

"Are you sure?" Cliff is asking. "He has to be on his *stomach*?"

"Yes." Nick scrolls through instructions on his phone screen. "It says on this medical site that lying on your stomach takes pressure off the back nerves."

Jason steps around Nick and sees Kyle over to the side of the dining room, out of the way of foot traffic, stretched out on the hardwood floor—flat on his stomach.

Lauren hurries past with a rolled towel. "Here," she tells Kyle. "Rest your forehead on this. To keep your face off the floor." She tenderly lifts Kyle's head and settles the towel beneath it.

In disbelief, Jason puts the lamps on top of some cartons and walks over to his incapacitated friend. "Kyle, listen," he says. He keeps his voice low so as not to make Kyle feel any worse than he apparently already does. "You were a union *shipbuilder*, for God's sake. Your arms are *jacked* from flipping all those pancakes at the diner. Just, just …" He looks at the mess of furniture and boxes in the Bradford house, then back at Kyle. "Get up, bro. Work it out."

"I can't, Barlow. Nick looked online, and this is the best immediate treatment. Prone on a very hard surface."

Jason straightens and considers his former best man. If there's one thing Jason knows, it's that Kyle Bradford will strong-arm just about any situation life throws at him. He's not one to back down. "Shit, Kyle. This is not like you. If it's *that* bad," Jason says, pausing to bend lower and talk even quieter, "let me take you to the walk-in clinic. Get things checked out."

"No! As soon as I can move a little, I'll sit up. Just give me some time, would you? Let the spasm calm down."

"Hey, man," Nick says as he inches closer to Kyle—all six-feet-two of him flat out in jeans, a tee and work boots. "Aren't you embarrassed lying there like that?"

Kyle manages to glare at him, then groan before answering. "I left my dignity at the door a long time ago with you guys."

Just as Jason is about to pick up the two lamps he brought in, his cell phone rings. "Everybody! Quiet for a sec," he shouts after seeing on the caller ID that it's his producer on the line. "Trent," he quickly says into the phone, leaning into the call. As he does, Cliff and Matt are maneuvering a sofa through the front door, making all kinds of racket, all while yelling to Kyle that they've got the couch, in case he wants to sit there. So Jason covers his other ear to better hear. "Sunday?" he asks into the phone. "At the studio?"

"You have to work tomorrow?" Maris calls out from the kitchen, where she's wrapping an ice pack.

Jason lowers his phone and tells her he has to review Elsa's happiness jar footage. "We're under a tight deadline."

"Okay, babe," Maris whispers as she passes him to set the ice on Kyle's back. "Maybe you really should go to the emergency clinic," she then tells Kyle as she studies him laid out on the hardwood floor.

"No!" Kyle reaches a hand behind him and adjusts the ice pack. "Got to stay away from those places. I just need to rest."

"If you're sure ..." Maris says, breezing into the kitchen again.

Instead of going out the front door, Matt and Cliff step around Kyle on their way to the back. His situation's like a car wreck; they don't want to stare, but they also can't look away.

Neither can Lauren, who kneels beside Kyle now and presses a damp cloth to his face.

"That's nice," Kyle says. "Cooling me off, at least."

As Jason wraps up his call with Trent, a new commotion fills the house. It starts when Eva and Elsa return with armloads of take-out pizza.

"My word!" Elsa exclaims upon seeing Kyle on the floor. She leaves the pizzas in the kitchen, then rushes over and kneels beside him, asking, "What happened?"

After hearing snatches of *bent wrong* and *muscle spasm* and *threw out my back*, leave it to Elsa to quickly find a pillow and sit Kyle up. "Here, now. Lean against the nice wall." On her knees, she's adjusting and fluffing the pillow behind him. "You know what you have to do next?"

Kyle drops his head back against the wall and closes his eyes. "No."

"*Mangia, mangia. Che ti fa' bene!*" Elsa instructs him.

"Eat, eat," Kyle answers. "It'll do you good?"

"Ah, yes." Elsa stands then and turns toward the kitchen, where Lauren is already dropping a loaded slice of pizza onto a dish. "You've been studying your Italian handbook, I see."

Kyle shakes his head.

"No?" Elsa asks.

"He lost it in the move," Lauren explains as Kyle takes the pizza plate from her. "Can't find it anywhere. But believe me, he has every one of Sal's favorite sayings and proverbs memorized."

"A few things left," Cliff says after coming down the stairs, his shoes clumping on each step. "Coffee table and a couple of nightstands. Give me a hand, Barlow."

Jason does, and heads toward the back door with Cliff.

"Need something to drink with that pizza?" Jason asks when they pass Kyle on the way. He sits straight against the wall now, his legs folded at the knee, a plate balanced on top of them.

"How about a cold brew?" Kyle asks around a mouthful of food. "Maybe a little buzz will numb the pain."

Before Jason can say, "I'm on it," Nick walks up, looking winded from arranging the living room sofa into place.

"Nice job, Bradford," Nick says while squinting down at Kyle. "Dude, you got out of the whole move."

four

BEACH BLISS, JASON THINKS. TWO simple words for his version of paradise: lying in bed with his wife early the next morning. He hears the raucous cries of seagulls outside, feeding over the bluff. Maris lies beside him, toying with his hair. Her fingers lift strands of it, give a gentle tug, then run along the scar on his jaw to his neck. With his eyes still closed, he reaches for her hand, clasps it in his and brings it to his mouth to kiss it.

But it's not enough for Maris, who pulls her fingers from his grip and moves them up along his arm, to his neck. There, she hooks a finger beneath his chin and turns his head to hers so that she can give him a sweet Sunday kiss. One that she lingers with, pausing only to murmur softly between kisses, and to slip off his boxers beneath the sheet. Which has him deepen his kiss while cradling her face. His hands work their way down her neck, along her shoulders and back, before he lifts her satin nightshirt and moves over her.

"You're very beautiful," he says, then kisses her forehead, her cheek, her neck. His fingers tangle through her dark hair, his mouth meets hers.

It's when he pulls away for a moment to look at her eyes watching him, to touch a finger to her smile, that she tells him, "Don't stop."

So he doesn't.

He kisses her once, lightly. Then again, deeper, feeling her mouth open to his. But when she raises her legs alongside his hips, when her own hands stroke the gnarled skin on his back—another physical remnant of his long-ago accident—he does stop, once more. No kisses, no caresses other than dragging the back of his fingers along her cheek, down her neck and to her breast.

"I love you, sweetheart," he tells her, his hand tracing her face again, moving aside a strand of her silky hair.

"I know you do," she whispers back.

And that's it. Her insistent touches say the rest as she pulls him closer and they make love on a Sunday morning. Today, though, her low whispers, and her body's moves—beneath him first, then on top—take Jason aback a little, and leave them both breathless afterward.

"I can't get enough of you," Maris murmurs near his ear as she slides off him.

And she makes sure he's fully aware of that. When he lies on the bed with an arm tossed over his eyes, her mouth leaves surprise kisses on his body, kisses soft against the skin of his neck, his jaw, his belly. It's a moment he wishes could last long into the day.

Instead, he lifts his arm and opens his eyes, seeing the sun lighting the bedroom.

"What are you up to today?" Jason asks.

Beneath the sheet, Maris turns and lies on her back beside him. Still, her fingers run down the skin of his arm, her smile lingers. "Well. I'm putting together a get-well basket for Kyle, and I might tuck in a chapter from the manuscript for him to read. I'm really hung up on a few passages in the book." Her hand reaches over to Jason's chest and strokes his skin. "Do you think Kyle would be okay with that? I mean, he and Neil didn't exactly see eye to eye."

"Kyle was my best man. And he's actually handled a lot in life. He should be up to the challenge."

"Good. Because this particular chapter's missing something, and I can't put my finger on it."

"You think Kyle will?"

"Yes, especially since it's tied in with food."

Maris is quiet enough then for Jason to glance over at her, only to see her eyes closed as she lightly dozes. When he touches her shoulder, she continues. "Afterward, I'm off to Elsa's. Celia is coming back. I made the baby a chambray onesie."

Jason drags his finger along Maris' shoulder, to her collarbone, then back again. But he says nothing.

"And what are you up to?" she asks from behind her closed-again eyes.

A slight breeze drifts in the window, and Jason takes a long breath of the salt air. "Studio work at CT-TV, remember? We're behind schedule with the premiere and have to wrap things up." Back to reality, he finally sits up in bed and gets on his boxers—his Sunday morning paradise fleeting now. "Can't believe the show airs next week."

Maris turns on her side and props herself up on her elbow. "You've been running on fumes lately and need to rest, babe."

Jason gives the top of her head a quick kiss. "No rest for the weary, darling."

With that, he settles himself onto the bedside chair, hooks

on his forearm crutches and heads downstairs. It's time to let the dog out and put on a pot of coffee before grabbing a shower.

He does one more thing first, though. At the bottom of the stairs, he gives a long look behind him, back up those stairs, knowing that the past hour in bed with his wife was the last peaceful hour he'll have for a week, at least.

~

Even from behind his closed eyes, Kyle sees the morning sunlight. It doesn't help that it's their first day in the house and they don't have any window treatments up yet. He scratches his bare chest, then turns his head away from the window.

"Oh, man, that *natural light.* It's blinding."

"No, it's *beautiful,*" Lauren quietly insists beside him. "The way the sun reflects off the water like that." She removes her sleep mask and loops it on his head, pressing the satin eye-covering over his face. "It's all a matter of perspective."

"Well, that helps." Kyle shifts beneath the sheet and adjusts the sleep mask. "I thought things would go fast yesterday, but it was the longest move ever."

"How's your back?" Lauren nudges him to his side.

Slowly, Kyle rolls over with a slight groan. He can't even help it, the way that groan rises with the pain in his lower back. But he's got enough flexibility to lift the sleep mask, reach for his cell phone on the nightstand and call Jerry. "Can you cover the diner?" he asks when Jerry answers the call. "I threw out my back moving a hutch, and will be out of commission for a day or two."

When Jerry assures him The Dockside is in safe hands, Kyle

ends the call and tosses the phone on the nightstand. While still on his side, he pulls the sleep mask down over his eyes again.

In a moment, he feels Lauren's light touch on his back, pressing, rubbing, moving lower. "Here. Let me massage the kinks out." Her voice is soft behind him, and if he's not mistaken, there's an occasional kiss thrown into this therapy. "I don't want you ending up in the emergency clinic for this," Lauren whispers.

So Kyle takes a few deep breaths, closes his eyes and goes with it, trying to relax those stricken back muscles. Lauren's fingers circle his skin lightly, stroke his side, then move around to his chest as she presses closer. When her fingers work their way down his belly and slip beneath his pajama pants, his massage therapy suddenly turns very interesting.

"Better?" Lauren kisses his shoulder then, too, before gently lifting that sleep mask off his face and tossing it off the bed.

"Little bit."

And it's true. Everything seems a *little* better with her touch: his back, his fatigue, even that darn natural light. Kyle looks at her behind his shoulder, rolls over and kisses her deeply. "Back to the beach," he says, nuzzling her neck, her hair, "and back to easy summer lovin'."

Cliff sits up in the bed, a perfectly fluffed pillow behind him as he leans against the headboard. He closes his eyes while chewing, focusing solely on the pancakes' flavor. Only Elsa can make Sunday morning breakfast in bed so grand. The aroma of a cup of fresh-brewed coffee rises from his breakfast tray, and his toast is buttered and lightly jammed—just the way he likes it.

Of course, Elsa does have an ulterior motive. With his eyes still closed as he savors the sweet pancakes, he feels the mattress shift when she slides herself nearer to him. Oh, her anticipation is palpable in the quiet room. Other than chewing, he doesn't move, though; his hand rests on the breakfast tray across his lap; the cool sheet covers his relaxed legs.

And he knows, he just knows, Elsa's studying his face for *any* small reaction. So he opens his eyes.

"Well?" she instantly asks. Wearing a leopard-print caftan, she's leaning close, her honey-highlighted brown hair swept back off her face. "Which one do you like better? Blueberry or chocolate chip? I need to know for when the inn's open for business."

Cliff sinks his fork through the blueberry stack and lifts another pancake heap, holding the dripping fork idle above the plate. "The chocolate chip is sinfully good, but it sneaks up on you. It's very rich." He eats this next mouthful. "Mmm. And there's nothing more New England than blueberry pancakes in a seaside inn." He sips his coffee, still considering his palate. "It's a toss-up."

Elsa reaches over for one of Cliff's overloaded pancake plates. "Give me whichever you're not eating." She wastes no time settling in, sitting against the headboard beside him and scooping up a mouthful of the chocolate-chip pancakes.

They're quiet, then, in Elsa's bedroom. The sun is shining through her paned window; a sea breeze drifts in. After all that furniture-moving at Kyle's yesterday, Cliff's glad to have this leisurely morning to rest his weary bones. Beside him, Elsa digs in for another forkful of food.

"I can get very used to this," Cliff admits while dragging some pancake through the melted butter and maple syrup pooled on his dish.

"Don't get too comfortable," Elsa warns around a mouthful of food, all while holding up her finger as she chews. After washing down the fluffy pancakes with a sip of orange juice, she continues. "The inn's opening soon and reservations are already coming in. So now, testing this Sunday breakfast food, I'm feeling stressed! There's still *much* to do."

That's all it takes for this blissful morning in bed to end. This moment when Elsa anxiously sweeps back the sheet, sets her plate on the nightstand, gets out of bed and reaches for Cliff's shirt—left hanging on a chair back last night.

"You better go," she's saying while shaking out the shirt's wrinkles. "I've got to vacuum, then arrange the dining room. Celia's coming back today from visiting her father in Addison. It's only been a few days, but oh, how I've missed her and the baby!" With Cliff's shirt draped over her arm, Elsa walks to her dresser and brushes her hair. After that, she fusses with the neckline of her leopard-print caftan as though considering what to wear, then spins around toward him. "I bought a crib mobile for the nursery. It has silver and gold stars on it, just like in the sky over the sea. And I picked up a few things for Celia, too."

"Need a hand with anything?"

"No. Out you go." She tosses his shirt onto the bed and nudges his shoes closer. "I'll be busy today. Shoo! *Shoo!*"

Yes, it was too good to be true, this lingering in bed with a breakfast tray over his lap, enjoying sweet food and Elsa's company. Just like that, he's ousted. But he takes his time, putting on his clothes from yesterday, including the heavy shoes he wore to move the Bradfords in. He ties the shoelaces slowly; resets his wristwatch. Anything to linger here with Elsa a minute or two longer. But she's opening drawers and her closet as though he's already left.

Well, after all those pancakes, the walk home will do him good anyway, to burn off those syrupy calories. It's only a few blocks from the inn back to his temporary digs in the beach association trailer.

Outside, the sun is up, mist rises from lawns, and an early robin chirrups in a tree. The problem Cliff's been having lately is that between Elsa renovating her inn *and* having a new granddaughter, there's little time left for him on her day planner.

Still, he'll take what he can get, including the perfect night they had, and morning too.

Perfect ... Until he walks a block in that morning sunshine and a car pulls up beside him while tooting the horn. He glances over at Nick in the security cruiser.

"Taking the walk of shame, Commissioner Raines?"

"The what?" Cliff asks while still walking along the side of the sandy road.

"Walk of shame, boss." Nick motions back to the inn, then to Cliff's wrinkled outfit—the same exact clothes he wore yesterday during Kyle's move. Nick says nothing more. He just waggles a finger at him and drives toward his guard post at the railroad trestle, where he'll log incoming vacationers' names and license plates.

"Walk of shame," Cliff mutters, looking down at his wrinkled pants and casual shoes. "What the heck?" he asks while watching Nick's departing car.

By the time he climbs the few steps to his steel trailer door, curiosity has gotten the best of Cliff. It's enough to have him fire up his work computer, sit in the office chair and do a quick search before anything else—including shaving. *Walk of shame*, he types in, then adds, *definition*.

"Are you kidding?" Cliff scrolls through a few explanations of the term. Is that how he was perceived this morning by anyone who saw him walking? As someone skulking back home after spending the night engaged in casual sex? *Unplanned* intimate behavior, as indicated by the absence of a fresh wardrobe change?

Cliff clicks off the computer and goes to the window, looking out at the cottage-lined beach roads. My goodness, he thinks. Do folks here see him that way? As some *philanderer*, sleeping around with the Stony Point women?

Eh, what does Nick know, anyway? He's just a young whippersnapper.

Because, well, what about if Cliff's night was actually *planned*? By him *and* Elsa? And what if it *wasn't* meaningless behavior they engaged in, but tender? And *loving*?

"Of all the cockamamie … Walk of shame," he mutters again while returning to his desk. Back at his computer, he types in *overnight duffel* on a popular shopping site. The bag has to be something discreet enough to hold a fresh change of clothes that he might keep at Elsa's. He finds a canvas duffel with pockets for a phone charger, some toiletries, even a pair of shoes.

With a quick click of the *Add to Cart* button, Cliff then selects two-day shipping. Anything to keep the Stony Point gossip at bay.

After an early shower, Celia puts on her striped seersucker blouse over distressed denim shorts. When she opens the blinds in her old bedroom in Addison, morning sunshine streams in. Every day, it's a wish come true—for her daughter to have sunshine in her days. Celia moves beside the crib her father had set up for her visits home. She's so thankful that he agreed to buy her little yellow bungalow and make it his own. As a widower, it's the perfect place for him, small and easy to maintain. It enables her and Aria to live where they belong, too: in their own cozy guest cottage behind Elsa's inn at Stony Point. It's exactly what Celia needs, with the loving support of family and friends always nearby.

Smiling, she looks at Aria in the crib now. Wearing a snap-up sleeper, the baby's tiny fingers are fisted, and her chubby legs bend and kick. Celia's hands gently slide beneath her daughter and lift her up.

"*Buongiorno!*" Celia says as she holds the baby close. At the same time, she remembers how she heard that exact word herself all last summer, from Salvatore DeLuca. They'd wake up together in her rented beach cottage on the marsh and that would be the first thing Sal would say to her. *Buongiorno, bella.*

This morning, she says it to his child.

Holding her sweet Aria close as she walks her to the sunny window, Celia feels nothing but love—finally. Because in the past two years, she's been divorced, left not trusting love. Then she unexpectedly fell in love again, and lost that very love. Now?

Now she kisses her baby. Now she's in love again.

Celia coos to Aria, then clicks the seashell wind chime that she brought with her. Aria loves the click-clack sound of the moving shells. Of course she would, just like Sal loved everything about the beach.

Finally, the voice of Celia's father comes to her from out in the kitchen.

"Made you breakfast, Celia! Your favorite, scrambled eggs."

Celia lowers her mouth to Aria's tiny, soft ear. "We're going home today, Aria!" she whispers. She carries the baby out to the hallway, heading to the kitchen. "Back to Stony Point, my little love. Back to the beach."

five

A FEW HOURS LATER, CELIA picks up the winding Shore Road toward Stony Point. She'd looped Aria's wind chime over the car's rearview mirror, and the cream-colored shells delicately clatter in the light sea breeze coming through the window. Leaving Addison's red barns and white picket fences behind, they drive past bait shops and ice-cream stands. A heron flies over a lagoon edged with swaying marsh grasses. The salt air is thick here, a tonic Celia deeply inhales.

If her life now were ever depicted on the silver screen, isn't this coastal view the perfect start to that movie? Yes, for the opening credits, the camera would pan all of it rolling by her car: sea and sky … a peaceful bliss waiting here.

Since Celia's made Stony Point her home for the past several months, the film might be called, well, it would be called *Celia's Return.* Yes, she likes that. Because though she's been back at the beach and settled in, this time she's returning from only a brief visit away. As her car nears Stony Point, a director's assistant might raise the clapperboard, identifying this as *Scene: Reunion, Take: One.* And this time, as always now, it's with someone special in the car. Whispering *Aria,* she glances back at the baby in her car seat.

Meanwhile, that director, he'd be ordering the cameras to shift from the sweeping coastal vista to a close-up of Celia, driving. What better way to capture emotion than on the nuances of her face, her eyes? On the tears that often fill them. Like right now, when she turns beneath the stone train trestle leading into the private beach community. Oh, Lauren knew last year, when explaining the tangled lives at this little beach. Celia will never forget her friend's words of warning. *When you arrive under that railroad trestle alone, you will one day leave here with either a ring, or a baby, or a broken heart.*

The thing is, Lauren had no way of knowing that Celia would become the first person in Stony Point history to leave with all three—which she did last summer after Sal's death. She left here then with his sea-glass engagement ring on her finger, and a broken heart deep inside—unaware that she was also pregnant at the time.

So that camera close-up would capture a world of emotions that Celia just can't conceal. But lately, happiness somehow tops them all. Like today, when she stops at the guard shack and Nick approaches.

"Hiya, sweet pea," he says to Aria in the backseat while tapping on the window. "Did you enjoy visiting with your grandpa for a few days?"

"She sure did," Celia tells him through her own open window. "Sat outside in the yard, got some fresh country air!"

Nick pats the car's roof. "Good to see you both back, Celia."

"Thanks, Nick." She puts the car in gear as he steps away. "It's wonderful to be here."

Nick salutes her as she drives down the cottage-lined street.

On this mid-June day, pots of geraniums sit on front steps; welcome flags wave beside screen doors; robins and blue jays perch on the edge of garden birdbaths. She slows the car to take it in and point out the pretty sights to her baby. "Look at the birdie singing," Celia says over her shoulder. "Chirp-chirp!"

But nothing feels as much like bliss as when she pulls into the inn's driveway and spots her little gingerbread cottage behind it. Does the imaginary movie camera catch that moment? The moment when Celia's head drops against the seat back? She can't help it, the way a slight smile comes and her eyes momentarily close—as though she need not look anywhere else for tranquility. Elsa included this guest cottage as part of her inn's extensive renovation so that Celia and Aria could live close by.

Not that Elsa had much choice. Last fall, Celia had planted herself in the ramshackle guest cottage, only hoping to convince Elsa to stay on here in Stony Point—*and* to hire Celia as assistant innkeeper. The job would be perfect for her, bringing her experience as a home stager to Elsa's Ocean Star Inn.

Then? Well, then the baby changed everything.

Celia takes in the renovated two-bedroom bungalow sitting on a stone foundation. The cottage's new pale yellow cedar shingles will slowly weather in the salt air. Wide white trim edges the windows … windows that let in breezes, and birdsong. A diamond-shaped stained glass window brings colorful sunbeams inside, a rainbow of sunlight Celia loves to show Aria.

After being away for only a few days, it all feels new again.

Even seeing Elsa waiting for her on the little cottage front porch has Celia smiling and waving. Elsa was the very first person she met when she arrived here last summer, the first person to make Celia feel at home. Like she's with family. Elsa has that way about her.

One thought hasn't escaped Celia since. Isn't it ironic that Elsa *became* her actual family, being the loving grandmother to Celia and Sal's baby girl. And in a sense, becoming the mother Celia's long missed, too.

As soon as Celia's out the door, Elsa rushes to meet her, and hug her warmly, and help her unstrap the baby from the car seat. To welcome them home.

~

Official hurricane watches have been posted, so it's certain now. It's coming. But he had been certain of it for days. The storm's arrival is apparent by the heavy damp air that hangs, still as a curtain, over the coastline. Not to mention the eerie lighting. Thin cloud cover casts a gray hue to the landscape. All of it, that damp gray pause in the weather, is the notorious calm before the storm's arrival. Making it the perfect day for their hurricane clambake.

"Guess what?" Lauren asks.

Kyle glances up from reading Neil's manuscript just as she breezes onto the front porch. She wears a tank top and frayed denim shorts, and is all dust-covered and sweaty from unpacking.

"What?" Kyle asks, his eyes dropping to the story on the loose, typed pages.

"Celia's back!"

Then, nothing. At least, not that Kyle notices. He's sucked right into this novel already. After reading a few lines, though, Lauren interrupts him.

"How is it?" she whispers.

Whispers, he notices, because in the last fifteen seconds she inched over to him and is stealing a peek at the papers he holds. "It's friggin' awesome, actually," he tells her. "Maris is doing a bang-up job. I'm just a page in, though, and it's only one chapter."

Lauren sits on a wicker chair beside him, leaning close to see the story. "And what does Maris want you to do?"

"Something happens over a dinner. I have to give cooking details to bring authenticity to the scene." Kyle glances at the manuscript pages, then adjusts the heating pad he leans on to relieve his thrown-out back. "But I just started. Right now, the friends are gathered together at this particular cottage, which reminds me of the cottage on the beach. The last-standing one on the end?"

"Probably the most iconic Stony Point cottage."

Kyle nods. "Definitely. So anyway, from what Maris told me, a clambake is about to begin as they await a monster hurricane's arrival."

"A clambake? When a hurricane's coming?"

"Yeah. Sounds like something we would've done, back in the day. A clambake with the gang, instead of taking precautions."

"Right. I could just picture it."

"Me, too. And I guess some drama goes down between the friends at this clambake. So I'll jot notes, like how the characters need to cook the food over a bed of seaweed, which should be rockweed. Its little pockets rupture while cooking and release sea salt for flavoring." Kyle lifts the pages from his lap.

"Okay, okay. But set the scene for me."

"Well. It's the calm, right before the storm. Eerily calm. Weather watches have been issued, but the power isn't out yet. The clambake will be on the beach, outside the cottage. The friends are staying there for a reunion, apparently in that cottage on the beach that's withstood every hurricane to come up the coast. And the guys just now dug up a barbecue pit in the sand, and loaded it with rocks and firewood."

Lauren reaches over and lifts a manuscript page. "Does it bother you to read Neil's story?"

"Bother me? Why?"

"Because even though it's a novel, it isn't *exactly* fiction. We're probably all in it. And there's a lot of history between you and Neil."

Kyle takes the page from her and sets it on the pile. "But it's *our* history, too, Ell. A history that brought us back together, so it's the least I can do to help with the book." Kyle lifts Lauren's hand and draws a finger down the lifeline on her palm. "The past, well, it is what it is. So I can manage clambake details."

"Speaking of dinner, we're going out tonight. To Elsa's inn."

"I thought she was bringing us a dinner here, with my back out and you busy unpacking."

"She was. But I want to see Celia and the baby. So we're eating there, instead."

"I don't know if we should, because I can't move that good." He shifts in the wicker chair. With the occasional throbbing still bothering his back, he could sit on this porch facing the bay all day. It's so soothing, the way a slight breeze works its way through the window screens.

"Get real, Kyle," Lauren says while slapping his arm. "You

managed to move just fine in bed this morning."

"That's different."

"No, it's not. And it's the best thing for you to move. You've got to gradually increase your range of motion—"

"I know, I know. Or the pain will persist."

"We'll walk to Elsa's, slowly. You can breathe that sweet salt air." Lauren stands and tucks a loose wisp of hair into her topknot as she walks back into the living room. "Cures what ails you," she calls over her shoulder.

"What about the kids?"

From the living room, where Kyle hears a moving carton being sliced open, she answers. "Taylor's watching them all day, over at Eva's, so I can unpack."

"Maybe you should go without me, Ell." Kyle tests his back then, cautiously standing with his hands on his hips.

Lauren returns to the porch doorway right as he stretches his arms and tries twisting from side to side. "You'll either walk to Elsa's, or I'm driving you to the emergency clinic. Make a decision while I take a quick shower."

Kyle waves her off, then sits back down and loses himself in the manuscript once more. The guys get a roaring fire going in the sandpit as they prep for the clambake instead of for the storm to come.

"That's a wrap."

Jason still can't believe it. The whole pilot episode for his new TV show is, yes, wrapped up. Later that afternoon, he rolls back his chair in the production studios at CT-TV and shakes hands with Trent. Eight months have passed since Jason won the award for Best Coastal Architect; eight months since Trent from CT-TV started hounding Jason to host this home-improvement program.

"We're good to go. Viewers will love this," Trent says to him now after watching Elsa's happiness jar segment. "The premiere is all set."

"That's it?" Jason asks, looking at the technicians still working at the control panels.

"Sure is. Nice job, Barlow." Trent stands up, finishing the last drops of his coffee.

Jason stands, too. "Can't believe we're done. Seemed like there was always one more room to finish at the inn. One more segment to film." He lifts his leather messenger bag and hooks it over his shoulder. "Thanks, Trent. Couldn't have done it without you."

"I'll get you that copy for your sand-chair premiere. When is it, anyway?"

"Next weekend," Jason says. "Saturday night."

"Nice idea, showing it right on the beach." Trent picks up a few papers from his studio desk. "Once this airs, and you become a local celebrity, don't you be going diva on me."

"Me? Diva?" Jason pulls his keys from his pocket. "I'll try not to."

Together they head out of the studios. Jason shakes Trent's hand again, still not quite believing that the project is done. The CT-TV camera crews documented it all these past months, filming every bit of Elsa's renovation—from its scrappy start as a run-down, weathered cottage to its finale as a grand seaside inn.

As he crosses the parking lot toward his SUV, Jason's phone dings with a text message. It's from Maris. *Hey, babe,* he reads. *Dinner out tonight, at Elsa's. She's having Lauren and Kyle over. Can you make it?*

Walking across the pavement, Jason waves to Trent when he drives past, then types on his phone. *Just got out of the studio, so perfect timing. Still in Hartford, be there in an hour.*

OK, will save you a seat, Maris answers.

These Sunday dinners have become a favorite of Jason's. Over the past year, the gang's Meet and Eats slowly shifted to the inn. As he picks up the highway and heads back to the beach, he wonders what recipe Elsa cooked up today. She's made it abundantly clear that all the beach friends have become her official taste-testers. They're part of her prep work, because Sunday dinners will be a mainstay for her guests once the inn's open. Elsa wants every meal to be mouthwatering.

One thing's for certain. After sitting in a television production studio all afternoon, Jason's ready for a seaside dinner, windows open to the salty breeze, talk and laughs rising around Elsa's big dining room table.

In no time, he's exiting the highway and turning onto Shore Road. With its marshes and bait shops, ice-cream huts and boat marinas, driving this road is like living a flashback of Jason's very life. Every sight he passes holds some summer memory—some carefree, some not so much. Last August, he cruised this very pavement on the back of Sal's Harley-Davidson, the wind whipping his hair, the salt air pungent. It was a rare afternoon of pure freedom, much like the days when Neil was alive and Jason would hitch a ride on his brother's bike.

A month later, Jason drove this same road in a funeral procession as Sal was laid to rest.

Since then, Jason's traveled his *own* difficult road to get to this hard-earned place, to where the tide's finally turned once again.

~

In the guest cottage, Celia puts the baby in for her afternoon nap. She winds up Aria's music box, opens the window to let in a sea breeze and lightly closes the door behind her.

"She's sleeping," Celia whispers to Elsa, who's rinsing the lunch dishes in the cottage kitchen. "This should give us enough time to assemble the baby suite my father bought." Celia motions to a box on the living room floor.

"Baby suite?" Elsa asks.

"Yes. It's a playpen with a built-in bassinet *and* changing station. Look!" Celia turns the box to show Elsa the photograph on it. "Perfect to keep at the inn, for when Aria is there. Help me put it together?"

Elsa dries her hands, straightens her black V-neck tee over flower-print capri leggings, and joins Celia in the living room. Then, like everything they do together, the pieces are pulled from the box and, one by one, carefully assembled.

"I have news, Celia," Elsa tells her while snapping on the playpen's top rails. "We have a definite grand opening date for the inn. Even though I'm having some family events prior. But the *official* date is Labor Day weekend."

"What?" Sitting on the couch, Celia drops the assembly instructions. "In *September*? But that's three months away! We'll miss so much of the summer season."

"Oh, but you're wrong, Celia." Elsa reaches into the playpen and snaps the base into place. "We'll actually *have* the summer season. You and I will, with Aria."

"I don't understand."

"It's simple, actually. Like Salvatore often said last year, we need to savor time. He did, in the short months he was here." After pressing the mattress pad onto the base of the playpen, Elsa sits on the sofa beside Celia. "And with everything we've been through, first with losing Sal, and then with your pregnancy, on top of *all* the renovations here, we really need to savor these summer months together, with Aria. Quietly. She's just born, and so very young."

In the silent pause that comes next, Celia knows that more than anything else, Elsa's dearly missing her own son right now.

"Life is precious, Cee," Elsa finally says. "So what I really want is for you to immerse yourself in Aria's life during these fleeting summer days."

"Are you sure?"

"Of course I am. It's what Sal would want, too. Our inn guests will come in September. It's a lovely time to visit the shore. And this way, you and I will be rested and ready to open our doors then." She squeezes Celia's hand. "Okay?"

Sometimes a hand squeeze is not enough. Celia couldn't have had a more special wish come true than to have three months of uninterrupted time with her newborn daughter. So she embraces Elsa at the same time that her eyes fill with tears. "Oh, Elsa. Yes. Yes, September is okay."

"*Perfetto!*" Elsa brushes a tear from Celia's cheek, then returns to the nearly assembled play yard in the middle of the living room floor. "Also," she says while securing the mattress pad with Velcro strips, "a full year will have passed since Sal's death by then. So we'll be ready for a new beginning."

"Which in Sal's words was to open the finest seaside inn on the Connecticut shoreline."

"Yes. I'm even thinking of having the priest from St. Bernard's give a small service here to bless the inn and its grounds, right before we open."

"That sounds so beautiful," Celia says as she picks up the assembly instructions again. "You think of everything, Elsa."

Just then, a car door slams outside the cottage. "That must be Lauren and Kyle," Elsa says. "I'm having them for dinner, since Kyle hurt his back yesterday and poor Lauren's working so hard unpacking all alone."

Celia goes to the window and presses aside the lace curtain. "No, it's Maris. Wait. Someone else is pulling in, too."

"Maris? She called earlier, but I thought she was stopping by later on." Elsa gets up from where she was kneeling on the floor and joins Celia at the window. "Must be Lauren behind her."

"No." Celia leans closer to the window for a better look. "No, I think it's Eva and Matt?"

"Seriously?" Elsa moves to the other window, this one by the front door.

"Mm-hmm. Because look! *There's* Lauren and Kyle." Celia points toward the street. "It looks like they *walked* here."

"How do you like that?" Elsa rushes to the door and steps outside onto the porch of the little guest cottage.

"Yoo-hoo!" Eva calls as she emerges from her car and raises a platter. "I brought dessert!"

Celia comes up behind Elsa and looks out past her shoulder. "Did you know they were *all* coming?"

After they give a wave to the crowd apparently arriving for Sunday dinner, Elsa turns to Celia. "No, not definitely. But I had my suspicions. So here's an Innkeeper 101 lesson for you to remember," she quietly says. "Always have more chairs *and* food than you think you'll need."

six

ANOTHER INNKEEPING LESSON ELSA MUST remember to tell Celia is this: Always keep a basket of seashells on hand. They add just the right ambiance to any seaside dining room table. As her guests drift in for their Sunday dinner, Elsa is leaning some of those sun-bleached shells against the brushed-silver lanterns glimmering on either end of the table. When she returns the basket to her hutch, she sets it beside one very special Mason jar—her wish capsule. The glass jar's filled with sand and white starfish, and tiny rolls of paper tied with twine. Each roll holds a private wish they each made last summer, when Elsa decided not to sell her big old cottage. They all agreed to let a year pass before opening the wishes and seeing if they came true. Elsa often wonders what secret desires her friends and family wrote. But it's not time yet.

She's simply glad to have this room bustling with voices and life again! It's just what she'd hoped for when, during the inn's months-long renovation, she made a few critical decisions. One of those was to keep her long, wood-planked dining table and distressed-navy French country chairs. Certain décor styles work in a coastal inn, like this furniture's shabby elegance.

Another decision was to let Jason go ahead with his vision, as she trusts him implicitly. He opened up the dining room wall with floor-to-ceiling windows facing the distant beach. Of course, in typical Jason style, he first raised the ceiling to accommodate a second, smaller row of paned windows above the taller, lower ones.

The result? Sweeping views of sea and sky … perfect to dine and linger by.

And by the time Elsa's setting the second dinner platter on the table, candles are flickering and Maris, Eva and Matt are seated, right as Lauren and Kyle walk in.

"Oh, Kyle," Elsa says as she rounds the table and pulls out a chair. "This chair's for you. I've added a comfy pillow for you to lean on, to help your back."

"Thanks, Elsa." Kyle sits, eyes the table and lets out a sigh. "Very nice of you."

"Okay, then! I think that's everything," Elsa tells them all as she sets out the salad tongs and serving utensils. "Fresh-baked bread, green salad with cherry tomatoes, and mac and cheese. Help yourselves, my friends."

"Elsa DeLuca," Kyle says after stealing a sample of the main course. "You're too modest. This is so much more than mac and cheese," he says around a mouthful.

After sitting at the head of the table, Elsa unfolds her linen napkin and sets it on her lap over her flower-print capris. "You have a discerning palate, Kyle," she says while dropping a spoonful of the gooey shell pasta on her dish. "This is my specialty, *caprese* mac and cheese, which means I added tomato wedges, mozzarella and basil for a little taste of Italy. You like?"

Kyle sits back as Lauren heaps a scoop on his plate. "Keep

going," he tells her while nodding at Elsa and lightly kissing his fingertips.

So Lauren tops Kyle's dishes with salad, hunks of crusty bread and the cheesy macaroni. "And where's Celia tonight?" she asks with a glance at Elsa. "I can't wait to see her baby again!"

Elsa stands and starts pouring wine into all their glasses, making her way around the table. "She's home right now."

"Still in Addison?" Eva asks, looking up at Elsa beside her, filling her wine goblet. "I thought she was back."

"She is!" Elsa turns to Matt's glass then. "Home is here, now. She's in the guest cottage."

"Oh, Celia made it so cozy in there," Lauren muses. "With that white paneling, and the weathered tables looking worn smooth by the sea. And those roped glass fishing globes like we have in the diner? She stacked miniature ones in bowls. It's just so pretty!"

"The baby was napping," Elsa tells them once she sits again. "Celia wanted to wait for her to wake up, then feed her before coming by here."

"Aria is so precious," Maris says around a mouthful of the mac and cheese.

Matt nudges Eva to hand him the serving spoon, then helps himself to another large scoop.

"Easy, easy," Eva whispers. "Save some for Jason."

"I had no time for cooking today," Lauren says after a sip of wine. "So I really appreciate this, Elsa."

"It's the least I can do for my new beach neighbors." Elsa glances over at Lauren. Wisps of hair have escaped from her messy topknot; a faded denim shirt covers a thin tank top; her gray eyes look tired after a day of unpacking. "A nice meal will keep your energy up."

"Absolutely." Lauren drags a hunk of bread through the cheesy mess on her dish. "And it's delicious!"

"Second that, here. This is so good," Kyle says while raising a heaping forkful dripping with melted cheese. "It's really helping my back spasm."

"Slow down, Kyle!" Lauren gently lowers his arm. "You'll get indigestion if you eat too fast."

But Elsa doesn't mind. This is the true taste test now: to see how much the room quiets. Because in this group of friends that never lacks for conversation, and small talk, and beach gossip, the only thing that silences them is a good meal on the table.

So Elsa gauges the decibel level as they're all digging in. The you-could-hear-a-pin-drop quiet means delicious food beat out the talking. Success. Her caprese mac and cheese will definitely be on her Sunday Dinners Menu.

"I never had a casserole this incredible," Maris manages to say as she's swiping her fork across her plate. "Are these your deck-pot tomatoes in it?"

"No," Elsa explains. "It's too early for my own tomatoes. But the lettuce in the salad is mine. And the basil in the casserole is from my little red herb pots, which Celia nurtured beautifully back to life last fall."

Then? Then only nods happen as the food is savored and dunked and salted and buttered and devoured. Silverware clinks on dishes; wineglasses are sipped from.

Until suddenly, there's a new noise.

"Oh!" Maris says, setting down her fork and pulling her dinging cell phone closer. "It's Jason, texting me." She looks at the phone screen. "He's here in the driveway." She still reads silently, but only laughs then.

"What's so funny?" Eva asks as she empties a forkful of cheesy macaroni into her mouth.

Maris looks around the table, where everyone has stopped mid-eating and waits for her response. "He wants to know if the vultures left him any food!"

"That's it." Elsa stands and lifts a china plate from the chipped-paint, built-in cupboard beside the table. Then she heads to the kitchen for a napkin and silverware. "I'll go and make him up a fresh plate."

No sooner is she in her kitchen than a knock comes at the front door, a courtesy knock that simply precedes the door swinging open.

Elsa leans to the side and glances down the front hallway. "Jason? Back here. Come on in!" she calls out.

"I picked up a hitchhiker," Jason announces from the dining room.

When Elsa brings in his dish and place setting, Jason's beside Maris, bending and kissing the side of her face. His hand rests on her shoulder as he takes in the feast on the table.

But that's not what gets her smiling. It's Cliff, sitting in the chair beside Elsa's, that has her grab another mismatched china plate from the hutch.

"Heard something about your specialty macaroni and cheese," Cliff says to Elsa as he tucks a napkin into his shirt collar. "Sure beats my grilled cheese sandwich on a hotplate."

Colors are always softer at this time of day. In evening's light, they take on the hues of a watercolor painting, misty at the edges, wistful as a summer memory.

Memories of which Celia has plenty, both sweet and sad. Which is what makes this moment all the more difficult.

Her baby is strapped into a cloth carrier against Celia's chest, and Celia touches wisps of her daughter's dark hair. "Oh, Aria," she whispers, then takes a deep breath. "I wish I was as relaxed as you." Her finger moves to the infant's cheek, which she lightly strokes.

Because Celia's not relaxed. Walking into this big, rambling cottage tonight is not like walking in and just being with Elsa, talking inn business. Or talking about Aria. Celia glances up at the renovated building; at the new windows illuminated by lamplight; at the large covered deck extending off the turret; at the lengthening shadows at twilight. Those shadows hold echoes of laughter, and tears; hold vague silhouettes of dancing, and embraces.

Tonight, everyone's here. The whole gang. Just like last summer, minus one.

Minus Sal.

And seeing the beach friends together, Celia will remember how they all loved Sal. Especially Jason, who was like a brother to him. What a tangled web of summer memories. With another shaky breath, she raises her hand and knocks on the door while opening it. She hears Elsa call out, right away.

"Celia? Back here!"

Walking down the dark hallway, Celia notices the dining room walls' distressed white paneling. It glimmers in the low light as an intimate dinner is underway. There are voices chatting, and silverware clinks on plates. As Celia hesitantly turns into the dining room illuminated only by lanterns and candlelight, all the women get up from the table and crowd around her and Aria.

"Ooh, she's so dear," Eva whispers while cupping the baby's head. "Hello, Aria. And look at that darling cap you have on!"

Celia touches the lace-trimmed cap. "It's to keep the sea damp off her head, in the evening."

Lauren shoulders Eva aside, bends low and smells the baby's head.

"*Ahem.*" Matt peers across the table at Kyle.

Celia looks from Kyle to Matt, who is now raising an eyebrow, too.

"Watch it, Kyle." Matt motions to Lauren, still bent close to the baby's head. Lauren inhales as her eyes flutter closed. "That's what I was warning you about."

"What?" Eva asks, looking back over her shoulder at her husband.

"Never mind," Matt tells her. "You come here and sit down, away from that pretty baby putting crazy ideas in your head."

"Matt!" Eva returns to her chair and slides it close so that she can get all cozy leaning into her husband. "Don't be silly," she purrs. "You think I want another baby now?"

Matt gives his wife a double take. "Exactly."

But what Eva can't see, which Celia does, is Matt pointing a cautionary finger at Kyle.

"Oh! Celia!" Maris clasps Celia's arm, then turns to the server, where lagoon-grass bouquets fill two white pitchers. "I made something for Aria." Maris pulls a tiny outfit from the tissue in a shiny pink gift bag.

"You *made* this?" Celia asks.

"Even though I don't design clothes anymore, I still love to sew." Maris holds up the denim outfit. "It's a chambray onesie!"

Celia takes it from her and turns it, running her fingers over the soft fabric. "That is so thoughtful, Maris. Aria will look *adorable* in this."

Lauren inches even closer, her arms outstretched as she cuffs her denim shirtsleeves. "Can I hold the baby?" Without waiting for an answer, she begins gently lifting Aria out of the cuddly carrier strapped around Celia's shoulders.

But something's going on between the guys at the same time. Celia happens to glance at Jason right as he elbows Kyle while nodding toward Lauren. So Celia looks at Lauren, who is smitten with Aria as she reaches her hands around the baby—while Aria's still strapped to Celia! Loosening one of the carrier straps, Celia helps lift Aria out.

"Actually, Lauren," Celia tells her as Lauren rocks Aria in her folded arms now, "it's really nice that you're holding her because I want to ask you something."

"Oh, sure." Lauren doesn't look up at her, and doesn't stop fussing with Aria … stroking her cheek, touching her tiny fingers.

With Lauren so intently focused on the baby, suddenly Celia gets it. The guys are utterly tuned in to some baby trance that comes over the ladies when they're near a newborn. It has Celia smile, not so much at the way Lauren holds Aria close while bouncing her very slightly.

No, it's more at the looks of panic on the men's faces as they're unprepared to handle this baby influence on their lives. Or on their *wives*, whose yearnings might instantly change their comfortable and familiar routines.

Celia steps closer to Lauren and strokes Aria's arm. "Lauren?" But there's nothing except cooing coming from Lauren. "Lauren, hon?" Celia whispers.

Finally, Lauren looks at her.

"Okay, that's better," Celia says with a warm smile. "Now listen. You were one of my first beach friends here, and so I would be completely honored if you might do something for me."

"Sure, Cee. Anything." Lauren looks from Celia to Aria's face and lightly touches the baby's chin. "You know that."

"Anything? So you'd even consider being Aria's godmother?"

"*Consider?*" Lauren's eyes instantly fill with tears. "Are you *kidding* me? I was hoping you'd ask me! Yes, yes, yes. Absolutely, yes." She bends and kisses the side of Aria's head, inhaling deeply as she does. "Hello, my sweet little godchild," she murmurs while cuddling the baby.

"All right!" Kyle punches the air and everyone turns to him in his cushion-laden chair. "You knew which couple to pick, Celia. The new *power* couple in this beach town." He sits against his back-pillow, then straightens his shoulders.

"What are you talking about?" Jason asks mid-chew.

Yes, *mid-chew*, Celia notices. Jason's so concerned with this new development threatening his Stony Point status, that he apparently doesn't have time to swallow first.

"I'm the godfather, man," Kyle says, right as Lauren sits beside him with Aria. He reaches over and gives Aria's tiny hand a gentle shake.

If he wore suspenders, Celia swears Kyle would have his thumbs hooked on them, looking pleased as punch. She smiles and unstraps the cloth baby carrier from around her shoulders.

"The godfather?" Cliff asks from beside Elsa. "How so?"

"By association," Kyle explains. "If Lauren's the god*mother*, I'm the god*father*. Right, Celia?"

The problem is, she'd asked Lauren on the spur of the moment. Celia starts walking to an empty chair at the far end of the table. "Well—"

"Wait!" Matt interrupts. "I've got rights, too." Every head silently turns to him now, waiting to hear his defense. "Godfather rights. Eva was Sal's first cousin. And Sal would want to keep the godfather in the bloodline."

Kyle sets an elbow on the table and points directly at Matt. "That's such bullshit and you know it."

"Whoa, whoa! Baby in the room." Sitting beside Kyle, Lauren holds Aria close and presses a hand to the baby's delicate ear. "*Language!*"

As if he didn't hear Lauren, Jason instantly picks up the godfather thread and runs with it. "Matt, if that's the case—if Sal would want the godfather to be part of the family—Maris was Sal's first cousin, too."

"Gentlemen." Elsa lifts her napkin and presses it to her mouth. "Are you really fighting to be … *godfather?*"

"Damn straight." Matt quickly turns to Celia. "I mean, *darn* right. Celia, listen." He takes a breath, then turns on every bit of his state police rule-enforcement tone. "When is this christening going to happen?"

"Well, I'm not sure exactly," Celia admits. "Later in the summer, I guess."

"Okay," Matt continues. "Just don't give the title away without any thought. It has to be *earned!* You need to do right by the Italian."

"Order!" Everyone looks to Cliff at the end of the table as he bangs a serving spoon as though it's a courtroom gavel. "Order in the room!"

"Stuff it, Judge," Kyle tells him. "I'm it. And if there's any duel, it'll be between me and Barlow."

"*Objection*, Kyle." As he says it, Cliff partially stands, then slowly sits again.

"Cliff?" Elsa asks while setting her hand on his arm. "Shh, stay calm."

"Never you mind." With that, Cliff removes Elsa's hand from his arm, fully stands and points across the table at Kyle. "Because I'm the closest relative Sal *almost* had. I would've been his stepfather, if things with me and Elsa moved past dating."

"Dating?" Kyle stands then, too. But slowly, with a hand on his back. "You mean your *wooing*?"

"Absolutely," Cliff tells him. "It's leading somewhere. Right, Elsa?"

Elsa simply shrugs and waves him off.

Which leaves Celia feeling like she's watching a tennis match, the way her head keeps whipping from one to another to another. Because as she finally makes it to a chair and sits, the guys press on with the godfather pursuit.

Cliff, after turning up his hands at Elsa, looks to Kyle again. "I'm telling you, I could've one day been Sal's stepfather."

"*Could've.*" Everyone looks to Jason, who is sitting back in his seat, wineglass in hand. "Could've is the operative word. Never actually happened, Commissioner, so tell it to the court."

When there's a sudden electronic squawk, Celia jumps, as does Cliff and probably half the table, the harsh squawk is so intrusive.

Cliff lifts a walkie-talkie from his belt and raises the radio to his mouth. "Nicholas," he says into the unit. "Come in."

"Just lowered the flag at the boardwalk," Nick's voice

echoes through the walkie-talkie, followed by a long beep. "You need me for anything else, boss, before I clock out?"

"I'll call you back after the godfather deliberation." Cliff nearly clicks off, but is stopped by Nick's instant response.

"The *what*?"

"We're deciding who will be Aria's godfather."

"Where are you?" Nick asks. After a second when only static sounds, he continues. "I thought you were home somewhere."

"I'm at Elsa's." Cliff looks at the adamant, stubborn gang sitting at the table. "Everybody's here."

"And you all hold off making that decision. I'm on my way over," Nick says. His voice is muffled through the small speaker. "Because I clearly should be Aria's godfather. Sal rode with me in the security car and we monitored the community *together*. Heck, he was my *paisan*!"

Cliff paces and heads to one of the tall dining room windows, as though he might see Nick approaching outside. "Wait. Nicholas! What about guard duty?"

There's no response, only steady static on his handheld radio. "Nick?" Cliff shakes the walkie-talkie, then presses the call button so that a piercing ringtone sounds. "Nicholas? Do you read me?"

Celia hurries to Lauren when Aria fusses. The baby's face scrunches as she begins to cry, which gets Lauren to gently return her to Celia's arms. And with good reason. In two seconds flat, Lauren is spewing some maternal wrath on the men.

"*Commissioner Raines!*" Lauren stands with one hand on her hip, one hand jabbing the air toward Cliff. "*You* are upsetting the baby! What decibel is that thing on, anyway? No normal human being needs their walkie-talkie that loud!"

"Sorry." Cliff fumbles with the unit, then hooks it back onto his belt.

"Get out now." Lauren aims her pointed finger around the table at the men. "All of you! You're upsetting Aria."

"Not only Aria," Celia says quietly, nodding in Elsa's direction.

All heads turn to Elsa sitting silent at the end of the table as everyone fights to be godfather to her son's child. Tears line Elsa's cheeks; the room goes silent.

"Aunt Elsa?" Maris says as she rushes to her side.

"It's just sad," Elsa explains over the baby's fussing. She glances at Celia holding Aria to her shoulder and rubbing the whimpering baby's back. "It's sad," Elsa continues, "seeing how much you all love Sal … and are fighting over him." She takes a long breath. "Yet he can't be here to see this."

Cliff pulls a handkerchief from his pocket and gives it to Elsa.

"It's okay," Maris whispers to her.

Elsa dabs the hanky to her tear-streaked face. She looks at Kyle, Matt, Jason and Cliff before speaking. "I think we need some quiet girl time, if you fellas don't mind."

Wordlessly, Eva stands and points to the doorway. As she does, all the men push back their chairs.

Oh, but Celia sees it, how Jason manages to grab another large forkful of that mac and cheese as he rises. It's as though he needs it for some godfather stamina as this argument is being moved to other quarters.

"Out!" Lauren says. She points to the doorway as well, her finger unwavering. "All of you. And your *walkie-talkies,* too."

seven

BACK IN THE DAY, THIS place was called Foley's.

Downstairs, the cottage was a market, stocking food and essentials for the beach community. Foley and his family lived upstairs. But it was the old man's grandson who got special attention. The kid was a little rough around the edges, so Foley tacked on an addition to keep an eye on him, and all the Stony Point teens, too. So much of the beach gang's history went down in that little hangout room as the friends spent many summer nights there ... playing pinball, having a brew, sharing laughs and stealing kisses—even throwing a few one-two punches when words got tense, egos threatened.

All these years later, if Jason had to name his biggest accomplishment with the inn renovation—the one feat for which he is most proud—it would be the old Foley's back room. Because he did it; he pulled off the nearly impossible. With structural changes all around it, and redesigns that moved adjoining interior walls, this hangout room from their youth remains utterly unchanged—even as a surrounding turret took shape.

Yes, from the dusty pinball machine in the corner; to the

original, creaking wood-planked floor; to the refurbished screen door; to the restored restaurant booths and even the dorm-sized refrigerator where they used to stockpile a six-pack or two, it's all here. Some of the old walls and sliding windows have been replaced, but still the original blueprint was honored and replicated.

Which was no easy triumph.

Every *design* cell of Jason's itched to update the windows, or reconfigure the far, shadowy wall. Or better align the outside doorway to the deck. The list goes on.

But at the same time, his heart insisted the room be left untouched. This way, the whole gang can walk through the door, snap open a can of beer and reminisce with summer ease.

Or hash out a conflict. Plenty of those went down in this dusty room, too. Oh, he can practically see the ghosts if the dim lighting's just right, or the dust swirls just so in the glow of the jukebox, or the floor creaks in a certain way. Words have flown here like knives; silences have festered in these walls for days; drinking glasses, or Neil's drumsticks, or decks of playing cards have been swept off tabletops, mid-argument.

~

Tonight's no different as the men all settle in the old back room once more. The lights are low; windows are slid open; warm sea air drifts in.

"Rock, paper, scissors to decide?" Nick asks. Still in his guard uniform, he caught up with them right as Lauren kicked them out of the dining room.

Jason shakes his head as he shovels in a mouthful of that caprese macaroni and cheese. He managed to nab his plate off the dining room table and sneak it in here.

"Nice. Rock, paper, scissors," Matt says as he snaps open a can of beer. "Except that's only good for two people."

"Winner advances through rounds with everyone," Nick explains before swigging his own brew.

"Too complicated," Jason decides. He gets up and grabs a cold can from the mini-fridge, amazed that Elsa actually keeps it stocked for them. That she tolerates their antics here. "How about a pinball tournament?" Jason asks with a nod to the illuminated pinball machine in the corner. "Surefire way to decide Aria's godfather."

"No way." Kyle moves over when Jason sits beside him again in the booth. "You always get the highest score. No one'll beat you."

"Exactly." Jason tips his beer can to Kyle's, then digs back into his cheesy dinner.

"No pinball." Kyle sets his elbow on the table and flexes his muscles. "More like arm wrestling. Brute strength wins." He eyes Jason beside him. "Right now, let's do this."

"How many times do we have to tell you?" Matt asks from where he stands and leans against the countertop. "Your biceps are twice the size of anybody else's."

"Level the playing field, man," Jason tells Kyle as he knocks Kyle's arm off the table.

"Hey." Kyle links all his fingers and stretches his arms in front of him. "I'm only capitalizing on the assets."

When Maris walks in with a plate of pastry and a carton of ice cream, Jason motions her to his table. "Over here, sweetheart."

"What *is* that?" Kyle asks, leaning close to the strawberry-swirled cake.

"Strawberry cobbler," Matt says. "Eva and Tay went strawberry picking. My wife's got pounds of berries to use up."

"Good way to keep her mind off having another baby," Jason tells him while swiping a hunk of bread through the cheesy macaroni dregs on his dish.

"No!" Kyle interrupts. "Strawberries are an edible aphrodisiac. Someone at the farmers' market once told me that."

With a raised eyebrow, Jason says, "Really, now …"

"*Seriously*. One evening, Matt, you'll be looking for a midnight snack and Eva will seduce you, feeding you one plump red berry at a time. Next thing you know, you've got an X-rated kitchen."

Oblivious to the talk, Nick slides into the seat across from Jason and eyes the strawberry pastry on the table. "Come to papa, where's my dish?"

"Guys, do you hear yourselves? It's *just* fruit. Anyway, here's some ice cream to have on the side." Maris sets down a large serving spoon and a stack of paper plates. "So did you decide who'll be Aria's godfather yet?"

"No." Kyle pulls the cobbler closer to him.

"Why not?" Maris asks. "It's really not that big of a deal. What's a godfather even do?"

She stops then, when they all turn and silently look at her.

"What?" she asks.

Jason only shakes his head, making her wary, so she backs up a step.

"You don't get it?" Jason asks his wife, pointing the last of his cheesy bread at her.

"Well. Being godfather is more an honorary title, isn't it?" She looks from Jason, to Cliff, back to Jason. "It doesn't really *mean* anything."

"Jason."

The voice is low, and comes from behind him. Jason turns to look at Matt still leaning against the countertop.

"I hate to say this, but do you even know who you married?" Matt asks with a nod toward Maris.

"Barlow was blinded by her beauty," Nick suggests.

Jason shrugs. "Yeah, that's a fair accusation," he says with a wink toward his wife.

"Are you kidding me, Maris?" Kyle asks while slicing the first of the cobbler. "You ever watch the movie? *The Godfather*?"

"Once." She backs up a step further, then turns toward the quiet jukebox and presses in a coin. "But that was a long time ago."

Watching her, Jason figures she's trying to distract them from their godfather interrogation by playing a good-time record. Quickly she picks a song, some summertime bluesy tune about driving on the highway, the miles rolling out beneath a wronged broken heart.

Doesn't work, Jason notices. He's finished his mac and cheese, leans back and cuffs his sleeves. The guys don't even notice the music. Instead, Kyle drops a serving of strawberry cobbler on Nick's paper plate.

"We're talking about being Stony Point's *Don*," Kyle reminds them all.

"Don? What the hell's that?" Nick asks, then scoops a spoonful of cobbler.

"Top dude, man. The boss." Kyle adds a heaping portion of the flaky, fruity dessert to his own plate. "The family leader. It's a position of deep respect."

"And fear, too. No one crosses the boss," Cliff adds.

"Maris!" Eva calls from the dining room. "Hurry up, coffee's percolating."

Maris quickly punches in another song or two on the jukebox. "Now listen, guys. Celia finally settled down Aria. So keep it chill in here," Maris tells them while rushing to the shadowy room's doorway. "I have to pour the coffee."

"Nice out," Matt tells her as they all wave her off.

But it's once they're digging in to their strawberry cobbler drizzled with melting vanilla ice cream that Kyle persists with the godfather issue—and with why the title should be his.

"Don't bother," Jason says while waving his spoon at him. "The title's custom-made for me."

"Bullshit." Kyle drags a spoonful of cobbler through the ice cream on his plate.

"What we have to do," Cliff says, "is rein this in. And we've still got time. Celia mentioned the christening would be later in the summer."

"Okay." Kyle nods across the table. "Well, Nicholas never even watched *The Godfather*. So he should be disqualified."

"No, no. Give him a chance. What we need is a movie night," Cliff suggests while dropping another scoop of cobbler on his plate. "It'll be a refresher for all of us."

"Perfect." Matt has hoisted himself up and sits on the countertop, plate of cobbler in lap. "We can try out my new man cave and watch it there."

"Really?" Nick asks Jason. "You finished redoing Matt's attic space, on top of the inn reno?"

"That's what I'm saying. I get shit done." Jason turns up his hands, then nods to Kyle to add more cobbler to his plate. "Which means I'm godfather material. Got all you losers beat."

"Not yet, you don't. So first … the movie. We need to watch it. And second," Kyle continues, refilling Jason's plate while brushing off his bogus godfather claim. "I need a badass binder."

"A binder?" Cliff looks around the room, glancing through the doorway out into the hall. "Elsa's got all kinds in her office, for the inn business."

"Grab me one when you get a chance." Kyle raises a spoonful of dessert, but holds it aloft, thinking. "See? Now *that's* godfather material. Giving critical orders like that."

"Critical?" Nick scoffs.

"Hell, yeah. I need Cliff to snag me a binder. How else can I keep track of things? And in the meantime, get ready for some serious competitions. We're talking a month of contests, rivalries, whatever you want to call them. I'll log each winner in the binder. Fair and square, whoever wins the *most* competitions will be granted the godfather title."

"Are we really going there with *contests*?" Jason asks, lifting his beer can for a swig. "Because I'm so the man for the job."

Cliff eyes him across the table. "Says who?"

Kyle shoves Jason out of his way, walks to the front of the room and puts his hands up for silence. "Sorry, Barlow. The coveted title will go to the winner of the godfather … The Godfather Tournament of Challenges! That's it."

Nick gives a sharp whistle at the same time that Matt cheers from the sidelines.

"It's the *only* way to decide who will be the *Don*." As Kyle says it, he air-quotes the word. "A Tournament of Challenges, Stony Point style. Then, and only then, will we know who will be the esteemed godfather to little Aria … Salvatore DeLuca's one and only daughter."

eight

JASON HASN'T BEEN SLEEPING WELL. With his cottage reno show's premiere just three days away, along with an exploding to-do list prepping for it, his stress has amped up. And keeps him tossing and turning, sweating, fighting against the bedsheets.

By Wednesday, he seeks calm where he always does—on the beach. This time, he sits beneath the shade pavilion on the boardwalk. Madison lies at his feet as Jason jots random thoughts for his premiere-night speech. A notepad is in his lap, a pen in his hand, and an empty beach before him. Saturday night, that beach will be overtaken by a sea of folding sand chairs. Each one—low profile; multi-position; highbacks and compacts; striped and solids of every bright color—will be occupied by someone waiting to hear his words.

Not yet, though. Behind him now, a gentle creaking noise rises. It comes from the boat basin, which moors about fifty boats. At one end, the little marina narrows to a wide creek that feeds the lagoon. The other side of the marina leads out to Long Island Sound. And in the basin, unseen currents move the little motorboats and cabin cruisers and fishing skiffs so that they pull against the pilings to which they're secured. As Jason struggles with his speech, the boats creak and sigh, sounding like some sort of sea fish.

Jay. You'll do fine, he hears his brother's voice as the boats talk behind him.

"It's our thing, bro," Jason quietly answers. "Yours *and* mine. Renovating old cottages. Stoked to bring it to this new level, but I never had to worry about an audience before."

"Who you talking to? The dog?"

Jason glances at Nick approaching at the same time Maddy sits up, her tail swishing across the boardwalk planks. "Something like that," Jason says as he pats the German shepherd's shoulder. It's apparent Cliff's rules and regulations have swung into high gear already this season. Nick's khaki button-down shirt with black epaulets is nicely creased, as are the black uniform shorts. "Looking sharp, Nick," Jason tells him. "What'd you do, iron your uniform?"

"Yes, okay? It's part of our dress code, thanks to Bradford."

"Kyle?"

"He gave Cliff some business pointers the other day, at Elsa's dinner. Explained how a polished, professional image evokes authority. Shit, the dude said he even irons his chef aprons! Put the idea in Cliff's head, and now all our threads have to be cleaned and pressed."

"Seriously? To patrol the boardwalk?"

"Word is we've got some whackos in this little summer paradise here." Nick sits in the shade beside Jason. "So Cliff doesn't want his security staff's authority missed by anyone. You know, *The rules are the rules.*"

"And you've got to enforce them."

Nick scratches the dog's ears. "That's right," he says, nodding toward a ruckus further down the beach. "So what's going on there? Those kids sneak in? Because I'll have to get them out, if that's the case."

"No, relax. It's Eva's daughter, Taylor. She's having a sweet-sixteen party with some friends at Elsa's inn."

Nick looks again, squinting out from beneath the shade pavilion. "Ah, sixteen. Those were some good times."

"Hell, yeah." Jason shoves Nick. "When was that, about five years ago for you, kid?"

"Hey, don't mess with authority." Nick stands and checks the time. "Okay, good," he says while straightening the heavy silver wristwatch that Sal left to him. "I've got a minute to scope out the boats." He points behind the boardwalk to the marina. "That one's legit, on the end."

Jason turns around and takes a look. "I like a Whaler, myself. My parents got me and my brother one, back when we were kids, twelve or so. We horsed around on the Sound. It was a nice little boat."

"No shit." Nick pulls his cell phone from his pocket and scrolls through his photos on the screen. "Check this out then."

Jason takes the phone and gives a low whistle when he sees a classified ad for a used Whaler similar to his old one. "What're you doing with that?"

"Thinking of buying it."

"Really, now …" Jason lifts his sunglasses and holds the phone closer for a better look. "Pretty hefty sum for you, no? $4K?"

"Nah. That's not the price. The real price is OBO. Or best offer. *That* I can swing."

"But a boat?" He hands Nick his phone. "You don't have any cash. You just finished college."

"Right. And I got a check from the 'rents. It's burning a hole in my bank account, I'm telling you. Listen, I'm the first in the family to graduate, don't forget."

"What a graduation bash Elsa threw your family at the inn last month. Great practice for when she opens up."

"It was friggin' awesome. And now it's time to splurge." Nick flicks his phone screen to enlarge the ad's photo. "My first official *adult* splurge, and it's going to be this boat."

"For real? What about your student loans?"

"I'm paying those, too. With my paycheck. Want to come with me?"

"Where?"

"To look at the boat. Got an appointment this afternoon, when my shift's done. Going to see this dude named Bud."

Before Jason can answer, his email dings. It's a message from Trent with a list of more instructions to keep him from sleeping at night: write a CT-TV promo post; get a picture of the renovated inn for the station's social media; confirm interview schedules for local news programs.

"Well. You game?" Nick asks.

"Where's it at?" Jason, still reading his own email, doesn't look up.

"Sound View. Off Hartford Avenue."

Okay, so now Nick's got his attention. "Damn, now that's a blast from the past."

"You busy?"

Scanning his email again, it's obvious his to-do list is out of control. "Always busy," Jason reminds him. "Could use some of your internship help, assisting me."

Nick pockets his phone and straightens an epaulet. "Sorry. I graduated, man. College internship's done. Must say, you worked me to the bone on Elsa's inn reno, but it got me some nice college credits."

"And I can't put you on the payroll until I see how the pilot goes. My series hinges on that. Then we'll talk."

Nick's walkie-talkie suddenly squawks, followed by Cliff's voice. "In the meantime, *that's* my boss this summer. Guard work's bringing in those paychecks covering my student loans." Nick lifts the walkie-talkie and starts to walk away. But before answering Cliff, he turns back to Jason. "So hey, you coming later?" Nick asks over his shoulder. "We'll go together to check out that Boston Whaler."

Jason hesitates while glancing first at his speech notepad, then at his cell phone loaded down with emails. On top of everything else, he can't forget Vinny. "Don't know. I have to give my brother-in-law a hand, too."

"Vincenzo?"

"Yeah. He and Paige are renting a cottage, and he needs help unpacking a few big things."

"Bring him along. Just pick me up at my guard post at one," Nick calls back. "At the trestle. I'll open your door and hop in."

When Jason nods, Nick waves him off and continues his shift, answering Cliff on the walkie-talkie while patrolling for any infringing vacationers on the sunny beach.

Before Jason gathers his pad and pen to head to his barn studio, he sends a text message.

Yo, Bradford, he types. *What's up today?*

In no time, Kyle texts back. *Another day of bed rest. Think I'll be good to work maybe tomorrow.*

Jason reads the message, squints out at the sparkling blue water of Long Island Sound, then back at his phone. *Want to go look at a boat?*

~

The shack's wood-boarded interior walls are painted white, but streaks of the wood grain show beneath the paint. Hurricane lanterns and candles line the wall shelves, and Maris lifts one of the lanterns. Even though sunlight shines through the weather-beaten four-paned window, she lights the wick in the lantern and sets it beside her table. A curl of smoke rises from the flame, and Maris thinks Neil probably spent many hours working on this manuscript by candlelight. Doing the same is her way of summoning his influence on the words.

Except lately, even candles don't help.

Sitting in front of her laptop, she nudges Jason's prized pewter hourglass beside it. She'd flipped it when she sat down to write today, and the sand grains steadily flow from the top glass bulb to the bottom. Its timed deadline often gives her creativity a nudge.

Still, nothing.

No writing inspiration. Nada. Zilch.

So she retrieves some dusty, salt-coated seashells from a wicker basket. Neil must've picked them up on the ragged beach where this shack once sat, nestled in dune grasses. She scatters a few shells around loose manuscript pages—*anything* to rouse her muse.

The problem is that Neil didn't finish his novel. When he died in the motorcycle crash ten years ago, it's obvious he'd been in the thick of writing this—fully intending to return to it in the days following the accident. Of course, he never did. And now Maris is unsure where to take the storyline … where Neil would want it to go.

So she paces Neil's private shack retreat until the grains of sand are depleted in the hourglass' top bulb. Since nothing's helping her write here, she extinguishes the lantern and walks across the backyard to her loft studio. When she'd been a denim designer, sketching helped spark ideas. Something about her hand free-drawing back and forth, giving shape to vague images, did the trick.

And it's a trick she also employs with novel-writing. Except instead of calling them fashion sketches, these are her *character* sketches. So she unlocks the barn studio, walks quickly across the planked floor through Jason's work area—past his drafting table, his framed photographs of completed cottages—and hurries up the stairs, managing to give the mounted moose head's nose a pat for luck.

Thirty minutes later, still nothing. No new ideas, no plot twists.

Yes, her worktable—a slab of barnwood nicked and notched from intense denim-cutting sessions—is covered with character sketches. And sure, her new sketches are lovely: one, a pencil rendering of her main character trying to secure a hurricane shutter over a window; the other, a charcoal delineation of waves rolling close to the story's cottage on stilts.

But it turns out that what her character sketches do is this: They remind her of the denim campaigns she *brilliantly* helmed for years as director of women's denim for Saybrooks Department Store.

Before she quit.

Maybe Jason was right; maybe it was one of those rash decisions made in grief, after Sal died. Maybe she never should've left denim designing.

But she can't talk about it to her aunt, Elsa, who is so preoccupied with her new granddaughter.

And she can't talk to her sister, Eva, who is busy with Tay's sweet-sixteen party, then leaving for a getaway at Martha's Vineyard.

And she definitely can't talk to her husband, Jason, about this horrible writer's block when the best thing that's ever happened to him is going on … right now! His TV show is to premiere in just days.

"Oh my God," Maris says while sinking onto her stool, right as the crying begins. "What did I *do*?" she asks herself between sobs, and while enough teardrops fall on a sketch to smear the pencil lines. She hasn't written a new page all week.

In the midst of her crippling insecurities, a loud knock comes at the door downstairs, right before the double slider opens.

"Knock, knock!" a voice calls out.

Still crying, she hurries to the loft's railing and looks down below. "Cliff?" He's standing there wearing khakis and a polo shirt, his gold-stitched COMMISSIONER cap on his head.

"Maris. I thought maybe Jason would be here. I'm dropping off my DVD of *The Godfather*." He waves the disk in the air.

"Oh. You can leave it on his desk," she says, then clears her throat while swiping away tears. "He's not home."

Cliff, watching her, hesitantly climbs the stairs to the loft. "Is everything all right?" he asks once halfway up, when he takes off his cap, too. "You seem upset."

Her eyes sting with more tears when Cliff reaches the loft.

"Please," she says. The DVD is still in his hand, but instead of taking it, she turns away to hide her tears. "Please don't tell Jason, Cliff."

"Tell him what?" He walks toward her worktable where her pencil sketches are strewn about.

"It's just that ..." she begins before pressing away even more tears with the back of her hand. "I think I made a huge mistake taking on this book to write."

"You mean, finishing his brother's manuscript?"

Maris nods. Now that she's actually admitted her doubts to someone, the floodgate opens and she can't stop blathering. "And Jason's so busy with his TV project, you have to swear not to tell him."

"Well, of course. But are you sure? Maybe he can help you."

"No! I can't worry him, not right before his pilot episode airs. He's worked too hard for me to go and mess it up."

Cliff fidgets with his COMMISSIONER cap and backs up a step, because okay, who wouldn't back away? She must look a wreck, blubbering, her eyes all bloodshot from stinging tears, her voice breaking. "Everybody thinks it's glamorous writing a book," she tries to explain. "But it's not. It's harder than anything else I've ever done. And completely overwhelming."

"Maris, we're all confident that you'll get it." After setting down his cap, Cliff picks up a sketch of one of her characters—a man hurrying away from a cottage in wind-driven rain. "That you're doing a fine job."

"It's not that I can't do it," Maris says as she takes the sketch from Cliff and glances at it before setting it down. "It's about honoring Neil's vision, you know? Except he's not here for me to run things by. And who am I to read his thoughts?"

"But you were friends with Neil, right? So you must have

an idea of his thinking." Cliff walks around her table, straightening one character sketch, picking up another.

"Really, Cliff. What's the point of all this toiling?" Maris starts collecting up her sketches in a messy pile. "I'm not getting paid, and who knows if the book will even get published—"

"Maybe you're trying to, you know," Cliff interrupts, "see across the Sound before you're there. That's pretty intimidating. You have to set sail, first. Do you have an itinerary? Or keep a journal, logging one step at a time?"

"No," Maris whispers, lest she start sobbing again. "What I'm doing is retyping Neil's manuscript, since his was all done on the typewriter in the shack. So as I retype it on the computer, I finish incomplete chapters, and tinker with passages while I work toward the ending. Each day, I pick up from where I left off."

"That sounds pretty involved. You need to keep an itinerary, like Elsa does. Treat the book like a business."

"Okay. I can try that."

Cliff pulls a handkerchief from his shirt pocket and gives it to her. "And maybe talk to Jason."

She only nods, dabbing her tears with his hanky.

"Where *is* Jason?" Cliff asks while lifting his cap and setting it on his head. "I can get him for you."

"He's at Sound View Beach. But no, I really don't want to worry him, especially not this week. He's been working *so* hard."

"Wait. He's at Sound View?"

She nods again, still dabbing her eyes. "Looking at a boat."

"You're getting … a *boat*?"

"What?" If only, Maris thinks. If only she didn't have to

face the dreaded blank page and could simply drive around looking at boats. What a grand life. Instead, Maris sits at her stool and picks up a pencil while holding that handkerchief clenched in her other hand.

"Oh, no. *We're* not getting a boat." Maris glances over her shoulder at Cliff. "Nick is."

nine

"PARK THERE." VINNY POINTS THROUGH the windshield to the vacant on-street parking spaces.

"Wait," Nick says as Jason veers his SUV into one of the spaces. "Bud's place is the next right. He said it's just off Hartford Avenue."

"Well, I'm parked now. So we can walk." Jason kills the ignition. "Shit, I haven't been to Sound View in a few years. Lots of memories here."

As he says it, two car doors slam behind his SUV. He gets out and waves to Kyle, who parked behind him, and to Matt, behind Kyle. "What are you doing here?" Jason asks Matt, who walks over in his state police uniform, minus the hat.

"Kyle texted me. Thought it would be fun to make a pit stop before getting to work."

"All right," Kyle says as he walks over holding a black three-ring binder. "Let's go, then."

"What the hell's that?" Vinny asks, nodding to the binder.

"Oh, right. You weren't at Elsa's that night, when this was arranged. The binder's to log our godfather competitions." Kyle gives a sweeping motion to the tiny cottages and colorful storefronts lining the beach street. "And this place is prime real estate."

"For what?" Nick asks, walking closer while eyeing the binder.

"For accruing godfather points." Kyle gives Vinny the Tournament of Challenges lowdown, then pulls a pen from behind his ear and points it at the opposite street corner. "You've got a bocce court, there." When they all turn, Kyle continues. "And I saw a sign when we pulled in. Something about an annual Frisbee-throwing contest on the beach."

"Now that's right up our alley," Matt says. He follows behind Nick, who checks his watch and heads toward his afternoon appointment. "Add that one to your binder, Bradford."

While they walk past cottages crammed too close, and little beach shoppes selling cheap sunglasses, penny candy and blow-up rafts, Kyle jots notes as the competition deliberations continue.

"Don't forget the infamous beach doughnuts. They've got the best on the Connecticut shore." Vinny points to Kyle's page of notes. "Add those to your list, too."

"No way are we doing a doughnut-eating competition," Jason insists when they turn onto the side street where Bud lives. "That's crossing a line of good taste."

Vinny looks at him and shakes his head. "They're not a *competition*. The doughnuts are *fuel* … to get us pumped."

"Okay, pipe down, fellas." Nick turns to face them all. "Here it is," he says, nodding to a rustic cottage with a massive side yard. The cottage is dark brown, with an open front porch trimmed in white. "This is where the boat is."

"Damn," Jason says while surveying the yard and its mown lawn. "You could fit another cottage in that yard. It's huge, something you don't see too much of here. Most of the yards are postage stamps."

"Double lot," Nick explains. "Bud told me he takes the overflow from the beach parking lot on weekends. Twenty bucks a car."

"Nice gig," Kyle comments, considering the yard. "Looks like his Whaler's there, near the back of the cottage."

"How you doing?" a voice calls out, and they all look to the front door where a man in his thirties just walked onto the porch. The screen door slams behind him. "Nick?"

"This is it, guys," Nick whispers. "Back me up on my lowball offer." Nick turns and crosses the yard as this Bud dude walks down the steps and shakes hands with him, then leads them all to a boat trailer holding a small white Whaler. Its interior is freshly painted a turquoise blue, and the wooden dash and bench seats have been sanded and varnished.

As Jason stands beside Nick, listening to Bud explain how the vessel has a new battery and new fuel lines, someone pulls him back by the arm.

"What's up?" Jason turns and asks Kyle, who's motioning him close.

"Now that's *perfect* for our competition," Kyle whispers, nodding to the used boat.

"A boat? For the godfather competition?" Jason looks at the Whaler sitting on a rusted trailer. "How so?"

Kyle's eyes are locked onto the vessel, even as he opens his black binder and begins writing. "Can't you see it, out on the open water?"

"See what?" Jason asks him.

"*Tubing*, man. A rad tubing contest, right on the open sea."

Forty-five minutes later, Jason realizes no tubing contest will be undertaken. Nothing will be competed on the open sea, as Nick leaves Bud's property without sealing the deal.

"Come on, Nick," Matt says as though trying to change Nick's mind. "It looked pretty sweet."

When they walk to the end of the block and turn onto Hartford Avenue, Nick unhooks his sunglasses from his pocket and puts them on. "I was distracted by you guys, the way you kept changing the subject. Talking with Bud about the bar on the beach, and how much cash he pulls in on a hot Saturday, parking cars. And then, Jason, well, you let me down. You had a Whaler once and didn't even help negotiate."

"Hell, when Bud mentioned Vecchitto's Italian Ice, shit, I forgot all about that joint. Best Italian ice around. Used to go there with Neil."

"Exactly. You talking about Italian ice didn't help lower the vessel's price," Nick goes on. "What it did was give *Vinny* a chance to inspect the boat, and now *he* wants it."

"Where is Vincenzo anyway?" Kyle asks.

"For crying out loud. Check it out." Matt points halfway down the block where Vinny approaches them while eating something. It's a flat piece of buttered fried dough resting on the top of his outstretched fingertips.

Jason shakes his head. Leave it to Vinny to find the food. Good food, too. Well, cholesterol on a plate. But still.

As they descend upon Vincenzo and his cuisine, Cliff Raines drives by and beeps his horn.

"What's the boss doing here?" Nick asks, turning as Cliff parks his car at the curb.

"Who cares?" Kyle hits Vinny's shoulder. "Hey, give me a piece of that."

Vinny turns away. "Get your own," he says while ripping off a hunk of the golden dough with his teeth.

"Where? Because man, I can't stop eating since living here in all this damn salt air." Kyle squints further down the street. "Gives you a friggin' appetite, I'll say."

"That little stand, next block." Vinny hitches his head in the general direction. "Place called The Beach Shanty. Come on, I'll show you."

He does, and ten minutes later, the five of them are chowing down on warm fried dough thickly dusted with powdered sugar. They're walking the sandy street's sidewalk leading to the public beach, where a honky-tonk bar sits right on the sand. The bar is in a low-slung blue building with large window frames lining the walls. But no glass panes are installed; the window openings are left empty to let in the sea breeze.

Finishing their fried dough, the men walk across the beach, around to the front side of the bar. There, a large gray deck is covered with round tables, stools and groups of people in shorts, tank tops and bathing suits. A small stage butts up against the deck, and a local band plays nostalgic tunes beneath the blazing sun.

"Ah, bliss," Kyle says after they cross the hot sand and sit beneath an umbrella at one of the deck tables. "One beer, to wash down the dough."

"Four drafts," Jason tells the waitress, "and a soda for Matt, our state trooper ready to clock in."

"Make it five drafts," a slightly winded voice says behind them.

They all turn to see Cliff catching up, holding his own half-eaten fried dough—his piece slathered with pizza sauce and cheese. He pulls over a chair and sits beside Nick.

"What are you doing here, Judge?" Kyle asks.

After folding the last of his sauce-covered dough into his mouth, Cliff holds up a finger while chewing. "I could be asking all of you the same question," he finally manages around the food.

"Shouldn't you be enforcing ordinances?" Jason presses. "Or helping Elsa with something at her inn?"

"Ha." Cliff shifts in his seat before taking off his sunglasses. He uses his shirt fabric to wipe a smudge on the lenses.

"*Ha?* What's that supposed to mean?" Nick asks him.

"What it means," Cliff begins, then pauses as he rests an arm on the table, "is that my relationship with Mrs. DeLuca has fallen to the wayside. She's much too busy lately, and we've been drifting apart."

"Bullshit." Jason turns and scrutinizes him.

Cliff puts his sunglasses back on, then pulls them off to inspect a lens before putting them on once more. "I'm just saying. Between her new granddaughter, and Celia living there, and inn preparations, there's no room left for me. Not right now, anyway."

"You've really got to man up, Judge." Kyle leans across the table and lowers his voice. "Move things along in the romance department."

"Just get a ring on that finger," Jason advises him. "You'll be all set then."

"Yeah. Lock it down, boss," Nick adds.

"In due time." Cliff glances toward the band striking up a raucous summertime number. "So tell me about this boat of yours, Nicholas."

"How'd you know I was buying a boat?"

"Heck, there are no secrets at Stony Point," Cliff says. "You're aware of that, aren't you?"

"A boat. Can't you just see it?" Jason asks as the waitress deposits a tray of drinks. He picks up a frothy glass and takes a long swallow. "Maybe do some night fishing out on the water, instead of from the rocks?"

"Absolutely." Kyle opens his black binder and grabs his pen. "I'd buy myself a new rod for that. Let me pencil in a fishing contest for this godfather competition."

"Hey, fishing?" Nick asks as he slides over his draft beer. "It's not *your* boat. It's mine."

"Except you didn't even get it," Vinny reminds him. "And Bud says someone else is looking at it tonight."

"Eh," Jason says. "That ain't nothing but a lie, to try for a quick sale with Nick."

"And I'm *thinking* about it." Nick sips his beer. "It'd be a nice way to get some peace and quiet from that daffy beach community of yours. *And* figure out my life now that I'm done with college."

"Cheers to that," Cliff tells him while tipping his beer glass to Nick's.

"What are you going to do with yourself," Matt asks, "now that you're a college grad?"

"Don't know yet." Nick looks out at the beach beyond the bar, nodding at Long Island Sound rippling beneath the afternoon sun. "Which is why I'd use my boat like Sal did. Drift a little out there and do some thinking."

"Drift?" Jason asks.

Kyle jumps right in, too. "You don't even know how to drop anchor, dude."

As Nick denies that, and as they finish their beer and walk

back along the beach road to their cars, the guys don't let up on Nick.

You'll need to take a boating safety course, and get your state certificate.

Do you even know how to swim?

Where will you keep this vessel? There's a mile-long waiting list for the Stony Point boat basin. Nobody ever gives up their slip.

Can you even read a chart and navigate the Sound?

"Ever think about celestial navigation?" Kyle asks after they've walked two blocks. "I read that if you can plot a course by the stars alone, you'll never need a compass."

"My brother was into that shit." Jason eyes some run-down buildings while talking. "Neil read up on it in one of his dog-eared books. An old copy of H. A. Rey's *The Stars.*" They keep walking and approach a long, boarded-up building. Its wood-planked white walls are faded; the windows are covered with weathered plywood; random vines climb its walls to the low roof; a lone broken chair sits outside one of the dark doors. "Hey, check it out," Jason says, stopping in front of the abandoned structure. "Isn't that the old arcade?"

"Yeah. Out of business." Kyle looks over. "They closed it up last year, at the end of summer."

"Too bad." Matt stops and considers the neglected building. "Eva and I used to go there. Shot some hoops, played lots of Skee-Ball back in the day. Rode those padded bumper cars."

"Me, too. They had the best video games. When we were kids, we'd load up on tokens and play for hours," Jason says. As he scrutinizes the building, noting the peaks at both ends, and the vertical wood siding, isn't it funny … If he listens carefully, he swears he can hear whispers, and echoes of laughter as the building's shadows waver in the summer sunlight.

"I've never been there." Cliff lifts his sunglasses and squints over. "Would've made for a great godfather competition stop."

"Ahem."

They all turn to Kyle, who is opening his trusty black binder. He nods to the corner lot across the street, a few yards past the empty arcade building. So they all look at the manicured bocce court there, then back to Kyle—who is already headed to the framed playing area. Several colorful bocce balls wait, seemingly just for them. There's even a mounted score post with a clipboard attached to record each player's points.

Kyle wastes no time declaring *this* their first official godfather competition.

As he distributes a ball to each of them, he also gives bocce history, saying that the game was actually depicted in a painting in an ancient Egyptian tomb.

But it's as he explains the rules about standing outside the frame when you throw your ball, and as he chooses who will throw out the first target ball, that's when it happens.

Jason can just see it coming.

The afternoon sun beats down on them. Fingers are flexed and arms stretched. Kyle clasps his hands behind his neck and surveys the playing court. Arguing ensues: *It's all in the wrist*, and *No, it's about control, man.*

As the players elbow each other to move over, and then roll a practice ball onto the court amidst hoots and hollers, Jason knows.

As more practice balls of blue and red and yellow roll along the court, bouncing off Cliff's, then ricocheting into Vinny's, Jason knows without a shadow of doubt.

A serious bocce battle is about to begin.

ten

THURSDAY MORNING, CELIA PUTS ON a straw fedora and sits alone on her stoop. Rays of morning sunshine reach her, and a robin in the dewy lawn sings a cheerful song. When Celia listens carefully, she also hears the whisper of the dune grasses edging Elsa's yard, near the secret path leading to the beach.

It's that sound that makes her wistful. Was it only last summer that she'd sit on the little dock behind the cottage she was staying in? The cottage was right on the lagoon, and those swaying marsh grasses whispered and sighed during those days when she fell in love with Sal.

"Hello!" a voice calls out now.

Celia tips back her fedora and sees Lauren coming up the walkway to the guest cottage. Her blonde hair is in a loose side braid, and she wears a long sundress with flat sandals. As if reading Celia's mind, she also carries a tray of two take-out coffees.

"Come on up," Celia says as she slides over and pats the stoop beside her. "Have a seat."

"Well, this is nice." After handing Celia a coffee, Lauren sits on the stoop, holds her coffee cup on her knees and takes a deep breath of the salt air. "I just dropped the kids at Parks and Rec for a beach treasure hunt today. Thought I'd swing by here and say hi to you and the baby."

"I'm really glad you did."

"Where's Aria?" Lauren asks as she lifts her sunglasses to the top of her head. "Napping inside?"

"No. She's with Elsa this morning." Celia nods toward the inn.

"Oh, that's sweet. I'll bet Elsa's whipping up something delicious in the kitchen—with Aria no doubt listening to an earful of early cooking advice from her nonna!"

"Probably! I was just on my way over there. But first, you can give me the scoop, Lauren. Because I hear the godfather competition got underway with a bocce game yesterday?"

"Did it ever." Lauren sips her coffee. "From what Kyle said, the guys got really intense. I mean, Cliff even used a *ruler* to measure the bocce balls' distance to verify the points. You know how particular he is about enforcing the rules."

"And who won?"

"Vinny."

"Vinny … I barely know him."

Lauren shifts and leans against the railing post. "He's a great guy, married to Jason's sister. And with a name like Vincenzo, I'm not surprised he won *bocce*!"

"It's kind of funny how they all want to be Aria's godfather. Sal would've gotten a kick out of that." Celia sips her hot coffee. "How many competitions do the guys have planned?"

"Kyle said about a month's worth."

"A month? Holy cannoli!"

"Yep, this should get interesting." Lauren sets her coffee

on the top step and slips off her sandals in the warm sunshine. "I'm so glad you moved back here, Cee," she says. "I like having my beach friend around again."

"Me, too."

"And Elsa helps you with the baby. She's delighted to be a grandmother!"

"Elsa's so cute, Lauren. You know how she became a Justice of the Peace so she can have weddings at the inn? Well, what she sometimes does is read to the baby from her JP handbook. Her voice is all soft and soothing, like she's reading a nursery rhyme. Instead, it's wedding formalities she's memorizing!"

"So actually, one of Aria's first read books is all about love."

Celia gives Lauren's arm a light pat. "Let's go get Aria now. It's almost time for her morning nap, anyway."

"I thought you'd never ask!" Lauren is quick to grab her coffee, rush down the steps and head in the direction of the Ocean Star Inn. Her long sundress flutters in the breeze as she pulls on her sunglasses.

"Speaking of books," Celia says as she catches up beside Lauren, "did you hear the latest about Maris?"

"Kyle just read a chapter from the novel she's working on." As she says it, Lauren stops at Elsa's *inn*-spiration walkway. She carefully kneels in her dress and picks up a fat piece of chalk. "Maris needed pointers on a food passage."

"But there's more." Celia moves closer to her friend and lowers her voice. "From what Cliff told Elsa, and Elsa told me, Maris had a private breakdown yesterday."

"About what?" Lauren glances up from the message she's writing across the walkway. "Jason?"

"No. It was about the book she's writing. Neil's old manuscript."

"Come on. It's an amazing thing she's doing, honoring Neil that way and co-writing it."

When Lauren sits back and reads her inspiring phrase, Celia does, too. *Salt Air and Not a Care!* "Maybe Maris needs some of your advice." Celia nods to the chalked words.

"But everybody's so supportive of her," Lauren is saying as she stands and brushes chalk dust off her hands. Together they walk toward the inn's back entrance.

"Even so, now she wonders if it's a big mistake, and might even quit the project, I guess. Do something else … maybe work with Jason."

"She *said* that?"

"I heard it from Elsa, who heard it from Cliff. Maris said she's ready to dump that manuscript right into Long Island Sound!"

"No!" Lauren grasps Celia's arm and actually stops walking with the shock of hearing this news. "I cannot believe that!"

Celia shrugs and takes off her fedora, right as she opens the inn's door into the kitchen. "Trouble, trouble," she says. "You never know what's going on behind closed doors."

The sand-chair premiere of Jason's cottage-reno show is two nights away, and Maris says he needs something new to wear.

Which was exactly his argument last fall when he resisted signing on with the show: that he wouldn't be able to simply be himself. He didn't want to have to fuss with his appearance. To shave when he didn't feel like it. Cut his hair. Wear appropriate business clothes.

"That's just silly," Maris told him this morning. "We'll go

to the outlet stores in Clinton after lunch and find something nice." She walked over to him drinking his coffee at the kitchen table and slid the back of her fingers along his three-day shadow of whiskers. "Something … *you.*"

And he knew he was doomed. Shopping with Maris for just the right look would turn into an all-day affair, and his itinerary was too crammed already.

"No, that's all right. I'm … going with Kyle," he lied. "Kyle said he'll pick something out with me, maybe grab a shirt for himself."

"Are you sure?" Maris asked as she headed out the kitchen slider toward the shack for her morning writing session.

"We're on it." Jason lifted his coffee cup and nodded. One dashed-off text message later and a plan was in place to meet Kyle after his shift at the diner. Jason thought ahead, too. He'd wear the same pants he'll wear at the Saturday premiere. That way, he wouldn't have to mess around with his prosthesis while trying on clothes. This would be a shirt-only mission.

So here he is, spending a Thursday evening shopping, at his third outlet store already.

Jason stands at the narrow mirror inside his dressing room. A long, tubular light is mounted on either side of the glass. Seeing his reflection up close and illuminated, he buttons a short-sleeved madras shirt, then tucks his dog-tag chain behind it. But when he steps closer to the mirror, it's not the shirt Jason notices so much as his face. His skin looks pasty, and there are slight circles beneath his eyes. Shit, is he that shot? He steps right to the mirror and draws a hand over his jaw. When he hears Kyle whistling, he knows he's returned with more things to try on.

"Glad you could make it tonight, man," Jason calls out, still at his mirror. "Shopping with Maris would've been an ordeal."

"Tell me about it." Kyle shuffles and rattles the shirt hangers before pushing them past the curtain for Jason. "Women."

Jason takes the two new shirts from Kyle before leaning even closer to the mirror for another scrutiny of himself. He presses back the skin near his eyes.

"Come on," Kyle says right as he gives three raps on the wall. "Let's see your threads."

Still considering his reflection, Jason tugs the madras shirt's short sleeves. The woven plaid fabric fits well, but he's not sure it's the right look for him. Or maybe it's not that. Maybe he's bothered by his tired face in the mirror. "Hell, I took a week off and I'm more stressed than ever."

"What gives?" Kyle asks from outside the dressing room.

"I was supposed to *enjoy* this week before the premiere. Go to the barber's, buy some new clothes, work on a speech. And I've done nothing but worry." Jason turns and gives another sidelong look at his reflection, including his needs-a-trim wavy hair that hasn't made it to the barbershop yet. "I'm better off when I'm overworked."

"You'll be fine. What about shoes? You good?" As he asks, Kyle slides open the dressing room curtain.

"I don't need any shoes." Jason looks over as Kyle holds up one more shirt for Jason's consideration.

"Your wife letting you go to the premiere all unkempt like that?" Kyle lightly slaps the side of Jason's head. "Got that mountain-man thing going on again, I see. Thought you went to the barber's."

"Not yet. But hey, guy, you've got something on *your* face," Jason tells him while touching his own chin, right below his lip.

Instantly, Kyle's hand goes to his chin as he leans in front of the illuminated mirror. "This?" He turns to Jason while pointing to a shadow beneath his lower lip.

"Yeah."

"That's my soul patch. Trying out a new look this summer." He hangs the last shirt and checks out the bit of hair beneath his lip in the mirror again. "Seriously, what do you think of the patch?"

"Well, right now it could look like a birthmark … or a bruise. Might need some work, Bradford."

"And I could say the same for you." Kyle shakes his head, then reaches out and flicks Jason's shoulder. "The shirt's really not cutting it. You might look better in something with long sleeves."

"See?" Jason winces at his reflection. "I knew it. Nothing's working." He takes off the madras button-down right then and there. "Look at that," he says while holding up the shirt. "It has *pink* in the pattern. I didn't notice that before."

"Wait. Is the pattern the same on both sides of the fabric?"

"What?"

"Check. See if the pattern is identical on each side. If it isn't, I read in one of those fashion magazines that it's not an *authentic* madras." Kyle squeezes into the dressing room and takes off the black tee he cooked in all day. "Here, never mind and just give me that." He puts out his hand.

"You can have it." Jason tosses him the fancy shirt, lifts his faded concert tee from a wall hook and pulls it on while leaving the dressing room. After straightening the shirt and adjusting his dog-tag chain again, he waits on a padded bench for Kyle. He also pulls a pen and paper from his back pocket and jots an idea for premiere night, then clicks his pen. *Click-click.* "You want to swap places with me?" he calls out to Kyle. "Write my speech?"

"No, thanks," Kyle mutters from behind the dressing room curtain.

"That's all I've been doing lately, writing speeches. For Sal's eulogy, then the architect award gala last fall. Now this." *Click-click-click.* "What I could go for right now is a smoke." *Click.*

"Hey, hey. We quit those, bro. On New Year's Day. Made a pact at The Sand Bar, remember?"

"Yeah, well." Jason clicks his pen again. "Just one couldn't hurt."

"No, man. You know what you have to do?" Kyle asks, still behind the curtain. "Get that speech written. Do what Elsa told me when I was working on your best man speech. Write from the heart. No gimmicks."

Jason shrugs, pen in hand, but doesn't say anything. Just sits with his elbows on his knees and fidgets. *Click-click-click.*

Suddenly the dressing room curtain sweeps open. Kyle steps out, reaches for Jason's pen and easily snaps it in half before dropping it in a trash bin. Then he turns to the three-way wall mirror and adjusts the madras shirt that he wears loose over his black chef pants.

"*I'm* buying this shirt. It looks better on me than you." Kyle turns and glances over his shoulder at the back side, before eyeing Jason. "Try on those other shirts I brought in." He hitches his head toward the dressing room. "One oughta do the trick, then we're done. And tomorrow night? It's fishing night. First one of the summer."

"I don't know, Kyle." Jason returns to his dressing room and slides the thick curtain shut. "I have to get ready for Saturday and have a boatload of stuff to do," he says while pulling his concert tee over his head again.

"No. What you need to do now is just unwind," Kyle says from the waiting area. "Clear your calendar for Friday night fishing, dude. Cast away your troubles, straight into the sea."

eleven

NEIL WAS AN OBSERVER.

It's an indisputable fact, evidenced by the shelves of leather and canvas journals lining Jason's architect-studio bookshelves. And now, even more journals line the shelves of Neil's salvaged shack. Earlier this afternoon, Maris paged through one. It felt clandestine as she unlooped a salty string of fishing line from around the leather cover. The private journals in the old shack had never been seen before, except possibly by Lauren. It's with Jason's blessing that Maris is slowly reading them. Her finger follows along the lines of Neil's slanted cursive; her mind absorbs his observations of run-down shingled cottages, and his thoughts of life near the sea, and his secrets kept close.

All of which Maris is also finding in Neil's book.

Yes, Neil was an observer. And whatever he observed in his daily life, he then brought to the manuscript—tucked into dinner scenes, and settings, and conversations, and narratives. Knowing this helps Maris to understand his writing process. Which helps her to move his story along.

So she decides to assume Neil's writing routine and become an observer, herself.

With that in mind, on Friday evening she walks along the sunset beach. She has a little time before she's supposed to meet up with the ladies at the inn. Gently breaking waves wash over her feet; the salt air and call of the gulls are the same backdrop as the book's. She soaks it all in—observing, observing. Then she pauses on the secret path leading through dune grasses to Elsa's newly renovated, but still unopened, inn. With the sweeping grasses whispering at her feet, Maris pulls her own brand-new leather journal from her tote and jots down what she sees.

The challenge is this: Anyone can simply note the white tents set up for Jason's TV show premiere tomorrow night; or the catering equipment and tables; or the sloping lawn of the inn's grounds; or even Elsa, Celia, Lauren and Eva setting out decorations a day early. Together, they're dangling paper lanterns and twinkly lights.

The trick is to find the *magic* in what she's seeing. The story. The sadness in Celia hanging Mason jar candles from tent spokes.

Or the secrets hidden in Lauren's painted driftwood centerpieces.

Or the hope in the tiki torches Elsa sets on the edge of the lawn.

Or the mysterious reason Eva is off to the side, intently on her cell phone.

Line sketches accompany Maris' jotted words as she observes the scene. Slowly she walks up the path, moving closer while sketching and writing, until finally her presence is detected.

"Maris!" Elsa calls out as she hurries over. "How *are* you?" she asks while hugging her.

Maris pulls back with a small smile. "Okay." Before she barely gets her journal and pen tucked back into her tote, Lauren is walking up with a pitcher and glass in her hands. She wears a white lace tank top over frayed denim shorts.

"Want some lemonade?" Lauren casually asks.

Oh, but Maris is not fooled by her nonchalance. It's too insistent, and is accompanied by worried glances to the others.

"Everything okay, hon?" Lauren lifts the pitcher so that lemonade and ice cubes clink into the glass.

"Hey, Maris." Celia walks over holding her daughter, right as Maris takes the lemonade from Lauren. "Aria says hi!" She lifts the baby's hand and waves it in Maris' direction. "You still plugging away at that novel? I so need a book to read when Aria's napping."

Elsa, wearing a sweater tied around her shoulders, takes Maris' arm and leads her closer to the tents and tables. "You've been writing all day? I hope you're keeping up with your nourishment. There must be snacks good for the writing muse, no?"

The thing is, when her aunt turns to raise an inquisitive eyebrow at Maris, it can't be missed how Elsa *first* throws a furtive glance at Celia and Lauren.

"You know," Elsa continues as they walk toward the inn. "Some food to get the wheels spinning differently?"

"Kyle says blueberries work." Lauren rushes ahead and sets the lemonade pitcher on a table, then turns back to Maris. "So how about blueberry muffin snacks? Blueberries are … are … good for the mind! Something about their antioxidants. Yes, they can really help, Maris!"

"Lots of things can help," Celia says from behind her. "Taking walks, for instance."

Maris stops. Stops dead in her tracks in the middle of Elsa's lush, sloping lawn. Stops so suddenly, Celia nearly bumps into her, but veers around in the nick of time. Further up the hill, the inn rises in shadow, looking dark and gothic in the low lighting.

"Wait just a minute." Standing stock-still, Maris eyes each of them. "You're all in on something, aren't you? Because you're *obviously* trying to help me. But … help what?"

From the side of the yard, her sister rushes over then. "Oh my gosh, Maris!" Eva says. "You can*not* quit writing."

"What?" Maris squints at them through the evening's lengthening shadows. Out past the secret beach path, the horizon is pale lavender.

Eva doesn't answer her right away. She simply stands there in her cropped black skinnies and denim jacket, then quickly takes up every bit of Maris in a huge embrace, one that rocks back and forth, too. "Don't worry," Eva whispers when she pulls away and brushes a strand of hair from Maris' face. "I just texted your husband and gave him a piece of my mind. He's been so greedy with that spotlight. He's all *my* TV show, *my* cottage, *my* producer. Jason needs to share the spotlight with you, because what you're doing with Neil's manuscript is *so* honorable."

Maris takes a step toward the inn. Then another. As she does, the women close in on her, blocking her from moving away from them. Eva touches her hair again; Lauren and Celia lean close, their heads tipped, concerned smiles on their faces. Elsa motions for her to sip from her glass of lemonade, which, okay, Maris does. *What the heck is going on here?* she wonders at the same time. She's never seen the women like this.

"What you're doing takes courage," Lauren insists.

"Even if you don't know where the story's going," Eva assures her. "Because don't worry, it's going somewhere."

Celia shifts Aria on her shoulder. "Elsa already has a reserved empty shelf for your book, in the inn's gift shop. Reserved!"

"What?" Maris turns and looks at all of them again.

Suddenly, she gets it. They all know her secret—that she's been having a really hard time with the writing. "How in the world would any of you know I've got writer's block?" Maris asks as she sinks into a folding chair beside a catering table. "I mean, I only told Cliff when he walked in on me a little upset. And even then, I just *mentioned* that I was having a hard time."

"And he told me *all* about it," Elsa says as she crouches beside Maris and touches her arm.

"And Elsa told me," Celia admits as she gently bounces the baby.

Lauren lifts a sweatshirt from a chair and slips her arms into the sleeves. "And Celia told me."

"And," Eva chimes in while shaking her cell phone in the air, "they all told me!"

"Your husband needs to support *you*, too," Elsa tells Maris.

As she's pulling another chair over the lawn to be close to Maris, Eva continues her rant. "Jason's so self-absorbed. I've always said that."

"Jason?" Maris looks at Eva as she sits beside her. "*My* Jason?"

"That's neither here nor there," Elsa insists as she grabs a nearby chair, too. And suddenly the others are pulling over chairs and sliding them to Maris' side. "Now listen," Elsa continues as she sits and points to the inn's illuminated turret. "Celia and I set up a special writing nook for you. There's a nice table at the window, and a chair, and pillows. The inn won't be open until September, so you'll have a solid month or two of quiet time in your own space. Especially if you need to get away … like on a writing retreat."

"You did that for me?" Maris whispers. In the dusky evening light, she looks up at the turret's third-floor room. There's only one thing its windows face, and that would be the distant sea. "That's so sweet of you."

And though they brush it off and act as though the gesture was nothing, Maris knows. Yes, she's always felt these women were the best people in her life, and now there's no denying it. At the slightest hint of distress, they all swoop in like birds, wings outstretched to lift her up.

But it's Lauren who surprises her then, when she leans close, takes Maris' hand in hers and looks her in the eye.

"Now be honest with us, hon. Do you really need help with the book?" she asks. "Or maybe you need a little marriage counseling? Sometimes when you and your spouse go in new directions, the marriage can drift apart."

"What?" Maris stands up and walks back and forth in front of them. "No. No, Jason and I are fine. Really! It's just that we Barlows don't always handle stress that well."

"Stress or not, I texted Jason, telling him to step it up!" Eva shakes her fist in the air. "Where is he, anyway? I wouldn't mind talking to my brother-in-law face-to-face."

"Jason?" Maris asks. "Well, he's at The Dockside. Kyle keeps a plate warm for him on Friday fishing nights. Which are starting up tonight. And he's really *fine*. It's not Jason that's on my mind."

"Of course, dear." Even though it's Elsa who says it, all the ladies nod and stand for a group hug.

The magic of it is that it works. Their hovering and fussing and supporting make Maris feel better. These special women lift her doubts. Lord knows her anxiety lately has been crippling—going from director of women's denim to debut novelist! It's felt like walking straight off the bluff without knowing how deep the water is.

But this early summer evening, in the misty light, with fireflies flickering and the dune grasses whispering, what Maris knows is this: Elsa, and her sister, and Lauren and Celia? They are her life buoys, always keeping her gently afloat.

~

"How's the leg?" Kyle asks.

Jason glances over his shoulder at Kyle, who's finagling his fishing line, pulling some gadget or gizmo from the tackle box. That one question has come every Friday fishing night for the past couple of years, and apparently this year is no different. When Jason doesn't say anything, Kyle looks at him and turns up a hand, waiting.

"Fine." Jason shifts his stance as he leans against a boulder. "It's fine, Kyle."

"Not too damp out tonight, bothering the *moncone*?"

That word, well, it's a bittersweet reminder that Sal is always somehow still with him. Even out here, night fishing. Jason remembers Sal explaining the Italian word. It was on a hot summer morning a year ago, when Sal stopped by his house. Jason was in a bad way that day, bothered by phantom pain and snapping at Sal, telling him to essentially mind his own effing business. But Sal would have none of it as he watched Jason cross the room on crutches, then sit and attach his prosthetic left leg to his stump. Maybe he saw Jason wince; maybe he saw his edginess brought on by memory, and pain, and a jam-packed itinerary slowed down by his leg. Sal didn't let up.

Stump. Stump. It seems so harsh, Sal had said after watching Jason fuss with his below-the-knee prosthesis. *Mon-cone-ay,* he'd said then.

Mon what? Jason had asked, with little patience, no less.

Moncone. It's Italian, for stump. Mon-cone-ay. Because sometimes you just have to soften things, cousin. If only for yourself.

Shit, he'd learned a lot from Sal last summer. Now he looks back at Kyle, his best friend always checking in with him.

"Too damp tonight? No, Doc," Jason assures Kyle. But his friend's loyal concern does get Jason to secretly move his leg and double-check that everything's feeling the way it should. "All's good."

"Okay." Kyle goes back to digging in the tackle box. "But you just say the word if you need to move, or leave." A moment's silence, then, "You know."

As they find nooks in the rocks to set down their cooler, and snacks, and tackle box, Jason wonders if Kyle's thinking the same thing he is: another summer of fishing; of casting off in the shadows, or beneath the light of the moon; of drinking a beer and chewing the fat while life goes by. Now Madison's collar jangles as she noses through seaweed on the exposed rocks. Low in the sky, a heavy, waning moon rises. It shines a soft light on Long Island Sound.

"Good to be back here, starting another fishing season," Jason says as he casts off for the first time. His line whistles out over the water.

"It is." Kyle moves down closer to him on the rocks. "Not

the same without our *paisan* here, though. Had some fun times fishing last summer."

"Absolutely." Jason raises a beer can and looks to where Sal would drift in his rowboat late at night, floating at sea, beneath that moonlight. "Here's to Sal. *Salute*."

Kyle lifts his can, too, then reaches for a bag of chips and container of salsa he'd brought along. "Man, my appetite is crazy since moving here."

"Salt air does that." After a quiet few seconds, Jason's cell phone dings. He sets down his fishing rod and reads a new text message. "It's Eva, going ballistic for some reason." In the dark, he shifts his stance and flicks the phone's screen, reading aloud. "*You are in big trouble, mister*." After a few seconds of reading silently, he looks at Kyle. "Blah, blah, blah. *This conversation is not over*, she says." Jason looks at his phone, then at Kyle beside him. "But the conversation is also one-sided, so it *is* over." As he says it, Jason returns his phone to his pocket. "Wonder what that was all about."

"Uh-oh. Sounds like your sister-in-law's gotten word about Maris."

"What are you talking about?"

"You kidding? Your wife is all worried, ready to throw Neil's manuscript into Long Island Sound and you're clueless?"

"Something I'm missing here? Throw out the manuscript?"

"Rumor has it Maris is ready to go back to denim design, dude." Kyle holds the bag of chips out to Jason. "Lauren wondered if maybe you guys were having marital problems."

"What?"

"I wasn't going to say anything, but now that Eva let the cat out of the bag with that text message, well, you can tell me.

Being that I was your best man and all."

"Marital problems?" Jason grabs a handful of chips and tosses a few in his mouth. "Maris is worried? Where did all this come from?"

"Lauren heard it from Celia, who must've heard it from Elsa."

"Elsa? How would Elsa know anything about my personal life?"

Before Kyle can answer, a flashlight beam cuts through the shadowy evening. It bobs along, shining on the rocks as Cliff makes his way across them.

"What's going on, fellas?" Cliff asks when he nears. He wears a light zip-up jacket and sweeps that flashlight beam across their gear. "Food on the rocks? The dog, too, off leash? Summer's here and you two are back to breaking every ordinance in the Stony Point handbook."

"Put it on our tab," Jason tells him as he picks up his rod and reels in his limp line.

"Duly noted." Cliff walks near the tidal pools and smaller rocks, then looks up at them. "Got an extra fishing pole?"

"For a price," Kyle haggles. "Excuse the fines and you can help yourself to one in my truck bed." He nods his head toward the dead-end Champion Road beyond the beach, where his pickup is parked curbside.

So the commissioner *and* former State of Connecticut judge is easily bought, Jason thinks. Because Cliff leaves, and minutes later returns with a fishing pole. After Maddy checks him out and gets her ears rubbed in the process, Cliff stands close to the water, baits his hook and casts his line straight into the moonlit swath of sea.

"Big night tomorrow, Jason," Cliff says over his shoulder.

"I announced the sand-chair premiere in the newsletter and folks were still RSVP'ing this morning."

"That right?" Jason asks as he tosses a potato chip to the dog. Maddy catches it midair before scrambling further out on the rocky ledge. "Expecting a crowd, then?"

"You bet. Ready to be a local celebrity?"

"Best as I can be." Jason scoops his own chip through the salsa and takes a bite. "Just fine-tuning the speech," he says around the food.

"And how's Maris?" Cliff turns again and squints at Jason through the darkness. "Feeling any better?"

"See?" Kyle asks with a shove to Jason's shoulder. "I'm telling you, *everybody* knows, bro."

"And just what exactly *do* you know about Maris, Commish?" Jason asks across the rocks.

Cliff fiddles with his fishing line, reeling it in a bit, then stopping. "Nothing much, really. I stopped by your place the other day to drop off my DVD of *The Godfather* and I guess it was a bad time. She was upset at how her writing's going."

The strange thing is that Jason had no clue his wife's been troubled. So he reels in his line and walks closer to Cliff. "What do you mean, *upset*?"

"Crying enough to use my hanky. She seemed more afraid than anything else, from what I could tell, about finishing the novel the way your brother intended. And I just mentioned it to Elsa."

"Oh, no," Kyle groans.

"What?" Cliff asks, shielding his eyes in the dark and squinting up to Kyle.

"Don't you get it?" Kyle gives his taut fishing line a tug and reels in the slack. "That's all it takes with the women. Mention something personal and it starts out one way, then gets blown completely out of proportion! Next thing you know, it's time for serious damage control."

Cliff looks at Jason, who is now beside him. "You better fix things when you go home tonight, Jason."

"Fix things?" Jason crosses his arms and leans back, feeling somewhat defiant now. "I didn't even do anything. Wasn't even aware."

"Exactly." Kyle toys with a fish on his line; he lets it have its way, swimming out deeper. "But you *should* be aware. Bring her flowers or something."

Jason checks the time on his cell phone. "She's at Elsa's now. They're all decorating for tomorrow night's post-show party."

"The last thing you want is to be in a fight for your premiere," Cliff advises him.

"But I just talked to Maris at home, before I went to the diner for supper." Jason walks back to his fishing rod, opens the tackle box and baits his hook. "We're *not* in a fight."

"Might be now," Kyle and Cliff say at the same time.

"Depends on how the women spin everything." Kyle hitches his chin at Jason, then turns to his whirring line. "I mean, look at that text from Eva," he calls out as he reels in the fish.

"Shit." Jason checks the time on his cell phone again. "Maris won't be home yet. I'll still fish. They're biting tonight." As Jason casts his line, Kyle reels his in.

"What's biting?" Cliff asks. "Striper?"

"No. Not too many stripers yet." Kyle pulls his line out of the water as the hooked fish flips and struggles. "A little fluke," he says while releasing the barbless hook and letting the fish swim off.

Jason watches Cliff reel in a slack line. "Put a good weight on the line, and keep the bait moving low. You'll get one."

Nodding, Cliff changes the weight on his line. "Perfect night for a godfather challenge. Your brother-in-law coming fishing tonight?"

"Vinny?" Jason asks. "He's at the cottage with Paige and the kids, and my mother. She came up from Florida for the TV pilot. They all rented a place here together."

"So Vincenzo's home with his wife and mother-in-law?" Kyle whips out his cell phone and starts typing.

"Who you texting?" Cliff asks.

Kyle glances at Cliff, then resumes typing. "Matt, Vinny and Nick," he says. "A group text." His fingers fly over the phone as he talks his message aloud. "*Grab your fishing poles and meet us on the rocks. ASAP. Biggest catch wins a godfather point.*"

That's all Jason needs to hear. It gets him to reel in his line and scope out the rocks for a premium spot to cast off. He also snags a cold can of beer and the bag of chips, but stops to put fresh bait on his line, too—stacking the odds in his favor. With his fishing rod in one hand and the rest in the other, he maneuvers further out on the stony point. Some of the rocks are slippery, but he knows this terrain from a lifetime of living on it. A beam of light from the Gull Island Lighthouse sweeping across the water helps him gauge his choice location. Finally he finds a good-sized boulder to lean against, one where he can set down his gear, get comfortable and cast easily to the prime feeding spots.

Because he knows. With Nick, Vinny and Matt on their way, oh, does he know.

Kyle's already getting the handheld scale out of the tackle box.

Nick will surely show up wearing his mesh fishing vest, the fabric loops ready to secure his fishing rod, each vest pocket stuffed with spare line, hooks, bobbers and sinkers, line scissors.

Matt will no doubt be wearing his old wading boots so he can walk right into the Sound.

And Cliff will have them all stand, ready to cast, as he shines a flashlight and checks his stopwatch.

Oh, yes. It's on.

A frenzied fishing fiasco is about to go down.

twelve

LATER THAT NIGHT, MARIS FEELS like a new person. The women all lifted her up and chased away her doubts as they decorated Elsa's inn for Jason's television debut tomorrow. Driving home in her golf cart now, Maris relishes the sight of summer cottages lit up for the season. Lamplight spills from windows; folks sit with a cool drink or around a card game on screened front porches; couples take a late-night walk on the sandy roads.

When she finally pulls the cart into her driveway, it's obvious that Jason's home from fishing. A few tiki torches are lit outside their deck, so she knows he's still up. Gathering her tote and the leftover strawberry-cream-cheese turnovers Elsa sent home with her, she walks across the deck and goes into the kitchen through the slider. Inside, the lights are low, the house quiet. As she drops her tote and keys on the kitchen counter, Maris catches sight of the dining room table. Beneath the black lantern-chandelier, the table is set with dessert dishes and glasses.

Which is when she knows. Jason's fear of Eva is showing itself. Her sister came to her defense in a text-message rant, and now he's trying to keep the peace at home. He must think he's in serious trouble.

"*Time to have some fun*," Maris whispers, just as Jason walks into the kitchen.

"Sweetheart," he says. "How'd it go at the inn?"

"Hmm?" Maris glances at him, then fusses with her tote. "Oh, fine. Any luck fishing?"

"It turned into a godfather challenge," Jason tells her as he opens the refrigerator. "Everyone showed up and cast for the biggest fish."

"Really. Who won?"

Jason takes a swig from a bottled water, then recaps it and puts it back in the fridge. "Cliff. He bagged a big blue. Man, he did all right."

"Oh." Maris takes off her wristwatch, then plugs her cell phone into a charger on the kitchen island. Jason's too quiet, walking on eggshells with her. So the guys must have filled his head with the same gossip she heard from the ladies. When she moves to the sink to wash her hands, her back is to him so he can't see her smile as she toys with him … just a little.

And her silent treatment works. Because suddenly Jason reaches his arm around her and takes her hand, dishtowel and all. "Come on in the dining room for some ice cream." He hitches his head in that direction, then tosses the towel on the counter. "I got your favorite."

"I'm not that hungry." She throws in a small smile for good measure, still enjoying his efforts to keep things smooth between them.

"Come on." He tugs her hand. "Let's talk. We haven't talked all week."

"True … But everybody else has, haven't they?" Her small

smile grows then; there's just no stopping it. "Eva scare the shit out of you?"

Jason steps back and eyes her closely. "So you're not mad at your *fame-hungry* husband who has the whole beach thinking we're on the brink of a nasty divorce?"

"No, Mr. Barlow. Never." Maris reaches her hand up to his neck and gives him a kiss. That's all, just a kiss before grabbing Elsa's strawberry pastries and heading to the painted farm table in their dining room.

All the while, Maris hears how Jason laughs to himself on his way to the freezer. But there's something else, too. "Eva's a tough one, Maris. Intimidating as hell and very protective of you," he calls out as he gets their ice cream. "Everyone needs someone like that in their corner. Be glad you have her in your life."

"Oh, I am. Believe me, I am."

As she waits, Maris uncovers Elsa's wrapped plate and sets it beside a pillar candle flickering on the table. She can't miss how Jason meticulously chose two summer placemats and arranged candles to set a nice mood. The crystal ice-cream bowls are a wedding gift they just got around to opening a week ago. Still, she turns her head and looks around the room—at the server covered with a stack of china dishes, and some of her character sketches, and marsh grasses and cattails spilling from a tall ceramic pitcher. Something's got her attention, but she's not sure what.

Finally Jason comes to the dining room and sets down the ice cream he must've bought earlier, in fear, at the convenience store. After sitting in a chair near hers, he scoops the ice cream into their bowls.

"So you're not throwing Neil's manuscript into Long Island

Sound, then?" he asks as he lifts a spoonful of some decadent coffee-swirled frozen concoction.

Maris assures him that she isn't. "Only old Maggie Woods did that. Didn't your brother witness it?" Beneath the lantern-chandelier, she gets a dish from the server and puts one of Elsa's strawberry turnovers on it for him. And as Jason takes it, and breaks it in half before adding a dollop of ice cream, they talk.

"Oh, man, he did," Jason says around a mouthful of food. "Must be fifteen years ago, now."

"I remember it went through the whole Stony Point pipeline back then."

"Yeah, it was classic. One winter day, Neil saw her toss her computer in the water, probably thinking it would clear her shady past. She thought no one was looking, but that's a common misconception here at this little beach. Someone's *always* looking."

"Isn't that the truth."

"So Neil got ahold of Vinny, our trusty tech guy. They dug that computer out of the Sound and Vinny pieced the hard drive back together. It was crazy, the stuff she had on there. Even passages of Neil's writing, lifted from a journal she stole. It was all marked up with her notes."

"There are definitely no secrets here." Maris scoops up a mouthful of ice cream while listening to Jason talk. But there's something more she's picking up on.

As Jason lifts another dripping spoonful of his now ice-cream-laden sinful pastry, their talk veers from Neil and the manuscript, to the gang worried about them, to the big celebration planned for the next night.

"Maybe we were both really stressed out this week," Maris

says when Jason sets down his spoon and reaches for her hand on the table.

"Maybe." His thumb strokes her skin softly.

Maris can't quite get what it is that she's sensing in the shadowy room. Beyond, in the living room, hurricane lanterns flicker on the mantel beside a barn star and conch shell there.

"All set for tomorrow, babe?" she whispers, turning her hand in his easy hold and stroking his fingers now.

Jason nods. That's it, just nods. Still his fingers entwine with hers, and touch her arm. He shifts in his chair and leans closer. His face is shadowed with whiskers, his dark eyes watch her. "Dance with me?"

A smile comes, then. Because, yes, that's what she's been picking up on—very soft songs from their jukebox. The music's been a subtle undercurrent playing jazz numbers, and bluesy summertime tunes, the whole time they've talked.

Jason leads her down the paneled hallway toward the side alcove housing their vintage jukebox. Its silver trim glimmers in the low light; its music plays on. When he takes her in his arms, she presses close right as the needle settles on another old record. A slow song plays, one about missing sweet loving. Jason's arms hold Maris close and they move into the living room, where candlelight flickers in the darkness.

"So everything's okay?" Jason asks as his fingers tangle in her hair. "I mean, *really* okay?"

Though it is for her, she hopes it is for him, too. She nods, then sets her head on his shoulder until his finger lifts her chin up toward him and he bends to kiss her. His hands cradle her neck and reach beneath her hair as the kiss deepens and their dance stops.

Which is when the night somehow changes. The darkness

fills with whispers: a sea breeze sighing through open windows; Jason murmuring against her ear and leading her up the stairs. They walk side by side—his arm around her, his mouth pressed close, his words hushed.

Upstairs, the whispers and kisses don't stop; instead there's more. In the dim light of their bedroom, their touches grow more insistent as Jason lifts off her shirt; as she unbuckles his belt; as they move in near-darkness now, to the bed. Beneath the window, Maris feels the salty breeze still coming in, fluttering the curtains, whispering secrets in the night. It makes her feel alone with Jason, completely alone in the summer night, as his voice says her name, as his fingers touch her skin.

Outside there is only the sea, its waves breaking on the distant bluff.

thirteen

OVER FIVE HUNDRED CHAIRS.

It's a sight Jason will always remember. That's how his television show premiere stays with him, in certain visuals.

Like the sand chairs lined up across the beach this Saturday night—chairs stretching in neat rows all the way from the boardwalk to the high tide line. Some chairs have blankets draped over the backs; some have coolers of snacks beside them. Nick and Matt direct the chair-toting crowds to set up their seats in successive rows until each is filled.

But that's not all. Every square inch of the boardwalk bench is also filled with people wanting to see Jason's cottage-renovation show. Especially since the first renovated cottage is a Stony Point landmark: the old Foley's place, being given a new prominence.

And Jason will remember Cliff patrolling the boardwalk, occasionally lifting a silver whistle and giving a short warning when someone brings a dog, or tries to move some of the chairs. Jason has to admit that Cliff is going above and beyond, enforcing the rules to accommodate all the folks here.

Further down the beach, he'll always remember the dark

shadow of Elsa's Ocean Star Inn. It's set back off the sand, behind sweeping dune grasses. During the hour before the debut of his show, the inn is intentionally dark.

Even waiting in the first row of sand chairs stays with him. His family sits beside him: Maris; his mother; his sister and brother-in-law, Paige and Vinny. Elsa has a choice first-row seat, too, with her assistant innkeeper, Celia. From behind him comes the low murmur of hundreds of waiting voices, including Eva's words as she leans forward and says in his ear: *Good luck!* And there are a few slaps to his shoulder, too, from Kyle, Nick and even Patrick from The Sand Bar.

Every sight he registers, as though each is a photograph in his mind. There's Trent from CT-TV welcoming everyone to the pilot episode airing seaside, and sharing how the public television station has high hopes to continue the series. Then comes Trent's introduction of Jason as the show's host, which prompts Jason to stand and turn to the crowd behind him.

Everything is a snapshot in his mind: his arm raised in a wave; the blank movie screen filling a large frame on the sand; Maris beside him, watching it all with a wide smile.

Everything. Until the boardwalk lights are turned off and the movie screen illuminates with the show about to begin.

That's when he *hears* it.

As the crowd's applause fades to silence, waves lap along the shore. Over and over, splashing onto the sand, then hissing in a frothy retreat. But one whisper blends with those rhythmic breaking waves.

Here we go, Jay.

Jason swears he hears it—his brother's voice. It's clear enough for him to glance toward the water, and the sky above it. He's not sure if anyone notices his discreet salute except for Maris.

After that, everything blurs. On the screen, the program opens with a montage of images of the inn—prior to its renovation. The building is shown in all its shabby glory: weathered shingles, some nearly blackened with the salty dampness; water-damaged roofline; rusted window frames; sun-faded trim; scaffolding and overgrown landscaping concealing the hydrangea bushes and sweeping dune grasses.

The next segment touches upon both his and Neil's passion: the historical elements of Elsa's cottage—from the structure itself, to its original use as a cottage and market. That history is followed by Jason working in his backyard barn studio, drawing up blueprints for the cottage's renovation as well as referencing Neil's journals and scrapbooks. It all seems so long ago now, those early days when the camera crew first arrived at his home on the bluff.

The scene shifts then, to the inn, as Jason meets with Elsa to review his new design. At this point on the dark beach, Jason leans over from his sand chair and extends his hand to Elsa, feeling her heartfelt return-squeeze. On the show, months are compressed into minutes as the cameras capture the ensuing demo work. Walls come down. Cabinets are ripped out. Floors are lifted. Dust and debris fall and the newly designed structure rises. Master carpenters and electricians, tile workers and landscapers—his crew could not have been more dedicated to preserving and rebuilding Elsa's inn.

Once every last cedar shingle is nailed into place; every black roof shingle set down; every window sealed; every room decorated with driftwood centerpieces, vintage Mason jars and nautical accents; every stone placed in an impressive rock wall, the camera pans out. Showing how the renovated cottage fits the locale, the Connecticut shoreline landscape is toured—

from its marshes and saltwater bays to the sandy crescent-moon-shaped stretch of Stony Point. Favorite hometown restaurants are mentioned, spotlighting Jason and some of his construction crew eating lobster rolls and fried clams at waterside tables.

Continuing the local angle, Jason visits nearby landmarks, including Old Lyme's Florence Griswold Museum. In explaining its prominent role in American Impressionism, he notes relevant artwork as well as significant features on the museum buildings' architecture. A Colonial Revival house draws parallels to the renovated inn at Stony Point. And all he thinks of is Neil when he points out the museum's shingled Chadwick artist studio, looking like a larger version of Neil's seaside shack.

Sunlight was important to the Impressionist painters, Jason explains on the movie screen. *And is equally so to coastal architecture, in the way light changes a building's appearance as the sun moves across the sky.*

All of it, though, the entire program, is a blur. Until the very end.

Until Elsa's happiness jar segment airs, showing the heart and soul she brings to every corner of her inn. Demonstrating her precious beach jars, she talks about preserving guests' memories among the shells, sand and sea glass. It's a segment that has Elsa lean forward and catch Jason's eye, her fingers to her lips as she sends her love his way, across the row of sand chairs between them.

Finally, at the close of his television show's debut, a message rolls onto the black screen. White letters form the words, stirring in their simplicity.

In Memory of Salvatore DeLuca, Beloved and Missed.

Once that line fades in silence and the boardwalk lights

come on, Jason stands. Celia is one of the first people there for him, her eyes filled with sad tears. She hugs Jason, saying, "Oh, how Sal would've loved to have been here. You know that, right?"

Jason hugs her a moment longer, then backs up, nodding and getting choked up himself. The whole time, he feels his friends' hands slapping his shoulder from behind; hears their genuine words of congratulations.

As Maris stands beside him then, Celia gives his hands a quick squeeze, hugs Maris too, then meets up with Elsa again.

And now it's time. Months of hard work are behind him, and it's time to acknowledge everyone who worked with him through it all. So he begins walking. Maris stays with him, ever at his side as they cross the sand. Beneath the boardwalk pavilion, a microphone waits; the crowd watches.

By the time they get to the boardwalk, a standing ovation has erupted. Maris cannot be happier for her husband. Beside him, she holds his arm when they step onto the boardwalk. Stony Point's movie screen is dark now, but further down the sand, new lights illuminate the skyline. Elsa's inn, set just off the beach beyond swaying dune grasses, comes to life. Each window shines now; balconies glimmer with twinkling lights; porches glow beneath paper lanterns hung from the ceilings.

As Maris and Jason move across the boardwalk, people cheer and whistle. He's gracious, nodding to some, saluting to others. But for one person in particular, Jason stops. Maris looks through the shadows and sees a silver-haired man with a weathered face. She instantly recognizes Ted Sullivan, with whom Jason shares such a storied journey. It was Ted, after all, who caused the accident that took Neil and nearly destroyed Jason's life.

Yet this same man reached out to Jason almost a decade later—his open heart leading to Jason renovating his cottage, which led to a prestigious architect award, which led to this night alone. In a rare twist of fate, Ted Sullivan secured a second chance for Jason Barlow: hosting CT-TV's cottage-renovation show. And yes, it's Ted's open heart that's made the two men unlikely friends.

As Ted rises from his bench seat, Jason takes his handshake and turns it into a warm embrace, both men slapping the other's shoulders.

Maybe that's why these moments are so immensely special, and spending them with Jason means everything to Maris. When she reconnected with him a few years back, he was utterly withdrawn and closed off to people. His world had paused at the violent scene of a roadside crash on a hot summer's day.

And now, this night.

When they approach the microphone, she stops and tugs him gently back. "I love you," she whispers into his ear, then kisses him, before nodding to the waiting microphone. The night is all his now, and he deserves the spotlight.

So she steps back and watches him go. His outfit is pure Jason: tan linen blazer over a pinstriped oxford shirt, with jeans. The blazer sleeves are pushed up, shirt cuffs folded back, and yes, she sees the glimmer of his father's dog-tag chain around his neck. Maris knows. That chain is his connection to the past—to his Vietnam War veteran father, and to Jason's brother, Neil, who also wore that same chain when he was alive.

Jason glances back at Maris once he nears the microphone. He runs a hand through his hair, which is wavy in the damp air close to the sea. Standing at the mic, his hand moves to behind his bowed head while waiting for the crowd to quiet. When it does—with a few random whistles cutting through the night—he pulls a paper from his pocket.

And it's just as Maris had hoped.

Because before they left their house earlier, she managed to secretly tuck a message in with his own notes. She included one specific word they used in their wedding vows two summers ago. *Always.* She said it that evening in the church when she spoke about the waves of the sea always being there, no matter where life takes them. That no matter how far they journey, those waves forever break on the beach.

What's stayed with her ever since was the way her groom's eyes filled with tears when she said those words at the altar. And so she wanted to connect this special night with that one.

Watching Jason now as he opens his paper, she knows he *does* see her words simply by the way he touches them, seeming to read them again. So in her mind, she reads what he's reading, too. The words she wrote …

Neil would be so very proud, Jason. We both love you … always.

When he looks over at her in the shadows, their eyes meet and he presses a hand to his heart, mouthing the word. *Always.*

Which is all that matters.

Maris sits on the boardwalk bench and watches Jason turn to the crowd. His deep voice rises, extending his gratitude to Elsa DeLuca for allowing him and his dedicated crew into her daily life. And for keeping them well-fed, too, with her own brand of sweet delicacies from her kitchen.

After a round of applause and hoots from his satiated

construction crew, Jason continues. He brings his late brother into his speech, crediting Neil's influence on his work. He mentions how Neil believed that the sky is a critical architectural component that needs to be incorporated into every design.

"On Elsa's job," Jason explains, "it was the expansive sky over the sea that influenced a significant part of the inn."

All eyes turn to the sky beyond Jason then, out above the water. The sun has set and the heavy moon hangs low over the Sound. A few stars smudge the twilight horizon; the sea is calm beneath them.

"My brother always reminded me to include a view of the sky in my designs. Ever changing, the *sky* is the true masterpiece. And so, the Ocean Star Inn's new turret, with three levels of windows facing the skyscape over the sea, is a tip of the hat to Neil. And ..." Jason holds up his hand to stop the growing applause. "That turret does something else, too." He squints out at the dark beach until he spots Elsa with Cliff, watching him from the sand. In a message to Elsa, Jason motions to the dark, rippling water before continuing. "Elsa DeLuca named her inn for a very special phenomenon—ocean stars. Unlike celestial stars, ocean stars appear each *morning* when sparkling sunlight reflects off the water, giving the illusion of stars shining on the sea. Those stars are now visible to any guests ... from the turret."

Once the applause subsides, Jason invites everyone to walk down the beach, at the water's edge. He assures them the sandy route will be illuminated by solar lights edging the tideline tonight.

"The lights lead to a path through the dune grass, direct to the grounds of the Ocean Star Inn. Please stop and say hello to Stony Point's new innkeeper, Elsa DeLuca. While you're there, her assistant, Celia Gray, will be giving tours of the inn. So you can see up close the renovations undertaken on the show."

When Jason extends his gratitude once more, Maris stands and takes his hand to walk the beach. Their friends and family are lingering at the water; she sees them all there. A private party awaits both them, and the television staff, beneath the white tents at the inn. Food and drink will be had by all, beneath the summer's stars.

As she and Jason cross the sand, Maris feels him press a kiss to the side of her head. She squeezes his hand, knowing he deserves every bit of honor this night holds.

Celia did it. Yes, she cuffed her jeans and walked the water's edge with all the friends. It felt so good to let the cool salt water splash on her feet. Shimmering light fell on the sand from candlelit Mason jars hung on decorative piers along the way.

But with all the joyous celebration tonight, there was a touch of sadness, too. Walking with her sandals clutched in her hands, Celia couldn't help but think that Sal would have loved this perfect night. Transforming his mother's rambling cottage into a seaside inn was so important to him. And so, as Celia gives countless tours of the building tonight, in her heart, each is in Sal's honor.

Once the tours are done, and after Celia helps Elsa serve dinner and dessert, she says her goodnights to everyone. Lastly, she turns to Elsa.

"You know that you and your son have changed my entire

life, dear Elsa," Celia says, hugging her close.

"And so have you, Celia. My *famiglia* now. You and your beautiful daughter."

For a moment, the two women are silent in an embrace. Celia holds on a little tighter upon hearing Elsa's one small sob. Oh, how happiness and longing for Sal mix together on this touching night.

Celia gives a sad smile and another quick wave to any lingering friends, before hurrying to the guest cottage. After seeing off Taylor, who was babysitting Aria, Celia goes inside and closes the front door. Her cottage is quiet; the baby is in her crib. She's moving around, though, and making cooing noises, so Celia walks to her daughter's room.

"Hello, precious," she whispers while leaning into the crib and stroking Aria's face. "I hear you were a *very* good girl for Taylor. You even finished a whole bottle for her!"

Reaching up and winding her star mobile, Celia then dims the bedroom lights. Above the crib, pretty silver and gold stars spin and turn with a crescent moon. "Time for sweet dreams," Celia whispers. She pulls a light blanket over her daughter, before resting her hand on the side of her face. "Hush, now. Goodnight, little one."

When Celia turns to the window to close it a bit, she sees paper lanterns still illuminating the white tents on the inn's distant grounds. Twinkly lights still glow on the inn's deck and porches; tiki lights still edge the lawn.

It's a magical moment … one that takes her breath away. Because after a long, dark year, Celia finally sees how the light always, always, eventually shines through.

fourteen

BY WEDNESDAY MORNING THE FOLLOWING week, Kyle's back spasms have subsided and he's returned to work. While at the diner's big stove flipping flapjacks and scrambling eggs, he also keeps an eye on the door, expecting Jason to stop in for a coffee and cruller at any time. By now, he's usually parked on one of the red-cushioned counter stools. Last check, though, no Jason. Instead, Kyle noticed that the fog still hadn't lifted, and he couldn't even see the sailboats in the harbor down the street. He adjusts the watch on his wrist. By noontime, for sure, the sun will be burning off that hovering silver mist.

But the fog drives folks in for a hot breakfast, so he's busy at the stoves. A few eggs are cracked open on the griddle, sunny-side up; his tongs turn sizzling bacon; bread pops in the toaster nearby; plates heavy with French toast and omelets and hash browns wait for the waitress to deliver. He's *so* busy that he actually misses Jason walk into the diner, and does a double take when he sees him sitting at the counter. His friend looks a little worn around the edges—his face needing a shave; vague shadows falling beneath his eyes; his chin propped on his two hands in front of him, along with his telltale stress sign. Yup, Jason keeps drawing his thumb along that faded scar on his jaw. So Kyle's sure to find the most sugar-coated cruller in the pastry case for him as he walks out of the kitchen.

Which is when he notices something else. Jason keeps clearing his throat.

"What a week it's been," Jason says when Kyle sets down his cruller. A cruller Jason instantly breaks into thirds before pausing, then raising his eyebrows and turning up a hand to Kyle while motioning to the spot where a coffee mug *should* be sitting.

"Right on it, dude," Kyle tells him. First he wipes his hands on his chef apron, then grabs the coffeepot and pours Jason a steaming cup. "How's the leg in this damp? It's pretty raw out there."

"Yeah." Jason shifts his position on the counter stool. "I feel it on days like this. My leg can get stiff."

"Well, be careful. Take it easy," Kyle advises him. "You hear me?" he asks.

Jason nods. And as soon as Kyle turns to put the coffeepot back, Jason's got a cruller piece dipped in his mug. "It's tough, though," he's saying while dunking. "I'm busier than I've ever been. Radio interviews, a TV appearance on that local afternoon news program." He takes a bite of the soggy cruller. "Just came from taping that one," he says around the food. "They'll be airing it tomorrow."

Kyle sips his own coffee, then leans against the counter. He crosses his arms in front of him and listens to Jason ramble. So this is why he's dressed up—a white button-down shirt beneath a navy blazer, cuffed jeans, serious watch.

"It was for their *Benefit Connecticut* segment," Jason explains.

"You know the one. When they feature products or events that specifically promote this great state of ours."

"Sweet, man. I'll have to tune in. So what'd you do? Sit at the roundtable with the cohosts? The two news anchors?"

Jason nods while pulling a paper napkin from the silver dispenser. "Nice folks. They showed some clips from my first episode, talked about my father's old barn studio where I draw up the blueprints, and asked the right questions about the show's format. You know, the historical angle with the cottages, the local attractions, and the before-and-after of the inn." He dunks another cruller piece into his mug, dipping it over and over again while clearing his throat.

"Hold that thought, guy." Kyle grabs a quick swallow of coffee and walks back to the kitchen. There, he gets a green apple from the refrigerator, slices it into wedges and brings the plate out to Jason. "Eat this." He nudges the plate close to his friend.

"What for?" Jason asks as he presses the last of his cruller into his mouth and wipes his hands on his napkin.

"Green apples get rid of phlegm," Kyle explains. "Noticed you haven't stopped clearing your throat since you got here."

"Seriously?" Jason picks up an apple wedge. "I'm just tired."

"It's more than that." Kyle steps back to let a busy waitress rush past, her tray held high. "You're doing public speaking now," he tells Jason. "So you need to learn the tricks of the talking trade."

"Like this?" Jason polishes off another apple slice. "Taking care of my voice now, are you, Doc?"

"Someone has to." Kyle crosses his arms again and eyes Jason closely. "It's no longer just you sitting in that barn studio, brooding."

When Jason starts to clear his throat, Kyle steps forward, holding up his hand. "Don't do it! Listen." He looks past Jason into the diner, then back at Jason again. "Try the panting puppy remedy," he whispers while bending close.

"Panting *what*?"

"Puppy. You know, like a dog pants? It sounds funny, but heck, I read about it in a health magazine. You stick out your tongue and lightly pant. It dries up the phlegm." Kyle glances at the patrons seated at tables behind Jason. Flatware clinks on dishes; a baby highchair is pushed to the end of a booth table; salt and pepper are being dashed; forks full of hash browns are dragged through ketchup. "Try it. No one's looking."

And Kyle kind of figured it was coming, the way Jason discreetly flips him off.

"What I need is a fishing night to relax," Jason counters, then sips his coffee. "Friday night can't get here soon enough to cast my line and have a cold brew."

"No, man. You forget already?" When he hears one of his cooks ring the bell from the stoves, Kyle turns and picks up a tray of three waiting plates heaped with bacon, eggs, pancakes and toast. He hands it to the waitress hurrying over for her orders. "Friday's mafia night at Matt's," Kyle continues then. "We're breaking in his new sports shrine to watch *The Godfather* on that big-screen TV of his. Didn't Cliff drop off the DVD at your place?"

"That's right. At least Eva will cook up some good grub, too."

"No, no, no." Kyle shakes his head, then grabs a doughnut from a glass pastry case. He leans on the counter behind him and takes a bite. "You're so out of the loop, guy. Eva's taking Taylor to Martha's Vineyard, remember? They're staying with

Eva's adoptive parents for the long holiday weekend."

"Damn, I forgot. Okay, we'll order takeout, then. Grab some grinders to go with the movie."

"And do *not* forget. This Saturday is my housewarming party. Everyone's coming, should be a good time."

"Maris and I will be there." Jason clears his throat again, then promptly reaches for an apple slice.

"Why're you so nervous, anyway? The sand-chair premiere was epic."

"It was. Now I'm waiting to hear from Trent to see if viewers across the whole *state* loved it. CT-TV won't give the green light for a long-term contract until the pilot episode's final numbers come in."

Kyle picks up a messy newspaper left behind on the counter and tosses it in the trash. "So what's next, if the show gets picked up?" he asks while wiping crumbs from the countertop with a damp cloth.

"I've got a pile of cottage-reno submissions waiting for review. If we're approved, life goes into overdrive." Jason pauses, with a throat-clear slipped in, too. "I'll need to get started on the next project, like, yesterday."

"What a huge commitment, and it's stressing you out." Kyle glances back toward the kitchen when someone drops a dish behind him. "Shit, do you even *want* that TV show?"

"Hell, yeah. It's a challenge, pushing me out of my comfort zone," Jason says with a check of his watch. "But it's also a damn high, taking my work to that level." He downs the last of his coffee while standing to leave. "Plus it's always better for me to be busy."

"Hey, we still on for this afternoon?" Kyle asks as he heads back to his stove and a pile of breakfast orders. "You got any interviews you need to prep for instead? Because I can handle Nick and his boat on my own."

"Oh, no." Jason takes a few bills from his wallet and leaves them beside his plate, grabbing the last few apple slices as he does. "I cleared my schedule for that one."

If the only way Cliff Raines can fit himself into Elsa's schedule is to tag along on her inn chores, so be it. That's right. Because when it comes to matters of the heart, Cliff apparently has no shame.

Which is why he's standing idle in Elsa's garden as she's kneeling on her foam cushion. A multi-pocketed apron is looped around her waist, short dotted gloves protect her lovely hands, and a blue bandana holds back her thick brown hair. Alongside the wide stone walkway, clay pots of varying sizes are chock-full of red geraniums. The blossoms stand tall, top-heavy with flowers rising from lush green leaves.

"In Milan," Elsa says as she plucks a dead blossom off a plant, "the cobblestone and brick roads are *filled* with flowerpots like these. Ancient stone buildings line those roads, and the pots sit beside doorways, and beneath shuttered windows, and on the stairs of stoops. Everywhere, splashes of red flowers against the brown and gray stone walls. Oh! It's very pretty to see. There's something so old-world about the sight." She sits back and eyes all her mismatched pots, then looks up at Cliff standing there holding her weed bag. "You really should visit Italy sometime."

"Maybe we could go together," he suggests.

Before she even has a chance to answer, though, Elsa's cell

phone rings. It's Maris, who Elsa talks to briefly before turning back to her deadheading and pruning.

"Is Maris feeling better these days?" Cliff asks, following along beside Elsa and picking up her garden debris as she weeds.

"Yes," Elsa says while tugging a stubborn tuft of grass from a crack in her walkway. "She's doing wonderful now, typing away in her writing nook in the turret." Elsa hitches her head toward the upper windows. "It's amazing how a change in latitude brings a change in attitude! She's burning up the keyboard, clicking away."

As Cliff opens his mouth to talk, Elsa's cell phone rings again. This time, it's a guest calling, wanting to book a room at the Ocean Star Inn. When Elsa writes their name and number on a notepad from her garden apron pocket, Cliff manages to deadhead one of the plants while waiting. Then he adjusts the black COMMISSIONER cap on his head.

"How is it that you're getting the inn's business calls out here on your cell phone?" he asks when she hangs up.

Elsa glances over from jotting a reminder in her pad. "I have a special business phone plan that redirects the inn's calls." She's busy dotting her i's and crossing her t's on that darn note. "Sal always told me to not let one phone call go unanswered. A missed call is a lost customer." Wasting not a second, she then grabs a metal can, lifts up a scoopful of some muddy mess and sprinkles it beneath a hydrangea bush.

"And what is that?" Cliff nods to the scoop overloaded with brown granules.

"Coffee grounds! They add acidity to the hydrangea's soil, which helps the blossoms turn blue." She sprinkles another scoopful beneath a bush. "Kyle told me that when I offered to transplant one of my shrubs to his new house. For good luck."

When her phone rings yet again, she sets down the coffee-grounds can and answers that call.

And the next.

When she *does* resume weeding or clipping, it's a plant at a time, a branch at a time, a weed at a time. Because in between each yanked weed and snapped blossom, that darn phone rings like it's on a loop. And Elsa kindly addresses each caller.

Can I call you in ten minutes, when I'm inside and have my ledger in front of me?

Call me back and leave your name, number and requested dates on my voicemail.

Yes, I see on my calendar that your days fall midweek. And my midweek specials do offer lower rates.

And so on and so forth, with an occasional apologetic smile tossed Cliff's way like she's throwing a bone to a dog. Somehow, she does manage to work her way past the hydrangeas, grabbing dead blossoms between rings. Each caller must think she's sitting comfortably at the inn's check-in desk, calendars and reservations in front of her.

Not bent over on her knees on the stone walkway, that calendar she keeps checking being a handy-dandy pocket-sized one *also* tucked into an apron pocket.

"Ha!" Cliff inadvertently says.

"What?" Elsa asks, momentarily lowering her cat-eye sunglasses and eyeing him over the frame.

Cliff motions to her apron. "That's not a garden apron. Well, it used to be. I remember the time last summer here in your garden, when there was a bee on your lovely shoulder, and, well … never mind that. Because apparently that's your *business* apron now. I'm surprised you don't have a computer tucked into one of the pockets!"

"Now that's not a bad idea." Elsa presses her gloved hand into a wide pocket, as though gauging its size. "Maybe a tablet might fit?"

But she doesn't even have time to answer herself! Another call stops her. And after each call, she slips her phone into one of those several multi-use pockets on her garden apron, before watering a hydrangea with a sprinkle from the hose, or moving a geranium pot into the sun.

"No, there's no swimming pool here," she says to the next caller. "But the beach is just steps away!"

When she begins explaining how there's a *secret path* through the dune grasses, making one feel almost like walking in a seaside fairy tale, Cliff does just that.

He walks away.

That's right. And being so engrossed in her inn business, Elsa doesn't even notice.

So Cliff keeps walking to the front of the newly renovated inn, completely out of her sight, where he dials the inn's telephone number on his *own* cell phone.

"Ocean Star Inn," Elsa answers.

"I'd like to make a reservation."

"For when?"

"Sometime in the next few days."

"Oh, but we're not open yet. We won't be having guests until September."

"Elsa! It's *Cliff*!" he says, still standing in front of the inn. The sun is finally burning off some of the lingering fog, and he can tell the late-June day will be warm.

"Cliff?"

"Yes. I'm trying to book a date with you. You're always on

the phone, so I thought I'd *call* you to get ahold of you."

When she doesn't respond, he lifts the rim of his cap and peeks around the corner of the inn. Just barely, though. Enough to see her spin around looking for *him*. So he ducks back.

"Where are you?" she demands. "Come here and talk to me in person!"

"Nope." Cliff walks across the front yard to a shady spot. "If I hang up, you'll get another call and I'll be kept waiting."

"Okay, fine."

So he leans to the side to see around the corner of the inn again. This time, Elsa's silently walking the other way, bent sideways, apparently trying to catch a glimpse of him hiding somewhere.

"How about Friday?" she asks. "A Friday night date for a little while?"

"No. No good," he tells her, still watching her looking for him behind her stone wall. "Friday night is mafia night at Matt's. We're watching *The Godfather*."

"What?" She spins around, getting him to duck back again and stand flat against the front of the shingled inn now, pulling his cap low. "Clifton, what's gotten into you?" she asks. "You're Mr. R and R. Rules and Regulations. And now you're going to … *the gangs*?"

"Elsa. It's part of the process, of getting to be godfather to your granddaughter. So why don't I pick you up on Saturday, instead? We can go out for a couple hours before Kyle's housewarming party. We'll get a coffee, have a bite to eat, enjoy some laughs."

"Can't I just watch *The Godfather* with you on Friday?"

When he takes one last look around the corner, Elsa is standing with a hand on her hip, the other holding her cell phone. Still looking for him, she squints in the direction of the path to the beach.

"A movie night with you would be nice," she's saying while tiptoeing toward the dune grasses.

"Absolutely not," Cliff tells her as he heads toward the street to get back to work. Because can't he just see it: the beer, and belly scratches, and bawdy remarks during the movie. Okay, the man-sized portions of some cholesterol-laden food, too. Not to mention, the foul language, the rowdiness. "That room at Matt's will be all testosterone territory."

"Clifton. You're being ridiculous."

"No. No, I'm actually not." He's walking on the sandy road now, right as the sun breaks through the mist. "No women allowed there! I'll pick you up on Saturday instead, for a surprise outing." On his way back to his industrial trailer, he tells her, "And now I have to hang up and get someone at the Rec Department to deliver the popcorn machine to Matt's."

Later that afternoon, a movement catches Maris' eye. She's sitting in Neil's old fisherman shack; rays of sun come through the paned window. And even though her hands have been working diligently at the keyboard, the motion outside stops her typing. She goes to the window and sees that it's Jason backing his SUV down the driveway, which gets her to yank open the shack door and run to the yard.

"Jason! Wait up!" she calls.

The SUV stops and his window lowers. "I thought you were at Elsa's writing nook at the inn." He leans out, watching her approach.

"This morning I was. Now I'm working here. I needed some of Neil's journals." She raises a hand to shield her eyes from the low sun. "And it helps when I give myself a deadline and flip over your hourglass. One hour, one chapter," she says while walking to Jason. "Where are you headed?"

"Sound View, with Kyle. We're meeting Nick there. He's finally buying that boat from Bud. At least, if the dude accepts his OBO."

"O-B-O?"

"Or best offer."

"Can I come?" Maris stands at the driver's window now. "I'm starting a new chapter and a change of scenery would do me good."

"Sorry, Maris." Jason pulls his sunglasses from the visor and slips them on. "No women allowed today."

"But it would be an adventure! We used to have adventures before we got so busy." She reaches in through the window and slides her fingers through Jason's needs-a-cut, wavy hair. He's changed out of his work clothes and is more casual now in an old college tee and black utility shorts. "Remember?"

"No can do." He puts the SUV in gear. "It's all boat stuff with the guys, for Nick."

Which she doesn't quite get, this boys' club mentality. *No women allowed. Boat stuff.* But Jason's so drawn to it all, he doesn't even hang around to hear her argument. Instead, in his boys' club trance, he slowly rolls the SUV backward to the street.

Still, Maris keeps pace with it, walking alongside his open window. "But I'll just tag along quietly. I won't even *say* anything—"

"Listen, sweetheart." Jason checks his watch and slightly steps on the gas. "Kyle's waiting. Got to run."

"But—"

When he simply waves out his window, Maris stands there, hands on hips, and watches him go. Once he's on the beach road, she turns to the shack beside their barn studio. The two structures are such a contradiction in architecture: one a brown-planked New England barn, the other a silver-shingled fishing shack. But weathered buoys of reds and yellows and greens hang on their outside walls, connecting them aesthetically.

Glancing back once more at Jason's diminishing vehicle, Maris has a sudden idea. So she hurries to the shack again and lights a couple of hurricane lanterns. Beside her laptop, she sets a conch shell on one of Neil's open journals. And when she sits at the keyboard, the first thing she does is flip the pewter hourglass so that the sand grains begin to drop.

And finally, she begins typing a new passage in the chapter she'd been working on.

"No. No women allowed," he says as the hurricane descends. "Just us guys. He's upset after she broke things off, so we're going to look for him. Plus the wind's really kicking up and power lines are down, so it's not safe. No women allowed on this trip, sweetheart."

With that last line, Maris actually hears her husband's voice in the written words. She pauses and glances out the shack window, whispering, "Thanks, Jason."

fifteen

"WHY, CLIFTON RAINES!" ELSA EXCLAIMS Saturday morning. "How'd you ever pick such a paradise for our summer date?"

"Seriously?" Cliff asks as they walk among long tables set beneath canopies at the local farmers' market. "Paradise?"

"Oh, yes. This is so … so *bucolic.*" Elsa gazes over at the white ranch fence running across a distant sloping lawn. Behind the fence, black-and-white cows graze. And on the other side, canopies keep the sun off of tables covered with jars and vases of fresh flowers for sale. There are daisies and delphiniums, irises and peonies.

She looks at Cliff, then, and sees how pleased he is with his date choice. It shows in that dimple giving away his slight smile. But the shadow of whiskers, a mix of silver with some black, hint at something else … The guys must've been up late the night before, riveted to their prized movie—*The Godfather*. The vision of *that* has Elsa smile, too. "All these barns, and native produce, tucked into the hills of Lyme?" She takes his hand and keeps strolling. "But it could all look like the rolling hills of Michael Corleone's Sicily, too, I suppose."

Beside her, Cliff's voice is low. "I've heard this is the only Connecticut farmers' market located on an actual one-hundred acre working farm."

Elsa stops at one of the produce tables and picks up a head of broccoli, sniffs it and closes her eyes with pleasure. "And to think I've never been here," she admits when she sets down the broccoli and moves to the native lettuces. "This fresh food will be wonderful for my inn recipes!"

"Let's get a coffee first, and you can buy some things on our way out." Cliff takes Elsa's arm and leads her back into the sunshine. "That way nothing will spoil."

She agrees, and they walk past more tables, some covered in checkered linens and lined with green berry baskets. And she can't help it; she stops at the Bailey's Berry Farm table to sample the fresh blueberries. "Ooh, scrumptious! I'll be back for more of those," she tells the young woman in cuffed denim shorts and a spaghetti-strap tank top there.

"I'll be waiting," the woman assures her with a wink. "Just ask for Megan."

Elsa nods and together, she and Cliff walk toward the farm café. It's inside a barn up on a slope past a winding stone wall. Off to the side are mountains of brown and black bark mulch the farmers sell to landscapers and homeowners alike. As Cliff and Elsa meander up the hill, goats tugging at tufts of scraggly grass bleat at passersby.

"Really, Cliff. I'm sure you never thought a date looking at goats would be my thing." She looks back at the furry animals. "But I can assure you, this is so charming. And nostalgic for me, too."

"Nostalgic?" Cliff asks as they near the big red barn. Its doors are open wide on this summer morning, and the aroma of fresh-brewed coffee wafts outside.

Elsa glances back at the penned animals. "Sometimes in Italy, farmers herded their goats across the streets, from one field to another. When Salvatore was just a boy, we'd sit on a rock wall and wave at the goats from the roadside, listening to their little hooves march past."

It amazes her, sometimes, how the briefest of scents, or sights—like that of the goats—can bring her right back to Sal in some strange way.

They continue on and finally reach the café. The coffee line is long, though, so Elsa tells him her idea. "You wait in line. I'll go outside and grab a picnic table in the shade."

"What do you want to eat?" he asks, motioning to a long table of doughnuts, pastries and pie slices.

"Surprise me!"

He agrees, and so Elsa heads out. It's pleasantly warm, which has her glad she wore her fitted denim capris with a simple white blouse today. First stop? She visits the goats again. This time, she cuffs her shirtsleeves and reaches into the pen to give a black-and-white goat a soft pat on its nose. "*Thanks for the memory*," she whispers. When she eventually makes her way to the picnic tables, Cliff is heading there from the barn. She can't miss him, with that checked short-sleeve button-down he wears over twill shorts, and so she gives a big wave.

"I'm starved, being outside in this fresh air. What'd you get me?" Elsa asks as he sits beside her at a picnic table in the shade. She reaches to the take-out tray and lifts out one of the coffees.

"Something to satisfy that sweet tooth of yours." Cliff reaches into a white bag and pulls out a big lumpy doughnut, which he sets on a paper plate. "Fried cinnamon-cider doughnuts. A specialty here."

"And I can see why," Elsa tells him around a quick mouthful. The warm doughnut simply melts in her mouth, with thick sprinkles of sugar and cinnamon adding just the right sensation. She takes another bite, then pulls her cell phone from her purse. "Maybe I should check in with Celia, though. I've been gone an hour, and it's so hard leaving Aria behind when I go out like this." She gives Cliff a quick smile as she explains. "They're my family now."

"Wait, Elsa." Cliff puts his hand on her arm. "Celia can reach you if she needs anything. Let the two of them have some quiet time, maybe?"

After a long moment, Elsa relents. "You're right, of course." Then she tucks her phone away. "It's just that sometimes I feel like a new mother myself. In my late fifties, no less … with this beautiful surprise baby!"

"I know, but let *Celia* mother her child. Because you need some quiet time, too. Like this." Cliff motions out to the farm before them. Pools of shade fall beneath tall trees around the coffee barn. Beyond, people in shorts and sandals roam the market area, browsing fresh fruit and produce as well as crafts—old painted buoys, dried flower arrangements and such. "So drink up and relax," he says, lifting his own coffee cup.

Elsa hesitates first, but then she *does* relax. It isn't easy though. Not when she wants to hover over Aria, and put a pretty outfit on her, and be sure she's eating enough. Then, if Elsa were home now, she'd maybe clip a tiny flower barrette in her granddaughter's hair before settling her in the stroller for a walk with Celia.

Instead, Elsa forces herself to just breathe and be in the moment. *This* moment today, right here beneath the sun, goats bleating nearby, good food at hand.

Until Cliff suddenly stands beside her.

"Okay," he tells her. "Like your son would say … *Andiamo!*"

"What? Let's go?" Elsa raises her nearly empty cup. "But it's so nice here. And now that I'm relaxing, I'd like another coffee."

Cliff lifts his leg over the bench seat and collects their napkins and plates. "Maybe in another life. We've got things to do, woman. Let's go now!"

"Go?" Elsa looks up at him as he stuffs things into the white doughnut bag. "Go where?"

"Dollar General, next to the Henny Penny gas station."

"We're going *shopping*? At a dollar store?"

Cliff simply hitches his head at her to get up.

"But your trailer has *enough* trinkets. All those mounted seashells, and new chair pads, and that faux wreath," she says while grabbing her purse. At which point, she has to hurry after him because, seriously? He's already walking away in that checked shirt of his, making a beeline to the parking lot.

"It's not for my trailer," he calls over his shoulder. "I need decorations for your golf cart."

If she only knew what the rush was all about. Elsa is trotting now, *and* managing to tip up her cup to catch its last drops of delicious coffee. "Wait. *My* golf cart?"

"Yes! Your golf cart, for the July Fourth golf cart parade. It's an annual thing at Stony Point."

"Well, yes. I know." Now she's finally beside him and grabs onto his arm. "But I didn't sign up."

"I did. My golf cart's in the shop."

"So you signed *me* up?"

By this time, and at this ridiculous pace, they're already at Cliff's car. He's holding open the passenger door, motioning for Elsa to get inside. When he then runs around to get in behind the driver's seat, he's talking as he opens his door.

"Listen." He clips his seatbelt and puts the car in gear. "The golf cart parade is today, and your golf cart's awfully available. So you can just let your boyfriend *borrow* that golf cart for the next godfather competition."

"Why, Commissioner Raines. You tricked me! Here I thought we were on a holiday date, and that you were romancing me—or what's the word I hear the fellas tossing around, thinking I don't hear? *Wooing* me, maybe? And instead you're just *using* me for my wheels."

"Are you mad?" Cliff throws her a quick glance as he speeds along Shore Road, headed to the dollar store.

Elsa meets his look, then pulls her big cat-eye sunglasses out of her purse. "Of course I'm mad!" she insists while perching the sunglasses on her nose. She sits straight and crosses her arms in front of her. "Which means *I* get to choose how we decorate my cart."

Oh, and isn't she the picture of cool, getting her way with conviction.

Sure, that is until Cliff burns rubber turning into the dollar store's parking lot, making her body sway as Elsa gives him a double take. He leans to the side, his sunglasses propped on top of his salt-and-pepper hair, his hands madly turning the steering wheel. After a quick glance at the road behind them—a glance of *disbelief* at how he ever got here so quickly—Elsa unbuckles her seatbelt and lets herself out of the car.

But she bends down low and leans inside to tell him one

more thing before he gets out. "And FYI, Mr. Raines. Don't you be calling yourself my *boyfriend*," she says, air-quoting the word, "when you don't even commit to *proper* dates." With that, she slams the door, tucks back a strand of windblown hair and heads in to the store. "*That's* a title you'll have to earn."

Something about the day feels like pure Americana to Kyle. His kids, Hailey and Evan, are in the yard making paper chains out of construction paper, cutting strips and looping them together. When each long chain is assembled, they drape them across shrubs and bushes in the back of the house. Meanwhile, Kyle's putting a vinyl tablecloth over the splintery picnic table the previous owner left behind. The table covering is bright red and splashed with exploding stars of blue and white and silver—looking like fireworks streaming to the sky. How many families across the country must be doing the same right now, decorating for their Fourth of July barbecues?

Yes, Kyle Bradford's living the American dream.

Though his barbecue isn't *really* celebrating Independence Day. Today's more the official day of their housewarming. A year ago, this was an event he *never* saw coming as he and Lauren looked at cottage after cottage; wood-paneled room after wood-paneled room; fixer-uppers of every size and shape. He'd lost all hope of ever finding a beach home, until they came across this sweet bungalow on Stony Point's Back Bay.

Now, as he clips the corners of the tablecloth to the table, his cell phone dings. When he sees it's a text from Jason, he sits for a moment to read the message.

Yo, Bradfords. You really need to get to the beach parking lot, pronto. No delays. Andiamo!

"Shit," Kyle whispers. He wastes no time hurrying over to the kitchen window at the back of the house. Lauren's inside getting her potato salad made for this afternoon. But Jason's message sounds important, so Kyle finds a pebble and tosses it up at the window. "Ell, you there?" he calls through the screen.

"Kyle?" Lauren leans close, and he can see her hair's in a topknot as she preps in the warm kitchen. "What are you doing throwing rocks at the window?"

"Never mind. Just listen to this." He reads her Jason's text message. "I hope everything's all right. They need us in the parking lot, right now."

"But Kyle," Lauren says. She holds up a dishtowel as she dries her hands. "We're so busy. And the kids are decorating."

"We *have* to go! Something happened, and I don't know if they got in an accident or what."

From behind Lauren, her mother's voice calls out. "You go," she insists. "Dad and I will watch the kids."

"Mom, are you sure?" Lauren turns around to ask her mother. "There's so much to do here."

"Yes, I'm sure! It sounds like your friends need you. We'll take care of all this."

So minutes later, Kyle and Lauren are walking the sandy roads to the beach parking lot. Lauren's flip-flops snap briskly as they hurry along. "Maybe we should've driven," Kyle says as they occasionally jog a few steps.

"With the Fourth of July traffic here?" A golf cart toots its horn as it passes them. "We'd never find a place to park!"

When they finally round a bend to the parking lot, the

street's even more crowded with families walking, and toting wagons and carts of beach gear to the sand. A line of slow-moving cars tries to maneuver around them.

"Look." Kyle squints and points to their friends huddled together in the middle of the parking lot. He can't miss Jason, Maris and Matt shielding their eyes and keeping a lookout. They wave Kyle and Lauren over once they spot them.

Lauren lifts her sunglasses for a moment, then trots to them quickly. "Is everyone okay?" she asks.

"What happened?" Kyle rushes up behind her.

Jason eyes them both, then looks at the others waiting with him. "I'll tell you what happened. You ready for this?"

He turns then, and together he, Maris and Matt carefully lift a beribboned cover off a gleaming, freshly waxed golf cart. "Happy housewarming!"

"What?" Kyle stops dead still. "Are you kidding me?"

"Oh my God!" Lauren walks closer to the cart. "Really? You mean, this is for us?"

"Happy housewarming, dude," Matt tells Kyle as he slaps his back.

"You shouldn't have." Lauren runs her hand along the side of the cart. "I mean, these golf carts don't come cheap."

"No worries. It's a few years old and was a good price, so everyone pitched in and got you two this bad boy," Jason says.

"Everyone?" Lauren asks while climbing in the passenger side.

"The whole gang," Maris tells her as she stands beside the cart. "Nick and Cliff, too. Oh, and your parents even chipped in, Lauren! Because we're all really glad you're here at Stony Point full-time now. And we wanted you to have authentic beach wheels as our housewarming gift."

Jason shakes Kyle's hand. "The Bradford family will be tearing up the sandy streets now."

A shake's not enough for Kyle. Not for this. He hugs Jason, slapping his back and laughing at the same time. "What a surprise! But damn, it's too much."

"Nah. You guys deserve it," Jason says as he hands him a key. "You busted your asses to find a place here."

So Kyle sits in the driver's seat, sneaking a hand to wipe a tear slipping down his face, too. "Hell, this machine's got all the bells and whistles."

Jason grabs onto a roof-mounted handle and leans in to point out the dashboard gauges, all while Maris and Lauren check out the backseat where her kids can sit.

"It's even got hooks to attach your sand chairs," Maris explains.

But what suddenly takes the cake, for all of them, is the *other* golf cart that skids to a stop beside Kyle's new wheels. A cloud of parking lot dust rises as the driver cuts the wheel in a sharp turn during the maneuver.

And *what?* Kyle glances over, then bends forward in his seat for a better scrutiny. A massive blow-up swim raft in the shape of a happy blue fish is mounted atop that golf cart's roof; red-white-and-blue foil garland drapes off the roof edge; balloons bob and … Can it be? Twinkle lights outlining the golf cart actually blink on and off!

And in the front seat, Cliff and Elsa look at them from behind the biggest, cheapest, plastic sunglasses you could imagine.

"Son of a bitch," Jason says under his breath.

"What's going on?" Kyle asks him as Matt starts inching away.

"Well, Kyle," Maris says as she slowly walks around his spiffy new golf cart. "The good news is that you have your very own golf cart."

"And the bad news—" Jason begins.

"Oh, no. Wait." Kyle wipes his forehead with his T-shirt sleeve. "Let it just be good news today. For my housewarming."

"Sorry, guy. It's never just good news at this beach." Jason pats Kyle's shoulder, then continues as Matt suddenly returns in the fully decked-out Gallagher golf cart—which Eva so must've decorated before leaving for Martha's Vineyard. Matt's cart is made to look like a rolling wave, with blue-painted cardboard cutouts of a breaking whitecap attached to each side of the cart. He idles on the other side of Kyle's new wheels.

Which gives Maris just the minute she needs to retrieve *her* cart from where it had been parked off to the side. Its red-white-and-blue patriotic flags and balloons bob and wave in a gentle sea breeze.

Jason backs up a step as he heads to Maris in their decorated cart.

The reality of the situation starts to settle on Kyle. These guys are absolutely up to something. Oh, he can't be fooled.

Jason's next two lines clinch it.

"The bad news, Kyle, is that you have half an hour to decorate your mean machine for the golf cart parade." Jason gets into the driver's seat as Maris shimmies over to the passenger side. He guns his golf cart's electric engine and briefly lowers his sunglasses as he squints over at Kyle, silently watching all this unfold.

"That is," Jason adds, "*if* you're game to compete in the godfather competition about to begin. *Best Decorated* snags the point."

Before Kyle can even get in a word, Jason and Maris take off and leave the rest of the crew in their golf-cart dust.

sixteen

NOW THIS IS SOMETHING MARIS never saw coming—a genuine traffic jam in Kyle and Lauren's own yard. A half hour after the Stony Point golf cart parade, cars and golf carts are speeding down Bayside Road all willy-nilly. Heck, it's a veritable frenzy as streamer-strewn carts and honking autos jockey to be first, turning into the Bradfords' driveway. If these assorted vehicles were all bumper cars, a load of fun collisions would be happening as push comes to shove in the traffic mania.

She and Jason cut off Matt and Eva to get in line, with Nick and Vinny pulling up the rear in their golf cart parade entry—Nick's security cruiser! They'd opened the trunk and attached their décor to the trunk edge and top lid. *If* Maris would classify cutouts of shark teeth as décor. Two cardboard shark eyes are attached to the top of the trunk door, and a huge fake shark fin is mounted on the car's roof.

Eye-catching, but still. It's not a golf cart, and so instead it's been dubbed the Loser Cruiser by all the friends.

As vehicles pull up in front of the house, little Hailey waves for everyone to follow the parking attendants: Lauren's father and Evan. Together they direct those vehicles into a parked line on the driveway, and another beside it.

"Who won?" Paige runs over and asks before Maris and Jason even get out of their golf cart. "I was making dessert and missed the parade."

"Nice to see you, too, Paige," Jason says to his sister when he climbs out of the cart.

"Whatever, Jason." But Paige hugs him and gives his cheek a kiss, then brushes it off with her fingers. She also winks to Maris standing beside her patriotic-themed golf cart. "So who won?" Paige persists.

Jason drops his keys into his cargo shorts pocket. "In the official Stony Point parade, Cliff actually won honorable mention."

"Oh, not that. I mean the godfather competition! Who won the point?"

"Cliff, again." Maris sighs while nodding to Elsa's golf cart, bedecked and adorned and streamered in all its fishy glory.

"Again?" Paige asks, walking over to Elsa's cart with Maris. "Cliff won *another* point?"

"I can't believe Cliff's leading the godfather competition," Vinny admits as he comes up behind Paige. "Bagged a blue fishing, and had the best golf cart, too. With a *blue* on its roof!"

"No one can beat the DeLuca touch, with its secret ingredient," Elsa says as she gets out of the passenger seat and lifts those cheap sunglasses to the top of her head.

"Which is?" Cliff asks.

Elsa winks at him. "Me!"

In the midst of all this, a golf cart horn rings out as Kyle and Lauren steer their new beach wheels into the driveway. Evan and Hailey run over to see it. They climb in and out of the backseat, begging for a ride.

"Later, kids," Kyle says as he ruffles Evan's hair. "After we have something to eat."

And so it begins. The voices and laughs and food and talk, all of it a part of the summer day.

Maris holds back and simply watches, much the same way Neil might have. It's a perfect method to observe intimate details that will fit any scene in his novel: be it the camaraderie of the friends gathered around the clambake as the wind kicks up seaside; or the lone deserter wandering off after arguing with his girlfriend; or maybe the women sitting on the cottage deck by lantern light as the storm approaches—their voices low, concerned; even the men's bravado in the face of a stormy night, as they recklessly bodysurf waves while throwing caution to that hurricane wind.

Now, as everyone walks around to Kyle's backyard decorated with construction paper chains and patriotic flags and tablecloths, Maris hears that very same familiarity she'll bring to the book.

"I've been painting rooms, and doing a lot of cleanup," Lauren mentions.

"Making the house your *home*?" Elsa asks while walking beside her.

"Definitely." They round the corner of the house, then, skirting an overgrown lilac bush. "Careful! Stay away from that stair," Lauren warns when they pass the side door. "It's loose, on my honey-do list."

"What?" Vinny asks Kyle as he catches phrases of the girl-talk. "Honeydew list? Like the melon?"

"No!" Kyle gives Vinny an easy shove. "Shit, more like *Honey, do this* and *Honey, do that.* Sweep the acorns, put down bug spray, tighten a screw."

"Oh," Jason adds. "One of *those* lists."

Yes, Maris takes it all in, making mental notes for her book-in-progress. She sees the colors of the day in the tall maple trees throwing shade on Kyle's yard, and in the brightly colored shorts and tank tops everyone wears. She smells that sweet salt air lifting off the bay, and later, wisps of barbecuing food after the guys fire up the grill. She hears music from an outdoor speaker. At this house sitting on Back Bay, someone set Otis Redding on repeat, with strains of *(Sittin' On) The Dock of the Bay* mingling with the sizzling grill and animated voices, and the occasional rumbling chug coming from the railroad tracks beyond the yard.

All the while, the tide rolls in across the street on the bay … the evening a long ways off.

~

Celia wheels the stroller along the sandy beach roads. It's a perfect July day to walk … all blue skies and golden afternoon sunshine. Why yes, this could be the view of a scene in her imagined life film, *Celia's Return.* The director's assistant would snap the clapperboard, identifying this as *Scene: "Hanging with Friends," Take: One.*

The filming might open with a tight close-up of the stroller's wheels turning over the gritty beach road. The camera would pull back then, showing the little baby carriage with Aria inside. She's wearing the chambray onesie Maris made, and has a bow headband in her hair. The baby makes cooing noises as they pass the shingled cottages. And so the ambiance being captured on film would be one of easy summer living.

Of bliss. Beach bliss. Panning out, another camera might film porch windows open to the warm air; pots of red geraniums sitting on stoops; garden whirligigs spinning in the sea breeze.

At the sound of Celia's voice, *she* would then become the film crew's focus. A cameraman on a dolly rolling along beside her would have his eye pressed to the viewfinder as Celia talks to her daughter.

"Look at that pretty one, Aria," Celia says. She bends low and points to a blue jay wind spinner, its wings lazily flapping.

When she turns the stroller onto Bayside Road, the first thing Celia notices is Kyle and Lauren's overloaded driveway, with cars and golf carts spilling onto the lawn. But the yard seems oddly quiet as she approaches.

"Hmm," she says to the baby. "I hope we didn't miss all the festivities."

Which is precisely when she hears a loud *Whoop!* coming from across the street. So she heads the stroller to the small beach on the bay. The closer she gets, the more voices she hears. The stroller wheels won't roll across the sand, so Celia unstraps Aria and lifts her out to carry her. All her friends are gathered near the water. The kids splash in the shallows; the women stand together on shore.

Suddenly, as though her imagined movie director is silently giving a rolling hand-over-hand signal to pick up the pace, a commotion arises. Once the women on the beach catch sight of little Aria in Celia's arms, they all hurry over and the rest of the scene unfolds, Celia right in the thick of it.

"Aria!" her beach friends quietly exclaim, touching the baby's cheek, giving her bare foot a gentle shake. "How pretty you look."

"I *love* that outfit," Maris says. When she puts out her arms, Celia gently places the baby in Maris' hold.

"Her onesie fits perfectly, too," Celia says.

"Aren't you a cutie!" Maris smiles while scarcely rocking Aria. "And look at that pretty bow in your hair."

"Oh, it's my turn," Lauren insists as she takes Aria in *her* arms and cradles her to her shoulder. "Mmm, you smell so sweet!" she says while putting her face to the baby's hair.

As the women fuss over her baby, Celia notices the narrow wooden dock. With its wood slats, it looks like a weatherworn boardwalk leading far out over the water. Jason and Cliff stand on the far edge. They're attaching some sort of towrope to a huge yellow tube at their feet. The tube is ringed with handgrips, and apparently Cliff just inflated it with an air pump there. He lifts the tube now and holds it up as Jason finagles the towrope and latches it on.

Along the shore, sand chairs are set out near the lapping waves, and further down the beach, a boat trailer is parked near some wild beach grasses. Hailey runs in the shallows while waving a red-white-and-blue pinwheel, and Evan walks along the beach with Paige and Vinny's kids, the three of them finding shells and rocks to drop into their sand pails.

Celia can't help it, then. Much as she tries to distract herself, she remembers last year's Fourth of July, and the barbecue she went to with Sal, back in Addison. It was at her neighbor's house there. Afterward, Sal and Celia lingered long into the night on the deck of her own little yellow bungalow. Sal lined up two-foot-tall sparklers across her backyard and gave Celia a very personal fireworks display when he set her dark yard a-sparkling.

Glancing now at Aria in Lauren's arms, Celia could never

have guessed a year ago where her life would take her in the ensuing months.

Could never have guessed the wrenching sadness and the soaring joy that would shape her days.

"What team are you on?" Lauren asks as she walks up to Celia.

"Team?"

"Team Kyle?" Lauren sets Aria back in Celia's arms. "Team Jason?"

"For what?" Celia asks.

Maris sidles over and gives her the lowdown. "Only for the latest face-off in the official Stony Point Godfather Tournament of Challenges. It's tubing today, with Nick's new boat." She points to the small Boston Whaler floating near the end of the dock. The men, all in bathing suits, huddle at the end of the dock. All of them, even Cliff!

Celia gives a worried glance at the way they're jostling each other, then turns back to the ladies. "This is getting out of hand, don't you think? Maybe we should just stop the competing. It really brings out something fierce in the guys."

Elsa not only lifts her sunglasses then, she also raises an eyebrow. "Oh, *that* ship has sailed, my dear," Elsa tells her. "So you just enjoy the ride now."

Jason walks off the dock and approaches the women on the beach. He wears a T-shirt loose over his navy swim trunks. And Celia sees that he's got some sort of waterproof cover over his prosthetic limb. So it's obvious. Nothing—nothing at *all*—is going to stop this godfather contest.

"Jason," Celia says. "Really, I don't want you to risk damaging your prosthesis on Aria's account. Maybe this tubing thing isn't a good idea."

All he does is shake his head with a small smile and turn up his hands. And Celia gets it; it's beyond his control now, the way the competition has taken over the men's lives. Obsessively.

"We're in a bind," Jason tells the women instead. He holds up a stopwatch. "We need one of you ladies on the boat to time each tuber. And to be our spotter."

"I'll do it," Maris quickly says. "Anything for plot point inspiration."

Taking the watch, she hurries along the dock and at the end, Celia notices Cliff help Maris step down into Nick's new boat. The vessel looks nice enough, all turquoise blue and white, bobbing on the water. It's actually a very serene sight.

But at the same time Maris settles in the boat's rear seat, the men's voices begin rising. Their excitement, and tension, can't be missed as they call out orders, and rib each other while vying for a position in line. Kyle must've won some coin toss, because he's first to get on the massive tube attached by that long towline behind the boat.

The secluded beach on Back Bay quiets then. Lauren's rounded up the kids to watch the tubing competition. Jason stands with Elsa, beside Celia, and also carefully observes the event unfolding. Waves lap on the sand; a seagull soars low. Celia hears the motor start up on the Whaler. She's glad that the guys are actually behaving themselves. Being ever safety-conscious, Nick gives a careful glance back at Kyle, then slowly moves the boat forward to pull the slack out of the towline.

So far, so good, Celia thinks. They're nicely keeping everything under control as the boat very slowly idles along. When Kyle calls out something to Nick, which Celia doesn't clearly hear, that's when it begins.

Oh, didn't she know it. There was no way this was going to be a placid, easygoing tubing event.

No, no, no.

At the sound of Kyle's words, Nick turns quickly from where he stands at the boat's steering wheel. He cups his hands at his mouth and calls out over the chugging motor, "You're going to fucking *die* out there, Bradford!" before turning back to the controls and opening up the throttle.

"Holy cannoli!" Celia instantly covers Aria's ears. "If this keeps up, Aria's first words will be nothing but filth! She'll have a *sailor's* mouth."

Jason steps over to Celia and extends a finger for little Aria to grip. He's standing in front of Celia and blocking her view of whatever antics are happening out on the water. "Listen, ladies," he says with an apologetic nod to Celia. Aria still tightly grips his pinky. "You might want to back up the children." As he says it, he motions with his other hand to Nick's boat spraying a wall of water in a sharp turn as he tries to dislodge Kyle from the tube.

The odd thing is how riveted all the women are, watching Kyle on the tube roughly bouncing over the water. He's lying on his stomach, arms outstretched as his hands grip the tube handles. Water rises around him when Nick turns the boat in such a way that he actually sends the tube airborne—with Kyle clinging to it for dear life. Hoots and hollers come from the guys at the end of the dock as Nick speeds his boat across the bay, Kyle giving everything he's got to stay attached to that inflated rubber ring.

"Really, ladies," Jason says. "At least head to the back of the beach." He pauses when the men's distant voices yell out, with a random expletive thrown in the mix, before he turns again to the women.

But he can't help it. None of them can—Celia included—the way they all freeze to watch this boat and bright yellow inflated tube skim across the bay in a silver plume of water.

"Trust me, you don't want to be too close." Finally, Jason pulls his finger from Aria's grip and looks over his shoulder at the bedlam on the bay. "Not when all tubing hell is about to break loose."

seventeen

THERE'S SOMETHING SO EXQUISITELY PERSONAL about a kitchen, something that lets your guard down.

That's what Celia thinks the following Tuesday morning when she's sitting in the inn's kitchen with Elsa and Aria. In his renovation, Jason was sure to include the massive island Elsa requested, and Celia gets why.

Because everything happens in the kitchen. Seriously. Everything happens around food prep, or sitting with a coffee, or over a meal. Even over the simplest of sandwiches. Yes, in the kitchen, life is dissected, problems solved, relationships mended, plans made.

Arguments happen, too.

Oh, did she have a doozy with Elsa last fall when Elsa was ready to sell her inn, pack her bags and leave Stony Point for good. Celia thinks their argument was a turning point, getting Elsa to slowly change her mind. The quarrel happened the morning Celia slammed a heavy leather portfolio on Elsa's kitchen table and told her to give it to any prospective buyers. *Just give it away and be done with it. Once and for all!* Celia had ordered then.

Inside that portfolio was the coveted Ocean Star Inn business plan, meticulously crafted by Sal's very own hand, in this very kitchen, over the course of the summer. His heart and soul filled that document, and if Elsa was set on selling her inn, Celia *dared* her to give away Sal's hefty proposal, too.

Words were thrown like daggers that day; tears didn't stop flowing. But within them, the truth was laid bare for Elsa. The truth of how much this inn meant to her only son. And somehow, when the dust settled after that painful morning, Elsa and Celia grew closer than ever.

So she loves hanging out in Elsa's kitchen on quiet summer mornings like this one, now. Aria sits strapped in her bouncer seat on the breakfast bar. Celia reaches over and strokes her arm, then turns to a project she's been working on. Next up? Tacking a thin strip of lace onto a piece of burlap.

"I still can't believe Kyle won the tubing challenge," Celia says to Elsa, who's standing at the garden window and watering her red herb pots.

"Me, too." Elsa wipes her fingers on a towel and gets a paper from the counter. "Did you see this?" She sets the page down on the island for Celia to read. "Cliff delivered my copy earlier."

And there it is, front and center on a special Fourth of July edition of the Stony Point newsletter: a photograph of Kyle Bradford airborne on the bay, the inflated yellow raft inches below him as he still holds on to those handles. Celia scans other photos of the golf cart parade and the fireworks display held on the beach, right in front of the inn. She glances at the residents' announcements of who's had a baby, and whose son or daughter graduated from college this past May. Even Nick's graduation is given a noteworthy mention by the commissioner, himself.

But it's the tubing picture that Celia returns to. "Kyle's such a big guy, over six feet tall," she says. "I don't know how he ever held on as long as he did."

Elsa is at the coffeepot now, lifting the steaming decanter. "The men want that godfather title very badly, Cee."

"Still." Celia shows Aria Kyle's picture, then sets down the newsletter. "I thought for sure Kyle would be the first to get dunked."

"Cliff even put a Godfather Tournament of Challenges tally on the bottom," Elsa says as she pours Celia a mug of coffee. "Showing how many points everyone has."

"Would you look at that?" Celia blows gently on her hot coffee and manages a sip. "Seriously? Matt won the *karaoke* competition? When was that even held?"

"Oh, it was a hoot!" Elsa takes her coffee cup and sits across from Celia at the island. "They had it here, in the back room on Sunday night. When you were visiting your friends Amy and George at their cottage."

"Shoot! I missed a fun one, then."

"It was. The jukebox was cranking, the windows open, music playing. Everyone had a lot of laughs. Secret votes were cast, and Matt was the clear winner. It was funny, because he's usually pretty staid, being a state cop and all. But he brought some fancy footwork to his performance and won the crowd over."

"How do you like that." Celia sets down her coffee and lifts the lace-fringed burlap, which she wraps around a Mason jar. "I just hope they don't take this too far."

"It's all done out of love, dear." Elsa reaches over and strokes Aria's hair, then notices Celia's handiwork with the Mason jar. "That is so pretty. A happiness jar for Aria's nursery, maybe?" As she says it, she stands and bends over to give Aria's cheek a light kiss.

"No." Celia straightens the burlap and securely attaches it to the jar. She uses a glue gun until the fabric is adhered. "After listening to all the guys' profanity Saturday at that tubing competition, I thought this was necessary. It's my official swear jar."

"Your what?"

"It's a swear jar. You know. Every time someone cusses in front of the baby, they have to put a dollar into the jar. And with the gang here, I figure that by the time Aria's eighteen, her college tuition should be fully funded."

Elsa smiles at Celia's savings plan, just as Aria fusses in her baby seat. Her little legs push and kick as she gives a whimper. When Celia looks at her, the baby's head is turned toward the open kitchen window, where a gentle sea breeze makes its way into the room.

"Why don't we put Aria in her stroller and walk across the boardwalk?" Elsa asks while bringing her coffee cup to the sink.

"Perfect. I'd love to."

"We can sit in the shade beneath the pavilion and Aria can breathe the salt air." Elsa stands at the window now, gazing out toward the distant beach beyond the dune grass. "Just like her daddy loved."

Maris leans on the railing of her upstairs loft studio. It's not too often lately that she and Jason are both working in the barn, together. She looks down at him sitting at his drafting table. He adjusts his swing-arm lamp and reads through some papers, occasionally looking at his cell phone, too. He's so intent on his work, he doesn't notice that he's being watched.

"What are you doing, babe?" she asks, smiling at how he slightly jumps. "It's awfully quiet down there."

Jason looks up at her, right as she tucks her hair behind an ear. "It's quiet up there, too. I don't hear any typing."

"That's because I'm *thinking.* It's part of an author's job, you know." She leans her elbows on the railing and studies him. His rack of finished rolled blueprints is close by, but he's not working on them. And his drafting pencils are all neatly lined up in their tray, untouched. "What are *you* doing?"

"Waiting."

"For what?"

"For my phone to ring."

"Jason!" Her fingers slide her gold star pendant along its chain. "I thought you were wrapping up work on your Sea Spray Beach project. The Nantucket-style reno?"

He discreetly slides his phone closer. "Can't focus right now. I'm waiting to hear from Trent about the show. To see if the numbers came in yet."

"Tsk, tsk." When he glances up at Maris, she blows him down a kiss. "What are you reading, then, while you wait?"

"Cliff's July newsletter. It was in our mailbox early. He got a good shot of Kyle on that tube."

"I'll bet." Maris watches her husband a little more. "I'm polishing up one of Neil's chapters. So read me some of Cliff's news. Maybe I can work it into the story."

Holding the newsletter, Jason quietly skims some of the boat-tubing article, then brushes past that to an announcement about Stony Point sweatshirts. "Now available at the Stony

Point Souvenir Shop," he says. "Keep the sea damp off on morning strolls, or sunset walks, with these fine sweatshirts."

"Hmm." Maris, still leaning on the railing, looks over her shoulder at her laptop. "Not bad. Not bad at all."

She walks back to her desk, sits down, lifts her hands over the computer keyboard and … thinks. Something has to happen, though. Something pivotal, in this simple exchange. Her fingers begin typing.

After she puts her arms through the sleeves, he loosely zips the sweatshirt on her before they continue walking the windswept beach. From the water, a fine salty mist blows and dampens her face. She tucks her hands into the sweatshirt pockets and finds something. Giving it a glimpse as she slightly pulls it out, it's obviously a postcard, with his handwriting on it. She slows her step and inches the card further out, just enough to read the familiar name of its recipient. Which is odd … because he said he didn't really know anyone around here.

As quickly as she'd begun typing, Maris stops. She runs down the stairs, giving the moose head nose a pat on the way. Madison scrambles up from her nap beneath Maris' desk and heads to the stairs, too. Her collar jangles as she runs down right at Maris' feet.

"Come on, Jason." Maris and the dog breeze past him. "Let's go out and get some air."

"What?" Jason looks up from the papers he's been shuffling around on his table. He spins on his stool and watches Maris head to the door, where she lifts Maddy's leash off a wall hook. "Wait. I just want to sit here. I have to … organize my architecture scales and … and sort through the mail."

By this time, Maris is at his side. "Nope." She tugs him up. "That phone will never ring when you're waiting for it. And anyway, I *want* one of those sweatshirts mentioned in the newsletter."

"Seriously?" Jason reaches back for his phone and drops it in his cargo shorts pocket.

Maris nods. "It's research. So it'll be a tax write-off, too." She hooks her finger on his belt, smiles and gives a tug. "We'll go to the Souvenir Shop. Isn't it run out of that big cottage on Ridgewood Road? Then we'll stop on the boardwalk on our way back."

"Okay, sweetheart." He takes her hand and heads to the doorway. "You're too beautiful to say no to, anyway." As he says it, he tugs her back and kisses her. Just lightly, though. One hand presses on her face, his other rests on her hip. He gives her that kiss, only one. Lightly, but it's enough.

~

Standing at the community bulletin board near the boardwalk, Cliff tips up the brim of his COMMISSIONER cap. The hot July sun is rising high in the sky, the day already a scorcher. Cliff scans the bulletin board for just the right spot to hang his latest Stony Point newsletter. After tacking it into place, he drops a handful more into the newsletter bin for vacationers' reading pleasure.

When he does, he also gets an idea. So he lifts out a newsletter and reads aloud.

"Bingo. Tuesday night, 7 PM. Hmm …"

"Who you talking to?"

"Nobody." Cliff looks over at Nick approaching. "Talking to myself."

"And I'm all freshly pressed, just the way you ordered. So where do you want me stationed today to assert my authority?"

Cliff glances at Nick and notices the ironed creases in his black shirtsleeves, and down the center of his black shorts.

"What do you think of bingo?"

"Bingo?" Nick lifts off his sunglasses and squints at Cliff. "You want me stationed at the *bingo* game tonight?"

"No. I mean what do you think of bingo for a *godfather* competition." He shows Nick the summer Boardwalk Bingo Schedule posted in the newsletter.

"That's for the kids, boss! They give out bubbles and boogie boards for prizes."

"Doesn't say it's for kids *only*. We can do something like, I don't know, first one to get a bingo wins a godfather point. Muscles I didn't even know I have are still aching from that tubing, so it'd be nice to keep it easy for this one."

"Yeah." Nick raises his hand to his chin. "I like that idea. Bingo!"

Cliff squints at Nick's chin and sees a patch of hair there. "You need to shave that, Nicholas. Rules are the rules, including the one stating no facial hair. Our guards are clean-shaven, which fosters professionalism and trust."

"Wait. Let's set this up first. Bingo night."

"Well … I'm not sure now. Because how can I get in touch with everyone in time? Bingo on the boardwalk is *tonight*."

"I'm on it, Commish." Nick whips out his cell phone and sets up a group text. "*From?*" he says while typing. "*The Boss. New Godfather Competition. Tonight at 7 PM. Sharp. Bingo on the Boardwalk. Be there, and hope for a lucky card!*"

"Look at that." Cliff steps away from the bulletin board and stands at the bottom of the few granite stairs to the boardwalk. Squinting against that hot sun, he makes out who he believes to be Jason, Maris, Elsa, Celia—hell, the whole gang seems to be sitting on the boardwalk bench. "You didn't even have to text," he tells Nick as he climbs the steps. "They're all sitting right here … slacking off on a perfectly fine workday!"

eighteen

DING, DING.

"That you?" Jason asks Maris, who is sitting further off, beneath the boardwalk's center shade pavilion.

At the same time, right beside him, Kyle says, "That mine? I think it's mine."

Both men pull out their cell phones and read a group text message from Nick.

"Bingo?" Jason asks, right as he hears footsteps on the boardwalk planks. He looks up to see Nick and the commissioner approaching.

"That's right," Cliff says with a slight smile giving away his amusement. "Bingo. We need to add it to the godfather tally."

"Tonight?" Jason asks with a glance to Maris. But she's in the shade, bent over the stroller while cooing to Aria. He gets a passing worry, watching his wife. Matt wasn't kidding when he said something comes over the women around Aria. But Jason's not sure he's quite ready for his *own* stroller on the boardwalk.

"Look how she loves it here," Maris is saying, her voice sweetly soothing. Even Maddy, lying at her feet, seems mesmerized by her voice. The German shepherd leans against Maris' leg, her tall ears listening.

"I know," Celia agrees. "Aria's really alert and seeing things now that she's two months old."

"And look how her dark hair has grown," Elsa quietly exclaims. She bends over from her boardwalk seat. "Wait. I think she *smiled* at me!"

Yes, there it is. That baby trance that descends on the women. Maris is purely lost in some foreign maternal world with Elsa and Celia right now.

In Jason's *man* world, Cliff's back to his courtroom behavior from his days as a judge. Jason can just imagine him in court, gavel in hand, as he listens to Cliff give the third degree to Kyle now.

"What are you doing here?" Cliff asks from beneath the brim of his COMMISSIONER hat. "Diner closed today, on this fine Tuesday morning?"

"Sheesh, I was at the farmers' market when my pickup crapped out on me. Couldn't get it started and needed a tow." Wearing his work pants and black tee in the hot sunshine, Kyle presses his arm to his perspiring forehead. "The tow-truck driver gave me a courtesy ride here, so I can use Lauren's car."

"When are you going to dump that P-O-S and get some new wheels?" Nick asks. He takes off his uniform cap and sits beside Kyle, giving his shoulder a shove at the same time.

"Yeah, Bradford," Jason adds. "I thought Sal gave you a hefty sum for that truck, with instructions to replace it. On him."

"Hey." Kyle stands and fans the fabric of his black tee over his chest. "We just bought a house, okay? So I've been busy?"

When Kyle waves to someone on the beach, Jason looks

out across the freshly raked sand, kept spotless in the summertime for vacationers. The sun is brilliant, midmorning, glaring off the beach and sparkling on the cool water. Jason squints to see someone tall and gangly trotting barefoot across the sand.

"Yo, Vincenzo," Kyle calls out.

"Shouldn't you be at the diner?" Vinny asks when he steps onto the boardwalk. He's got on his bathing suit and a tee, and quickly sits to cool his sand-burned feet. "Cooking up some good grub for the hungry folks there?"

"Ay yai yai. I'm on my way, I'm on my way." Kyle paces a little. "Just took a walk before getting Lauren's car, okay? Anyway, Jerry's got me covered at the stoves for an hour or so."

"You're on the beach early." Jason eyes Vinny all slathered with sunblock. "My sister got you reserving her space in the sand?"

"I just put up the umbrella," Vinny says while motioning to a striped sun umbrella, "when I got Nick's text." Paige and his kids wave as he points them out. Sand pails and tubes and beach towels are spread around them.

"Not a bad gig, Vincenzo, teaching at the high school," Kyle muses while looking longingly at the glistening water on this steamy morning. "You've got summers off."

"Yeah, but I coach all year. Different swim teams keep me busy. *And* bring in extra cash," Vinny explains.

"Where you renting this summer?" Kyle asks.

"Hillcrest Road. Nice cottage, but not much of a view. Makes up for it with a great porch swing and a horseshoe pit, too."

"No shit!" Kyle turns around and high-fives Vinny. "That

was our place last year."

"*Ahem.*"

The sound rings loud and clear from beneath the shade pavilion. And it's stern enough to get them all turning. Celia, wearing a sleeveless ankle-length sundress and her fedora, is lifting something out of Aria's stroller. "Gentlemen," she says as she walks over to them. "I want to show you something." She lifts a decorated jar high into the air, so that they can't miss it. "This is my brand-new, custom-made … swear jar."

"Your what?" Cliff asks.

Celia holds up a hand for silence. "Now *listen.* And listen good. Because from now on, every time one of you utters, let's just say … *colorful* words in front of my daughter, there'll be a price to pay. Because Aria is *not* going to grow up with a potty mouth." She stops in front of Kyle. "One dollar, please, for your latest infraction."

Kyle shakes his head, but he does it. There's no getting around Celia's insistence as she gives the jar a shake. Yes, Kyle pulls his wallet from his pocket and folds the first dollar into Celia's swear jar, also muttering something about Celia being as savvy as Sal when it comes to money and investments.

As he does, Vinny jumps onto the sand to head back to his family. "See you for bingo on the boardwalk later," he calls over his shoulder while prancing his burning feet, right as Jason's cell phone rings.

"Finally!" Jason stands up and answers. He leans into the call, pressing the phone close. "Trent? Hang on." Jason jogs down the boardwalk a ways, then circles back as his cell phone signal wavers. "What's that?" he asks, bending into the call, then lifting the phone high in the air before continuing. "Green *what*? You're breaking up. News light?"

Beep-beep-beep, he hears then, getting him to eye his phone closely. "Oh my God, Maris." He turns to where she's now standing in the shade. "The call got dropped."

"Go to the bench, Jason," Elsa orders him from beside the baby stroller. She points to a distant wooden bench set in a clearing on the rise where the dune grasses sway. "It's on a hill, the only place on the beach with a decent signal."

"Hurry!" Maris whispers, giving him a gentle push.

So Jason does, rushing to the bench and calling Trent back at his CT-TV office. They talk for only a few minutes. And when Jason returns to the boardwalk afterward, every eye is glued to him.

"Well?" Maris cautiously asks. "Are the numbers in?"

"Good news?" Kyle slaps Jason's shoulder, watching him closely.

Everyone—Nick, Cliff, Kyle and the women—all wait silently for Jason's answer. It's obvious how much they want this for him.

"Not good," Jason says, shaking his head.

"Oh no!" Maris takes his hand.

"No. It's more like … *great*!" Jason says with a slow grin, which prompts two shoves: one from Kyle, then from Nick on his other side. "Got the green light. CT-TV picked up the show for a year."

Maris gives him a quick hug and a kiss. "I'm so proud of you, babe!"

And between the guys telling him, *You're the man*, and *All right, dude*, and *Way to go*, Jason feels the backslaps and handshakes and takes the hugs from Elsa and Celia, too.

"Wait." He steps back, hands held up. "Wait, wait. There is one problem. Really, no horsing around. The series needs an official name. *CT-TV Cottage Redo* was just a placeholder on the premiere. Now that the show's a go, my producer wants something really catchy."

"Have any ideas, Jason?" Cliff asks as he shakes Jason's hand.

Jason considers the question while glancing at the cottages out beyond the boardwalk, near the winding footpath. They're the type of seaside homes his TV program might feature—grande old dames showing the wear of the sea and the permeation of its salty dampness on their coastal architecture. Though imposing in age and stature, the cottages—Nantuckets and Hampton-style colonials and even a stone-sided bungalow—bear the brunt of the sea. Brown cedar shingles on one are edged in black; the screened front porch sags with fatigue on another; sea-facing windows are permanently clouded with years of salty spray.

"Something cottage-y sounding?" Cliff continues.

"That'd be a start—" Jason says, before Kyle interrupts.

"Don't worry. I am *so* on it, bro." Kyle slaps Jason's shoulder again. "I'll check my dictionary for ideas, mnemonics. It has to be something cool, that will draw the viewer in."

As he puts his uniform cap back on, Nick walks to Kyle. "Great, Kyle. You'll be deliberating on this for three years. Just like your diner name issue."

"Kyle!" Elsa calls out from the shade, where she sits with Aria in her lap. "What'd I tell you about finding answers that way? Remember your best man speech?"

"I know, I know." Kyle pats his chest while nodding.

"That's right." Elsa kisses the top of Aria's head, before eyeing Kyle first, then Jason—as though her next words are really meant for him.

So Jason waits. When she pauses, he walks closer to where she sits beneath the shade pavilion.

"The best answers," she insists then with a wise look at Jason, "*always* come from the heart."

nineteen

"B-14." THERE'S A QUIET PAUSE, then louder, "*Bee-14!*"

Jason impatiently glances over at Taylor and Alison, the two Parks and Rec counselors calling the bingo numbers. He can barely make them out in the crowd, though. Being Fourth of July week, the boardwalk is the busiest it'll likely be all summer. And this Tuesday evening is a pure kiddie event. Freshly sunburned families gather with little kids and tiny tots—in shorts and tees, bathing suits and cover-ups—all wanting a chance to win a full card, or round robin, or four corners.

But in this sea of eager bingo-playing children, a pack of anxious guys clutching their own bingo cards sticks out like a sore thumb. Each of Jason's friends is rigid in their posture, straining to hear each announced number. Still, Jason knows this could be a quick and easy godfather point to clinch. Vinny must have the same idea, the way he keeps leaning too close to steal a look at Jason's bingo card. Close enough for Jason to elbow him back.

"Keep your eyes to yourself," Jason tells him.

"N-31," Taylor calls out from the far end of the boardwalk. "*Enn-31!*"

Jason checks his card. Nothing. On either side of him, all the guys sit lined up on the boardwalk bench. They were sure to keep Kyle separate from his family. Because not one of them trusts Lauren *or* Evan to sit beside Kyle. Who's to say they wouldn't do a discreet bingo card swap if one of them had a winning card? So Lauren and her two kids sit on the edge of the boardwalk, their feet in the sand. Little Hailey sits close to her mother, and a blanket covers their laps in the evening sea air.

Meanwhile, everyone sits tensely, not saying a word. Not Kyle. Not Vinny and Matt on one side of Jason. Not Cliff and Nick on the other, clutching bingo cards and clearly off guard duty. In the quiet, all Jason notices are roving eyes as one or another leans forward and glances at someone else's card. That, and occasional swats at mosquitoes.

"G-53."

Jason marks his card.

"*Gee-53!*"

"What'd she say?" Vinny asks in a spoken whisper.

"Shh!" Kyle scolds. The stress of it all actually has him perspiring, prompting him to press the back of his hand to his forehead.

"G-53," Matt says.

"When did Eva and Taylor get back from the Vineyard?" Jason asks him. "This afternoon?"

"Pipe down!" Cliff orders them as another bingo number is revealed. "Can you repeat the number?" he calls to Taylor, then leans over from his seat with his head tipped to hear.

With his card on his lap, Nick crosses his arms, all smug-like. "FYI. I only need one more for bingo."

"Big deal, kid." Jason waves him off. "Me, too."

Silence descends again. While studying his card, Jason hears only the gentle waves breaking across the beach, over and over again. A light breeze blows, carrying the early evening dampness lifted off the water.

"I-20."

A few murmurs rise, which Jason can't decipher. There's also a distinct *Yes!* as someone's card gets closer to a bingo.

Lauren looks at them over her shoulder. "How can you guys be as into it now as when you were ten?" she asks. When Kyle only shrugs, she lifts her cell phone and snaps a picture of them bent over their bingo cards. "Celia has *got* to see this," she says. "All this bingo drama … to be the godfather."

When the next number is called, Jason doesn't even have time to check his card. Not before a young boy sitting nearby shouts, "Bingo!"

"Good job, Carter," a woman beside him, likely his mother, says as she high-fives her son.

"Hold your cards!" Taylor warns the players. "Until we double-check!"

When this Carter kid rushes past him clutching his winning card, Jason leans back in defeat, his losing bingo card on his lap. "Son of a bitch," he says under his breath. But apparently not quietly enough. Because Carter's mother leans forward from her seat and catches his eye with a sharp glare before moving further down the bench, away from him and his bad influence.

"We have a winner!" Taylor declares. "Carter, help yourself to a boogie board."

As he does, Cliff stands and stretches, then sits again with his card. If Jason's not mistaken, Cliff's actually fidgeting with his good-luck domino. Everyone *seriously* wants this easy point.

Nick heads over to Taylor and Alison and switches his card for a new one.

"Clear your cards," Alison calls out. "This round will be a *regular* bingo."

And so Jason clears his card, sits back and silently begins again. Behind him in the boat basin, the docked vessels subtly rise and fall in the water. That pull of the unseen tide has the boats straining against the pilings to which they're secured. They creak and sigh against the wood posts. *Boat talk*, they've always called that creaking noise. Hearing it is comforting and eerie at once. Because with a glance behind the boardwalk, can't Jason picture two young boys there? As easy as that, with one evocative sound, he's lost in a memory of his brother.

~

Wearing shorts and tees, with sweatshirts thrown on at their mother's insistence, they walked around the marina. Shadows were long, and they kept to them so as not to be seen. They knew the rule: They could not go out in their Boston Whaler at night.

But they also knew that in 'Nam, there were no rules. Their father told them that countless times. So Jason and Neil silently climbed into their docked boat. And in the summer darkness, they became the soldiers of their father's Vietnam war stories. As night fell, random couples strolling the nearby boardwalk became the enemy, seeking them out. So they ducked! Suddenly, their little docked boat, pulling against the pilings, was their only cover. Jason and his brother lay there, sipping fresh water from a canteen, hunkered down in the swaying boat until it was safe to run.

"Now!" Neil yelled in a whisper once no one was in sight.

Grabbing toy rifles, they scrambled out of the boat. Bent low, the two of them crossed the beach—hitting the ground when Jason heard enemy fire coming from the distant trees. He felt his brother fall nearly on top of him, his arm reaching around Jason's shoulders, both their heads bent into the sand.

"I got you covered," Neil whispered.

Finally, they made it to the water. In the dark, they waded in to their waists, plastic rifles held above their heads as seawater sloshed around them. The water was cold and treacherous; their clothes were soaked and clinging to their bodies. Beneath their feet, fiddler crabs became swamp creatures scurrying away; rocks were swamp turtles. When the two brothers made it to the far end at the stony point, closer to the marsh, they emerged—drenched and dripping. Their voices low, they pointed in the moonlight to where the enemy might be hiding.

"Over there!" Jason said, whipping around. Neil fell to his knees, his gun aimed at wavering shadows.

It was risky, but they moved slowly beside their pretend jungle in search of any Viet Cong hidden among trees lining the beach, or in the marsh's sweeping grasses. The only noise above the buzzing and chirping night insects was their whispers. That and their toy guns vibrating with electronic blips rather than bullets—whenever they pulled the trigger on some imagined VC soldier detected behind a tree, or darting into the lagoon.

All it takes is that one creaking sound, boat talk in the dusky light of evening, to bring those childhood memories back to Jason.

"G-48. *Gee-48!*"

And suddenly, just like that, Jason's back in the bingo game. Especially when he hears Vinny beside him, muttering that the cards are rigged. Jason glances over and sees that his brother-in-law has barely any numbers covered. Further down the boardwalk bench, Cliff is intently bent over his card, marking his latest number.

"O-74," Taylor says. "*Ooo-74!*"

Wait. Jason almost misses it. That's the number he needs. He marks his card, leans forward and waves it in the air, yelling, "Bingo!" When Kyle gives him a shove, he gets up and walks down the boardwalk to have his numbers officially checked. Sharp whistles break out as the guys get Taylor's attention. Jason hears them shouting behind him: *Hey! Make sure he didn't cheat,* and *Don't trust him. He could've fudged the numbers!*

Finally Jason stands waiting at the end of the boardwalk, where Taylor and Alison review his card. He moves aside when couples out for an evening stroll squeeze past him, headed for the beach.

"Congratulations!" Taylor says when she hands him back his card. "It's a bingo!"

Jason nods, takes his winning card and returns to the guys.

"Uncle Jason!" Taylor calls out. "Wait!"

Halfway back to his seat, he turns around.

Taylor's standing, raising a huge, colorful tin of cheesy Fish Bites crackers. The blue metal can is covered with bright yellow smiling fishies. The can also looks half the size of Taylor—and with good reason. It's the cracker-snack's jumbo party-sized container.

"Don't forget your prize!" Taylor reminds him.

twenty

MARIS BELIEVES THAT ONE OF the best things Jason ever did was this: not take on Elsa's reno unless the contract contained one critical stipulation. As usual, he had the foresight to hold Elsa to this demand. It meant the world to Jason, to Maris, and to every single one of their friends here at Stony Point.

Elsa *had* to agree to leave the old Foley's back room intact and unchanged from its original design. Even as the rest of the cottage transformed before her eyes.

Turns out, Maris repeatedly heard during the inn's renovation, that stipulation was one of the most difficult Jason ever put into a contract. Because every design molecule in his body itched to move walls, change angles, shift doorways, upgrade windows.

The restraint required to leave the room alone became his highest challenge.

Sitting with Elsa and Celia in the back room this Tuesday evening, Maris sees that it was also one of his greatest successes. Walking into this space is like walking into a time capsule. A beautiful, misty, stardust-filled, spirit-hovering time capsule that never ceases to evoke the sweetest, and saddest, long-ago memories.

Now, just like then, the jukebox quietly plays summertime tunes. And like then, the brand-new sliding windows—identical to the old—are open to the hitching salty breeze coming off the distant water. Two platters of pastries sit on the table in the refurbished restaurant-style booth where they gather. As usual, tonight Celia and Maris are Elsa's taste-testers—sampling foods Elsa might serve once the inn's officially opened.

But through the doorway, Maris also sees other design details in this refurbished inn. Faded and distressed fishing buoys of red, green and yellow hang around the stone fireplace in the living room. And in the hallway, Lauren's grand painted staircase mural leads upstairs to the bedrooms. Bedrooms which are exquisite: one decorated with nautical blues and whites, the room done up with white wicker furniture; another bedroom with distressed-white shiplap covering the walls and ceilings, old lobster trap nightstands beside the bed, with sea-green linens on the mattress and a lantern-chandelier hanging from the white-beamed ceiling.

"You did a beautiful job with the décor, Celia," Maris says. "Guests will love staying here."

"Thanks. It helped that I did the decorating when I was pregnant with Aria, so I had that nesting instinct going on." As she talks, her cell phone dings with a text message. She slides the phone close, laughs, then turns the phone to Elsa and Maris across from her. "Check it out."

Maris looks at a second photo Lauren sent from tonight's boardwalk bingo event. The picture shows Jason waving his bingo card right as the rest of the guys toss theirs in the air.

"Looks like Jason won the godfather point," Celia says. "Wait, I see Taylor on the boardwalk, too. Does this mean they're back from the Vineyard, Maris? Tay and your sister?"

"They are. But it's unpacking day, so Eva will catch our next ladies' night."

Elsa takes a look, then slides the phone back to Celia. "Anyway, who do *you* want to win, Cee? After all, the men are vying to be godfather to *your* baby."

"You can tell us," Maris assures her.

"Oh, no." Celia shakes her head and sits back. "I'm remaining a completely unbiased witness to their shenanigans." Celia walks over to the countertop, where she checks the baby monitor. Aria is tucked into the playpen suite she and Elsa assembled. Thankfully it has a built-in bassinette, and the baby's asleep now in one of the extra bedrooms. "Let the chips—or should I say the godfather points—fall where they may. And we can get crafting, instead," Celia suggests. She turns around holding vintage jars found at the salvage yard. Celia's auburn hair is in a loose ponytail, and her blouse sleeves are turned back, her hands ready to snip and paste. "You don't mind helping us, Maris? These are happiness jars for the inn's gift shop."

"Not at all." Maris helps carry over decorating items: a bucket of sand, and scraps of burlap, lace, and a roll of twine. "These tasks actually help me with my book. I think differently when I'm busy like this."

"Are you feeling any better about the writing?" Elsa trims a piece of lace as she asks.

"Definitely. Your writing nook here is a huge help." Comfortable in the booth again, Maris bites into a key-lime brownie. She simply savors the tart lime-flavored filling before wiping her fingers on a napkin. "I can get away and focus."

"What do you hope to eventually do with the book?" Celia asks.

"Well, once it's finished and gone through edits, I really want to publish it." She presses the rest of the tangy brownie into her mouth, chews and gives Elsa a thumbs-up, then continues. "Because even though Neil wrote much of the novel ten years ago, it still feels fresh. I'm just padding scenes he didn't finish. I'm also working on the final third of the story, which he never had a chance to. He died before writing the ending."

"That's always so sad to hear," Elsa says while wrapping a thin burlap scrap around one of the jars. Her leopard-print reading glasses sit low on her nose as she fusses. "But it makes the story that much more special, reading his thoughts and words, no?"

Maris nods while covering a jar with lace now, her pastry appetite satiated—for the time being. Scraps of fabric and string dot the table; damp salty air drifts through the windows. "The problem is, even in Neil's journal notes, he gave no indication about the ending. So I'm uncertain where the story should go." She trims a piece of the lace. "Jason tells me to take one day at a time. And to really outline one *chapter* at a time, to steer the storyline."

"And will you look for a publisher?" Celia asks.

"Not sure. Because typically you'd need a literary agent first, and I'm *really* wary of that process. When I worked in New York, I had friends in the business. And from what they told me, it's risky to submit manuscripts to agents. Often, the best submissions are pipelined to the agents' existing author-clients to lift from."

"Wait." Elsa sets down her sand-filled Mason jar and whips off her glasses. "You mean, published authors actually *steal* from unsuspecting writers just seeking an agent?"

"Some do, yes. One author in particular built a publishing career that way. She wrote her books using conveniently cloaked material, all stolen from another writer's manuscripts. Manuscripts that had been *requested* for consideration by the literary agency. Of course, when the thieving author had to eventually secure work based on her own *inadequate* ramblings, her publishing contracts quickly dried up in an ugly end to a really corrupt career."

"Deplorable, having no morals like that," Celia says. "I don't know how that author sleeps at night."

"I'm sure she doesn't." Maris fusses with her lace-edged jar. "But you can see why I'm uncomfortable sending out Neil's manuscript. Because what book will I open a year from now only to find reworked passages of Neil's in someone else's story? I can't risk it."

Elsa slices two pieces of blackberry-crumb bars and sets them on plates. "I agree with Jason," she says. "One chapter at a time. And it's not the dark ages anymore. You have so many options for publishing the novel."

"And how about Jason?" Celia lifts her crumb bar and takes a bite. "What's next for him now that the show's a go?" she asks around the fruity pastry.

"Cottage submissions," Maris explains. Tempted again by another sinful dessert, she cups her hand beneath her own blackberry-crumb bar as she digs in. Her eyes flutter closed with the delicious flavor. "The network opened up entries on their website, so Jason's inundated with videos and applications vying to be the next reno. The producer, Trent, is working with him to make a selection, and they're under a real time crunch. They should be filming, like, *right now*, for season one. And instead," Maris says around another bite of the blackberry bar, "I'm sure he's in The Sand Bar celebrating that bingo coup."

"Of course," Elsa agrees. She gets the coffeepot from the counter and pours three cups. "Because it's also time to plan the next godfather challenge!"

Maris nods to the illuminated pinball machine in the far corner. "I'm surprised they're not headed here for a pinball tournament. Whacking those flippers, getting that thing ringing and whistling in their mania."

They have an easy laugh then at how the guys are methodical in tallying the points in Kyle's binder; and how they try to talk like the Don; and how this godfather title grew into such a *complete* obsession.

"What's the draw?" Celia asks.

Elsa shrugs, then lifts her coffee cup. "Did you ever see the movie?"

"I did," Maris says. "Years ago, with an old high school boyfriend. *The Godfather* was the movie on the beach."

Celia leans across the table and lowers her voice. "Want to watch it?"

There's a moment of silence as Maris and Elsa squint at her through the shadows and low lighting.

"When?" Elsa asks.

Celia shrugs. "Tonight? Because, I mean, the guys are vying to be godfather to *my* baby, but they keep shutting us out of the deliberations."

"I know. Like last week. *You can't come boat shopping.* And *You can't come to movie night*, Jason said. *No women allowed.*" Those three words, she deliberately air-quotes.

"Oh, I heard the malarkey, too," Elsa adds. "Cliff was sure to tell me something about Matt's sports room being all … *testosterone* territory!"

"Well," Celia decides as she stands and puts her hands on her hips. "We need to know what this godfather business is all about, and not be treated like second-class citizens."

"The way they keep us women out of their secret planning meetings, it's so sexist," Maris says. Then, well then she lowers her voice. "I have their DVD at home. It's actually Cliff's."

"Ooh." Elsa grabs her arm. "You go get it, and we'll set up here."

So an hour later, in Elsa's living room, the three chatting women gather in their comfy pajamas and terry flip-flop slippers. *We'll just see what all the fuss is*, they muse. *See why the guys are so taken with this godfather thing.* A bowl of hot buttered popcorn sits on the coffee table; Aria's baby monitor is set on a bookshelf; the room lights are dimmed.

Their words still poke fun at the men as a trumpet solo begins the film: *I'll be the Don,* they say around its foreboding melody. *Oh no, it's me. Because you're too much of a hothead to be godfather!*

But by the time the opening credits roll and the sad, but ominous, strains of violin start the movie, the room is silent, the women … riveted.

~

It's one of those warm summer evenings when the door to The Sand Bar is propped open to the salty sea air outside. Twinkly lights are strung around a blackboard, where the night's specials are chalked. On the bar's big-screen TV, a baseball game is unfolding as the batter hits a line drive, bringing home a run. A few of the guys at the bar erupt in cheers.

Kyle glances at the TV from their regular booth, then slides over his black binder just as Nick grabs a handful of Fish Bites from the canister on the table. Kyle reaches into the can and grabs some, too. "Bingo … bingo," he says while opening their godfather-tally binder.

"Log it, loser," Jason orders him. "Because I won the game that's as American as baseball and apple pie."

"Not quite, pal." Kyle sets down his pen. "First bingo game dates back to *Italy*, actually, in the 1500s. It's traced back to a lottery game there."

"Is that right?" Jason downs a few crackers.

"Damn straight. And if Sal were here, he'd let you all know that bingo has strong ties to *il bel paese*."

"Ah, yes. The beautiful country," Jason says while raising his glass in a toast to Sal.

Kyle obliges and does the same, then logs Jason's bingo point. It's gnawing at him that his own potential godfather title is slipping away. "But seriously," he tells Jason, "you won the laziest challenge, bro."

"Doesn't matter." Jason takes another swig of his beer. "A point is a point. And that's not sour grapes I'm hearing, is it?"

"Could be." Kyle lifts the beer pitcher and tops off his glass. "Hey, by the way, I came up with some names for your TV show."

"Lay it on me," Jason says.

"Renovating the Coast."

"What?" Nick squints across the table at Kyle. "That's a lame one."

"You got something better, punk?" Kyle swigs his beer. "Besides, I'm just tossing things out there. See if anything sticks. Like, how about Cottages in Connecticut?"

Jason shakes his head. "Sounds more like a *tour* of beach homes. Doesn't even indicate I'm renovating them." He nudges the giant-sized brightly colored cracker canister closer to Kyle. "Maybe eating more fish will help you think."

Matt reaches over and snags a handful of the little fish crackers. He tosses a couple in the air and catches them in his mouth. When Nick pulls the canister his way, Matt stops him. "Yo, Nick." Matt lifts a yellow fish cracker and takes aim. "Open up. Patrolman to patrolman."

Nick does, and doesn't the cracker hit its target.

"I'm sure your boss would be *really* impressed with your hidden talents, Nicholas." Jason sits back and gazes out into the bar. "Where is Cliff, anyway?"

"He'll be here," Nick says while popping another cracker. "Had to square things with a new hire on the payroll for the summer. Explain the night-shift routine."

"Well, Nick." Vinny points a finger at him. "You're really hangin' with the big boys tonight."

"Out past your bedtime?" Kyle asks as he reaches across the table and lightly swipes Nick's chin.

"Eh, shut up." Nick motions to Matt to toss another cracker his way and opens his mouth to catch it.

"Hey!" an irritated voice calls out from the bar. "Knock it off."

But Vinny's already sucked into these new hijinks. He flips up his polo shirt collar, lifts a cracker and aims it toward Kyle. "Who gets the godfather point?" Vinny asks. "The one who *tosses* the cracker, or the one who *catches* it?" When he zings it across the table, Kyle catches it in his mouth.

"Doesn't matter." The now-annoyed voice gets closer. It's Patrick approaching from behind the bar. He wears a black vest over a button-down, the sleeves shoved up to his elbows. And he's personally delivering another pitcher of beer. "I'm shutting this food-toss down. Next thing you know, one of you knuckleheads will be at the walk-in clinic with a cracker lodged in your throat." He sets the pitcher on the table and turns Kyle's monster binder. "What the hell is all this, anyway?"

Kyle pages through a few sheets of competitions and stats. "It's a sweet deal, man. Our godfather competition."

"What?" Patrick reads some of the contests, whispering *golf cart parade* and *fishing tournament.* "Godfather competition? For who?"

"Remember Sal?" Jason asks. He slowly turns his beer glass on its paper coaster. "Sal DeLuca? You met him in here, not long before he died."

"Sure." Patrick snaps the binder shut. "Great guy, that Sal was."

"Absolutely. And his lady had a baby," Jason explains.

"No kidding." Patrick slides over a chair and sits at the end of their table. A dim pendant light above it casts them in dusky shadows. "She's the singer, right?" He looks at Jason, straight on, raising an eyebrow while asking, "The one who was in here strumming that guitar last fall? Feeling a little loopy?"

"That's the one. Celia." Jason takes a long swallow of his brew in the shadowy bar. "She had a baby."

"Sal's?" Patrick quietly asks with a wary glance at Jason. "You never mentioned she was pregnant."

Jason returns the look. "I've barely been here, guy. The TV show's kept me plenty busy," he says. "But, yes. Celia had *Sal's* baby two months ago."

Kyle watches Patrick, then Jason, wondering what's being suggested between these two.

"Really." Patrick shakes his head. "Now isn't that a cruel twist of fate?"

"The worst," Kyle has to agree while waving Cliff over when he comes in through the bar's propped-open door. "The cards just never aligned for poor Sal."

"You talking about Elsa's son?" Cliff asks. He drags a chair over to the dark table and sits with them all.

"Yeah. Still miss the guy," Kyle says. "The Italian deserved so much more from life."

"Celia too, actually," Cliff adds while lifting the pitcher and pouring himself a beer. "The way she's raising that baby alone now."

Vinny jumps in, tossing back another handful of the cheesy fish crackers. "And their little girl needs a godfather for her christening day. So here we all are, vying to be the Stony Point Don."

"Got it." Patrick leans his chair back, arms crossed over his chest as he eyes the table. "And who's winning this racket?"

"That'd be me." Cliff straightens his shoulders, then tips his COMMISSIONER cap. "Right here."

Patrick drops his chair down. "*You?*"

Cliff simply nods.

"Is that right? Well, good for you, guy." Patrick stands and shakes Cliff's hand before spinning his chair back to its other table. "Just keep it easy over here," he adds while grabbing a handful of the crackers. "Play darts, shoot pool. Nothing requiring an ambulance, please. I'm trying to run a classy joint."

"Okay." Jason looks at each of them. "So the Fish Bite challenge is off. What's next?"

"Fish Bite challenge?" Cliff asks.

Kyle drags over the big tin and grabs a few crackers. "Eh, you missed it, Judge."

"And we need some ideas," Jason tells them all.

"I know." Vinny leans across the table, fidgeting with his lanky hands while considering something. "My students play it every year. The seniors do, right before graduating. But the competition gets pretty intense. You guys up to it?"

"What is it?" Cliff asks.

"The List." Vinny sits back then, waiting.

"What?" Matt asks.

"What the heck's that?" Cliff sips his beer. "The *List*?"

"It's an elimination game. Each participant has to take down opponents to advance. So it's well-suited to our," Vinny pauses and air-quotes the word, "*godfather* thing. You know," he adds with a shrug. "Because of the *elimination* part."

"Wait." Jason squints at his brother-in-law. "So we're going from bingo to … The List?"

"Sure." Vinny sits closer now and motions to Kyle to write this down. "Here's how it works."

Kyle grabs his pen and flips open his black binder. His hand moves across a blank page, keeping the rules in order. Every now and then, Jason leans over and points out details he missed while Vinny elaborates.

Kill or be killed, Kyle scribbles. *When you take down your target, you inherit their target, move up the ranks and keep advancing to winner.*

"Don't forget the safe zones," Jason quietly reminds Kyle.

Safe zones … your own property, because your children and significant others are there. Probably better they not witness this.

"What about a general safe zone, away from home?" Matt asks. "Somewhere easy to access."

The table goes quiet until Jason suggests one. "The boardwalk. Convenient location, multiple ways to get on it, too."

Meanwhile, Kyle writes their names across torn slips of paper and folds them in half. When Cliff offers his cap, Kyle drops the papers in it, then Cliff gives the cap a shake. Finally, one by one, they all draw the name of the person they have to eliminate.

"Keep it top secret," Vinny advises them while reaching into the cap. "No revealing identities."

"So if someone eliminates *you*, you're out of the game. Done." Cliff takes a peek at his folded paper before pressing it deep into his wallet. "But if you *eliminate* someone, you inherit *their* target, too?"

"Exactly," Vinny explains. "It's how you advance in the game. You have to keep eliminating someone."

"Wait," Nick says as he discreetly tucks his target's name into his shorts pocket. "We need walkie-talkies, then. Because we'll have to communicate when someone is eliminated, to be fair." He looks at Cliff across from him. "Boss? You've got some in the trailer."

"Well, I don't know now. Because those are official Stony Point business supplies, not intended for general use." Cliff shakes his head, then finishes his thought with a swig of beer. "And the rules are the rules."

"Raines." Jason looks at him and turns up his hands. "You in on this competition or not? Because true godfather candidates do whatever they have to do, *regardless* of the rules. Or they make their own rules, if you get my drift."

"Fine." Cliff checks his watch. "We'll stop at the trailer after here. But only if it's all on the sly, fellas. Off the books."

"Of course." Jason tips back his glass and downs the rest of his beer, then turns to Vinny. "Vincenzo, how do we actually eliminate someone from this *list*? What's the weapon of choice?"

Vinny lowers his voice again. "This shit gets serious now."

Everyone quiets and leans over the dark wooden table. Half-empty beer glasses are held close; the crack of a pool stick sounds from the back; a few men over at the bar have a good laugh.

"We have a few options. Like … shooting a rubber band at your target," Vinny says after surveying the room. "Or silly string, maybe. Squirt guns work, too."

"Now we're talking." Nick sits back and rubs his goatee. "Super Soakers!"

"Nicholas," Cliff interrupts, pointing to Nick's facial hair. "Regulations—"

"Wait," Kyle interrupts. He looks up from manically jotting down the rules. "Squirt guns? But from where?" he asks. "How can we get our hands on some, real quick? I mean, my son has one or two, but not enough for everybody."

Cliff's glare at Nick changes to a distracted slow smile now. A slow smile and a raised eyebrow. "I know just the place. Saw a whole display there when Elsa and I were buying golf cart decorations."

"Where?" Matt asks.

Cliff looks over his shoulder, as if to be sure no one's listening in on their plans. "The dollar store," he nearly whispers.

"Perfect," Jason admits, reaching across the table and shaking Cliff's hand to seal the competition deal.

Cliff nods and pulls out his car keys, first, then his phone—almost as an afterthought. He rapidly begins texting, stopping mid-typing to look up at everyone watching him. "Text your women, gentlemen! Because between walkie-talkie disbursement and squirt gun selection," he says as everyone's instantly grabbing their phones, "well, it's going to be a late night."

twenty-one

IT'S NEARLY MIDNIGHT BY THE time Cliff's back at his trailer-apartment. After emptying out his pockets—dropping his wallet and keys on a small dresser, then standing his good-luck domino on his nightstand—he changes into his favorite blue pajamas.

Only one dim bedside lamp is on, so the trailer is dark. A Dean Martin album plays on the record player. The singer's smooth voice pleads for the love of his life to come home … to his heart. While opening his futon and smoothing a blanket, Cliff sings along, softly. Because, heck, isn't that what he's trying to do? Hurry home to Elsa's heart by being her granddaughter's godfather? It would be such a special honor.

But apparently the other guys will do anything for that godfather honor, too, as evidenced by the array of protection Cliff has amassed to fight them off. His squirt guns are aligned neatly on his bistro table: a few water pistols, a dripping drencher, and his favorite—sure to hit any target within its forty-foot range—one extreme water launcher decked out with a viewfinder and foam-covered handles.

That one is so intriguing, he heads there to pick it up.

Lifting the bazooka to shoulder level, he peers through the viewfinder and imagines his nemesis on the other end, about to be dowsed.

And he jumps, nearly dropping the plastic weapon, when there's a sudden knock on his door. Cautiously, he sets down the water gun and walks through the pleated door to the business end of the trailer, passing his tanker desk and a few random chairs. He presses his ear to the industrial-strength steel door and listens for a sound outside, but hears nothing.

"Who is it?" he calls out with his hand on the doorknob.

"Your girlfriend!"

"Is this a setup?" Cliff asks when he recognizes Elsa's voice.

"What?"

Cliff flicks on an outside light and cracks open the door to see Elsa standing there. She wears a light sweater over a V-neck tunic pajama top and capri-length leggings. A black-and-white leopard print bandana is looped around her honey-highlighted brown hair, and terry cloth flip-flop slippers are on her feet.

"Are you trying to lure me off the property?" Cliff asks while bending and squinting past her. "Because as soon as I'm in the street, my eliminator can move in."

"What are you talking about?" Elsa glances back over her shoulder to where Cliff just looked. "No! On the contrary, I'm here to protect you. Let me in!"

Cliff reaches for her arm and gently yanks her inside before slamming the door behind her. Which is precisely when he notices some leftover pastry wrapped on a plate in one hand, and a small piece of luggage in the other. "Who says I need protection?" he demands.

"Cliff. When you mentioned your next challenge in your

text message earlier, we did some quick research."

"We?"

"Maris. And Celia, too. We were having a ladies' pajama party and watching *The Godfather* when you texted me." Elsa motions to her nighttime loungewear. "So after the movie, we got all the lowdown on this competition you're involved in. *The List.* And you need to keep your strength up for this one." Elsa raises the delicious-looking dessert. "Because I'm sure you filled up all night on those Fish Bites, which have *zero* nutritional value." She walks further into the trailer, then turns to face him. "You have to be strong. And ready!"

"Ready?" Cliff asks.

Elsa steps closer and lowers her voice. "To take down your target!" Her voice drops even lower with the rest. "Bring him to his *knees.*" Then? Then she sets her overnight bag on a chair and reaches for Cliff's arm. "Who'd you get?"

Cliff squints at her in the darkness. "That's confidential. I have to swear you to secrecy."

"Absolutely. Because I will *help* take down this target, no matter who it is."

"Okay." Still, he looks at her for a long second. Strains of Dean Martin float in from his secret, dimly lit apartment. "It's your favorite nephew-in-law," Cliff admits.

"Jason?"

He nods.

"Oh, dear."

When Elsa drops into a chair beside his work desk, Cliff thinks it's with defeat. Her posture changes as she slightly slumps, still holding that pastry dish in her hand.

"He's a crafty one," Elsa continues while squinting over her shoulder at him in the shadowy room. "He'll be onto you in two seconds flat." With that, she quickly stands and heads through the accordion-style door to his little hidden trailer-apartment. There, she moves his water guns to the counter and sets two plates on the bistro table. "You better have some of my blackberry-crumb bars. Here," she says while folding a napkin.

Cliff stops in the doorway and watches Elsa. Something about her actions seems too rehearsed. "Blackberry-crumb bars?"

"And key-lime brownies, too."

"That sounds awfully suspicious."

Elsa looks over at him as she sets a fork on top of the folded napkin.

"Like you're sweetening your way to the inside," Cliff says with a sidelong squint. "Next I'll see you having an egg sandwich with *Barlow*, in cahoots with *him*. I'll bet you're wheedling for inside information, just to get the godfather that *you* want. Because you're too attached as the child's grandmother. So … So …" He steps closer and whispers. "Maybe I lied, and Jason's just a red herring to throw you off."

Before Elsa can even defend herself, Cliff hurries out to the trailer's reception area and picks up her one piece of luggage. "Take your overnight bag and get out!"

"You can't be serious."

"Oh, I am." He hurries straight to the bistro table and hands her the luggage, folding her fingers right over the handles. "I've said too much already, clouded by your beauty, and food and … *wiles*."

"You can trust me!" Elsa insists as she sets down the overnight bag.

Cliff picks it up again and presses it into her arms. "Out! I need to strategize and I don't trust that this isn't a setup."

"Oh! You don't trust *me*?" Elsa starts walking away with her luggage before she spins around and snatches up her pastry dish, too. "I never did trust *you*, Commissioner Raines. With those … those … *blue* eyes of yours."

"Seriously?" Cliff takes her elbow and walks her to the door, where he stops and turns to face her. "My *eyes*?"

Elsa shifts her pastry dish in her hand. "Yes. Your icy blue eyes. Which you match your sleepwear ensemble to, I suppose?" Her own eyes drop up and down his body, taking in his navy-blue-with-white-piping short-sleeved top and matching shorts pajama set, before looking at his face again.

At which point, Cliff opens the steel trailer door, the one with a pretty twig wreath on it. A wreath with a cream ribbon woven through the twigs. A wreath Elsa hung to soften the look of the door and make it feel somewhat homey. Now she brushes straight past him and heads down the few metal steps to her golf cart parked there. Her slippers flip and flop harshly on each step.

"Wait! Elsa!" Cliff goes outside to the top step and stops right there, afraid to leave his property lest he be taken down by a hidden squirt gun lifted to someone's eye. A water pistol with a finger on the trigger, ready to unleash a stream of water on his chest—and instantly eliminate him.

Elsa hesitates, her back to him. But she gives in, he sees it, and slowly turns with a smile on her face.

A smile that could win Cliff over under *any* other circumstance.

On *any* other night when he might take her in his arms and have a little waltz to Dino still crooning inside. Then maybe some canoodling afterward.

"I knew you'd have a change of heart," she says, still smiling as she returns up the stairs. Her smile lights up her whole face, even reaching her sparkling eyes.

"I did have a change of heart, Elsa. I *did*." With that, he grabs her pastry plate. "A change of heart for your blackberry-crumb bars!"

Quickly, he backs into his trailer and closes the door behind him—being sure to lock it. In a moment, he walks past the reception area, past the tanker desk and metal file cabinet, through that pleated door to his tiny bistro table.

He does something else, too.

Passing a mirror on the way to the table, he gives a long scrutiny to his, well, his *blue* eyes that apparently undermine Elsa's trust. He steps close to the mirror and squints at himself, but only until that pastry plate gets his attention. And once sitting all by his lonesome at the table, Dean Martin singing about the moon low in the sky, Cliff does it. He lifts the wrapping on a sweet mound of blackberry-crumb bars drizzled in a pool of glazed cream cheese, shrugs, takes the fork and lifts a hunk to his mouth.

~

Wearing only his pajama pants, Kyle stands in front of the bathroom mirror and brushes his teeth. "For crying out loud," he says when he knocks the tube of toothpaste off the sink and it spins to the floor. He rinses his mouth and spits out the water. "Who uses pedestal sinks, anyway? They're too small."

Lauren's voice, sounding distracted, comes to him from the bedroom. "But in a small room, they take up less space."

"Right." And in *this* room, there's barely *room* for himself.

Kyle bends over and scoops the toothpaste off the floor. When he straightens, his shoulder bumps into the sink. "Damn pedestals leave me no space to put my stuff." He looks at his reflection while rubbing his shoulder, first, then running his hand across his bare chest. "I need a vanity. With storage."

"At least we have an *en suite*!"

Lauren still sounds distracted. So Kyle leans back and looks at her in the bedroom. With only one bedside lamp on, the room is shadowy. But he sees that she's wearing her satin nightshirt while propped up in the bed, one leg bent at the knee. His deluxe Super Soaker sits across her lap as she scrutinizes it.

"So, who'd you get?" she asks, finally looking over at him.

"Can I trust you?" Because if there's one thing Kyle learned from this night of planning, it's to trust no one. The List is a devious game. "You're the godmother, after all," he manages around the toothbrush bristles in his mouth.

"Kyle! I'm also your wife."

After another rinse and spit-out, he wipes his face on the towel. "Matt."

"Matt? You have to take down *Matt*? But he's a state cop. He knows this stuff and will have you pegged in three seconds flat."

"No he won't." The towel is soft, and so he presses it to his face with his eyes closed for a long second. "I'll be careful."

"Where is all this going down, anyway? These squirt-gun *shootouts*. Not here, with the kids watching."

"Don't worry." As he says it, Kyle drags his hand over his face and studies his soul patch in the mirror. The whiskers came in nicely, filling in to a thick tuft just below his lower lip. He lifts a small pair of scissors and clips a few stray hairs.

"Personal property is a safe zone," he says with his head tipped up to the light as he trims. "The boardwalk is, too."

After a quiet minute passes, Kyle brushes off his chin and looks out to the bedroom, where Lauren is still eyeing the water gun in her lap. Folds of her nightshirt shimmer around that bent leg.

"This squirt gun is so huge." She lifts it as if to demonstrate. "Matt will see you coming a mile away."

"Nah. That one was only a decoy." Kyle walks barefoot to his dresser and opens the top drawer. "I'll show you what else I slipped into my cart."

"Who do you think has you for their target?" Lauren asks behind him, from the bed.

Kyle pulls a sleek green squirt gun out of a plastic bag. "Don't know, which is part of the suspense. No one can be trusted." He walks over to the bed and gives the squirt gun, this one pocket-sized, to Lauren.

"Wow." She turns the toy, then runs her fingers over it. "So everyone's armed with these?"

Kyle nods and sits on the edge of the bed. A slight breeze wafts in through an open window.

"I feel anxious *for* you." Lauren extends her arm, pointing the water pistol at the closet door.

"Listen," Kyle quietly says. He drags a finger along her arm, up to her shoulder. "Nowhere's safe. So trust no one, Ell. Everyone will be spewing lies to try to take down their target."

"When does all this begin?"

"Right now. Last man on The List gets the godfather point."

With the squirt gun in one hand, Lauren reaches up with the other and lightly strokes Kyle's bare chest. "It's like you're headed off to war."

"Yup. This could be our last night together if my eliminator gets to me first." He gently tugs the squirt gun from her fingers and sets it on the nightstand. Then he glides his hand along that leg bent at the knee and moves his fingers up her thigh, lightly caressing her skin. Outside the window, the warm night air is nearly still. But inside, Lauren shifts on the bed as she reaches for the drawstring of his pajama bottoms. A quiet moment passes when only her fingers loosen them. When she then shuts off the bedside lamp, Kyle leans closer and slips his hand over that silky nightshirt that's been shimmering and wavering over every gentle curve of her body. Beneath his fingers, the silky fabric is cool to the touch, and light as a feather. Finally, he pins her arms to the pillow as he moves over her. "Send me off with a smile?"

~

Jason hears an odd noise as he stands at his dresser. Leaning on one forearm crutch, he's emptying out his shorts pockets, dropping coins into a dish, setting his wallet on his valet.

And still, the noise.

Which gets him to look over his shoulder at Maris. She's lying on the bed, munching on those cheesy Fish Bite crackers. The party-sized jumbo tin is beside her and her hand is constantly scooping up more crackers.

That's what he's been hearing. Not her crunching, but rather her fingers scrabbling around the tiny crackers to grab a fistful.

"Darling, should I just hold that can above your mouth and pour those fishies in?"

"Jason!"

"Just sayin'." Instead he unstraps his watchband and sets the watch on his dresser.

"Are you really keeping your water pistol right beside the bed?" Maris asks then.

Jason turns and looks at his bedside chair this time. The chair that his prosthesis leans against, and the chair his gun is on, too. "Maris. That weapon has to be with me always. That's the nature of this whole godfather gig. Where I go, so goes my squirt gun."

"Who'd you get?" she asks after plunking a few cheesy fingers out of her mouth.

"Can I trust you?"

"Babe!" After she says it, a little indignant, her hand scoops out another handful of crackers. One by one, she drops them in her mouth.

"You have to promise to keep this under wraps." Jason hooks his other crutch onto his wrist and walks over to the bed. There, Maris is propped on her elbow while lying on her side, wearing a loose tee over black silky pajama shorts. He leans down and whispers, "I got the kid."

"The kid?" she asks, mid-chew.

He puts a gentle finger to her lips, then sits on the edge of the mattress. "Shh. *Nicholas.*"

"Why are we whispering?"

"Oh, man." Jason hitches his head toward the open window. There's only a slight sea breeze coming off the water tonight. The sound of easy waves breaking out on the bluff reaches him. "They could hear you," he explains. "Someone could be hiding outside our window. And, you know. Secrets carry in the salt air, especially here. Didn't you say you ladies watched *The Godfather* tonight?"

"We did. And shouldn't home be a safe place?"

"*Safe?* You need to watch *The Godfather Part II*. There's a scene when Michael Corleone and his wife are practically machine-gunned down in *their* bedroom. Ambushed!"

"Oh, that sounds awful. Attacked in their own home?"

"Right. Under a false sense of security." Using his crutches, Jason walks back to his dresser. "So you see? The enemy spies."

"Do you want me to talk to my sister and see if Matt got you for his target? She's back from Martha's Vineyard. Spent the day unpacking, but is having us over for dinner tomorrow."

"Eva?" Jason asks as he pulls his leather belt from his shorts' belt loops. "Darling, you're so sweet. But *so* naïve." He bends and drops off his shorts, then grabs his pajama bottoms from a dresser drawer. While on crutches still, he finagles one leg, then his stump, into his pajama shorts. "Your sister will defend her husband to the very end."

When Jason walks back to the bed, Maris is still processing this new competition, The List. He moves his squirt gun onto the nightstand so that he can sit on his bedside chair. In a moment, he unhooks his forearm crutches and leans them alongside his prosthetic leg.

Maris, meanwhile, is pressing the lid onto the cracker tin before setting the jumbo can on the floor. He hears her voice as she slides it away. "So I can't trust the girls?" she asks. "Not even Elsa?"

"*Especially* not Elsa!" With that, he shuts off the light, stands on his right leg and climbs into bed. In the darkness, he leans close to Maris, runs his hand through her hair, then gives her a kiss. His hand cradles her face as she lengthens the kiss. Finally, he pulls away and whispers into her ear. "Trust nobody."

twenty-two

IT'S GOING TO BE ONE of those summers, Jason can just tell, when the heat won't let up. Every day is the same: glaring sunlight beating down on the sand, on dried-out lawns, on every plank of the boardwalk. Bees lazily hover; birdsong wanes. By late morning, the air is always oppressive. Relief can only be found by getting yourself into the sea for a dip, a swim, a wade.

So the next day, he's not surprised to see a few familiar faces on the beach. He'd spent most of this Wednesday morning in the air-conditioned TV studio reviewing cottage photographs and videos with his producer, Trent. Problem is, after sitting for hours bent over computer screens, Jason's leg aches right at the stump. So on the way home, he stops on the boardwalk safe zone for a walk. It's best for him to keep his leg moving, to keep the muscles limber. After lunch, he'll review more video applications in his barn.

But while on the boardwalk, suddenly Jason's day takes a twist. This moment is the precise reason his squirt gun is tucked into his cargo shorts pocket. He lifts his sunglasses to the top of his head and spots his target crossing the beach.

Nick can't be missed. He's dressed in full security uniform from head to toe: security cap, khaki short-sleeved shirt with black epaulets, black shorts, black sneakers. As he patrols the beach, he waves to a few vacationers. He's also enforcing his boss' motto: *The rules are the rules.* It's obvious by the way Nick points to a sign indicating that no food is allowed on the beach. A reluctant couple picks up their cooler and carries it away, most likely straight back to their cottage.

But still, something about Nick is off. He's too intent while walking across the sand. His leisurely, chatty ambling is missing. Instead, Nick's tense. His hand shields his eyes from the sun as he hurries along and watches someone in the distance. So Jason follows his steadfast gaze.

It's Vinny.

Which means Vinny must be Nick's target.

"Score," Jason whispers when Nick fusses with some highfalutin water pistol discreetly tucked into his belt. Seeing it brings Jason to his feet, keeping his own squirt gun pressed to his side as he moves down the boardwalk. Out on the sand, the beach is crowded with colorful umbrellas and large inflated rafts and vinyl swim rings, not to mention the sand pails and plastic toy boats scattered around blankets. So from the boardwalk safe zone, he keeps losing track of Nick maneuvering all that beach gear.

While all this spying is happening, Jason also pulls his cell phone from his pocket. He tips it in the sunlight, thankful to see a few bars of service—enough to text Maris. *Get the golf cart and wait for me on Champion Road. Behind the dunes, near the stairs. I need a quick getaway.*

Once more, before leaving the blessed safety of the boardwalk, Jason scopes out the situation. First he drops his sunglasses back on, then spots Nick chatting all friendly-like with Paige while Vinny sits in his sand chair. But it's a ruse. Paige and their two kids appear to be heading to the rocks, maybe for some crabbing. They each hold sand pails stuffed with string and small nets. Nick plays it up and pats one of the kids on the head while he still chats with Paige.

Which gives Jason time to hurry onto the sand and sneak around the vacationing families. He has to keep Nick in his sights, while not risk being seen himself.

As Nick keeps glancing over his shoulder at his target, Vinny gets wary. He scans the beach—prompting Jason to duck behind a large, striped umbrella—then stands and adjusts his sand chair. So Jason hurries closer, almost walking into a father and daughter building a sandcastle. After passing them, Jason trips on an inflated tube and nearly falls until his hand hits the sand and rights his balance.

And suddenly everything is a blur.

Because when Nick waves off Paige and turns to Vinny, he's also pulling that water weapon from his belt. Vinny wastes no time. Hell, he wasn't captain of his high school swim team for nothing. He takes a running leap into the water just as Nick raises his plastic pistol and takes aim.

It's now or never, with the way Nick is preoccupied with his target: Vincenzo.

Jason closes the distance. His eyes stay locked on Nick as Nick unleashes a continuous stream of water at Vinny—who is swimming safely beneath the water, evading Nick's ammo.

So it takes Nick by surprise when the back of his own head gets doused. As does his uniform shirt. Confused, he twists around and grapples with his sopping shirt, then looks up to see Jason standing mere feet away, still squirting.

"Ah, shit." Nick says, dropping his plastic pistol. "You got me."

"Shh." Jason holds a finger to his mouth.

Meanwhile, his brother-in-law is madly swimming *not* to the swim raft, but beyond it—to the big rock jutting out of the deep water! To get there, he manages to dive beneath the buoyed rope designating the swimming area. Vinny's every stroke is urgent, as though his life depends on it, with nary a glance back.

So he missed the entire shootout.

"You're eliminated, Nicholas," Jason says while tucking his squirt gun into his pocket. "And it looks like Vinny's mine now. But he's never going to know that because he never saw *who* took you down." Jason unclips his walkie-talkie from his belt and hands it to Nick. "Don't let on that it was me, and I may be able to finagle you more work on my show."

"You blackmailing me, Barlow?"

Jason steps closer, his fingers grazing the scar on his whiskered jaw. "Just making you an offer you can't refuse."

When Nick hesitates, Jason gives the two-way radio a shake. So Nick takes it, presses the button and holds the unit to his mouth.

"Hurry up," Jason insists while lifting his sunglasses to the top of his head and checking on Vinny, still swimming.

"Nick reporting in with a heavy heart as I announce that I'm now … eliminated." He checks his watch. "Time? 11:50 AM. Waterfront."

Before he can say more, Jason snags the walkie-talkie and half runs across the beach. He needs to get out of Vinny's view before his brother-in-law puts together what just went down. It's best if Vincenzo doesn't know that it was Jason who took out Nick. Anonymity is its own weapon, leaving targets unsuspecting.

Sweating now beneath the relentless July sun, Jason quickly winds around families and beach gear and kicked-off flip-flops and porta-cribs set beneath shade canopies. He climbs the granite steps toward the dunes, where he spots Maris driving the getaway golf cart. She barely screeches to a stop before he hops in, and off they go—leaving a cloud of sandy dust in their tracks.

~

Now that his pickup's air conditioning has crapped out, Kyle's not sure how long he can hold on to this jalopy. Especially with the sweltering New England summer they're having. The heat feels like a physical assault; every day, there's no escaping it. Not on the beach, not in the evening, not in the shade.

So with both his truck windows rolled down, a stifling breeze reaches his face as he turns into Maritime Market's parking lot. It's been a long day behind the diner's hot stoves, but the heat's even worse here. Waves of it rise like a mirage off the black pavement. Even the *thought* of walking across the parking lot has him sweating, so he parks as close to the door as he can. At least it'll be cool inside the store.

Parked, he starts cranking up the windows, but stops. "*Nothing to steal in this rusted piece of tin, anyway.*" Instead, he checks his cell phone for Lauren's text message to see how many yogurts she needs him to buy.

When he eventually gets out of his truck, there's no variation in the temperature. The heat is just solid, like he's beneath a blanket of it. But a shopper catches his eye before he shuts the truck door. It's Matt, following behind Eva wheeling an empty cart toward the store.

"*Yes!*" Kyle whispers while swinging back into his truck. "Opportunity knocks." He quickly calls Lauren and talks in a low voice. "My target just came into sight."

"Matt?" Lauren asks.

"Should be an easy nab. He's with Eva." Kyle squints through the perspiration dripping off his forehead. "I'm in Maritime's parking lot, so I guess Eva's back from Martha's Vineyard. She and Matt must be loading up their fridge for tonight's dinner." He leans out the window when they enter the store and disappear from view. "I'll be home in a while to watch the kids while you're at their place."

"You're seriously not coming with me?"

"Are you kidding? And risk being assaulted with some random squirt gun aimed at me from behind the shrubs? Or from the marsh grasses there? No way. And I'm beat from being on my feet all day. So what do the kids want for dinner? I'll pick something up here."

After adding to his grocery list, Kyle starts the truck and cruises around the parking lot to find a better space for his ambush. He decides on a space diagonally across from Matt's vehicle and pulls in between two SUVs, which conceal his pickup. Three squirt guns are on the passenger seat.

But this is a dire situation where only one will do the trick: the bazooka-blower. He picks it up and positions himself with the water-gun's barrel resting on his now half-open window. It's critical that Kyle remain hidden, though. So he tugs his *Gone Fishing* cap low on his head. Next, he stretches across the dusty dashboard, grabs his sunglasses and gets those on, too.

All that's left to do is wait.

It doesn't take long.

The Gallaghers' flashing car lights get Kyle's attention. There! Eva is aiming her remote at the vehicle to unlock the doors. She and Matt move behind their SUV as she hands Matt bags to load into the cargo area.

There's no telling how long they'll be in clear view, so Kyle doesn't waste any time. He pulls the trigger on his super-duper-bazooka-soaker and silently sends a powerful stream of water straight across the pavement.

And … bull's-eye! Matt's back is drenched.

"What the—" Matt gripes as his arm reaches around to his soaking shirt.

When he and Eva both spin around, Kyle yells out, "Got ya, dude!"

"Kyle?" Eva looks from him to Matt, then brushes the excess water off her husband's shirt.

"Oh, shit," Matt says while glancing over his shoulder. "Damn, he got me."

Which is when Kyle sends one more squirt his way, direct to his chest, for good measure.

"Come on," Kyle calls. He hooks a finger from where he still sits in his truck. "Get over here. And no funny business, you two," he says as he flaunts his water weapon.

Though Eva waves him off and continues unloading her grocery cart, Matt knows he's now eliminated. His sinking realization is obvious when Matt unclips his walkie-talkie from his belt and crosses the pavement.

Ah, defeat is sweet when it's someone else going down. Kyle gets out of his truck, laughing. But not laughing enough to prevent him from giving an order. He adjusts his cap while squinting at Matt. "Announce it, Gallagher," Kyle says.

Matt raises the walkie-talkie to his mouth. "Matt here, reporting my untimely elimination outside Maritime Market. Incident occurred while unloading groceries. Cause of elimination? Bazooka shot, straight to the back."

Kyle steps closer and reaches out his arm to show Matt the time.

"Time of demise?" Matt continues. "3:57 PM. My last advice?" He glances over at Kyle's pickup truck. "You are safe nowhere."

"Who do I inherit?" Kyle asks him as he heads toward the store. "Who's your target?"

"The judge, man." Matt lifts a loaded bag from his wife's arms. "Cliff Raines," he calls over the bag.

twenty-three

IF THERE'S ONE PERSON MARIS never tires of seeing, it's her sister—Eva.

Watching her now from a distance, Maris tears up. It surprises her how that happens. But the tears, she knows, are tears of loving relief. Because for thirty *years*, she and Eva believed they were merely beach friends … only to find out three decades later that they were actually sisters.

How close they came to never knowing that truth.

Standing on the deck, her sister wears a blue-and-white striped top over cuffed denim shorts. Her layered auburn hair is freshly streaked blonde in the latest edgy style she favors. As usual, Eva's setting out dishes and silverware, ready to tend to Maris and the gang.

Oh, doesn't Maris know it as she rounds the corner of Eva's beach home to the backyard. Eva is definitely the nurturer of them all. And apparently is always on the lookout for her sister, too.

"Maris!" Eva calls as she runs to meet her in the yard. "It's *so* good to see you," she says while hugging Maris.

"You too, sis. How was Martha's Vineyard?"

"Amazing." Eva takes her hand and they turn toward the deck. Weathered-and-distressed fishing buoys hang from the deck rails in the misty evening. White twinkling lights are strung around the spokes of the large patio umbrella, casting a soft glow beneath it. "Theresa and Ned are all settled in at their new condo. And it was great to have a girls' getaway with Tay there."

"Where is my favorite niece?" Maris asks.

"At Alison's. You know how that goes. She has to catch up on all the Stony Point gossip," Eva says while walking up the steps to the deck. "You have to come with me to the Vineyard next time. For a research trip! Maybe you can set a novel there."

Maris leans on the deck railing and looks out at the lagoon. Secretly, she knows. All the setting and sights and stories she'll ever need are right here at Stony Point. In the early evening light, the marsh grasses are unmoving beside inlets of seawater gently flowing past.

Without answering, she reaches over and simply squeezes Eva's hand.

Until a pesky mosquito lands on her arm. Maris swats at it.

"Oh, the mosquitoes are terrible lately!" Eva exclaims. "But those citronella candles help." She walks to the table and gets two candles, each set in a silver pail. Those she puts on the deck railing, away from the food. "Hey," Eva says over her shoulder while lighting the wicks. "Where's Jason? Working?"

"No. You're not going to believe this." Maris walks over and begins folding napkins on the patio table. "He's missing out on your delicious meal because he won't put himself at risk with that elimination game. So he's staying home. Out of sight, and safe."

"What? Now that's ridiculous. And anyway, I planned this dinner *before* their latest godfather competition."

"Doesn't matter, Eva. Jason said to tell you that, unfortunately, your dinner will actually be with the departed. The only men who'll show up are the ones who are off The List. Matt and Nick."

"Are you serious?"

Maris nods as Nick rounds the corner and approaches the deck. He wears standard summer fare this hot July evening: camouflage shorts, a tee and flip-flops. "The competing's gotten that fierce," Maris lets Eva know. "Any guys still in the game won't risk it."

"If they showed up here," Nick explains when he joins them on the deck, "it would be too easy a pluck-off."

Eva looks past them both. "Wrong, guys! Because here come Paige *and* Vinny—who's still in the game."

This Maris has to see to believe, so she whips around and there's Paige beside, yup, her tall and lanky husband. "Vinny?" Maris steps closer.

Nick is shaking his head as he high-fives Vinny. "But you're not safe here, guy. You crazy? Someone can do you in."

"Oh, Maris. Nick." Paige looks up at her husband and shrugs. "Vinny will dive into the marsh before he misses a free pizza dinner. He *is* a swimming coach, after all."

At that moment, Elsa, Lauren and Matt walk out through the kitchen slider and join them on the deck.

"Kyle and Cliff won't come either," Elsa announces as she sets a plate heaped with crispy orange potato slices on the table. "Sweet-potato chips," she whispers to the inquisitive faces directed at her delicious-looking concoction.

Lauren finishes up sending a text message, then tucks her

cell phone into her fringed tote, saying, "They're both at home, looking over their shoulders and plotting their next moves."

"Sheesh," Eva says as she starts setting out plates from a stack on the table. "This competition's getting out of hand. I'm not sure it's setting the right tone."

"I beg to differ." When everyone stops and silently looks at Elsa, she continues. "You have to understand that it's all about defending *famiglia*. Because let's face it. Though none of the guys are related to Sal, not by blood, they were his friends. His *good* friends, a different kind of family." She raises a wise eyebrow to them all. "And to Sal, as you know, family nonetheless. One I believe *The Godfather's* Don Corleone might deem worthy of honor."

"Absolutely. Friends, family," Maris says as she takes a seat at the patio table and looks at Elsa, at Paige and Vinny, at Lauren. "The Don would be right." Maris lifts Elsa's plate of sweet-potato chips and passes it around. "You're all nothing less than family to me. And I mean that with all my heart."

A chorus of *Amen, sister* and *Ditto here* and *Isn't that the truth?* is murmured in unison as everyone digs into Eva's fresh garden salad and Elsa's chips and dip. The talk meanders then, from Maris' novel-writing to possible names for Jason's TV show. Tiki torches illuminate the evening; forks clink on dishes; Verdicchio pours freely.

"How's moving-in coming along?" Eva asks Lauren.

"Fine." Lauren sips her wine while squinting across the table at Eva. "It's fine, but I was wondering … Do you guys ever get a funny smell in your houses here, near the sea? I know our house is *like* a cottage and still needs work to bring it up to date, but sometimes I notice a stale smell. A little musty, maybe."

Nick lifts an overloaded handful of the crispy sweet-potato chips, along with a dollop of sour-cream dip, then holds up his hand as he chews. "Are you sure it's not Kyle?" he asks around the food. "Sneaking cigarettes again? He and Barlow made a pact and quit, but who knows?"

"No, Nick." Lauren tucks a wayward strand of hair into her side braid. "No, it's not that. It's something in the house."

Elsa refills a few of their wineglasses. "Be sure to really clean things up, Lauren," she says while pouring. "When I moved here, I cleaned for weeks. Bleached everything. Had my cleaning gloves on and scrubbed like the dickens. People in this beach area seem to leave their places in such shambles, and it's up to the new owners to inject positivity and cleanliness."

"Air out the rooms, too," Maris suggests.

"I try," Lauren tells them. "But some of the windows are stuck. Those are on Kyle's honey-do list to fix. You know, *Honey, do this; Honey, do that.*"

"Yoo-hoo!" a voice calls out then from the shadows.

They all turn to see Celia pushing Aria in her stroller across the lawn. The women leave the table and are instantly beside her, touching the baby and talking softly.

"I'm really glad you're all here," Celia says with a twinkle in her eye. "Because I need you to mark your calendars for Aria's christening! It's on Sunday, July twenty-fourth. At St. Bernard's Church."

"Oh! That's where Jason and I were married!" Maris says as she gives Celia a light hug.

"I know. Your wedding, *and* I went to Neil's memorial mass there," Celia answers, right when Lauren lifts Aria from the stroller. "Sal's funeral was there, too," Celia adds with a certain sadness, "and since he's Aria's father … Well, a lot of our history is already tied to the place. *And* it's such a beautiful church, so close to the sea. Of course, you're *all* invited."

"It'll be really special, Cee," Maris whispers. "Sal would've loved it, with the way the sea air drifts in through those stained glass windows."

Celia squeezes Maris' hand, then turns toward the marsh. And Maris can't help but think that she's picturing Sal sitting in his rowboat there, the way he used to, taking Celia for evening rides in the lagoon.

"Come on," Lauren quietly says. She's holding the baby to her shoulder and very lightly bouncing her. "Let's bring Aria to the dock to look at the water there."

"You go," Maris tells Celia and Elsa. "I'll help Eva set out the rest of the food."

By the time a large pizza is arranged on a platter, and a dish of barbecued chicken wings is lightly sea-salted, they're all gathered again. Celia also brought a baby seat for Aria, one with dangling rattles and soft puppies hanging over it. The baby's little fisted hands pump the air as she watches them. Meanwhile, everyone else reaches for the deluxe pizza and sides.

"So I was with Matt when he was taken down," Eva says while lifting a heavy pizza slice and setting it on Matt's dish. "It was actually pretty shocking when it happened. Just knowing you're in someone's sights, unaware, was an eerie feeling."

"How'd *you* get eliminated?" Matt asks Nick. "And get crossed off The List."

Nick folds a slice of pizza in two and holds it aloft. "It happened when I was in the middle of trying to nail *Vinny*. Wasn't watching my back, but my eliminator was."

"Which was who?" Vinny pries.

Nick shakes his head, then bites into the loaded pizza slice. "Oh, no," he says while wiping his chin. "That's classified information. But, hell, he got me good, man. Right on the beach, with witnesses and all."

"And I figured it would be safe here tonight," Vinny says as he scoops up a handful of sweet-potato chips, "because my potential eliminators—Kyle, Jason and Cliff—are wusses living in fear and paranoia." As he pops a chip or two in his mouth, he adds, "My goombah, Salvatore, believed you have to *live* life—and I am! If those other guys show up here, like I said, I'll just dive into the marsh."

"I don't know." Matt's voice is rather ominous. "They're cunning, those three. You're playing with fire, Vincenzo."

"Eh." Vinny stuffs half a slice of pizza in his mouth and, casual as can be, gives Matt the Italian salute—one hand gripping the biceps of the other arm, which he's raising into a vertical position.

Elsa shakes her head, whispering, "*Gesù, Santa Maria! Il gesto dell'ombrello.*"

"What's that?" Maris asks, leaning close across the table.

"Ah, yes. The gesture of the umbrella." Elsa gives a wink to the women at the table. "The Italian way of not-so-subtly saying … *Up yours!*"

~

"I knew it," Jason whispers from where he stands beside Eva and Matt's rambling Dutch colonial. He wore dark shorts and an old black tee to blend in with the shadows. An overgrown lilac bush also helps keep him hidden from view. The sun will set soon, and it's the dusky hour. But in the light of the flickering tiki torches, he can clearly see Eva's patio table. "*Somebody* would cave for that food." He turns, then, and heads to the front of the house. "Who else, but Vincenzo?" he says to himself.

As he goes to the front door, Jason pulls out the extra key he snagged from Maris' key ring. Maris and her sister both have keys to each other's homes; they're in and out of them so often. After unlocking the Gallagher front door, he pauses to get his bearings. Only a few lights are on, so the rooms are dim. Glancing around, he hurries straight up the stairs, taking two steps at a time. When the kitchen slider scrapes open and someone calls out something about salad dressing, Jason ducks into an upstairs bedroom and presses his back against the wall.

Seriously? Standing there with his heart pounding, the moment feels like some night straight out of his teens when the gang pulled their share of beach stunts. Like when they stole old Commissioner Lipkin's boat one Fourth of July and got lit out on the Sound. In his late thirties now, Jason thinks his shenanigan days should be behind him.

But, no. They're not. Not when it comes to being godfather to Sal's daughter.

So while standing there motionless, Jason squints into the darkness. No lights are on here, upstairs. But it doesn't matter; he knows every detail of this upper level since designing Matt's sports shrine in the attic.

Which is where he's headed now. He takes the next set of stairs to the attic and stops again. Now he pulls out a pocket flashlight and uses only that narrow beam to see, so that he doesn't trip on anything. From where he stands, he glimpses the attic window illuminated from the deck-dinner below.

Those dancing tiki-torch flames, and the twinkly lights strung around the deck … all cast a glow to the windowpane.

Now he just has to silently get there. He walks slowly across the new hardwood floor, passing the sofa and recliners; the mounted brass sculpture of a bull's head that Sal gave Matt; the big-screen TV where they watched *The Godfather*, and adopted the movie's dialect and attitude in a rowdy night of beer-drinking and, okay, food-gorging.

Finally, he stops at the attic window and looks down at the gathering outside. Everyone's there except for Cliff and Kyle—wise men, indeed. They obviously learned a lesson or two from the Corleone clan that night.

More so than Vinny did.

Jason slowly lifts the window screen, but instantly stops when it squeaks. Stops and steps back into shadow. "Damn it," he mutters.

"What was that?" Nick asks from below. "A bird?"

"We get lots of wildlife on the marsh," Eva assures him. "Could have been a kingfisher settling down for the night. They have a squeaky whistle like that."

"I've always loved it right here," Lauren says, motioning her fork to the marsh grasses. "It would be a perfect place to set up my easel, or come up with scenes for my painted driftwood pieces."

"Oh, definitely!" Eva's voice carries. "Anytime you want. You just come on by."

Jason inches closer to the open window again. Down below, he hears Eva talking about Martha's Vineyard, and how she and Taylor went horseback riding right on the beach.

"Okay," Jason whispers then. "Easy does it this time," he says while gently lifting the screen. "Almost there."

Once the screen is fully lifted, he leans against the wall beside the window, lifts the barrel of his super-soaking weapon and gets Vinny directly in his sights. Then, while holding his breath so as not to move a single muscle, he stands fully in the window and pulls the trigger.

"What the hell?" Vinny asks. His hand quickly goes to the back of his head.

"Uh-oh." Celia leans over and lifts Aria's swear jar out of her stroller. "One dollar, please."

Vinny pulls out his wallet and drops a couple of singles in the jar, all while twisting around and looking at the sky. "Is it raining?"

Nick turns and looks back, too. "Raining on your dinner parade," he says while pointing upward. "You're a goner, Vincenzo."

Jason, still standing in the window, gives a piercing look with a wave, then hurries downstairs and makes his way through the house and out to the deck. All he hears are the voices saying his name, asking how he got upstairs, wondering if anyone knew about this.

But he ignores it all. Because it doesn't matter, none of it. What matters is getting to that darn twinkling patio table covered with a spread of divine food that he sadly missed. Once there, he first tugs Aria's little foot and says, "This one was for you, cupcake."

Then? Then his expression drops as he silently hands Vinny his walkie-talkie.

"Say it." Jason nods at his brother-in-law.

Vinny snatches the radio from him. "Vinny here," he announces into it. "It's been a good run, but it's all over now. Time of list elimination?" He grabs Jason's left arm and squints at his watch. "7:48 PM at the Gallagher cottage, overlooking the marsh. A lovely evening, really, for my sad demise." He pauses with a wistful breath. "Cause of elimination? Liquid trauma to the head. Final advice? Follow your gut, not your stomach. Over and out."

"Jason!" Maris says. "You can stay now. Come on." She pats the empty chair beside her.

"No, sweetheart," he says, then kisses the top of her head. "It's not safe here."

"Well, at *least* stop by our rented cottage," his sister, Paige, calls to him. "You can say hi to Mom and the kids, who you haven't seen in how long?"

Jason shakes his head. "No can do, Paige." He snags a few sweet-potato chips before turning to Vinny. "Vincenzo, who was your target?" he asks while scooping the chips through the sour-cream dip.

Vinny sets his gaze on Lauren for an apologetic second, until he spots Jason inching away.

"Your best man," Vinny tells him. "Kyle Bradford."

Jason hesitates before stepping closer once more to snatch a large slice of pizza. Standing there, he bites into it while considering Vinny. But only for a second, until he turns and takes the pizza with him as he slinks back into the shadows of Stony Point—where there's no longer any safe place to be.

twenty-four

THOUGH CELIA WAS HOPING FOR a cooler day to take Aria's first formal beach portrait, it isn't to be. The heat that has settled on Stony Point holds steady, making one day indistinguishable from the next. It's all bright sunshine, blue skies, and no breeze lifting off the water.

So Friday morning, she and Elsa set Aria's things in the shade beneath a large umbrella on the sandy beach. There's her baby carrier and blanket. And a few rattles and toys to get Aria's attention as the photographer prepares to snap pictures. He gets down on his knee and adjusts his camera, all while Celia settles Aria in a pretty wicker basket Elsa brought along. It's set on the sand, with a soft beach towel folded into it. Now Celia fusses first with the towel edge spilling over the basket top, then with the dark curls of Aria's hair. "Good?" she asks the photographer as she steps back.

He nods and lifts the camera to his face, then shifts to a different angle and begins snapping pictures.

"Smile, Aria!" Elsa crouches nearby and waves a plush stuffed seagull. The baby wears Maris' chambray onesie and has a white lacy sunhat on her head. "Come on, love!" Elsa encourages as she touches the soft fluffy gull to Aria's skin.

Which does the trick. With sand and sea spread behind her, a smile fills the baby's face as she kicks her little bare legs and pumps her arms while nestled in the basket. She coos, too, and even her brown eyes sparkle.

All the while, Celia stands off to the side, watching. When a motion catches her eye, she looks over to the inn's turret. Maris waves down at her from the window in her writing nook, so Celia waves back and blows her a kiss.

And she knows, then. Turning back to the expanse of Long Island Sound, Celia knows. This summer has held some of the sweetest and slowest days of her life. Though the inn's extensive renovation is done, Celia's so glad that Elsa insisted they take some private, peaceful time before opening for business.

Because, truth be told? Celia's grief still comes. That emotion has been like a wave that recedes, but always returns again.

Like right now, while watching her baby girl on the beach. Standing there with her arms crossed in front of her, Celia feels that painful stab of sadness, just wishing, *wishing* Sal could see his beautiful daughter nestled in a basket on the beach.

As though she senses Celia's longing, Elsa looks over at that precise moment. Then, after a few words with the photographer, Elsa picks up the baby and brings her to Celia. They stand close, and quiet. Celia fusses with Aria's sunbonnet before Elsa places the baby in her arms, then squeezes Celia's hand.

"I asked the photographer to take something very special." Elsa's voice is almost a murmur. "A seaside mother-daughter portrait."

So wearing her fedora and flowing sundress while barefoot in the sand, Celia carries Aria to the lapping waves of the Sound. She walks right in and wades ankle-deep. Though no breeze blows, gentle waves splash at the hem of Celia's dress as she cradles her Aria in the sea.

And she hears Elsa saying one word. It's the same word she imagines Sal would tell Celia, if he were watching her. His voice would be low, his look unwavering. *Sorridi.* Smile.

For Sal, Celia tries. When the photographer wades right in and snaps candids, Celia slowly spins with Aria embraced to her chest. As she twirls, it happens—yes, like a wave pulling out to sea. Her grief recedes and a smile returns. The beautiful part of it all, she can feel it, is that her smile is wide, though her heart bittersweet.

And sunlight sparkles on the water all around them, ocean stars, in this rare, magical moment. A bit of beach bliss, indeed.

~

"Thank you," Jason says while walking along the tideline on Sea Spray Beach.

As he says it, he glances at Ted Sullivan beside him. In his seventies, Ted's silver hair looks even lighter beneath the bright sunlight, and the deep creases lining his face rise with his smile. But he shakes his head, too, as though about to counter Jason.

"No, seriously," Jason persists as he stops walking. "Those are two words I never thought I'd be saying to you, Ted."

"You don't ever need to thank me," Ted tells him. He scoops up a stone and skims it out on the water.

Jason watches. Three skips. "Oh, yes I do," he insists.

"Because so much started with you. Let's face it, my renovation of your cottage actually got you to nominate me for that architect award. Which I *did* win, leading to this television show where I essentially get to restore tired-old beach homes to their deserved glory." Jason holds up his hand when Ted starts to interrupt. "Let me finish, Ted. Because you should know that ultimately, what started with you asking me to renovate your cottage did what nothing else could do."

"What's that?"

"It brought my brother back to me."

"Neil?"

Jason nods. "I told you how I felt like I lost him again when Sal died. I didn't hear my brother's voice anymore. His vague whispers in the breeze. Or his words in the breaking waves when I walked the beach. You know, whether they were real or not … or just memories of things he used to tell me … who knows. But, nothing. Then, renovating Elsa's inn for the show, so many times I felt Neil *right there*, swinging a hammer, too. During the whole project, I sensed his presence. And I'm really proud that now so many people will get to know Neil's story, and see his vision, through the episodes. What a way to honor my brother's legacy, with that show." Jason picks up a stone, joggles it, then skims it out over the sea. With no wind, the usually rough surf here at Sea Spray is calmer today. Four skips. "Which is why I'm here now, Ted." He lifts his sunglasses to the top of his head and squints over at Ted beside him. "I wanted to tell you this in person. I got the green light for a whole season."

"No kidding. Terrific!"

"So I have something for you and your wife." Jason reaches into his cargo shorts pocket and hands Ted an envelope. "A gift certificate to have a nice dinner out, on me. Because without you, Ted, none of this would've happened."

Ted takes the envelope, then gives Jason a warm hug, slapping his back while telling him, "Congratulations!" When he pulls back, they start walking the beach again. "That's *really* good news, and well deserved. So what's next?"

Jason hooks two fingers in his mouth and gives a sharp whistle. His German shepherd, who had just loped into the water, turns back. "Maddy!" he calls, so the dog gives a shake and runs down the beach toward him. "What's next?" Jason repeats. "That's the tricky part."

"Something I can help you with?"

"No, I'm on my own with this one. Because not only does the show need an official name, it also needs a bona fide, real-deal cottage renovation to get underway. And I'm not seeing one in the submissions. You know, nothing I feel connected to."

"Can you pick one that *wasn't* submitted? Maybe use a client of your own?" Ted asks.

"I did just sign on a new job," Jason tells him while he snaps on Maddy's leather leash. "But it's too small. A tiny little beach box." They start walking again, this time with the dog beside him—though she does manage to reach the water and keep her paws wet. "The bungalow is about six hundred square feet. Smallest I've ever renovated. So it won't work for the show. But it's an easy project to handle—raise the roof, add a loft and windows—all while I'm on the hunt for a meatier reno."

"And under deadline, I assume?"

"Absolutely. I've got two weeks to come up with the best cottage ever."

"No pressure."

Jason laughs. "Shit, you got it."

"Well, come on," Ted says as he hitches his head in the direction of his beach home. "Have a sandwich at the cottage. We'll hash out some ideas."

"Wish I could, Ted. But I've really got to go. I'm stopping down the street at your neighbor's cottage, which is just finishing up. Vintage hurricane shutters were installed, and I'm project manager on the job, so need to check on it." He gives Maddy's leash a tug and veers up the beach toward the street. "I'll catch you next time, definitely."

"And I'll hold you to it," Ted says. He shakes Jason's hand. "Congratulations again. Always good to see you, Jason. I'm really happy things are going well for you and your wife."

Jason is, too. Or he's getting there, anyway. He's feeling happy about Maris working on his brother's novel. That's something Jason never saw coming either, but he loves skimming Neil's words, and hearing Maris read the book aloud. Those late-night sessions with Maris propped in bed beneath lamplight, her soft voice delivering Neil's passages, are just about perfect. Jason lies beside her—his arm crooked beneath his head, his eyes closed—and simply listens to the rhythm of the story, of Neil, while the warm sea air drops in through the open window.

And the cottage-renovation show? Jason couldn't ask for a better direction to take his architectural career. So yes, he has much to be happy about.

But still, he knows. Too many hard knocks have come his way during times when he let his guard down. When he sat back and relished some small happiness that settled on his life. Which is why he knows better than to trust happiness. Because doesn't he also know that on any day, at any minute, life can go and spin out from under you. Just like it did ten years ago when he and Neil were happy, comfortable in the business they were building. And then Neil's Harley spun out from beneath them. At the hands of Ted Sullivan, no less—an innocent man who had a heart attack behind the wheel of his car, crashing into their lives in so many ways.

Happiness has come only in fleeting moments since then.

Now caution reigns in its place. So once he's home in his barn studio, diligently reviewing cottage submissions, he takes a break to text Maris in her writing nook at Elsa's. She must be working at the turret window, the sea out in the distance. *Hope you're having a good writing day*, he messages her. *Love you.*

It's his way of being cautious—saying vigilant words, being sure his loved ones are okay. It's all that matters to him.

When he gets back to his video submissions, though, when he looks at everything from cabins to huts, from tidewaters to Nantuckets, that wariness is still there. A damn niggling that, yes, is keeping his elusive happiness at arm's length.

So he rolls back his big desk chair and drags a hand across his whiskered jaw—his thumb finding the faded scar there—before walking to the double slider. It's open wide, letting in the distant sound of surf on the bluff. Letting in birdsong and a neighbor's slamming screen door.

Letting in any noise upon which his brother's voice might hitch a ride.

"Talk to me, guy," Jason says. "I can't seem to nail down the next project." The tall maple throws shade on the backyard, and Maddy sits in her kiddie pool, which Jason had filled with water earlier. The dog's muzzle rests on the pool edge, and she snaps at an occasional bee or fly that buzzes past. The day, in this heat, is eerily quiet. Just a couple of birds chatter in the tree branches above the dog pool.

You'll know, Jason hears right as a neighbor starts up a lawn mower. So Jason steps outside onto the deck and leans on the railing. In a moment, he takes a deep breath of the salty air and closes his eyes.

Every cottage tells a story, Jay.

When the dog stands and slowly turns in the pool, Jason looks over at her. Maddy's paws slosh through the water, making splashing sounds as she settles back down.

The right one will speak to you.

Are his brother's words a memory from when they'd hash out business plans years ago? Jason reaches up and drags his father's dog tags along the chain on his neck.

The thing is, it doesn't really matter how the words come. All that matters is that they do, freeing him to salute the sky before turning back to his studio to review the rest of the submissions on his desk.

twenty-five

AFTER HE GETS HOME FROM the diner Friday evening, Kyle lifts a ceramic pitcher from a carton. He hands it to Lauren, who places it in their dining room hutch. Two shelves are covered with stacks of their china plates, cups and saucers. On the top shelf, she's arranged larger serving platters and bowls. Slowly, they are getting all their things unpacked in their new year-round beach home. Dishes, linens, off-season clothes, tools and gadgets.

"How am I going to nab Cliff?" Kyle asks while handing her a silver-rimmed coffee cup. "He doesn't think anyone knows that he *lives* in the back of that trailer he also works in. So he's *always* in a safe zone."

Lauren takes a large plate from him. She runs her finger around the edge. "You'll have to get him when he goes out."

"Right. Except whenever he goes out, he's always on the boardwalk—another safe zone."

Lauren is quiet, her back to Kyle. Finally she turns to him while holding another plate to her face. "Smell that?" She hands him the dish. "I just got a whiff."

Kyle brings the dish close and smells it. "It's musty. Like

the house has been closed up."

"Elsa says to give everything a good cleaning," Lauren says as she takes the plate back. "Maybe you can powerwash the roof and gutters. And clean the windows, too."

Kyle lifts the fabric of his tee and fans his chest. "Add it to my honey-do list, would you?"

When the kids start banging around in the living room, Kyle steps over two cartons and takes a look. Hailey is blowing bubbles in the house. "Hailey-copter. Outside with those." He hitches his thumb to Evan, who's swinging his plastic baseball bat at the bubbles. "You too, buddy. Out back."

"But Dad," Evan argues as he flops onto the sofa.

Kyle eyes him. "Either outside for a few minutes before it's dark, or take a bath and go to bed. Your choice."

"Fine." Evan stands and drags his bat toward the kitchen. "Will you throw the ball for me?"

"Not tonight, slugger. I'm helping your mom unpack things." Kyle heads to Lauren and her boxes. "And stay in the backyard, where I can keep an eye on you," he calls to his kids.

"Finally," Lauren is saying as she rummages in a carton. "I'm so sick of that instant coffee and have been looking *everywhere* for this." She unwraps crumpled paper from a coffee decanter. Her hand runs along a fine line in the glass. "Oh, shoot. It's cracked."

Kyle pokes around in the box. "Probably not enough packing peanuts. Must have broke in the move."

"And it's for my favorite coffeepot. Now I need a new one." Lauren sets it on the table, then brushes a damp wisp of hair off her perspiring face. "Can you go get one? The hardware store carries them."

"Now?"

She smiles. That's it. Just smiles.

"I know," Kyle says. "*Honey, do this.*"

Lauren plants a light kiss on his cheek and musses his hair, too.

"I'll be back in an hour," Kyle tells her. He pulls his keys from his pocket. "Need anything else?"

"No." Lauren returns to her hutch-fussing, restacking smaller dishes off to the side, but stops. "Wait! Why don't you take the kids?" she asks. "Because you *were* kind of crabby to them before."

"It's this damn godfather challenge, The List." Kyle glances out toward the street to be sure it's safe to go outside. "Has me tied up in knots, waiting to get shot."

"So this would be good! Who's going to shoot you with the kids in the car? And they'd like to go for a ride."

"No. Not this time."

"Why not?" Right as she spins around, Lauren catches him lifting a squirt gun off the table. "It's Cliff, isn't it?" she asks as Kyle walks to the front door. "You're going to take him down?"

"Going to try."

Lauren runs out to the front yard when the kids catch wind of his leaving. She takes Hailey's hand in hers.

"Can I come, Daddy?" Hailey calls out, tugging at Lauren's hold.

"Not tonight, princess," Kyle says over his shoulder. "But I'll bring back ice cream," he tells them before getting in his pickup truck and waving them all off.

Because, seriously? The pressure's suddenly on. Shit, if he still smoked, he'd light up right now. Instead, he sets his walkie-talkie and squirt gun on the front seat.

First order of business? Cruise the Stony Point roads in search of one wily fox always evading him—the judge.

"I'll never get him," Kyle mutters as he leans down and squints out at the cottages and bungalows. It's another warm evening, and some folks are just returning from the beach. Big inflated tubes are hooked around their arms, beach towels draped around their necks as their flip-flops scuff along the sandy street. "My days are numbered," he whispers with no sign of the commissioner.

Finally, heading out to the hardware store, he pulls up to the guard shack at the railroad trestle. Nick stands in the shack's doorway. His uniform hat is tipped back, a clipboard in hand.

"What's up, Nicholas?" Kyle asks through his open truck window.

"You still on the The List?" Nick air-quotes the words with one hand, the other holding that clipboard. "Because this isn't a safe zone."

Kyle checks the rearview mirror to the shadowy street behind him. "Yeah, I'm still in the game. What are you up to?"

"Waiting for the boss."

"Raines?"

"He brings me a new log sheet for incoming renters every Friday night. So I can log their cars when they arrive tomorrow."

"Cliff's on his way now?"

Nick checks his big silver watch. Kyle recognizes it as the one from Sal. "Should be here any minute," Nick says while squinting at the time. "Why?"

Kyle doesn't even answer. Suddenly every second is critical, so he pulls his truck to the curb, gets out and clips his walkie-talkie to his belt.

"Oh, no," Nick's saying as he backs into his guard shack. "I can't get caught in the crossfire. Cliff's my boss!"

Kyle waves his submachine water-gun at Nick like he means business. "Get out of there." He motions with his squirt gun again. "*Now.* And take my keys." As he says it, he tosses the key ring.

Nick snags it as the keys jangle midair. "No, man. I *won't* be a part of this."

"You already are. So leave." Kyle yanks his security guard friend out of the little gray-sided booth with its paned window and pretty blue shutters. Ironic that it looks like a quaint fairy-tale cabin, given what's about to go down in it. Kyle starts to work his way inside the cramped space. "Take my truck for a ride." He turns sideways to fit his six-foot-two frame through the doorway. "And don't you come back until you get Cliff's walkie-talkie announcement of his demise."

Once Nick drives Kyle's old pickup beneath the stone railroad trestle and straight out of Stony Point, Kyle settles in. He partially closes the door of the tiny guard shack, then sits on a stool inside. From his vantage point, he can barely glimpse out the window. Right beside the shack, there's a large painted sign listing all the street names in the beach community—Sea View and Hillcrest, Bayside and Champion—with arrows beside each pointing either left or right. Beyond that sign is the arched train trestle.

And right now, in this shadowy evening hour, all's remarkably quiet. There's just Kyle, perspiring in the very close confines of the guard shack. Which is kept particularly tidy. A few wooden shelves hold clipboards and papers, a telephone, a flashlight, basic supplies and such. Kyle angles his body so that when Cliff approaches, he won't notice him inside.

Finally, a car door slams. With just a peek out the window, Kyle can't miss Clifton Raines walking up with papers in his hand.

"Nick!" Cliff calls out while glancing at the paperwork. "Here you go. You've been waiting for these."

Still sitting on the stool, Kyle kicks open the door. "No, Judge. *I've* been waiting … for *this*." He sits with his bent arm on his knee, his water blaster pointed at its target. "It's *judgment* day," he declares while pulling the trigger. A steady stream of water hits Cliff in the head and chest.

"Damn it," Cliff says while jumping aside, but he's too late. And drenched. The surprise of the attack has him drop his papers, which he scoops right up and gives a shake. Droplets of water fly off them. "Damn it all to hell! I *just* printed these."

Kyle finagles himself out of the stuffy guard shack and holds out his walkie-talkie. "Do it."

"I never even saw you there." Cliff looks past him. "Didn't stand a doggone chance."

"Announce it." Kyle steps closer, arm still outstretched.

So Cliff does. He snatches the walkie-talkie. "Commissioner Raines here," he says into the unit, "slowly wilting from a shot to the heart. Time of elimination? 6:14 PM. Place? Outside the guard shack." He shakes his head, as though not believing his sad fate. "I've been eliminated from The List right at our own landmark stone trestle. My final advice?" He looks back at his security cruiser, parked beside the shack the same way it is every single Friday evening. "Vary your routine, people. Over and out."

"Who's your target?" Kyle asks. Not wanting to waste any time, he grabs back his walkie-talkie. "Spill it."

Cliff squints up at him. "Jason Barlow is your nemesis, now.

You two boys are in the final showdown."

Just then, Nick pulls under the train trestle in Kyle's truck. When he parks at the guard shack, Kyle yanks open the door, orders him out, jumps in and drives away—leaving Stony Point's defeated security team in his dust.

twenty-six

WHETHER HE LIKES IT OR not, Jason's in overdrive again. His schedule is backed up from here to kingdom come. How can it be Tuesday already? He worked all weekend, and hasn't had a day off in God knows how long.

Standing at his dresser mirror, he employs his shaving gauge. All that's necessary is to drag a hand along his face. If skin is visible beneath his whiskers, he's good for another day without picking up a razor. He leans close to the mirror, slightly turns his head and squints at his reflection.

"Good enough," he whispers before heading over to his bedside chair to put on his leg.

Except it's not there.

"Ah, shit," he says, remembering he left it downstairs late last night. Maris had found him sitting in his chair in the living room with only a dim light on and a tumbler of Scotch in his hand. After crouching beside him and asking if everything was okay, she gently removed his prosthetic limb, lightly stroked his leg and moved the ottoman close, so he could keep his stump elevated.

After he told her he'd be upstairs shortly, she left his

crutches by his side and went to bed. *Shortly*, for Jason, turned into one more shot of whiskey, just enough to unwire him and get him drowsy enough to go to bed. Which he did. But the prosthesis stayed downstairs.

Now, after dressing in cargo shorts and a plaid short-sleeve top, he does it.

Even though his wife has warned him plenty—not that he's ever listened. Warned him to take it easy coming down the stairs on his forearm crutches. The way Jason rushes, it gets Maddy nipping at the crutches as though they're a threat. Maris says it's just a matter of time before he falls.

Still, using his crutches, Jason flies down the stairs. And, that's right, nearly stumbles head over heels when that damn dog's nipping jaw breaks his momentum. Jason's two hands grabbing onto the railing barely stop the fall—and even then, only after he practically twists around backward while holding on.

Part of his rush stems from his cell phone; it's been dinging with emails and text messages since he buttoned his shirt. The last time he checked, it was Trent asking him to drop by the studio that afternoon. *Serious brainstorming for next project is in order*, Trent had reminded him.

Once making it safely to the bottom of the stairs, Jason sucks in a deep breath to slow his still-pounding heart. Then … the decisions begin.

First up? Leg on, or food in?

That's how busy he is. He's actually stopped thinking in complete sentences. And the first decision of the morning calls for a compromise. Grabbing his prosthesis and its gear, he drops it all in the kitchen.

But food-in wins.

He grabs a powdered doughnut from the box on the

counter, where he also puts his cell phone. Leaning on the counter while biting into the white, sugary pastry, he flicks through his cell phone messages. His powder-covered fingers aren't helping, so he wipes them on a paper towel before continuing. Answering some, deleting and saving others, all while downing a second doughnut.

Thankfully, Maris brewed a pot of coffee. Before pouring a cup, Jason sits at the table. He rolls his silicone liner and sock over his *moncone*—as Sal had kindly called his stump in Italian, trying to soften the reality of Jason's left leg ending below the knee. Just the thought of Sal sitting here in the kitchen those mornings last summer, and being deeply concerned with his injured leg, has Jason miss him again. What he wouldn't give to be bullshitting with the Italian on this busy day.

Instead, Jason's hands methodically flatten and align the liner and sock. Reaching for the prosthetic limb, then, he presses it onto the end of his leg.

But the fit is a little off today. He notices this when he stands and things feel snug. Which gets him to sit again and scrutinize his leg to be sure there's no swelling going on. Because if his leg bothers him, everything else will, too. Maybe he just has to get going, a tactic preventing random swelling—as using the leg muscles keeps all the fluids moving.

So when his phone dings again, he stands, pours one coffee for himself in his travel mug, and one for Maris, who must be in the shack cracking out another chapter.

"Hey, babe," Maris says with an easy smile. It still takes Jason by surprise when he steps into the shack … and this private world of Neil's. Because it clearly *is* Neil's. It can't be denied; everything—from the old hurricane lanterns to worn leather journals to the vintage typewriter—hints at his brother.

Jason sets a coffee beside Maris' papers. "You're up early," he says, then picks up a few of her manuscript pages. "I'm assuming the writing's coming along today?"

"It is! I got a few new pages done already." She pushes back in her chair, sips her coffee and watches him read some of her work.

The sprawling cottage, raised high on stilts, faces the water. It's the last-standing cottage on the beach, all the others having been washed to sea by previous hurricanes. But the angular shape of this one saved it by deflecting storm winds and water. Its blueprint will be put to the test again with this storm. While the waves roll onto the beach now—right beneath the cottage, no doubt—he stands at the window facing the rocky ledge. The wind whips against the glass pane, bringing a salty sea spray to everything it touches. The cottage is taking a beating. It's how his life's been feeling these days. Beaten down from every direction.

Maris stands beside Jason and points to the passage. "Neil started that scene," she says. "But he didn't finish it. That's what I'm working on now, filling that one in."

Jason flips the page over, then skims it again. "If Neil could pick a cottage for my show, I think that would be the one he'd go for. The last-standing cottage on the beach. The sole survivor. What an episode that could make."

When Maris takes the papers and sits again, she agrees. "It's really intriguing how it's the only cottage left on the sand." She sips her coffee, then straightens the papers Jason had lifted. "Where you off to this morning?"

"Beach Box. It's close, over on Ridgewood Road, so I'm taking the golf cart. Have some preliminary sketches to review with the owner." He notices the pewter hourglass sitting beside her laptop then. How often did his father flip that hourglass, all those years ago? On good days, it was simply to give Neil, Paige or Jason an hour of his time to beachcomb, or toss a ball with them. On bad days, and they always knew by the emotions that preceded it, his father would turn the hourglass to give *himself* an hour to collect his thoughts after some war memory or flashback unhinged him. Those were the times when he'd sit alone, out on the bench he'd personally built on the bluff overlooking the sea.

Jason notices now that only a few grains of sand remain in the hourglass' upper bulb. "Timing yourself?" he asks before leaving. "Lots of minutes have passed."

Maris nods, then flips the hourglass. "That sand is my deadline. I work best with a visual pressure to beat the clock."

Jason steps closer, touches her shoulder and bends to kiss her goodbye. "And you work best … in a bathing suit?" he asks as his fingers move aside the beach cover-up on her shoulder to find her navy swimsuit there. He strokes the skin beneath it.

"Okay." Her hand reaches up and covers his. "I was hoping you wouldn't notice." Now she spins around and smiles up at him as she unzips the cover-up and flashes her bathing suit: a navy tankini, the deep-V top having little polka-dot spaghetti ties at the hip, and a polka-dot belted bottom. "I'm on my way out to float in my tube. With Elsa."

"Seriously?" Jason pulls back and crosses his arms. "You're both just going to *float*?"

"Yes!" Maris shuts her laptop and neatens her papers before standing. "I got up early to meet my word count, and then I'm checking in with Elsa to see how she's doing." Maris touches Jason's whiskered jaw. "So we're not *just* floating. We'll have a nice water-talk." Her hand lowers as she drags the back of her fingers to his neck. "You know that's part of the reason I quit denim design—to be present." She smiles, then tucks her brown hair behind an ear. "Like Sal was," she whispers.

"Was he ever." Jason reaches over and toys with Maris' gold star pendant.

"So I'm spending time with Elsa this morning." Maris steps closer. "Hope you're not mad," she whispers again.

Jason's hand moves from her pendant, up along the chain, to her shoulder once more. He lowers the cover-up and strokes her skin there. "How can I be mad at you, sweetheart?" As he asks, his fingers run down her arm, and back to her shoulder.

Maris murmurs something; he's not sure what. Because she says it right beneath the kiss she leaves on his neck, first, then another on his face.

Okay, so … a little fooling around, or get to his overloaded work schedule?

The question lingers only until his hands cradle her neck when he kisses her back. The kiss deepens enough so that even when his cell phone dings, he keeps kissing. His hands, too, keep touching. When she links her arms behind his waist, he drops that cover-up off her shoulders and slips down a strap of her bathing suit. Another ding of the annoying cell phone in his pocket can't stop him from nuzzling her neck, then her bare shoulder. All while feeling her close. Feeling her fingers tangle in his hair as she drops her head back, whispering his name.

In between the dings and rings of his cell phone.

But somehow, Maris does it; she takes his face in her hands

and kisses him at the same time she steps backward to that cot along the side wall. Her mouth opens to his with each step that she tugs him along. It's as though she doesn't even hear his phone demanding some attention of his—some reply to contractors, or the salvage yard, or Trent. How easy would it be for him to step away, to take a much-needed breath and check those mounting phone alerts?

Or would it be better to slip her bathing suit right off? Hell, it would be so damn easy, anyway. Just let his fingers drop from those shoulder straps and run down her sides, skimming her breasts, feeling her hips as he'd lift the swimsuit top off.

It's clearly time for the day's second decision.

Answer phone, or morning sex with his wife? It doesn't help that Maris pushes the conflict when, still kissing him, still murmuring, she gets him to that sweet cot.

Just as his phone rings again.

And okay, sometimes it's really nice to have someone make a decision *for* you.

Like Maris does when, still kissing him, she slides his cell phone out of his pocket and shuts it off. But that's not all she does. Oh, no.

She also lifts off her navy swimsuit top, slowly, as she sits on the cot. Slowly enough for Jason, with only the briefest glance at his watch first, to then lower the polka-dot belted bottom.

~

"What time is it?" Kyle calls out from the upstairs linen closet. On his Tuesday morning off from the diner, he's stacking the linens that Lauren already unpacked and washed.

"Nine-twenty," Lauren tells him. She squeezes past behind him, stopping to tuck in a loose corner of sheet fabric. "Why?"

"Jerry went in early for the dairy delivery so I can get a haircut. But he doesn't want to work all day."

"You better go, then. I'll finish this."

"Okay, good." Kyle backs up and eyes the closet shelves. He likes everything organized—at home, at work. Everywhere. So here, winter flannel sheets are on the top shelves, out of reach until the colder months.

Lauren lifts another set of folded sheets from the laundry basket on the floor. "Can you drop the kids at day camp on your way? Take them there in the golf cart. They love riding in it."

The thing is, Kyle does, too. Cruising the beach streets in it reminds him of his high school days, when he and the guys would roll around here, windows down, maybe a six-pack in the back. They'd pick up their friends from different little bungalows and cottages on summer nights, then park the car in the lot behind the boat basin, or down by the lagoon, and hang out together. So he's always game for a golf-cart cruise these days.

And this cruise to the Rec area won't take long. There'll still be time for a quick haircut before the lunch shift at the diner. Once he's got the kids strapped into the rear seat of their new golf cart, he runs back inside for one more thing.

Because he *also* knows damn well that only one person remains on The List other than himself. And that would be Barlow—who will no doubt try to take him down, no holds barred. Rules will be tossed, honesty shook off, morality tested. Anything will go, all for the honor of being godfather to Sal's child.

For now, he can't trust Barlow as far as he can throw him.

"Ain't that the truth," Kyle says to himself as he settles his Super Soaker on the golf cart's front seat, then pulls on his *Gone Fishing* cap. "Got your lunch, Hay?" Kyle asks as he drives off, squinting into the sun.

"Yes."

When he glances back, his seven-year-old daughter is pressing wisps of blowing hair off her face.

Kyle reaches behind his seat and lightly slaps Evan's knee. "How about you, bud?"

"Yup. I got it." Evan lifts a tote from the seat.

"Good." The golf cart speeds along over the sandy beach road. "So what's happening at camp today?"

"Painting! Mommy gave me a smock to wear," Hailey says. "Just like she does."

Kyle slows up when a father lugging his overloaded beach gear needs to cross the street. "What are you painting?" he asks the kids after waving to the harried dad.

"Sand pails. Which is for *babies*." Evan gives his sister a slight shove.

"I am *not* a baby!" she yells back, still fussing with blowing wisps of hair.

"Now, Ev." Kyle rounds a curve and pulls into the beach parking lot, headed to the Rec area where the teen counselors wait. "Enlighten me why painting sand pails is for babies?"

"Dad! A sand pail? And then we're going to take our pails and collect things to put inside them. *That's* for *babies*."

"Listen, guy. Back in my day, sand pails were hot." Kyle parks and gets out to unbuckle Hailey from her seat. "They're for crabbing, son. So pick a good-sized one to paint. Big enough to put your crabbing line in, a small net, too." He looks across the seat at Evan and remembers himself at nine years old, always game to head to the rocks. And he *still* is, decades later, but with a fishing rod in hand, instead. "And when you collect things for that epic pail, find good sinker stones for your line. Maybe we can go crabbing on the rocks this weekend."

"All right!" Evan says as Kyle high-fives him. "I'm decorating *my* pail with skulls, so everyone will keep out of it!"

"Maybe your friend will, too. What's his name?" Kyle asks.

"Timmy. I can't wait to tell him."

It's all how you spin things, Kyle thinks as his kids grab their totes and run up to the camp area. Metal sand pails line a long table beneath a shade pavilion there. Paints, paintbrushes and paint pens are spread out around stencils and shells on the table. The kids will have a blast.

So Kyle waves them off, circles the parking lot in his golf cart and heads back to his house. On the way, though, one sight stops him.

Ah, shit. There's no way he can get to the barbershop on time now. Not when a familiar golf cart catches his eye. It's parked at that little Beach Box on Ridgewood Road. And he knows exactly *whose* golf cart it is by the dog decal affixed near the rear seat. Only one person has a dog sticker on his golf cart here at Stony Point. And that person would be his current archenemy, at least until Kyle knocks him off The List.

"The hell with a haircut," Kyle whispers. "You're going down, pal. This is it," he says to himself. It's hard to take his eyes off Barlow's golf cart, even as he cruises past it. "I got you this time."

Like that, his plan is set. Because it's important to think on your toes and outfox the enemy. How many times did Jason tell him his father's Vietnam tales with that thought at the heart of it?

So he'll outfox Barlow at his own game.

First, Kyle circles around Ridgewood Road again, but this time parks his golf cart beyond the curve, out of sight of the enemy's wary eyes. He sinks down in the driver's seat, pulls his shabby-looking *Gone Fishing* cap even lower and silently … he waits.

twenty-seven

AT BEACH BOX, JASON PUSHES open the front screen door. It squeaks on its hinges and slams shut behind them.

"I'm glad you're fixing up the place," he tells the cottage owner. They stand side by side while surveying the square, shingled building set back on a dried-out, sun-scorched lawn.

"Me, too. It's a little cottage, no fuss to keep. My wife and I can come and go easily and, more importantly, relish the beach."

Jason leans back and considers the structure. It's literally a brown-shingled box with not even a front porch to add any dimension. Two plain concrete steps lead down from the paned door, and mismatched windows fill the wall space on either side of that door. A tiny bungalow—with huge potential.

"We'll turn this little box into a beauty," Jason says when they shake hands.

"Thanks, Jason."

"I'll be in touch," Jason calls over his shoulder. He walks to his golf cart, secures his portfolio and sketches in the backseat and climbs in to head home. About a block later—a block where he passes a few people walking to the beach with tubes over their shoulders, umbrellas beneath their arms—he hears a sound, close. It's a golf cart practically beside his, so he speeds up.

But suddenly, this rogue golf cart *is* beside his, speeding along neck and neck. Which is when he gives a double take because, *shit*, it's Kyle! He's driving with one hand on his steering wheel and the other holding some monster water soaker—in an attempt at a drive-by elimination!

Do the opposite. Hide by day, patrol at night—that's what we did, Jason's father often told him and Neil. *Until we didn't. Until we did opposite of what the VC expected. And the night we didn't patrol and instead laid low, absolutely unmoving, was the night they got spooked and moved first. End of story, for them. Sometimes do opposite what the enemy thinks. To win.*

A simple lesson Jason never forgot. Especially now, when Kyle—his enemy—no doubt thinks he'll pick up the pace and try to outrace him.

So just as Kyle lifts his weapon and pulls the trigger, Jason slams on his brakes. The heavy stream of water from Kyle's behemoth water weapon sprays directly into … thin air, as Jason is now way behind him and pulling a hard-and-fast U-turn. His hands spin the steering wheel as he peels out and makes a beeline to the closest safety zone—the boardwalk.

Their tubes float and bob on the calm water of Long Island Sound. No wind blows to get them drifting. Maris and Elsa are pretty much idle, with floppy sunhats shading their heads, and their fingers dipping into the cool water. Beach bliss.

"What a warm day," Maris says. "All the beach umbrellas

on the sand look like lollipops from here."

"So pretty," Elsa agrees as she gives herself a gentle spin.

Their talk is as easy as the peaceful morning. Maris tells Elsa about the latest chapter she's finishing up in Neil's novel; Elsa tells Maris how the inn is already booked for September.

"Jason's show was nothing short of a marketing miracle! So many callers mention that they found my inn that way."

"Wonderful!" Maris drizzles cold water on her shoulders, then paddles closer to Elsa. "Sal would be so proud of what you and Celia have done to the place. And with little Aria living there, too. You've got three generations of strong women at your inn now."

"My favorite part is that turret," Elsa tells her. "Jason was so right to incorporate it, with all those windows facing the sea."

After a moment, Maris points to the gray cottage on the far end of the beach. It rises on the sand like a lonely sentry. She imagines that with the jutting angles of its architectural design, from the inside you would have a panoramic view of sky, sand and sea. A look-out cottage, keeping an eye on the beach. "I'll tell you a secret, Aunt Elsa. That's the cottage Neil wrote about in his novel."

"Really?" Elsa twists around and lowers her cat-eye sunglasses for a better view.

Maris nods. "This morning, Jason read a passage from the manuscript, and he said that if his brother were here, Neil would so pick *that* cottage for the show."

"It does need some work," Elsa observes while spinning her tube to face the distant cottage. "Like its better days are behind it. But it's not bad, though. She's still the grande dame of Stony Point."

"Oh, she is. Definitely *not* a crumbler like the dilapidated Maggie Woods hovel Jason tore down. This one would be perfect for his show." Maris reaches over and touches her aunt's arm. "It's kind of like how your place was. A little rough around the edges. Problem is, it's not one of the submissions."

"Maybe we can come up with some plan to get it submitted, at my next Sunday dinner. I need you and Jason to sample a new recipe for my future inn guests."

"Huh." Maris tips her face to the sunshine. "Good luck with *that.* Jason and Kyle are at a standoff with the godfather challenge. They'll never come to dinner and risk losing a godfather point." With her tube barely swaying on the water, Maris closes her eyes and feels the sun's warmth on her skin. "You won't see either of them at your table until only one name is left on The List."

"But those two are my best taste-testers!"

"They'll only talk to each other now in one of the safe zones. So you'd have to consider moving your dinner."

"Hey." Elsa gives a finger splash to Maris. "Would you look at that?" She points to Jason running onto the boardwalk right as they speak. "I thought you said he was working."

"He was." Maris sits up straight in her tube and paddles closer to shore. She squints across the sand, leaning to the side to see around the umbrellas and families and inflated swim rings. "Wait. There's Kyle, on the *other* end of the boardwalk! They must've had a squirt-gun shootout."

Elsa paddles her tube beside Maris'. Together they lift their sunhats and scope out the situation. "Well," Elsa quietly says. "If they're *both* on the boardwalk, the shootout was a draw, then. So my guess? Game's still on."

Okay, if Kyle had to admit it, he would. He really feels it as he approaches Jason on the boardwalk.

Damn, he misses his friend. They haven't talked in a week. No crullers and coffee early mornings in the diner. No bullshitting. No Friday night fishing.

"So this is what it's come down to," Kyle calls out, motioning his finger between them. "You and me."

"I thought you were at the diner and I was safe. You caught me off guard, dude."

Kyle sets his water gun on the boardwalk bench and sits beside Jason. "The way you backed out of that assault? Your fight-or-flight instincts are razor sharp."

"Lifetime of 'Nam stories. Not to mention the accident." Jason motions to his prosthetic leg. "Dockside closed today? Shouldn't you be manning the big stove and feeding hungry tourists?"

"Haircut morning, bro. But that's nixed now." Kyle runs a hand through his hair. "Jerry went in early for me. Truck was coming in with a dairy delivery."

"How's it going, using the old Dockside Diner name again? You see a difference in business?"

"Yeah, actually. I think it's the nostalgia factor, which works like a charm. You know, it's not just a diner. Now I'm selling *memories.*"

"With this heat, there must be a helluva line to get in." Jason lifts his sunglasses and squints out at the already-crowded beach. "No one wants to cook in these cottages. They're nothing but hotboxes in a summer like this one."

"No shit. The diner can barely keep up with the demand. I'm up to three deliveries a week. Today, Wednesday and another Friday."

"Speaking of Friday, we putting this godfather thing behind us in a free zone? Get some fishing done after missing out last week?"

Kyle stands and peers down at Jason. "Oh, nice try." He shoves his shoulder. "The *only* way I'm fishing is if one of us goes down first."

Jason slaps his hand away. "Won't be me."

Kyle takes a few steps backward, all while keeping his sights on him. He lifts his *Gone Fishing* cap brim, puts two fingers to his eyes, then turns those two fingers to Jason.

"Watching you, bro." Kyle stumbles when he says it, but recovers and continues walking backward down the boardwalk.

Until Jason stands and begins walking backward in the *opposite* direction. Slowly. After a few steps, both men turn and make a run for it. They fly into their golf carts and gun it out of there, each one headed home.

Each one, still in the game.

twenty-eight

BY THE NEXT MORNING, JASON has a plan. Something Kyle said actually gave him the idea. It's a perfect way to eliminate Kyle from The List, which would clinch another godfather point for Jason. But a few more details still have to be worked out.

Instead, Jason makes an early stop at the inn. From a distance, he sees how the new shrubs and beach grasses have grown in around the expansive front porch. A *new* porch, at that. His architectural blueprint included a grand overhang extending from the second level, providing much-needed shade from that hot New England sun.

With a quick knock at the door, Jason walks into the inn's lobby. "Elsa?" he calls out.

"Back here, Jason!" Elsa answers from down the hall.

So he drops his food bag in the kitchen on his way to the gift shop, where Elsa is tinkering with a bothersome shelf. Celia is there, too, bouncing her fussy baby who is lightly crying and twisting in Celia's arms. Celia hovers beside Elsa while trying to talk over Aria's complaining cries. Several other shelves in the small room are already stacked with Ocean Star Inn tees and hats.

"This shelf *has* to be level," Elsa is saying, her voice tense. "It's for something very, very special that I can't have sliding off."

"I've got a level in my truck," Jason says from behind them.

"No, that's okay," Celia tells him with a quick glance back. "I have a good eye." Then, she turns again, and this time walks to him. "Would you mind?"

"Helping with the shelf?" he asks.

She steps closer. "No. With the baby."

As she says it, she holds out Aria, prompting him to quickly cradle his arms. Celia wastes no time depositing Aria there before turning back to Elsa.

"Wait—" Jason starts to say. But the women don't even hear him. When Aria moves in his hold, he shifts his awkwardly curved arms. Seriously, he hasn't even held a baby since, well, since Paige and Vinny's kids were infants. And that's been several years now. So something about this seems *really* foreign to him.

Feeling somewhat uncomfortable, he looks down at Aria. She wears a pink-and-white romper with ruffled cap sleeves. But she's also quieted, and her gaze is locked onto his. Which makes him very conscious of his shadow of dark whiskers and hair curling over his collar, long overdue for a cut. Not to mention the scar along his jawline and any fatigue circles beneath his eyes. Cripe, he must look a wreck. Certainly bad enough to spook an innocent baby.

But, what?

He looks down again and the baby is cooing? And her hand is reaching toward his face. So he adjusts his hold and lifts her closer to his chest. When the baby still reaches up, he lowers his face and her tiny, soft fingers touch his cheek. What it does, seeing her dark eyes watching his so near, is this: It chokes him up.

Because he's never held Sal's baby before. Oh sure, he's touched her cheek with his finger. Or given her tiny foot a gentle shake.

But held her in his arms? No. And it feels absolutely so deeply personal … and heartbreaking. Because Sal will never be here, glancing over Jason's shoulder and looking at Aria *with* him. Will never see the sparkling dark eyes Aria inherited from her father. Her eyes laced with feathery eyelashes. Will never see her soft cheeks, pink-flushed this summer morning. In the warm air, her fine brown hair falls in lazy curls beside her face.

There's no mistaking it's Sal's baby in his arms.

Sal's.

The reality of that hits Jason now, and the sudden lump in his throat is painful. This little life he holds—she can't weigh more than twelve pounds—moves in waves of motion in his arms. A new life here *only* because of Sal. Salvatore DeLuca. A man who was like a brother to him.

The baby gurgles quietly, still looking at Jason's face. So with Elsa and Celia busy shelf-fiddling, he shifts his position to make Aria more comfortable. Rather than have her lie across his cradled arms, he sits her up—hooking one arm beneath her legs, while his other hand holds her shoulders and neck close to his chest. Her head is warm; her hair soft against his palm. While he holds her like that, her tiny fingers curl and close around his shirt fabric.

And he can't believe it. Cannot believe this baby of Sal's is in his arms. When his eyes burn at the thought, he first swipes away a tear. Then, well, then he bends close to the top of her head and just closes his eyes with the grief and joy that flood through him.

"Perfect!" Elsa calls out.

When Jason turns, he sees that she's eyeing her straight shelf while setting a glass jar on top of it. Celia reaches over to adjust it, and suddenly Jason's heart breaks for *her*. For what Celia must feel so often while caring for this sweet baby, alone. Which makes him shift Aria comfortably to his shoulder—with a new resolve.

Oh yes, he *will* be little Aria's godfather, come hell or high water. No way will he ever let Kyle clinch that title, not for Sal's beloved child.

Elsa suddenly catches Jason's eye and must recognize the emotion on his face. He can tell by the way she stops everything then, and instead slowly turns with her arms crossed.

"Isn't she something, Jason?" she asks.

Celia quickly looks, too, before giving a knowing nod.

"She sure is," Jason tells them as he presses a kiss to the baby's head. "One of a kind," he softly says when he gently places Aria back in Celia's arms.

After a quiet moment, Elsa motions to the shelf. "I said this will be for something very special, Jason. And I want you to know it's reserved for Maris' book. For as many copies of it that will fit here."

Elsa looks at Jason then, her own eyes filled with tears.

And Jason knows. Aria has that power, still. And he's sure she always will. The power to open up wells of emotion in certain people—Elsa especially. Her talk of the shelf is just a distraction from her tears.

"And I'm never putting anything on this shelf," she assures him, "until that book is published and ready. Hopefully, this sight will keep Maris motivated, too."

"Isn't that a great idea?" Celia asks him. "It'll be the perfect summer read for our guests."

"Speaking of ideas," Elsa says while setting down a screwdriver and then taking Jason's arm, "let's go eat. I have something to mull over with you."

He follows her down the hall toward the kitchen.

Celia, though, remains in the gift shop and pokes her head out the doorway. "Thanks, Jason," she calls. "You know. For helping with the baby."

"No problem." He gives a small wave from the kitchen, then turns to the bag of food he'd brought, pulling out paper napkins and foil packets of ketchup.

"You wanted to talk to me about something?" Jason mentions as Elsa pulls on her starfish-print oven mitts. "We were overdue for an egg sandwich, so I brought a couple." He holds up the bag. "Let's go on the deck, upstairs."

"Why?" Elsa carefully pulls a tray from the oven. "We can have our food in the yard, on the bistro table. Like we always do."

"No." Jason walks over to the stove, lured by the delicious aroma coming from that oven. "Seriously, I can't keep living like this."

"Like what?" Elsa steps back and swats his arm with the oven mitts. "Eating my food?"

"No, no." He moves closer and bends to see better. "What *is* that? Pizza? Maris will kill me if she knows I'm eating pizza in the morning."

"Oh, Jason." Elsa picks up a pizza wheel and slices a few

pieces. "This pizza is *meant* for breakfast. Look!" She drops a slice on a plate and hands it to him. "It's my eggs Florentine pizza. See the eggs? The yolks are just right, still a little runny. And there's some spinach, all with my white sauce." She grabs a slice for herself. "Come on. We'll talk outside over our breakfast." She moves to the center island and gathers a handful of napkins. "And you can tell me why you can't live like this. Is something wrong with your work?" she asks.

"No." Jason drops the ketchup packets and napkins back into the egg-sandwich bag. "It's not that. It's this hiding, from Kyle. You know, because of the godfather competition. That's why I can't eat outside. He could ambush me. Hell, I even phoned-in the egg sandwich order at the convenience store because I couldn't risk waiting in line and being whacked off by him."

As soon as he says it, Elsa gets it. It's obvious by the knowing nod she gives while making a sharp turn and heading to the deck off the infamous back room. They can relax on the inn's second level—out of any threatening squirt gun's range. It takes a few minutes of back and forth to the kitchen before they bring all their sandwiches and pizza slices and fresh hot coffee out to the upper-level deck. But finally, they sit in the shade of a small roof overhang, where the air is slightly cooler.

"Now that you're safe, try something new," Elsa says when she pushes his pizza slice closer. "I'll be serving this to my future guests here."

While Elsa preps her egg sandwich, squeezing a curl of ketchup on the gooey egg and cheese beneath the top roll, Jason bites into her newfangled pizza. All he can do is moan his pleasure as he leans back, chewing. Warm, salted egg, and olive-oiled spinach, all covered with cracked pepper are pure heaven in his mouth.

"Is there prosciutto on this?" he asks.

"A touch," Elsa whispers, her finger to her lips.

He takes another double bite and gives her a thumbs-up.

At the same time, she's laying into her croissant egg sandwich. Her eyes flutter closed when she says, "Oh my God." She manages some chewing, then digs in for another bite.

"Making up for lost time?" Jason asks her with a wink.

"I haven't had one of these in two weeks, at least!" she says with a vigorous nod—and with another bite. She wipes a drip of ketchup off her chin with the back of her hand.

While she's in her egg-sandwich glory, Jason reaches for another piece of pizza. The summer air is so still, sounds carry to the deck on its stillness: the plaintive call of seagulls; the clatter of the flagpole pulley as the flag is raised on the beach.

"Maris and I had a nice talk floating in our tubes yesterday," Elsa finally says around a mouthful of egg and croissant.

"Oh, no." Jason bites into the pizza and watches her suspiciously. "Sounds like some sort of collusion is happening."

"No, no. It *is* about you, but it's good." She sets down what's left of her sandwich. Well, sweeps it through a bit of ketchup and holds it over her plate. "Good. But maybe not easy."

"My father always said that anything worthwhile in life never comes easy."

"Smart man. So. With that in mind, here's my suggestion for you to mull over."

Jason nods, then bites again into his second pizza slice.

Elsa leans close and lowers her voice. "*Can* the CT-TV cottage submissions."

Which gets Jason to almost gag on his food. "What?"

"Can them. You know, for your show. Because listen." She sits back and lifts her coffee cup. After a sip, she elaborates. "My inn renovation was very personal, for the pilot episode. Which gave it a lot of meaning. So your next project *has* to be significant. Especially for the first *official* episode."

"But I'm still reviewing the submissions."

"You've already found it, Jason."

"I have?"

"It's the cottage on the beach."

"You mean the last one? Down on the far end?"

"Yes. The one your *brother* also wrote about in his *novel.* What a fantastic way to bridge *two* projects—yours and Maris'—with Neil at the heart of it."

"But the owners didn't apply."

"You can *ask* them. Can't you?"

Jason sits back and eyes Elsa now. A rolled bandana holds her hair off her face. And because she was working to set up her gift shop, she wears a long tee over black capri leggings, with slip-on sneakers.

Her expression, though, is serious and unwavering. And she's being awfully brazen about this project.

"I don't like to talk to people," Jason tells her. "Not if I don't have to."

"But you can be *very* persuasive. Remember trying to convince me to keep *my* cottage?"

"This is different. *Talk* to them? Ask whoever lives there to disrupt their lives with a massive home renovation? They're complete strangers." Jason stands and goes to the deck railing. From here, he can see some of Stony Point Beach in the distance, past the dune grasses. The sand is nearly white beneath the blazing sun; those ocean stars sparkle on the rippling water. When he turns to Elsa, he remains at the railing. "I don't even know their names, whoever it is that owns the place."

She shrugs. "Knock on their door. Simple as that."

"The cottage *is* historical, I'll give you that much. So that's a nice angle to play up for the cameras." He looks over his shoulder toward the beach again. The last-standing cottage rises on stilts there, near the rocky ledge where he and the guys fish. "It's not in that bad of shape, though," he counters Elsa.

"Bad enough. I gave it a good scrutiny. We floated past it in our tubes yesterday, Maris and I. And," Elsa says, raising her coffee cup in a toast, "we *love* the idea."

"You don't understand, Elsa." Jason sits again and swirls ketchup on his egg sandwich, then pats the croissant top back on. After cutting it, he places one half on Elsa's plate. Then he lifts his own half, but holds it midair, saying, "I'm not supposed to pitch my own projects."

"Says who? And what about the inn? That was your own project and everybody loved it. I'm booked through the fall now!" She drops the last bit of her egg sandwich in her mouth, then wipes her fingers on a paper napkin. "My reservation ledger is bulging."

Jason quickly finishes what's left of his sandwich and washes it down with a gulp of coffee. Because though his cell phone is set on silent, it hasn't stopped buzzing with messages the whole time he's been on Elsa's deck. Standing, he returns to the deck railing facing the beach. Down below, a hummingbird flits about in Elsa's tended flower garden. "I'm not sure." He checks his watch. "But I really have to get going now, so I'll think about it. Okay?"

She nods and waves him off, raising that extra sandwich half as she does. He starts to leave, but ah, yes. Sweet temptation has him turn back to snag one more slice of her eggs Florentine pizza. He'll bring it to the boardwalk. From there, his safe zone, he can better consider what Elsa just proposed.

Sitting on the boardwalk minutes later, Jason studies that lone beach cottage in the distance, right as he bites into the eggy pizza slice.

And right as Cliff Raines walks up the boardwalk steps.

"Seriously, Barlow? This may be a safe zone, but you're not safe from ordinances here. I'm going to have to ticket you."

"For what?" Jason asks as he stuffs the last of the thin-sliced pizza in his mouth and brushes the crumbs off his hands.

Cliff is already pulling his ticket pad from his cargo shorts pocket. He raises his sunglasses on top of his head, clicks his pen and peers at Jason. "Nice try. But no food on the beach, you know that." After jotting the fine on the ticket, he rips it off the pad and holds it out.

But something's not right, though Jason can't place what it is. When Cliff gives the ticket a shake, Jason snatches it from him. He stands, too, and leans closer to Cliff. "Something's off with you," Jason says while squinting at him. "Wait. You're blinking funny."

Cliff turns away, then quickly drops his sunglasses back on and resumes walking the boardwalk. He also pulls his COMMISSIONER cap down low while sternly saying over his shoulder, "Sweep up those crumbs before you attract any bees."

Jason does. With a paper napkin, he brushes off the bench. But not before throwing one more curious look Cliff's way.

twenty-nine

CLIFF HEARS VOICES. ONCE HE'D left Jason on the boardwalk, he drove the security cruiser over to Elsa's place. Outside the open windows there, he hears—wait—hears only *Elsa's* voice coming from inside. So she must be alone? He walks along the front porch to a large window and leans against the cedar shingles. Yes, it's Elsa talking. Reciting … wedding vows?

"Do you, Reginald," she asks, then pauses before continuing, "take this woman, Beatrice, to be your lawfully wedded wife?" Another pause, then, "To love, honor and cherish, in sickness and in health, for richer and for poorer, as long as you both shall live?"

Cliff peers over his sunglasses but can't see Elsa from where he spies through the window, so he goes to the front door and walks inside. He heads down the hallway because it sounds like she's in the living room. Once there, he stops in that room's doorway and suppresses a surprised laugh. Because Elsa, wearing a long black tee and leggings, faces a mop and broom propped beside the fireplace. Standing perfectly straight, she reads from the Justice of the Peace manual in her hands.

"Do your mop and broom need a witness?" Cliff asks.

"Cliff!" Elsa spins around. "You scared me, sneaking up like that." She turns away while tucking a loose strand of hair beneath her rolled paisley bandana, then sets down her guidebook. After another glare back at him, she snatches up her mop and broom. They clatter together in her arms. "It's just that I'm getting *requests* for seaside weddings now that I'm a JP. And I need to be prepared."

Cliff steps further into the room. "With a mop?"

"It's just a prop, Clifton. A *prop*." She looks at the pretend bride and groom in her hands, then heads to her broom closet off the kitchen. "I have to get into a zone," she calls back while hiding the pseudo newlywed couple. "To practice projecting my voice." When she shuts the closet door, Elsa asks over her shoulder, "What are you doing here, anyway?"

"I'm returning your pastry dish, from last week." He hands her the cleaned plate.

Which Elsa also snatches, obviously still flustered at being caught rehearsing to … a broom! In the kitchen, she opens one cabinet, then another, and drops the dish inside. Finally, she pulls out a stool at the massive center island and motions to Cliff.

"Take off your sunglasses and stay awhile, why don't you?" she asks.

It's the moment of truth. Right now.

This is what Cliff's been waiting for. He sits first, sunglasses still on. Elsa is filling a coffee decanter with water at the sink. This will be perfect, because he can begin explaining while her back is to him, and there's no direct eye contact.

"Something you said the other day really bothered me,

Elsa." Now? Now he has no choice but to set his sunglasses on the island countertop.

"Me?" Elsa asks over her shoulder, water still running.

"Yes. What you said about my blue eyes."

"Well, sometimes blue eyes can seem shifty." She shuts off the water and turns. "That's all. It's nothing personal."

"Okay." He clears his throat and does it. Yes, he points to his eyes. "So what do you think of *this*, Elsa DeLuca?"

"Cliff." She steps closer, squinting at his face. "What did you *do*?"

"I got new contact lenses. Brown ones." He opens his eyes wider. "Pools of milk chocolate, which I figured is the color of … trust. Just like Barlow's dark brown eyes."

Elsa quickly sets down the full decanter of water so urgently that the water sloshes over the rim. "Your eyes are *not* brown, Clifton Raines. They are bloodshot!" She grabs his hand and rushes down the hallway to a guest bathroom, where she pushes him in front of a wall mirror.

Okay, so the sight shocks even Cliff. He leans close, pulls at the skin beneath his eyes and scrutinizes his bloodshot reflection. "Of all the cockamamie …"

Elsa, apparently very worried, has already run to her room and returns now with her purse and keys clutched in one hand. When she passes the bathroom where he still scrutinizes his red eyes, she reaches in and grabs his arm, but keeps moving toward the front door—all in one urgent blur.

"I'm getting you to the walk-in clinic," she insists without looking back. "Pronto!"

After sitting in the clinic's waiting room; after filling out endless medical forms—which Elsa had to do *for* Cliff, who was having a hard time seeing; after watching other patients called in ahead of Cliff; after going through a handful of tissues wiping runny tears from Cliff's eyes, it finally happens.

Yes, hours later, the day quiets down.

In Elsa's favorite place, thankfully: her big, remodeled kitchen. A pot of soup simmers on the stove, and breaded pork chops bake in the oven. Outside her kitchen window, a seagull cries, and the seashell wind chime gives the slightest clicking-clatter in a breeze off the water. That's one thing she's noticed this summer. Sometimes at the end of the very hot days that have settled on Stony Point, a breeze visits only briefly as day changes to night. Just a stirring of the salty air during the blue hour when the horizon deepens to violet, the sky meeting sea in a soft pastel color.

"You really did that for me, Cliff?" Elsa asks while stirring the soup on the stove. She glances over at Cliff sitting alone in her dining room now. Two place settings are put out for their late dinner this summer evening.

"Yes, I did, Mrs. DeLuca."

Elsa absentmindedly stirs. "Nobody's ever changed their eye color for me before."

After a moment's silence, Cliff asks, "So can you trust me now? After all that?"

"Oh, you poor thing." Elsa sets down her ladle and sits beside Cliff—who looks a little lost, all by himself at her wood-planked dining room table. "Come to find out, you're allergic to the preservative in your contact lens solution! And then …

to have your pupils *dilated*, too! What a procedure! What a … What a day."

Cliff nods and reaches for the cup of tea Elsa had prepared for him.

"Over to the right, Cliff." She nudges the steaming cup closer to his hand. "You spend the night here, because you can't even see straight. I don't want you bumbling into things in that cramped trailer of yours."

They both look over when the side door swings open and Celia breezes in, holding Aria.

"Feeling better, Commish?" Celia asks with a sly grin.

Cliff, sipping his tea, somehow manages to make her out, then squints to Elsa. "Elsa! You told her?"

"*Everything*," Celia whispers as she pats Cliff's shoulder. "*Which is so sweet.*" Another pat, then. "And now, Aria came to say goodnight to her nonna."

Elsa stands and gives Aria's hand a squeeze. "Goodnight, little love."

And like that, with a hug or two, Celia and Aria breeze right back out to their own guest cottage behind the inn. So all's settled down with the day, though it's obvious Cliff's eyes still need some tender loving care. Elsa runs warm water over a small towel.

"Put this over your tired eyes," she softly says as she sits again beside him.

Cliff takes the towel, presses it to his face and simply sighs behind it.

"And Commissioner Raines? Don't you *ever* do that again." Elsa leans close and peeks under the warm towel at his eyes. "Because you know something? Your blue eyes are actually growing on me."

With that, she gives him a light kiss on the cheek, then gets back to her pork-chop pan in the oven, and pot of soup on the stovetop, and ladles and spatulas in the kitchen.

thirty

THE DAY HAS ARRIVED, AT last. Jason's patiently bided his time, ticking off the minutes, the hours, until his plan could be set in motion. His plan to oust his best friend—and best *man*, no less—from The List.

But for any of it to work, he has to get up on Friday morning before the sun even rises. He also doesn't want to wake Maris.

The first problem is the dog—following his every move, with an occasional growl and nasty nip at his crutches, too. So he loads up her bowl with kibble to keep her fat and happy. Then he brings his prosthetic leg and clothes to the enclosed outdoor cabana, where every summer he sets up a stool so that he can shower there. This way, the house will be quiet and Maris can sleep. After showering, breakfast is a blueberry muffin slathered in butter and heated in the microwave, wolfed down with a glass of orange juice, so he can tell Maris later that he met his day's fruit quota.

The dog is in and out with him, sitting on the deck while Jason eats, then shadowing Jason back inside. There, a quick glance in the bathroom mirror has him decide he's good for another day unshaven. Looking at his reflection, he drags his hand down his jaw, across the faded scar there, before quickly brushing his teeth. He's ready to leave by the time the sun just crests the eastern horizon.

Because the one thing Jason Barlow knows for sure is this: Kyle Bradford will be expecting his *early* Friday dairy delivery at the diner. Leaving no room for error, Jason snatches the only water weapon that will do the trick and heads out. Yes, he'll outsmart the enemy, the same way his father did time and again, simply to survive in the jungles of 'Nam.

Everything is planned as Jason hits the road. Everything down to the decoy vehicle, which is why he's using Maris' car. Kyle will never even recognize it if he spots it in the diner parking lot.

So this is it.

The plan has begun on this morning when Kyle Bradford will go down at Jason's hands. With every single detail thought out, Jason settles his monster aqua-assault weapon—freshly filled with water—on the front passenger seat, then drives beneath the stone railroad trestle and hangs a right on Shore Road. It doesn't take long to get to The Dockside because there's hardly any traffic at this godforsaken early hour. Deliveries happen at the diner's back door, so that's where Jason heads—the rear lot. But he kills his headlights first, to be as invisible as possible.

Then, there's only one thing left to do. He backs the car into a parking spot that affords a good view and waits.

It won't be long before that delivery truck pulls in and the deal will be sealed.

As will Kyle's fate.

Kyle still does something he's been doing for years, ever since he temped as a short-order cook at the diner. When he opens up for the morning shift, he still wipes down the counters, and fills napkin dispensers, and gets the morning's pans and utensils ready at the big stove. He thinks this as he straightens a stack of diner T-shirts. Even though the place was scrubbed down the night before, he always works his way through the morning cleaning routine. It's not only that cleanliness is next to godliness in his eating establishment.

It's that and something more. That cleaning routine is a quiet therapy for Kyle as his arm sweeps a damp cloth over countertops and booth tables. Any niggling thoughts or bothersome worries get swept away as he sanitizes and shines. Stepping back and scrutinizing his sparkling diner then, everything feels new and fresh—even with his life, somehow.

Once the spot-cleaning is done, and before checking on his Friday morning delivery, Kyle stops in his office and calls Lauren.

"Ell, I forgot to put away the Christmas boxes in the spare room. Leave them, and I'll carry them up to the attic when I get home."

"Perfect. Because I'm taking a break from unpacking," Lauren says into the phone. "Instead I'm loading up the golf cart and declaring this an official beach day for the kids. It's so hot out already."

"Tell me about it," Kyle says with a swipe of his damp forehead.

And doesn't he know it. Whenever he's ready for his first change of clothes *this* early, the day's sure to be a scorcher. Outside, it's the kind of pressing heat that makes its way right through the air-conditioned diner's walls.

So when Kyle hangs up, he peels off his black tee, balls it up and makes a hook shot into the trash can. "Score," he whispers, then lifts a new three-pack of tees off his side shelf. Just as he rips it open, the rear delivery door buzzer sounds.

"Coming, coming," Kyle mutters while pulling the new black tee over his head. He walks out of the office and passes the kitchen where he'll be stocking cheese and milk unloaded from that waiting truck. To get the perishables into the refrigerators, fast, he'll grab an extra hand truck and help the driver wheel in the dairy inventory.

"Hold your horses," Kyle calls when the buzzer sounds again. Everyone's a little impatient in the heat these days. Finally, he unlatches the rear diner delivery door and steps outside into the glaring early sunshine.

"Man, it's a scorcher, Bradford," the driver says after sipping from a bottled water. "Another day in the nineties, so let's get this unloaded before anything spoils."

"Bring it over. I'll give you a hand." Kyle waits while the driver backs the delivery truck to the small loading dock. Once the truck's aligned, the driver shuts off the engine, walks around and motions for Kyle that he's ready. Kyle approaches the back of the truck just as the driver unlocks the rear padlock, releases the latch and raises the roll-up door. As it clatters and grinds in its tracks, Kyle steps forward, until he's stopped dead by a stream of water hitting his brand-new black tee.

"What the—"

Suddenly he's sopping wet. So he squints into the shadowy rear of the truck to see someone standing there—dead center, spread-eagle—with two taut arms aiming a Super Soaker at Kyle's chest as though there's a bull's-eye right *on* his new black tee.

It's Jason, of course. Jason Barlow blasting a never-ending fatal stream of water at Kyle's heart, with an extra shot to the head for good measure.

Once he's just about depleted his liquid ammunition, Jason unclips his walkie-talkie. Oh, but that's not all he does. No, he's sure to have a smug, wicked grin, too, as he wordlessly hands the walkie-talkie to Kyle.

Kyle, after first wiping excess water off his shirt *and* face, snatches the little radio while never taking his eyes off of Barlow.

"This is Kyle Bradford reporting in," he says into the unit. "I've been eliminated at 6:05 AM. Place of demise—in true mafia style—rear door of Dockside Diner, behind a *delivery* truck." He pauses while throwing a glare at Jason, who has stepped out into the sunshine now, still grinning. And still holding his extreme water weapon. "Final words?" Kyle says into the walkie-talkie. "Thank *God* this challenge is done. You can all find your fishing rods for Friday night fishing on the rocks. We're safe to go now."

With that, he tosses the walkie-talkie Jason's way.

thirty-one

THE NIGHTS ARE JUST AS hot as the days. That's the kind of summer it is. Fishing on the rocks brings some sweet relief, but not much. Long Island Sound is barely moving; not a breeze lifts off it. Instead there is merely a heavy waning moon slung low over the water. It drops a misty swath of moonlight, and the thing is? Even that looks sultry.

Everywhere he turns, Jason sees the heat.

It's been bothering his leg, too. Perspiration at the stump is a problem on days like this.

But nothing can bother him *too* much today, not even that. Not after he took Kyle down mafia-style this morning. The moment was definitely one for the books.

"My delivery guy opened the truck's rear door," Kyle is explaining to Vinny, "and *bam*! Barlow laid into me with a fatal shot."

"*Niiice.*" Vinny casts his line out into that lone moonbeam dropping on the water. "How'd you ever get *on* the truck, Jason?"

Jason finishes up a clinch knot as he puts a hook on his line. "Money talks," he says while pulling the line tight. "And hell, it was worth the price." He looks over at Kyle and Vinny standing further back on the rocks. "Because I earned the blessed godfather point."

A sudden noise gets them all to turn. Cliff's scrambling over the low rocks. He's got his fishing rod in one hand, a basket in the other.

"Fellas," he says while approaching Jason. "Need to account for the Stony Point merchandise. Walkie-talkies, please." He sets down his fishing pole and lifts the small basket to Jason.

"Seriously?" Jason asks while unclipping the walkie-talkie from his belt. "I kind of like these little radios. There's something old-school about them." He holds it aloft over the basket without dropping it in. "My brother and I used to talk all secret code and shit with these things."

Cliff, silently, gives the basket a shake.

"Fine." Jason sets his walkie-talkie in the basket.

"Surely a man of your stature and prominence can afford to purchase his own walkie-talkie?" Cliff asks before he heads over the rocks to Kyle.

"Eh. It's not the same as illegally using the beach units," Jason remarks as he picks up his rod and scopes out a good place to cast his line.

"Matt around?" Cliff asks. "I need his walkie-talkie, too."

"He's working, as usual. Racking up the overtime," Jason says. "And where's *your* minion tonight?"

"Nicholas? He's got the late shift at the guard shack," Cliff tells him while crossing the rocks. "Said he'll swing by to check up on things here. See if the fish are biting." After the others deposit their walkie-talkies in his basket, Cliff grabs a beer from Kyle's cooler.

"I brought cannolis," Vinny tells him, motioning to an insulated tote set on a boulder. "Paige made them today."

"In this heat?" Kyle asks.

"Yeah." Vinny slowly winds in his slack line, and the clicking sound is almost like an insect buzzing over the water. "Paige said it was actually too hot to be on the beach. So she and the kids baked in the cottage all day."

"Your mother-in-law, too?" Kyle asks.

"No," Jason explains. "I brought her to the airport earlier in the week. Mom had a nice visit with Paige and me, but she's back in Florida now."

"Yeah, and I think Paige really misses having your mom around," Vinny tells him as he grabs a beer from the cooler. "So now she's tending to the neighbors instead, giving them some of her fresh cannolis. Which they loved."

"I'll bet." Jason could go for a cannoli right about now. That, or a cigarette—which he gave up months ago. But something about hanging out here on the rocks gets him craving a smoke, enough to pat down his cargo shorts pockets.

"I brought a bag of chips, too," Kyle tells Cliff. "Over there," he says, hitching his head.

Then? Nothing. Just the guys finding the boulder of their choosing to lean against, or sit on. Finding the prime spot to drop their line. The Gull Island Lighthouse beam sweeps over the misty water, catching in its path a lone rowboat paddling out in the Sound.

"I'm loving that sweet little cottage we're renting," Vinny mentions then. "You ever play horseshoes when you stayed there, Kyle?"

"Yeah, sure." Kyle sets down his fishing pole and walks over a few rocks to get closer to Vinny. "Let me ask you something, Vincenzo. You notice any odd smell in that place?"

"Smell? No. Just that sweet salt air." Vinny takes a long breath then. "Aah. Nothing like it."

"That's what I thought." Kyle pauses to dab perspiration on his face with a corner of his tee's fabric. "But Lauren's still noticing something in our new house."

"Is it the carpet, maybe?" Jason asks. "Old rugs can be musty."

"I started pulling some out," Kyle answers over his shoulder. "But the smell's still there. Ever run across that in your renos, Barlow?"

"Sometimes. Could be cigarette smoke. Pet odors, or even food smells." Jason tugs at his line when he feels a persistent fish toying with it. "The list goes on. Let me know if you need one of my guys to check on it."

Cliff, working on a cannoli and a beer, walks over to Jason. "Got a name for that show of yours yet?"

"Oh!" Vinny turns to Jason. "I've actually been thinking about this."

"Now that's a first, Vincenzo," Kyle remarks.

Vinny tosses a glance Kyle's way. "What is?"

"You. Thinking."

"Shut up, Bradford," Vinny mutters while snapping open his beer. "So Jason, I thought of something with a nice ring to it. Demo to Reno?" Vinny asks, tipping up his can for a swig.

"Has potential," Jason admits. "Not bad. But there's no cottage reference."

"Let's see." Vinny sets his can on a rock and digs for potato chips in the bag he's hoarded all evening. "What about … The Plan Man? You know, with your blueprints and all?"

"Nah." Jason waves off his idea.

Kyle gives a sidearm move and his fishing line unreels far out over the water. "You even settle on a new project yet?"

Jason looks back toward the beach. The lone cottage on the sand is dark tonight. Not a sign of life around it. In fact, the way it rises like a shadow near the patch of woods, he can barely make it out.

"Got my sights set on that one, right there." Jason nods to the gloomy-looking cottage.

"No shit." Kyle walks a few steps over and bends to catch a shadowy glimpse of it. "Last-standing cottage on the beach? Sweet."

"*Would* be, anyway. Problem is," Jason tells them, "it's not in the running. The owners didn't submit it as a project. So it's a long shot, but if I could ever seal that deal …"

Kyle gives Jason's shoulder a shove. "You've got balls, dude. Like the way you nabbed me off that truck today? You'll do it. Hell, your brother wrote about that cottage, too, in the novel Maris is working on."

"Now how'd you know that?" Vinny asks.

"She gave me a chapter to read, few weeks back. Needed some cooking pointers with a clambake scene." Kyle sits on a rock beside Jason and squints toward the beach. "It's an epic cottage, the way it's just stood there … when every cottage around it got swept out to sea in one storm or another. So it's got some sort of 'tude."

"Definitely," Vinny agrees while walking closer for a better look.

"Every now and then there's a light on," Kyle adds, "but I never see anybody. You know the owners?"

"No," Jason says. "Never connected with the folks there.

Place has always been a bit of a mystery." He looks back at the vague structure, a hulking shadow in the misty moonlight. "Especially the way it's the *only* cottage on the sand that survived the hurricanes."

Cliff maneuvers a few rocks closer, then sits against a large boulder facing the beach. "Not sure about that one." He quietly studies the cottage. "You really think it's a good idea to cold-call your televised cottage renos? You know, it *could* be insulting."

"Insulting? How so?" Jason asks.

"I mean, what if the owners take it the wrong way? Because let's face it, you'd be insinuating their property needs work and should be gutted. They might get offended."

"I guess they *could* take it that way," Jason answers. "But there's something in it for them, too. Discounted contractor work, local retailers offering free merchandise for the television plug."

Cliff squints over at Jason. "But surely you've got a stack of *other* parties eager for the chance." After a long moment, he looks out at that lone cottage again.

"What, play by the rules, you mean? And follow protocol?" Jason follows Cliff's gaze through the night's shadows, then looks at Cliff who's still preoccupied with the cottage on the beach. "The rules are the rules?"

Cliff glances at Jason, then back to the cottage. "Yeah. Something like that."

"Eh." Jason feels a sharp tug on his fishing line. "We've got a more pressing issue, anyway. Because I saw Celia today. She said Aria's christening is scheduled for next week."

"Already?" Kyle asks. "That snuck up fast."

"Yeah. So we have to settle this godfather thing once and

for all. And quick, because the godfather needs time to get a new suit, buy a gift."

"What are we going to do?" Vinny asks.

Cliff walks over to the chip bag and grabs a handful. "I had godfather status all locked down until Barlow tied the score. What's the tally anyway, Kyle?"

"Hang on, I'm on it." Kyle walks to his cooler, where there's also a tote holding their trusty black binder now crammed with competitions and stats and those winner tallies. He pulls a flashlight from the fish tackle box and shines it on the pages, flipping a few this way, then that. "Let's see. Cliff? Two points—golf cart decorations and fishing, from when you bagged that blue. Vinny, you're good for the bocce win. One point. Same for me. I've got a point for tubing." He flips to the next page. "Matt's got the karaoke point, and Jason? You're tied with the judge. Two points. Bingo and The List." With that, he slaps the binder shut and picks up his fishing rod. "So what's left?" he asks them.

"A baseball game?" Cliff suggests.

"No." Jason's line unreels as some rogue fish drags it out. "That'll take too long. We need the mother of all challenges, to finish this once and for all." He stands and grips the fishing pole with both hands as the line whistles. "You all free tomorrow?" he asks while pulling back on his catch.

"Tomorrow?" Kyle carries his fishing rod closer to where the water is sloshing on the rocks. "I'm booked all friggin' day. That new diner patio is hopping, man. Outdoor cuisine draws the crowds. Won't be free until after six, when Rob's coming in."

"Perfect timing." Jason reels in his taut line, his fishing pole bending with the strain of that resisting creature beneath the brine. "Because I have an idea for tomorrow night," he tells them as he lets the fish have more line before reeling it in. "And I know just the place."

thirty-two

WHEN YOU'RE CRUISING SHORE ROAD, Saturday night is a world of its own. Especially in the twilight hour, when the low sun casts golden rays on the passing marshes. There's something nostalgic about the sight. It's the weekend, after all, so on those marshes, guys paddle to a sweet fishing spot in their rowboats. Or just drift, maybe having a beer on the calm water. Couples linger over dinner at local seafood joints. Families take the kids out for ice cream. The stuff of memories.

"We should stop there," Vinny says from the backseat of Jason's SUV. He's pointing to a roadside ice-cream shack. Lines of people dressed in shorts and tees, flip-flops and sneakers, snake from the take-out windows.

Matt leans over for a look. "A.C. Petersen has *thee* best sundaes."

"Maybe later," Jason says as he drives straight past it. He still hasn't told them their final godfather competition is at Sound View Beach, so his friends are clueless about their destination. He gives a glance in his rearview mirror to be sure Cliff and Nick are keeping up behind him.

They pass another take-out seafood place, and a bait-and-tackle shop that also rents little motor skiffs for fishing. Shore Road, this main drag winding through the beach area, is dotted with dark taverns good for a quick drink; and shoppes specializing in vintage coastal décor—from weathered fishing buoys to seagull statues to wicker furniture. Then there are the secondhand bookstores and garden nurseries. Everything you could want during your stay at the beach. But mostly, green sweeping grasses of the saltwater marshes fill the view. Salt marshes fed by the changing tides of Long Island Sound.

No surprise, every turn *off* of Shore Road brings you to the shore, literally. The narrow sandy side streets are lined with shingled cottages and bungalows and shanties. Those streets lead straight to tucked-away beaches like Stony Point and Sound View, Hawk's Nest and White Sands—each a mere few blocks off the infamous main drag.

Shore Road gets you there. To the sea.

And to Jason's destination. Finally, he turns onto Hartford Avenue, leading to Sound View Beach.

"Seriously, guy?" Kyle asks from the passenger seat beside him. "We *did* Sound View. Vincenzo won the bocce game, remember?"

"It's not bocce this time," Jason tells him as he pulls the SUV into a curbside parking space and shuts off the engine. "It's this." With that, he nods toward the passenger window and a low, barnlike pavilion. Nods toward the Sound View Carousel's hand-painted horses just inside the wide-open doorway of that building.

"We're riding the *merry-go-round*?" Vinny asks from behind him as they all turn to take a look outside.

Matt pushes Jason's shoulder from the backseat. "You kidding us?"

"Nope." Jason gets out of the SUV. "And FYI, we're not *just* riding the carousel." As soon as his door is closed, the guys spill out of the vehicle. Cliff and Nick are fast approaching, too. Together they cross the sidewalk, scoping out the horses already. "We're going for the *brass ring*," Jason tells them.

"So what?" Nick asks. "The brass ring means you get a free ride. Big deal."

"It's more than that, dude. Listen," Jason begins.

Several picnic tables are arranged on a gravel lot outside the carousel. Big red sun umbrellas are open at each. Jason stops at a table and lifts his foot to the bench, all while considering the spinning horses. They're all jumpers, with their four feet curled beneath them as they rise and fall. Their mouths are open in whinnies, their ears back, their manes flying. Children's laughter and carousel music come from the little shoreline merry-go-round.

"Playing a bocce game. Or winning at bingo, or tubing. What the hell's it mean?" Jason turns up his hands. "Nothing, really. But grabbing the brass ring for Aria? Now we're talking. Grabbing the brass ring, hell, we're shooting for the best for her. The brass ring, man. It's all about living the good life." He turns and eyes the guys now seated at the table. "And without Sal around, it's up to us to help his daughter live the life *he'd* want for her. To live like she's got that brass ring every God damn day."

"Jesus, Barlow. That was some speech," Kyle says as he swipes away a tear.

"All right! Let's do this then," Nick says. "For Aria!"

"Wait. We have to review the rules." Cliff stands and squints over at the safety regulations posted outside the carousel pavilion. "And pay attention. Because any violation will be due cause for competition disqualification."

"Hurry up," Vinny pipes in. "Hours are from seven to nine, and it just opened. We need to get going."

"Okay, for starters," Cliff begins, "no standing to get a better shot at snagging the brass ring—which would be cheating. So stay seated on your steeds, gentlemen. And safety belts must be fastened."

"Come on, Judge," Kyle calls out. "That's for the kids, for Chrissake."

"Hey, just saying," Cliff warns him. "The rules are the rules, guy." He scans the rest of the list. "And here's a critical one. It says you *must* pull the ring with your *right* hand only. No left-hand grabs." Cliff looks at them all. "Oh, and finally? Disorderly conduct, according to the regulations, can result in a five-hundred dollar fine. All clear?"

"Clear enough," Jason says as he walks over to buy tokens. Once at the window, he turns. Kyle is right behind him, with Nick pushing past Vinny, and Matt standing with Cliff, who … wait. Is he *really* discreetly rubbing his good-luck domino—that scuffed-up talisman the commissioner once found in a parking lot? Okay, so what strikes Jason is this: For a crew so dead set against merry-go-round rides, they're *awfully* intent on getting started.

"Buy yourselves enough tokens," Jason advises. "Because this is it. We ride the horses over and over, until *someone* grabs that brass ring and wins enough points to claim the godfather title."

~

Though Jason thought this competition would be an easy coup, it's not.

As a matter of fact, it's the most nerve-wracking of them all. Because winning comes down to luck, so it's actually anyone's game. Not to mention, there are so many families with children here on a Saturday night, it takes a few rides before all the guys even get a horse.

Once everyone's mounted, a few of the rules are instantly tossed. Kyle makes that abundantly clear when he pulls the safety strap around his waist, only to be shy a foot or so. As they all are, on this kiddie ride. And as for the disorderly conduct thing? Well, Jason doesn't have much faith in that being observed, either, not if the scores are close. The rivalry might get cutthroat on the carousel.

Two things happen when the horses begin moving: the band-organ music starts up, and the ring dispenser drops into place. It's filled with dark iron rings—and only one shiny brass ring. Kyle sits on the horse directly in front of Jason, so Jason's able to keep brass-ring tabs on him. And Nick is a few behind him, easy enough to monitor with a glance back.

Problem is, ride after ride, someone *else* keeps getting the brass ring. Some kid, or a mother reaching for her young daughter, or a teenage couple.

Until finally, Jason leans over and swipes an iron ring, but sees the brass ring fall next into place in the dispenser. "Shit," he says when he turns to see the boy behind him miss the brass ring completely.

Because Nick is next, and he *won't* miss. But then he screws up when he nearly slides right off his leaping horse as he reaches for the coveted coup, saved only when his right hand quickly grabs the carousel pole to prevent his topple. At the last second, though, once he recovers his balance, he nabs it. Yes, his left hand stretches across to grab that damn brass ring.

"Sweet!" he yells as he waves the shining prize. "Score one. I'm catching up to you, Barlow."

His arrogance only lasts as long as it takes Cliff to dismount his horse and walk over to Nick. He nudges Nick's shoulder first, before extending his hand. "Turn it over."

"What?" Nick's horse rises and falls, all while Cliff's hand never wavers.

"You're disqualified from this round. Left-hand snag." Cliff gives his open hand a shake.

When Nick looks back at the ring dispenser, then forward to Jason, Jason hitches his thumb at him. "Loser," Jason calls out.

Cliff promptly turns in the brass ring to the attendant, then remounts his horse in time for the next ride to begin. Once the tokens are collected, the ring dispenser drops down and the competition begins again.

And quickly ends when a boy of about eight scores the brass ring, punches the air and whoops all at once.

"Son of a bitch," Jason mutters as the ride slows and comes to a stop.

Pressure's coming from all sides now, and Jason's not sure which is worse: being intent on securing the brass ring, or monitoring the others to see if they beat him to it. On the next round, he has to lean to the side, but he sees how Vinny and Matt both grab a dark ring. It's obvious by the utter dejection that drops over them once they realize it. Cliff goes for a ring, too, only to get the dark iron.

Meanwhile, Kyle's developed the same strategy as Jason. They both ride past the dispenser a couple of times and ignore the iron rings, hoping for a chance at the last brass. They also both know that if Jason snags it, he'll clinch the godfather title—three competition wins to Cliff's two.

So next time around, Jason watches Kyle on the horse in front of him. Eyeing the approaching dispenser, Kyle's body is slightly turned, his arm ready. A quick glance ahead beyond Kyle, to the dispenser, and Jason thinks the visible ring is absolutely the brass one.

Apparently Kyle does, too. His left hand holds the carousel pole as he leans to the side, his right arm outstretched well ahead of time—*perfectly* gauging that brass-ring grab.

Kyle's posture is loose, his arm angled just right, his finger ready to hook through that—God *damn* it—that shining brass ring he's about to secure. Jason can already see the smugness in Kyle's glance over his shoulder at him.

As the horses near the dispenser, Kyle raises his outstretched arm higher, and right before hooking the undeniably brilliant brass ring, he simply drops that hand to his lap and cruises on by, ringless.

Jason doesn't miss a second of it.

Doesn't miss a second of his best man rigging the game for him. When Jason reaches out and hooks the brass ring, it's Kyle who gives a sharp whistle, turning around with his arm outstretched to point out the official godfather.

~

"It's legitimate, man," Kyle says as they all leave the carousel. "You are Stony Point's newest godfather." When he grabs Jason in a faux chokehold, he quietly explains—so that only Jason hears. "It just felt right, man. Sal would've picked you, guy."

"Let me see that," Nick says, taking the shiny brass ring

from Jason. All the friends crowd around to check it out as though it's made of the finest gold.

"Nice of that attendant to let you keep it," Vinny tells him. "You put that ring in a safe place, *capisce*?"

Kyle stops then, on the sidewalk, and he does it. In the spirit of the movie *The Godfather*, he takes Jason's hand in both of his.

"Wait." Jason tries to tug out of Kyle's hold. "Tell me you're not."

"Oh, yes I am." Kyle bends then, and kisses the back of Jason's hand. "Godfather," he says while patting Jason's hand before releasing it. "We need to toast this momentous night. For you *are* the Don of Stony Point now, having won our Godfather Tournament of Challenges."

"Okay." Jason nods. "So, in the spirit of Italy, and in honor of Salvatore, there's no better toast than with an *Italian* ice."

"Yes!" Vinny says as he brushes past them and walks toward Vecchitto's Italian Ice stand. The sun has set, and twinkling and colorful lights shine on the sidewalk along this honky-tonk block of shops, and restaurants, and clubs. Passersby dressed in shorts and tank tops, sundresses and sandals, they laugh and talk easily. The street is busy with cars and motorcycles; a security ranger glides past on a one-wheel electric scooter.

In no time, they arrive at the white-sided storefront. Vecchitto's striped awning extends over the take-out window, and they crowd beneath it to read the menu of flavors.

"I remember Neil riding his Harley here. He'd cruise down Hartford Avenue on hot summer nights just like this one," Jason tells them.

"Oh, yeah." Vinny's first to get his paper cup filled with a mound of watermelon Italian ice, and already he spoons a scoop. "Thought he was so badass, getting a lemon ice."

"Only a true badass can pull off lemon ice on a Harley-Davidson, Vincenzo," Jason says as he takes his cup of blue-raspberry ice through the window.

Nick looks down the street to where the bar on the beach is hopping. People mill around on the sand and live music plays. "Your bro didn't even go to the bar?"

"Not always, dude." Jason puts his arm around Nick's shoulders as he explains. "See, we'd go to the arcade first."

"Wait." Nick turns and looks down the block. "The one all shuttered up?"

"That's the one," Jason tells him. "It was before your time, kid. Played pinball, Skee-Ball. Night's loser had to buy a round of, that's right, Italian ice."

As they talk and dig into their frozen delicacies, the live music from the beach calls to them. A local band's strains of guitar, and the beat of the drums beneath a July night sky—it all proves too much a lure. Spoons and cups in hand, they walk down the street and sit on a couple of benches right on the sand, barside. Rock-and-roll tunes play on from a small wooden stage; the bar's outdoor deck is crowded with patrons milling, talking, laughing; couples dance on the sand.

With Long Island Sound in front of them, and the Saturday-raucous bar crowd on the beach beside them, Kyle stands. He walks in front of both benches while eyeing Cliff, Nick, Matt, Vinny and finally, Jason. Then he raises his dripping cup to the starlit sky.

"A toast," he announces to them all. "To Aria's official godfather."

"To Jason," everyone somberly calls out as they each lift their Italian ices skyward. "*Salute!*"

~

It's late by the time the guys pile back into Jason's SUV. Jason follows behind Cliff as they drive Sound View's streets, going around the block to head out to Shore Road. The cottages here are stacked close together; porches are illuminated; folks linger outside in their yards on this warm weekend night.

Suddenly, though, Cliff's blinker is on and he's parking his car at the curb.

"Why's he stopping?" Vinny asks as Jason pulls behind him.

"Not sure." Jason inches the SUV closer.

"Think he has a flat tire, maybe?" Kyle wonders, squinting out into the night.

Matt leans forward from the backseat. "Maybe he can't see too good. I hear he had some problem with new contact lenses."

Jason kills the engine and everyone spills out of his SUV. The guys approach Cliff and Nick, already on the sidewalk in front of a small, white bungalow. Metal sunflower blossoms dot the cottage's blue window shutters; colored lights strung from the eaves twinkle in the misty night. And an extravagant garden of wildflowers of every color and height circles around the front and sides of the cottage, seeming straight out of a beach fairy tale.

Cliff and Nick stand beside a decorative wire plant cart with two thin wheels, and with mesh shelves lined with wire hearts. A beach umbrella is open beside the cart. Propped on the cart's top shelf, a hand-painted sign advertises *Flowers – $1.00 Bunch.*

There are other signs, too, leaning against the homemade stand. Painted peace signs, and a slab of white beadboard covered with another hand-painted message to *Spread Some Love.*

But it's the flowers that Cliff is carefully eyeing. White Shasta daisies and black-eyed Susans. Orange tiger lilies and red zinnias. Purple lavender and white phlox. All tiny bunches tied with twine and set in old jars and tin cans of water. The bouquets are obviously handmade from the cottage's abundant wildflower garden.

"What's going on, Cliff?" Jason asks. He stands beside Cliff and looks from him, to the simple summer bouquets filling the two wire shelves on the garden cart. On either side of the cart, light shines from solar lanterns hanging on shepherds' hooks.

"Wooing my lady," Cliff tells him with barely a glance. The flowers demand all his consideration.

"Wooing?" Vinny asks as he inches up from behind.

Cliff turns up his hands. "Don't you boys know *anything* about the art of romance? These here are one-dollar bouquets by the sea." He picks up a bunch of flowers. "And this one is special for Elsa DeLuca."

"Hey." Kyle, hand to the soul patch on his chin, walks around the cart. "You may be onto something."

"You mean, one single dollar will buy my way into Paige's heart again?" Vinny wastes no time pulling his wallet from his pocket. "She's been so busy baking cannolis for everyone, I have to win back her attention. Shit, all the neighbors want her to *buy* a place at Stony Point now, and be their *permanent* beach neighbor—and baker."

"Cannoli Cottage, man." Kyle shoves Vinny's shoulder. "Can't you see it?"

"Right," Vinny says with a shove back. "And you'd all want a seat on the deck."

But what doesn't escape Jason is how even with all the ribbing and shoving, the guys are drawn closer and closer to the twined bouquets. They touch the snapdragons, reach for the impatiens. On this warm July night, beneath the stars, they each pick a twine-tied bunch.

"Nicholas," Cliff says as Nick drops a dollar bill into the self-serve cashbox. "You keeping a secret from us?"

Nick lifts a bouquet in each hand. "What?"

Jason sidles close beside him. "Who's the lucky lady?"

Eyeing his two bouquets, Nick finally sets one down—holding onto the brightest, happiest-looking bunch of flowers there.

"You're buying a love bouquet, too?" Kyle drops a few bills in the cashbox for his own bouquet.

"That's right." Nick examines his small bunch of flowers set in an old, foggy jar of water. The summer blossoms stand tall, their velvety petals red and yellow and white. "For one very special girl." He walks toward the car, but stops briefly to face them in the dark while raising his flower jar. "My bouquet … is actually for little Aria."

thirty-three

THE SEAGULLS ARE FEEDING OUT on the bluff. It's one of Jason's favorite sounds, especially when he's in bed early mornings.

Holding a Mason jar filled with wildflowers, Maris leans back against the headboard and looks from the window, down to Jason beside her in the bed. Yes, she knows little things like that about him. Little things he simply likes.

The same way *Jason* knows that to Maris, little things like motley summer bouquets mean more than a dozen fine roses. Her fingers skim the velvety petals of a white daisy. "He loves me," she barely whispers when her finger touches one. "He loves me not," she murmurs when her finger moves to the next petal, stroking it rather than pulling it out.

Warm air drifts in through the open window, and the gulls have quieted. Still, as she moves from one petal to the next, Maris hears the slosh of easy waves breaking out on the bluff. "He loves me," she whispers again, her finger alighting on one petal, then moving to the next beside it. "He loves me not."

Suddenly there's a soft sensation on her arm. Jason's reached over and brushes her skin there.

"I don't say it enough," he says. "I love you, Maris. And I love having you around all the time. Especially after missing out on so much during our first year being married." His fingers rise up the soft of her arm, to her shoulder, then back down again. "You were away on business a lot."

Still holding the glass jar vase, Maris bends down and kisses Jason. His hand rises to her neck and tangles in her hair as he lengthens the kiss.

"He loves me," Maris says into the kiss, then pulls away and touches another petal on the white daisy. "He loves me not."

As she leans against the headboard again, Jason shifts onto his side and watches her. He crooks a hand beneath his head, his other hand toying with the silky fabric of her nightshirt.

Maris presses the daisy to the skin of her cheek, then lowers the vase to her lap again. "You know, in Neil's manuscript, he wrote about flowers. Right before the hurricane strikes, a few characters go outside the cottage and cut *all* the wildflower blossoms. They gather them up because they know the hurricane will decimate everything. So they bring them into the cottage—armloads of wildflowers—and the women find vases and glasses and jars to put them all in." She looks over at Jason and touches his dark hair. "The whole cottage is filled with wildflower bouquets when the hurricane strikes. So I'm going to put *this* pretty bouquet in the shack. It'll be my writing inspiration for the flower passage in the book."

"Tomorrow, you can."

"Tomorrow?"

"It's Sunday. Let's do something today."

Maris sets her bouquet-in-a-jar on the nightstand and lowers herself on the mattress. She turns on her side beside Jason.

"What do you want to do?" Jason asks.

"Besides lying in bed with you all day?" She kisses his jaw then. "How about if we walk down the beach to that cottage on the end. I'll come with you."

Jason toys with the braided gold chain of her star pendant. His finger traces along the length of it to the V-neck of her nightshirt. "Scope it out, as a potential reno project?" he asks.

"Uh-uh."

"No?" His hand leaves her neck and moves up to slip her nightshirt off her shoulder, which he lightly kisses.

"No. We can knock on the door and try to talk to somebody there." Maris looks over at the bedside clock and starts to sit up. "How about if we stop at The Dockside first for breakfast—which I'm sure will be on the house, with your new godfather status and all. Then we'll walk the beach."

"Okay." Before she can swing her legs out of the bed, though, Jason tugs her back down beside him. "But later." His hand glides along her side, to her hip, sliding that silky nightshirt fabric up at the same time.

Maris smiles and draws her finger along Jason's whiskered cheek. Because there's another little something she knows about him. So she leans close and kisses his neck, then his jaw, as he's lifting her nightshirt while skimming his hands beneath it.

Oh, yes. She knows.

Paradise for her Jason? A bit of Sunday morning bliss, in bed.

Once the waffles are made and syrup poured, Kyle walks around the kitchen table. He stands behind Hailey first, hands on her shoulders, and kisses the top of her sleepy head. When he moves to Evan's chair, his son squirms, so Kyle high-fives him instead. But he sneaks in a hair-muss, too, at the end.

"I'm off to work, kiddos," he says after turning on the countertop TV for them. "Don't forget to drink your orange juice, you hear me?"

When they quietly just eat without responding, Kyle glances over at them. "Be good for Mom today, and I'll bring you something from work."

"A toy!" Hailey calls out.

"Leftover brownies," adds Evan.

In his office at the diner, Kyle keeps a file cabinet drawer filled with dime-store toys—animal figurines and spinning tops and baseball mitts and plastic jewelry kits. He'll bring them both something tonight.

He finds Lauren on the front porch now. She wears frayed denim shorts and a black tank top as she stretches to string white twinkly lights around the porch windows. Her blonde hair is up in a messy topknot, with wisps already escaping in the heat. He knows that putting white twinkly lights in the windows was a dream of hers. Another tangle of lights sits on the porch table, beside her tin-can one-dollar wildflower bouquet.

"Don't those flowers look pretty there?" Lauren asks over her shoulder as she fusses with the lights.

"Pretty as you are, Ell."

"You going in to work now?" she asks. "Bet it'll be busy on a hot Sunday. When the ladies helped me paint this window trim last night, they all said they haven't been cooking in this heat." She tucks a wayward light. "Even—now here's a shocker—*Elsa* stopped cooking!"

Kyle walks closer to Lauren. "I've got a few minutes. Let me help you with that." He takes the string of lights and hooks them across the top of the window. After he does, he steps back right as Lauren flips the light switch and the paned window twinkles.

"Oh, so magical," she says, then spins easily around, arms outstretched, on the porch. "I'm putting them on *every* day!"

It's what she'd wished for, ever since the day they first looked at this house. *We'll hang little white lights around the porch windows at Christmastime*, Lauren had said as they toured the porch—when Kyle had a panic attack thinking of the financial commitment about to happen. *No, all the time*, Lauren had added, sounding pensive, yet full of hope, as she pictured the porch aglow.

When Kyle walks outside to his old pickup truck now, he glances back at the twinkling porch window, knowing one thing for certain. Yes, if nothing else in his mundane, workaday life, at least he knows this: Little dreams do come true, living on this bay of blue.

~

"Be sure to whisk the eggs," Elsa calls out from beyond the room divider.

Cliff, wearing an apron tied around his waist, finds his whisk in the kitchenette drawer.

"Whisking puts more air into them," Elsa continues. "So you'll have fluffier scrambled eggs."

Standing at the trailer's small countertop, Cliff gives the eggs a vigorous whisk, scraping along the bowl's sides, before pouring the mixture into a pan on his dual-burner hot plate.

The eggs sizzle nicely in the melted butter, and a comforting aroma rises. He'll let them set a minute, while quickly putting out two dishes and glasses on his bistro table.

When he's back at the hot plate, he notices the dollar bouquet on the countertop. Elsa had said his trailer needed the flowers more than her place, and so they brought them here last night.

And stayed here.

So he takes the pretty summer flowers and sets the bouquet on the table between their dishes. It gives just the right café touch to the cramped space. Cramped, or intimate, depending. After lifting and tipping the eggs so that they're perfectly scrambled, he divides them among their two plates, then returns the pan to the cooling hot plate.

All the while, though, Elsa is silent. No chatty comments come from the futon as she relaxes in her pajamas there. No remarks about what she'll do today, or if she needs to stop at Maritime Market for fresh food. No more talk about Jason being godfather, though *nothing* could stop her proud prattling last night.

Not a word comes now. Just silence.

He takes a peek beyond the room divider to see her lying on the futon, wearing her leopard-print glasses. The bedside lamp is on as she reads her Justice of the Peace guidebook. So Cliff leaves her be, and gets the orange juice carton from the mini-fridge to fill the two small glasses. He's happy just to have this quiet morning time with Elsa today.

Until Elsa unexpectedly rushes into the kitchen area, nearly knocking down his room divider. And … she's crying?

"What's wrong?" Cliff asks as he sets down the juice carton. "Your handbook brought you to tears?"

"No." Elsa sits at the table. She wears a light robe over her pajamas; her sleep-mussed hair is tucked behind an ear; her reading glasses perch low on her nose. "I'm crying from reading this text message from my sweet niece Maris." She sets down the phone that he suddenly notices she'd been clutching. "Cliff? How can life be so beautiful, but so aching at the same time?"

Now there's a question that anyone who lives a full and layered life will occasionally cross. It's a question that can either break your heart … or fill it with warmth. So since Cliff's not sure where Elsa's going with her question, he unties his apron and cautiously sits across from her.

"Everything's okay, I hope?" he quietly asks.

Elsa simply nods as another tear escapes. "Look," she says as she slides her cell phone closer to him. "Maris texted me a photograph of her christening gown. She and Eva both wore it at their christenings. Which I was at … both of them."

Cliff looks from the lacy gown pictured on the phone screen, up to Elsa.

"Maris wonders if Celia might have Aria wear the gown," Elsa explains.

"Do you think she would?"

With a wistful smile and tears still lining her cheeks, Elsa tips her phone back to consider the baby gown. "I don't know," she whispers. "But I *will* ask Celia." Elsa looks up at Cliff then, her eyes still spilling with tears. Tears hinting at the deep, deep connection Elsa has with her nieces. "I'm telling you, Clifton," Elsa quietly says, "what a beautiful sight that would be. The gown my sister June chose connecting her daughters with *my* granddaughter."

The words so move Elsa that—for the third time in as

many weeks—Cliff Raines does it again. Yes, he pulls his hanky from his shirt pocket … this morning for Elsa to dab her dampened face.

Sal once told Celia that he was very particular about what he kept on his bedside nightstand. It had to be something he could open his eyes to in the morning and feel good about. Could reach over and touch. Could smile at. A seashell from the beach, or his childhood toy sailboat, or a photograph of Celia.

So last night, after Nick dropped off Aria's dollar bouquet with the grand announcement that Jason would be the godfather, Celia put the little jar-vase of daisies and zinnias on a table beside Aria's crib. Those bright summer flowers will be the first thing she sees when she opens her eyes.

"Good morning, Aria!" Celia says now as she lifts her baby from the crib. Fluffy wisps of Aria's dark hair fall across her forehead. "Did you see your pretty flowers?" After kissing the baby's cheek, Celia lifts the simple bouquet and touches the velvety flower petals to Aria's skin. "Aren't they so soft?" Celia whispers as her baby smiles at the touch. "Look. Those are daisies, and a black-eyed Susan, too." She turns the glass jar. "And look at the red zinnias."

As they stand there in the sunlit nursery, a thought occurs to Celia. Gradually, her memories are beginning to feel happy again. It seems to have happened since coming back to Stony Point. And as she sits in the rocking chair and settles Aria on her lap, it's apparent. Her new moments of happiness might have something to do with sharing memories of Sal *with* her daughter now. No longer is Celia holding those sweet thoughts close to her broken heart. No.

She bends and kisses the top of the baby's head. Now, she has this.

"One time, your daddy brought *me* Sunday morning flowers." Celia's voice is soft, the words close to Aria's ear. "When I told him no one had ever given me a Sunday bouquet before, he was glad. Because he said that I would *always* remember it then." She looks over at Aria's dollar bouquet in its glass jar. The colorful blossoms seem to be smiling, too.

And Celia remembers holding her own bouquet. Remembers Sal, remembers his sailor's knot bracelet on his wrist as he set his hands on her shoulders, bent close and kissed her that morning.

"My flowers were in an old milk jar," Celia whispers to Aria. "Daddy said he bought them at a little roadside flower hut that reminded him of a storefront back in Italy …"

A hint of a salty sea breeze flutters the curtains as she tells her daughter the story.

thirty-four

WHILE TALKING ON THE PHONE Wednesday morning, Jason sits in his big desk chair and spins it to face the barn's open double slider. Outside, the blazing July sun beats down.

"What've you got for me, Jason?" Trent asks. "Narrowing down those cottage submissions?"

Jason leans back, thinking he has one of two things—either the perfect cottage in the palm of his hand … or nothing. Because when he and Maris knocked on the door of the cottage on the beach over the weekend, no one answered.

"I'm closing in on something," Jason assures Trent. But at the same time, his producer's closing in on *him*. With good reason, too.

"You know we're under deadline," Trent reminds him. "Need to be filming in August. Not to mention the legalities beforehand: releases, contracts. So lock it down, Jason. I'm counting on you."

"I'll do my best. Just sit tight."

"Guess I have no choice. In the meantime, we're still brainstorming names here at the station. Trying to get just the right branding for your show. And typically you would not have a say in this, but you were such a dog in the contract negotiations …"

Jason spins his chair back and brushes through a few papers on his desk. "The right lawyer works wonders," he says into the phone pressed to his ear.

"Tell me about it. So any of these names work for you?"

"Let me have it."

"Can-Do Cottage?"

"Nix."

"Okay. How about Summer House Arrest? It's got some edge to it, Barlow. Thought it might fly."

"Summer House Arrest? Sounds more like a teen reality show."

"Here's one, then. A Shore Thing?"

"What? It doesn't even mention cottages! And people would spell it wrong and end up calling it A Sure Thing."

"You're probably right. Well, you and that beach crew of yours come up with anything?"

"Not yet, but I put the word out." Jason straightens his papers, antsy to move forward with Trent, which means finding a way to negotiate a reno of the lone cottage on the beach, once and for all.

"Clock's ticking," Trent warns him. "So I'll be calling you for updates later. Don't go AWOL on me, guy."

AWOL. Right. Jason tried that, last summer. Days after Sal died, he definitely went AWOL. Absent without leave. Without much explanation. Just disappeared into the night, the evening after Sal's funeral. Drove as far away from memories, as far away from the sea, as he could get. But distance couldn't alleviate his pain. It did something else, though. Those forty-five minutes when he booked made Jason realize what a selfish son-of-a-bitch move that was. His leaving devastated everyone around him.

And he quickly ended up right back here, at the sea again.

Which is where he finds himself later that Wednesday morning—walking with the dog on the hard-packed sand below the high tide line. The ground is cool and firm beneath his gait. He'll never believe that any other place on earth can feel as soothing to body and mind. But this time, the mind part's not working; he has no clarity in his thoughts.

So maybe he headed here seeking out his brother's spirit. Because in the still heat hanging over Stony Point, there's no other place to actually *hear* that hushed voice. Not in the silent barn studio. Not out on the calm bluff. But on the beach, gentle waves roll ashore in easy splashes.

"You around, Neil?" he murmurs. Or thinks. His own voice is so quiet, it's hard to tell. "I need help."

Madison, though leashed, tries to veer into the water. Jason obliges. He moves closer and gives her enough lead to walk through the shallows.

What's up, bro? Neil's whisper comes to him just as the dog sloshes a bit deeper.

Jason strains to hear more. So he tugs the dog close again and heads back to the packed sand near the driftline—away from children splashing in the waves; away from boys boogie-boarding across the water-covered sand.

"Time crunch, bearing down on me," Jason says while lifting his sunglasses off the top of his head and putting them on against the day's bright skies. He and Madison step around families stationed with their beach gear at the water's edge. Near the rocks at the end of the beach, a seagull swoops low and gives a long, plaintive call.

That's a tough one, Jason swears he hears. *Can never fight time.*

Doesn't Jason know it. Hell, if he'd only had ten more seconds, ten years ago, Neil might still be alive. Might be walking the beach with him, figuring out how to secure the next renovation for his show. At the rocks, Jason leans against a large boulder and faces that lone cottage on the sand.

Just then, skimming the Sound's surface, a Jet Ski flies past. A silver plume of the sea sprays up behind it.

Remember, every cottage tells a story.

Jason tips his head toward the water, the voice. Problem is, telling *this* cottage's story isn't up to him. "It's up to the owners," he says under his breath.

Like shit, Jay.

A sun-bleached stick that washed up on the beach catches Jason's eye. After unhitching Madison's leash, he picks up the driftwood, hits it in his open hand while considering what to do, then throws the driftwood across the sand, in the direction of that one cottage. When his dog lopes after the stick, he follows behind her. Listening.

But the whole time, nothing more from his brother. No whispers in the waves, no hushed voice in their hissing retreat over the wet sand, no divulgences in a puttering distant motorboat.

So Jason slowly walks toward the cottage. It rises before him on stilts; a beached rowboat leans beneath it; the sun shines on the empty wraparound deck. As he walks the tideline, he rubs his knuckle across his scarred jaw while keeping the cottage in his sights.

Until he trips, such that he has to look behind him because, actually? It felt more like he'd been pushed. But no one follows him—no one you can see, anyway. There is only the meandering seaweed line he'd been walking beside. That, and the abandoned remnants of a sandcastle. So did he trip on leaning sandy battlements and fallen towers? Did he stumble in the shallow moat still encircling the castle? He looks behind himself again.

Or did his brother lightly shove him?

Jason stops, glances at the expansive sky over the Sound, gives a slight salute no one would even notice, then turns toward the cottage before him.

He hesitates only for a second before climbing the stairs to that deck, where he knocks on the door for the second time this week.

~

They're quiet, the two of them. Celia sits on the top step of her front stoop, and beside her, Aria is in her baby-bouncer seat. Her daughter's little hands stretch for the small, plush animals hanging from the toy bar across the seat. Silently, Celia reaches over and gives Aria's bare foot a tender wiggle.

Then? Then Celia settles the guitar across her lap and tunes the instrument. Holding one string down at the fifth fret, she plucks the next string with the other hand, then turns the tuning peg before plucking the string again. All the while, she hopes the fresh air might tire out the baby. Celia's fingers tune each string before she settles upon a familiar song and lightly strums. A lone robin chirps in the summer stillness, seeming to sing along with her melancholy melody.

But a motion catches her eye then. Holding a thin box, Maris walks across the inn's front yard toward the guest cottage. She wears faded denim shorts with a loose white tank top, her gold star pendant glinting in the sunlight.

"Hey, Maris," Celia says, still strumming. "You here to see Elsa? She's out meeting with the caterers, planning a feast for Aria's baptism."

"Sounds like my aunt." Maris climbs the few steps and sits beside Celia on the stoop. "But I'm actually here to see you. And I've got to tell you … Jason is thrilled to be godfather to Sal's child. He and Sal were so close."

Celia stops her song and slowly draws her pick across the guitar strings. "Jason meant the world to Sal," she finally says as she plays the opening notes of her reworked *Twinkle, Twinkle, Ocean Star*. "He told me Jason was like the brother he never had."

Maris reaches over and simply pats Celia's arm. "You look tired today." Maris sets the box on the porch floor behind her. "Everything okay?"

"The baby's been fussy the past few nights, not sleeping too well. It must be this heat. So I thought I'd sit out here on the stoop and let her breathe that salt air she was named after."

Maris turns to Aria and tickles her cheek. "You're not sleeping, sweetie?"

Celia watches her talk soothingly to the baby. Maris leans close and asks, "Are you playing with Mr. Birdie?" When she says it, she takes Aria's hand and taps her tiny fingers on the fluffy bird on the toy bar.

"Do you and Jason have any plans?" Celia asks.

"Plans? For what?"

"Little ones." Celia nods to Aria. "A playmate for Aria?" She reaches over and gives the bouncy seat a nudge, setting it in motion. "I guess they'd be cousins, if you had a baby, too."

"Right now, my book became my baby. I feed it, nourish it, and am raising it until I'll send it out in the world."

Celia strums slowly. "When you have a draft done," she says, setting her open hand across the strings, "I have some free time while Aria naps. I can read it, if you need a fresh pair of eyes to give it a look."

"That's really nice of you, Cee." Quiet then, Maris reaches over and touches Aria's hair.

"Do you want to hold her?" Celia asks.

"Maybe in a minute. I want to show you something, first." Maris reaches to the side for her box. She removes the top, carefully unfolds delicate tissue paper and lifts out a lacy christening gown.

"Oh, Maris! It's *so* beautiful," Celia quietly exclaims.

Sitting on the stoop, Maris drapes the gown over her knees. "I'm offering it to you for Aria to wear. It has so much history from Sal's side of the family. It's actually a family heirloom," she says while brushing a wrinkle from the gown's lace.

Quickly, Celia sets her guitar against the porch railing and lifts the gown. "How incredibly thoughtful, Maris," Celia says. "I'd love to have Aria christened in it."

Nodding, Maris explains. "I hoped you would. Because it turns out Eva and I were *both* christened in this gown. And making it even more special, Elsa was at each christening. With Sal, too, at Eva's." Maris reaches an arm around Celia's shoulders and pulls her close, saying, "So the last time this gown was worn, Sal was actually there. As a child."

Celia hugs her back before taking the gown from Maris. She holds it up to the sunlight, making the lace and sheer tulle shimmer. Then, with a glance at Aria in her bouncer seat, she whispers, "This will be perfect."

"Come on. Come on." Jason paces outside the door. He'd knocked twice, stepped back and waited patiently for a response, then knocked once more. "Damn it," he says under his breath now. Because the *one of two things* he thought he had for Trent will most likely be the second of the two: nothing. With each silent moment of waiting, the hope of having this cottage in the palm of his renovating-hands fades.

Apparently no one is home here. A blazing hot summer—and this cottage on the sand remains empty. So he shields the sun from his eyes and leans close to a large window beside the door. But because of the brightness outside, the cottage's interior is too dark to pick out any architectural details. Finally, Jason whistles for Maddy, clips on her leash and returns to the beach.

Before he gets far, something niggles at him, though. Enough for him to turn and look back at the cottage. Wait. Did a curtain move in the breeze? There … in an upstairs window. But there *is* no breeze. None at all. So he squints up at the second-level window where a lace curtain now hangs perfectly straight. Was someone standing behind it, someone who pressed the curtain aside and watched him leave? If so, they quickly dropped the curtain when he turned.

"Yoo-hoo!" a voice suddenly calls out. "Jason!"

He turns to see Eva water-walking with her daughter, Taylor. They both wear bathing suits, and look to be sidestepping a jellyfish as they scoot this way, then wade that way, out of the Sound.

"Hi, Uncle Jason," Taylor says. "And Maddy!"

Jason gives one last look back at that suspicious curtained window, then leads Madison to the water's edge. Eva gives him a light hug and Taylor goes straight for the dog, rubbing the scruff of the German shepherd's neck.

"Can I take her for a walk?" she asks.

Jason looks at the crowded beach. "How about to the rocks and back?" He hands her the leather leash. "Less people thataway."

"Cool." Taylor loops the leash around her hand. "Come on, girl."

"You behave yourself, Maddy," Jason tells the dog as he pats her shoulder before Taylor leads her away.

"And what are you doing here?" Eva asks him then. "Shouldn't you be working?"

"I *am* working, actually," he tells Eva. "Trying to connect with the family that owns that cottage." He hitches his head in its direction.

"That one? On the beach?" Eva lifts her sunhat and glances over at it.

"Absolutely. Would *love* for it to be my show's next reno. But I can't make any headway. Don't even know who lives there. Or if anyone even *does* live there anymore, seeing how it's been empty all summer."

"Somebody must. Because this spring, a lady actually stopped by my office. She asked about listing the property as a summer rental. I even had her fill out a spec sheet. You know, number of bedrooms, bathrooms, amenities like air conditioning."

"Seriously?" Jason lifts his sunglasses to the top of his head.

Eva nods. "Problem is, then she had a change of heart. I couldn't get a reason out of her. She just changed her mind," Eva says with a snap of her fingers. "Like that." Eyeing the lone gray cottage once more, she drops her voice. "You know, I *might* still have her contact information, which I *could* share with you. Even though it goes against my real estate principles."

"Principles?" Jason squints at her closely. "Principles, let's see, like breaking into Foley's a couple summers ago when it was on the market? And sneaking the party of all parties in the back room there? Or principles like using your lockbox code to check out cottages on the market, just to take photographs for your own design ideas?"

"What? How did you—"

"There are no secrets at Stony Point, Eva. You know that. Not to mention, I *am* married to your sister."

"Fine. Fine, you caught me red-handed then, *bending* the rules." Eva motions for Taylor to head back now. "But heck, we're family. So why don't you stop by my place and I'll see what I can come up with? Me and Tay are about ready for lunch."

It's a long shot; Jason knows it. But when a long shot is all you've got, you can't turn it down.

So he grabs onto that long shot and crosses the beach beneath the unrelenting midday sun. Maybe this way, he won't have to tell Trent later that, unfortunately, he's got the second of two things. He's got nothing.

The sun beats down on them, slowing their pace as they leave the beach and walk the few blocks to Eva's big Dutch on the marsh. The roads are gritty with sand; garden flags hang limp; waves of heat rise from withered lawns. The whole way there, Eva tries to remember details as Jason listens closely, in search of answers.

thirty-five

BUT NO ANSWERS CAME.

All Jason got from Eva was an old phone number, which he called.

A call that went unanswered, so he left a voicemail.

Which went ignored.

Reality bites hard when it's not as you'd hoped. Of the two possible things he had lined up for his green-lighted TV show, days later he actually *did* end up with the second: nothing.

Early Sunday afternoon, frustrated and disappointed, he finds himself standing outside the shingled walls of St. Bernard's Church. The salty breezes rising off Long Island Sound have weathered the shingles a dusty gray. Stained glass windows around the church are tipped open to let any of that same salty air drift in. Drift in, because there's not been much of a blowing sea breeze all summer long on the Connecticut coast.

Maybe he'll find answers here. Or pray for a miracle. Because St. Bernard's is the one place that's opened its doors to Jason at the most pivotal times in his life: Neil's memorial masses; Jason's wedding to Maris; Sal's funeral.

Today, he and Maris walk in for Aria's baptism. Jason wears a crisp checked button-down with his khaki suit. In the heat, his jacket is loose, a silk handkerchief folded into the chest pocket. Maris, wearing a pale gray sheath, is at his side.

The July afternoon, like every single one before it, is warm and still. At least the church, used only in the summertime for the swelling vacationing crowds, has swirling ceiling fans to move around the motionless air.

They enter the church vestibule, where Jason dips his fingers into the holy water font and blesses himself. Once Maris does, too, they walk down a side aisle. But halfway to the altar, Maris slows and pulls on his arm.

"Do you want to light a candle?" she asks, nodding to the tiered bank of votive candles in a side alcove.

"Actually, I do," Jason tells her. "For Sal, on the day of his daughter's christening."

Together, they veer into the alcove in the hushed church. Rows of candles—blue and cream, several of them lit and flickering—are on the tiered candle stand. Jason drops a few dollars into the offering box, then moves in front of the candles. Though he feels Maris waiting behind him, his thoughts are already elsewhere. It just happens; he can't even help it. The day comes back to him from last August when Sal was still here, still alive. In this very church, it was Sal who lit a candle for Jason's brother on the day of Neil's memorial mass.

But it's what Sal said then that still stays with Jason. It was after a morning spent greeting friends and family, and entering a church crowded with folks stopping and hugging Jason, with plans for a busy brunch after the mass. Sal summed up the hectic event once the church emptied afterward. He and Jason lingered behind, and were headed out through the side alcove …

"I thought this day for Neil would be more intimate," Sal said as he stopped at the bank of flickering candles. "But this is the best part, right here," he murmured after touching a lighted taper to a candle wick. "Lighting a candle."

Then he persuaded Jason to ditch the mobbed brunch to go drifting in Sal's rowboat in the lagoon. "To truly honor your brother," he said. "Being in one of his favorite places."

And that afternoon, beneath the summer sun, Jason told Sal stories of his brother as the rowboat floated; as dragonflies hovered near the marsh grasses; as a red-winged blackbird trilled; as a lone fish ruffled the water's surface.

Now, Jason touches a taper's burning ember to a blue candle's wick. As the flame takes hold, he thinks of the man he's missing deeply today.

"This one's for you, Salvatore," he whispers.

~

As Jason quieted, and first bowed his head in brief prayer, Maris backed up a few steps. She gave him his privacy as he thought of Salvatore; as he lit the wick, then quickly blessed himself once more; as she noticed muted sunlight illuminating the blues and yellows of the stained glass windows; and especially as she noticed the church filling with guests for Aria's baptism. There's Elsa, and Celia's father, and even Celia's hometown friends George and Amy.

But when Jason turns and nods that he's ready, she stops him.

"I've never lit a candle in church," she softly says.

"You haven't?"

In the shadowy space, she shakes her head and steps toward the votive candles. "How do you do this?" she asks over her shoulder.

Jason moves beside her. "You light the flame with thoughts of someone, here *or* gone. When you light the candle, it shows your intention to say a prayer for that person."

The flames hold Maris' gaze. Something about their flicker reminds her of starlight, twinkling in the dark night sky. Or ocean stars, even, flickering atop the dark blue sea. The burning candles are just as hypnotizing as celestial light. "So all these flames signify prayers being said?" she asks without taking her eyes off of them.

"Yes."

In a moment, Jason picks up a taper, lights the tip in a candle flame and hands her the taper.

Maris chooses a candle off to the side. She reaches over and touches her burning taper to the wick. And it's as though she's creating a new star; a tiny, fleeting star that she can find anytime she's here. Her eyes drop closed against stinging tears then, as she bends her forehead to her clasped hands.

Oh, Mom, she thinks. *How I wish you were here.*

The sunlight dropping in through the stained glass windows casts an unfamiliar illumination inside the church. It's the first thing Cliff notices, that bluish-green tint. Maybe because it reminds him of a sight from decades ago when he was a young boy. It was the day a deadly hurricane hit the state, and the morning sky had the same unfamiliar shade as the church does now. Surprisingly, it isn't the ocean swells that Cliff often recalls happening before that hurricane struck; or the whipping wind ushering in the massive storm.

No, it's the foreboding color of the sky. He remembers his mother telling him that the heavy storm clouds were filled with water. And the yellow light of the rising sun hitting those waterlogged clouds cast a pale green hue on the beach.

Later that day, the storm lived up to the ominous color of those skies.

Now, though, Cliff's in a rush as the church begins to fill up. With one more glance to the stained glass windows, he blesses himself and walks behind the pews in the direction of the candle stand. But he's a little surprised, too. He'd thought that lighting candles was an old-fashioned thing. So when he hurries down the side aisle to do just that, he's taken aback to see Jason there, holding Maris' arm after she touches a taper to a wick. Who'd have thought the kids would be lighting candles today? But he's glad for that, just the same. Glad that certain traditions carry on.

As Cliff passes them, he nods and pats Jason's shoulder. After putting a dollar in the offering box, Cliff looks at the candle stand and thinks of his son, Denny. Oh sure, they're close enough. Problem is, *distance* separates them. Finally settled in at Stony Point as the beach commissioner, Cliff finds he wants to spend more time with his son now. Being in St. Bernard's Church today, he remembers coming here for Sal's funeral. Surprisingly, *that's* who has him thinking of Denny.

Sal, who breezed into their lives last year and suddenly left before anyone was ready.

With that thought, Cliff lights a candle for Denny. Maybe he'll invite his son to visit on a Friday fishing night. The water would be lapping at shore, the moon rising low over the sky.

Yes. It might be nice sitting out on the rock jetty, together with his son. It's time now.

~

There's a veritable procession in the church today. But what Kyle notices is that so many familiar faces are making a stop at the flickering candle stand. From the pew where he's sitting, Kyle's been watching them closely. So closely that Lauren finally nudges him.

"What are you looking at?" she whispers.

In the hushed church, with only a soft strain of organ music filling the space, Kyle stands beside her and nods to the side alcove. "Let's go light a candle, Ell. Come on."

"Now?"

"Before the ceremony begins." He takes his wife's hand. "You're Aria's godmother, after all."

"Oh, good!" Lauren quietly says, following him out of the pew. "I'll light one for the baby, then." She catches up and loops her arm through his. "This is so beautiful, Kyle," she whispers while walking beside him in her ankle-length sleeveless sundress. "I'm so glad everyone's gathered together like this. For a *happy* occasion instead of a sad one."

When they get to the glimmering bank of candles, Lauren quickly lights one right in the center. A cream-colored one.

"For Aria," she murmurs, then dips her head for a long moment.

When she's done, Kyle lights his candle—one off in the far corner. He's sure Lauren thinks that his is for Aria, too.

But he doesn't tell Lauren that it's not.

Doesn't let on that once a month, he secretly stops in here before work—early—and lights a candle for someone who neither Lauren, nor any of their friends, would ever dare mention.

For the brother Kyle hasn't spoken to in over a decade, at least.

Hasn't seen, either.

Let alone uttered his name.

And he won't. Ever again. The *most* he can do, driven by some pathetic shred of conscience, is this.

Yes, he lights a candle with guarded, private thoughts of that brother.

When Lauren gently touches his shoulder, Kyle blesses himself and straightens his shirt cuffs beneath his suit jacket sleeves. He takes Lauren's hand and first glances to the altar, and the large crucifix hanging behind it. Then, together—while waving to a few friends on the way, while passing a confessional tucked into the side wall—he and Lauren walk side by side back to their pew.

thirty-six

"I DO," JASON SAYS.

The words come without hesitation, as he professes his faith in God as the Father, Son and Holy Spirit. Standing before the baptismal font with Lauren on one side of him, and Celia holding Aria on the other, he *does* believe.

There have been times, granted, when he didn't …

A decade ago, endless hours in his hospital bed after the motorcycle accident were the worst. Because no God, Jason felt, would subject such senseless loss on him, on his family. An accident that took not just Neil's life, but Jason's mobility, too.

For what? he'd asked God from behind closed eyes, able to only barely move. It was all he could do to even think. *Death and destruction inflicted on us, for what purpose?* he'd whisper in the dark of night, when only the dim illumination of hospital equipment lit the space around him. *Why?*

One time, his father—still alive then—sat with him well

into the night. He could figure that Jason was in a bad way, and that the nights were the worst. His father had lived through plenty of scary nights himself, sitting with wounded comrades in the jungles of 'Nam. He knew. *Pain is amplified in dark silence,* he used to tell Jason and Neil when they were boys. *It feeds off it, the pain growing with each passing hour.*

So in Jason's hospital room, his father sat in a bedside chair near the window. Long after visiting hours were over, he remained. Long after lights dimmed with only the late shift working, Jason's father was there, still. When Jason grew agitated with his pain, and grief, his father stayed with him.

"You take one day at a time, son. One day," his father said.

Wordlessly, Jason turned his head and squinted over at him in the chair. As he did, he felt the bandages pulling on his bruised face, and fresh stitches tight along his swelled jawline.

"That's all that matters," his father tried to assure him. "During the war, I'd get through one day in the jungles, then check it off that I kept myself alive. One day, then another. You can, too."

Still, Jason only silently met his father's gaze, then closed his eyes. He wanted sleep so badly, but there was too much else in the way. His body—battered and covered with road burns—ached; his heart was devastated; his anger seethed.

In the quiet, Jason's father reached over. His hand found some space on Jason's arm not monitored, not wired, not tubed. And when he did, he squeezed as though giving his own strength. "God'll get you through it."

Which is all it took, those five words. They unhinged Jason, when he'd thought he'd already hit bottom. His father's remark got Jason to struggle, to attempt sitting up, to thrash in his twisted hospital gown beneath the sheet. The most he could do was prop himself on his elbows and glare at his father. "That's fucking bullshit."

"What?" his father asked, leaning close and still clasping his son's arm.

"Bullshit. There *is* no God, so don't insult me with that crap." Exhausted, Jason dropped back onto the hospital bed, just sank down, flat on his back, and gazed at the ceiling. "Because, why, Man? Why'd You take Neil?" he asked, raising his hands with anger. "My brother, shit. Come on, God, who'd he ever hurt? And then my leg, too?" Jason glanced at the horror of it; at his left leg, with white dressing all the way up his thigh. Those bandages—tight and well-secured—wrapped around and around, from the top of that thigh down to his knee before stopping just below it.

Stopping where his shin *should* extend.

"Wasn't my leg enough for You?" Jason asked, his voice low. "You couldn't have stopped there, God Almighty, Heavenly Father?"

That was all he could manage. Because the thoughts, the *anger*, spent every bit of his energy. So he closed his eyes and said no more, doing nothing at all but breathe.

In a minute, or thirty—there was no way of knowing, as time was as fluid as the consciousness he moved in and out of—his father let go of his arm. Jason felt it, felt that sensation of his grip loosening. He heard the chair creak, too, as his father sat back in the shadowed room filled with blinking monitors, and tubes, and smells.

And silence.

Until Jason opened his eyes and looked over at his father watching him closely.

"So you *do* believe in God, then." His father said it without moving.

Jason simply turned his head away.

"If you didn't," his father persisted, "you wouldn't be asking Him those questions."

~

And here Jason stands now—beside Lauren as godmother—vowing to renounce sin, and professing faith in, that's right, in God as they renew their own baptismal vows.

Once the vows are said, they move to the baptismal font. Celia carries Aria there, the baby's gown draped in folds beneath Celia's arms. Together, the three of them—Celia, Jason and Lauren—support the baby over the consecrated holy water in the stone receptacle.

The church is quiet. Ceiling fans paddle the warm air above.

That's when it happens.

The robed priest administers the blessed sacrament. Invoking God in the cleansing of original sin, his voice is low, his words fluid. They're only a rhythm now, sounding like a brook flowing gently over stones. Calming, somehow. And that sound alone—that quiet, low rhythm of the priest's reassuring voice talking about God's presence and power—takes Jason back ten years to that same night in the hospital.

Standing in St. Bernard's Church as Aria is baptized, what he hears *instead* is his father's voice, talking late into that dark night, his voice as low and rhythmic as the priest's now.

~

A few months into my tour, his father began as Jason grew fatigued from his own wearied thoughts, *any notion of getting out of 'Nam was gone. All hope was dashed. No one was coming for us except the Viet Cong; the heat was, too, coming at us like an assault, the way we couldn't breathe sometimes. And the sweat? Sweet Jesus, jungle sweat so thick, you wanted to wipe it off your skin. Creatures, too, came at you. They never stayed off my body at night. That's all that was coming for us.*

Worse, even, was what you couldn't see—enemy presence. It kept me always wary. Any movement might reveal our location and so had to be calculated, or else we'd all be dead.

And at night? Usually the only light was enemy fire. But sometimes, you didn't know if it was the VC's or actually our own. Who was who. What was what. Day from night. Sleep from wakefulness. All you knew was that you had to get through twenty-four hours alive, then try again tomorrow. Because, yeah, all hope was gone, long gone.

Or so I thought.

Until one night, a night so goddamn dark I couldn't see my hand in front of my face, a buddy lurched beside me. He grappled through that blackness, shook my arm—hard—and pleaded with me.

"Teach me," he begged.

"What?" I turned, but couldn't see him there. There was only noise. Insects, buzzing so loud, the sound was a nightmare.

"Teach me. Please. I got nothing else."

"What are you talking about?" I whispered harshly.

"To pray. Shit, teach me a prayer."

I slowly sat up and squinted through the darkness.

"I hear you praying," he whispered. "I hear you saying religious words."

Hell, I didn't even know it. That's how desperate I was. Didn't even realize I was actually murmuring some pathetic plea to the Lord to get me through the night. Not until this guy told me.

"How do you do it?" he asked, his hand roughly shaking my arm.

"Pray? Didn't you ever pray?"

"No."

"How do you talk to God then?"

"I don't. Never did. Wasn't raised that way."

"You shittin' me?"

"No religion at home. Parents had none."

Well, I didn't know how a soldier could last a day, never mind months, without some kind of prayer in this hellhole. Even a made-up prayer. Didn't matter, as long as it gave you something to wait for—an answer to that prayer. So, hope, I guess.

And he'd lost all his, this soldier beside me. His voice cracked, his body trembled. I almost felt like I had to hold him down, that he was at the end of his rope and about to bolt into the jungle.

Off in the distance, enemy fire flashed. The sound reverberated, too.

That's what my life had come to. Lying in the blackness, waiting to be attacked, some random tarantula crossing my neck, sweat pooling on my skin. And apparently, without even realizing it, praying.

So I sank back down and raised my finger to my mouth. "Shh. Just breathe, man. Okay?"

"No, you got to teach me. What do I say? How does it work? Because I'm going crazy inside my own fuckin' head."

"Okay, okay. But breathe, first. And listen closely."

His hand still gripped my arm. And though I couldn't see, I knew his head was tipped toward mine. His breath came close and yes, I could smell the fear on it.

"Our Father," I said then, my words spoken slowly.

"Our Father?" I heard from beside me.

"That's right. Our Father, who art in heaven."

"Our Father, who are in—"

"Art. Who art *in heaven," I corrected him.*

"Our Father, who art in heaven."

"That's right. Think about it, man. Think of who you're talking to.

And of what you're saying." When I felt the motion of him nodding, I continued. "Hallowed be Thy name."

"Hallowed be Thy name."

"Okay." I paused, closed my eyes, then continued. "Thy kingdom come. Thy will be done."

"Thy will be done? Are you saying this shit here is God's will*?"*

"No. I'm saying you're going to do *God's will."*

"What? How? Look at this fucking nightmare we're in. I can't sleep, can't think. The whole place wants to just kill me. Where's God's will in that?"

"Listen. You want to believe in God or not? Because if you do, you believe in evil, *too. It exists as much as He does. And that out there?" I looked up at where I knew the sky was, even though I couldn't see it. Everything was black. Then I pointed toward the jungle. "That's evil. So there's both. Got it? Which is why you got to pray." When he said nothing, I went on. "On earth as it is in heaven."*

It came then, his voice; I had to strain to hear it. But he didn't give up on me.

"On earth as it is in heaven."

When we made it to the last line, when we said Deliver us from evil, well, he actually sobbed. That's right. A guttural sound came from him, one I don't know that I've ever heard before, as he said those words.

But I knew, shit I knew. He got it. He got the power of prayer. Understood that there was always someone to turn to who might deliver us from the jungle.

And that's how we spent that one night. Over and over and over again, reciting each line of The Lord's Prayer.

As Jason hears the priest say those very same lines now, leading them all in the recitation of The Lord's Prayer, he remembers his father's words early the next morning in the hospital. Like that night in Vietnam, when his father had recited the prayer over and over till dawn, his father also stayed with *Jason* until dawn.

To that soldier—someone who had zero faith, his father said, *none at all, I was rich. With my one little prayer. He made me see that I had a way out with it, a way to escape evil, or fear anyway.*

Every time he's said that prayer since, Jason remembers his father's story. That morning in the hospital, after his father went home, Jason lay in bed and looked down at his bandaged, decimated leg. Then he turned his head toward the light coming in through the window and whispered the words. At times since then, he's murmured the prayer in the dark of night, alone. When struggling to walk again. When overcoming a prescription-drug addiction. While sweeping up shards of a broken whiskey glass from the fireplace hearth.

Said it in bed; said it—head bowed—at the edge of the sea.

And standing here with Lauren, with Celia holding Aria beside him, and with Maris and the others in the pews behind him, he bows his head and whispers the prayer now, again.

thirty-seven

THIS TIME, ELSA'S RELIEVED NOT to be cooking. She's busy enough overseeing the caterer, as well as all the family and friends gathered at her beach inn after the christening. On the sweeping lawn, a long planked table the silver color of driftwood is set beneath a white canopy. For that, she's so glad. The sun's been warm, and the canopy kept them all shaded during dinner. Now, the catering staff lights tea candles nestled among white hydrangeas and greens across the center of the table. Dessert silverware set on linen napkins sparkles beneath the candle flames.

Just beyond the table, the Ocean Star Inn rises against a blue sky. The inn's shingles glow golden in the late-afternoon sunshine. In the windows, thin white starfish are propped in random panes, and lace curtains hang limp, waiting for a sea breeze. On the upper-level deck off the infamous back room, more candles glimmer in hanging Mason jars. Elsa imagines that once the sun sets, the jukebox will play and intimate starlit dancing will happen there.

But for now, everyone—everyone she loves—gathers on the wide veranda. They linger there, talking, laughing. Kyle, tie loosened, leans on the railing with Vinny; Celia, her auburn hair in a low chignon, sits with Lauren on a white wicker settee. Jason, suit jacket long gone and shirtsleeves cuffed back, relaxes on the porch swing with Maris, who is holding Aria, the baby's christening gown draped across Maris' lap.

When Taylor eventually lifts Aria to bring her to the guest cottage for a nap, the baby's gown hangs in soft, satiny folds. Elsa remembers holding her nieces in that very same christening gown so many, many years ago. Visions come to her then, of everyone gathered after church in her sister June's dining room … beneath a sparkling chandelier.

Like all those years ago, the sight of family and friends is before her again. She pauses to take it all in, knowing how fleeting moments like this are—which makes them all the more beautiful.

Just then, she jumps when someone takes her arm.

"I want to show you something," Cliff says from behind her. "Follow me."

Elsa does, holding Cliff's hand as he leads her around the inn's vast side yard, past her hydrangea gardens, alongside sweeping dune grasses to an expansive stretch of green lawn overlooking the distant Long Island Sound.

But there's more.

At the very edge of the lawn, a long row of white Adirondack chairs faces the blue water. Each chair is meticulously aligned, armrest to armrest, with enough chairs to seat the whole gang. It's what Elsa's been waiting for this past year—since losing Sal—seeing a sight like this that is filled with only happiness. Because today, all is good, and her loved ones will linger in these chairs, at the edge of the sea.

"You did this?" she asks Cliff.

He nods. "Jason, too. Early this morning."

"It's perfect. The perfect way to end a wonderful day."

What it does, that thought, is this: The whole way back to the dining table, Elsa can't stop smiling. Watching everyone take their seats again, their easy talk continuing as they eat ice cream and pastries while drinking coffee, she smiles through it all. By the time second cups are poured and it's time for Celia to open Aria's christening gifts, Elsa still smiles.

"Mine first," she says. Before giving Celia the gift, though, Elsa leans over and hugs her close. "Oh, Cee," she whispers into her ear. "How I love you and Aria both. And I'm so glad you're here."

Celia, teary eyed, opens the wrapped gift and lifts out two etched-star pendants on braided gold chains. Elsa takes one, stands behind Celia and clasps it around her neck.

"My goodness," Celia says, looking up at Elsa and squeezing her hand. "It's so beautiful."

So Elsa sits beside her again. She reaches over and touches the shimmering pendant. "One for you, one for Aria when she's older. Because you are both now a part of a very special constellation." Elsa tugs up her own chain from behind her blouse and shows the gold star pendant. As she does, Eva and Maris lift their star pendants, too. "You see … we're all connected."

Each thoughtful christening gift moves Celia, from the star necklaces to summery baby sunbonnets; from a pretty white child's prayer book to a fluffy stuffed bunny with floppy ears and a stitched smile.

But the gift from Aria's godmother, Lauren, takes her breath away. Celia holds it up for all to see. On a watercolor seascape, Lauren had painted silver ocean stars, then mounted the painting in a driftwood frame.

"You are my *very* best beach friend," Celia whispers as she hugs Lauren. "And I know right where I'll hang this, beside Aria's crib. She's napping now, Taylor's with her."

"I know, hon," Lauren says.

"But as soon as she's awake," Celia insists, "this is going straight into her room."

When Celia begins thanking everyone for the gifts, Jason stands and raises his hand. He takes a small present from Maris and walks around the table.

"A little something for Aria, special from me. The godfather."

"But, Jason," Celia says. "The trinket box from you and Maris is gorgeous. It'll hold Aria's star necklace. So I don't understand."

"You will." He sets down the gift, along with an envelope, and gives Celia's shoulder a squeeze before returning to his seat.

Celia watches him, then opens his note. She reads it silently, first, then presses it to her heart and closes her eyes against her tears.

"Celia?" Elsa asks beside her.

After nodding and taking a deep breath, Celia clears her throat and lifts the note.

"*Dear Celia,*" she reads, then pauses and pats her heart before looking down at Jason's handwriting again. "*To live as though you've grabbed the brass ring is to be able to smile, each day. Somehow, in some way. It's what Sal would've wished for his daughter, that brass-ring kind of life. There's nothing he ever wanted more than to see the people he loved smile. My wish for Aria, too, is that. When she looks upon this brass ring one day, may she hear her father's whisper … Sorridi. –Jason*"

After gently pulling wrapping paper off the small box, Celia opens the lid and lifts a short silver ribbon. Looped through it, on the other end, is the shiny brass ring Jason grabbed at the Sound View Carousel. The ring has been shined, polished and engraved with her daughter's name: *Aria Gray.*

Clutching the note and special ribboned charm, Celia walks around the table, arms outstretched. When Jason stands, she hugs him, so touched by his simple wish … a life of smiles for her and Sal's daughter.

"Thank you," she whispers close, before stepping back and turning to everyone at the table. "Thank you, *all* of you, for making this day so very, very special."

On her way back to her seat, Celia taps Cliff's shoulder and whispers in his ear. When he nods and walks to the inn's grand front porch, Celia waits until he quickly returns. In his hand is one of the Mason jars that held a burning candle there. He blows out the candle, removes it and gives her the empty jar.

"Excellent," she says as she sits again.

"Anything else?" Cliff asks. When she tells him no, he wanders over to the guys. They're stoking driftwood logs in a stone fire pit on the lawn, marshmallows close at hand.

"Celia?" Elsa asks. "Is this what I think it is?"

Celia nods. "And I hope you ladies will help me fill it." She snaps a small hydrangea blossom from a vase on the table, then tucks it into the Mason jar. "It's Aria's first happiness jar."

And just like that, the women reach for ribbons from the giftwrap, and a seashell from the centerpiece, and wispy blades of nearby dune grass, all of which get tucked into the jar. When it's almost full, Celia adds one last item. After reading Jason's personal note once more, she folds it, carefully presses the paper in the jar, and gently drops the brass ring inside, too.

thirty-eight

IT DOESN'T SURPRISE JASON WHEN everyone walks over to the Adirondack chairs he and Cliff had set out. Because it's that early evening hour, when the low light gives a rich depth to the green lawn, the distant blue seawater. The white chairs are stark against that blue … and it all beckons. All you want to do is be a *part* of that sight. Pick a chair, sit right down and breathe in that sweet salt air.

To Jason, beneath the late-day sun, those slatted backs of the empty chairs look simply like a photograph in an old, dog-eared album—a picture you'd run a finger across while gazing at it, remembering the good times of some summer evening.

Now, drawn to those chairs, they all cross the lawn: Kyle and Lauren, Matt and Eva, Paige and Vinny, Elsa and Cliff, Nick, Maris and himself. Most hold a glass of wine, some a plate of biscotti. Talk comes easy, laughter aplenty. In their summer dresses, the women leave their shoes behind and walk barefoot across the cool grass. The guys long ago pulled off their ties, undid shirt buttons, rolled back sleeves. There are enough white chairs for the whole gang, and each of them settles into one.

Kyle, holding a plate heaped with dessert seconds, sits with a sigh. "Ah, bliss," he says while taking in the blue water before him. "Beach bliss."

Vinny leans forward and motions to Elsa. "With these seats, you'll *never* get us to leave. Or your future inn guests, either." He rests his head back on the Adirondack chair before taking hold of Paige's hand beside him.

"It is nice, isn't it?" Elsa vaguely asks. It's obvious by her gentle tone that the sight of blue water, and deepening blue sky, has mesmerized her, too.

"Absolutely," Kyle says as he forks a hunk of some farm-fresh berry pie covered with whipped cream. "Since living here at Stony Point, something about this salt air gives me an appetite for *everything*. Food, lovin' … life!"

Their easy banter goes on as the horizon turns red, then fades to lavender. All the while, Maris talks about what she's working on in Neil's novel. And Lauren shares a photo her mother just texted her while babysitting. It's of Hailey and Evan holding their freshly painted sand pails. Nick agrees to take Cliff for a boat ride soon, in his little Whaler. Vinny deliberates going for an evening swim; it's that warm out still. And Kyle challenges him to a night race to the raft.

They don't go, though. Because the view from their white Adirondack chairs facing sky and sea keeps them seated, their voices quieting as wine is sipped, biscotti dunked, light kisses stolen, including Jason pulling Maris closer—his lips grazing the side of her face.

Something about it all—the whole evening, Jason thinks—is an ending. A *good* ending. Last summer, Sal's death flung their world off its axis. And it's taken this long, this many months, this many days of confusion and memories and resistance as they fought the truth of his absence, as they tried to hold onto some essence of him, before they finally made it back here again.

To the comfortable place they were in when Sal sat among them last summer. He'd insisted they were the luckiest people he knew to have this beach life … and each other. *You folks are very blessed*, Sal said then.

"Hello!" Celia calls from behind them now.

They turn, but no one gets up. Instead Celia walks over in her long sundress, the fabric fluttering like a wave around her legs. All smiles, she holds Aria on her hip.

"Everybody," Celia says as she rounds the front of the chairs and looks down the line of faces. "Say goodnight to Aria! It's bedtime."

As Celia walks along in front of the chairs, hands reach up to squeeze Aria's tiny foot, and clasp Celia's arm. Lauren stands and gives the baby a small hug. Elsa does, too, leaving a kiss on her granddaughter's cheek. Cliff salutes Celia and her baby, before finally, Maris and Jason stand and walk with Celia back toward her guest cottage. They talk about the day, the abundance of food, and the christening ceremony, before saying their goodnights near Celia's front porch.

The sun has set now, and Jason links his fingers with Maris' as they return across the inn's lawn to the others. A heavy waning moon rises over the water. The moonlight casts ocean stars on the gentle ripples of the calm Sound. A mist rises, too, as the air slightly cools from the heat of day.

"It was so nice being with everyone like this," Maris softly says, leaning into Jason.

He slips his arm around her waist as they approach the Adirondack chairs, where everyone is still settled in. Tiki torches flicker nearby; the murmur of voices carries in the salt air.

"Wait a second." Maris stops before they get to the chairs. She points toward the beach. "Jason, I think someone's there. Want to take a walk over?"

He looks to the main beach and sees that one lone cottage. A few of the upstairs windows are filled with golden lamplight.

Maris squeezes his hand. "We can go now and try to talk to whoever it is. Because who knows when they'll ever be back."

Jason steps closer and squints into the dark. He can make out the shadow of a vehicle parked beyond the cottage, so someone is definitely there.

"I'll go with you," Maris tells him. She tugs his arm now. "We'll cut through Elsa's secret path to the beach."

"No."

"No?"

Jason doesn't move. He simply looks at the distant vast shadow on that moonlit beach. The mystery cottage is merely a black silhouette on the sand. And though lamplight fills some windows, most remain dark.

"No," he says again.

"Why not?"

Jason glances at Maris, then back to the cottage. "I left a very clear voicemail for the woman who talked with Eva last spring. It's been a few days now, since I called. And I never heard back."

"Nothing?"

He shakes his head while watching the cottage first, then looking again to all those white chairs where his friends and family sit. They're relaxed, at ease, sipping wine. While talking, some lean into others; shoulders are nudged; hands held.

If he had to name it, that sight alone is contentment … an easy calm awaiting him and Maris in their empty chairs. A plain happiness.

Which can unnerve him, too. Because he learned years ago not to trust happiness. When you do, when you let your guard down and let that bliss in, life has a way of changing before your unsuspecting eyes. Of spinning out from beneath you.

He looks closely at his friends illuminated by the flickering light of the tiki torches around them. The flames cast dancing shadows that drop over a laughing face; a reclined pose; an animated conversation.

When he starts walking toward everyone seated with their drinks, Maris stops him.

"Babe. It's what you've been *waiting* for. Someone's in that cottage." She pulls him close, running her hands along his arms. "Are you *sure* you don't want to try to talk to them? Just a quick knock on their door, introduce yourself?"

"I'm sure." Jason tips up her face and kisses her lightly, then takes her hand and leads her back to their seats. Sitting again in a white chair beside Maris, beneath the darkening sky filled with tiny stars, he looks out at Long Island Sound and hears a noise then. A small boat putters on the water. Probably someone doing a little night fishing, a little drifting—and he thinks of Sal.

Of Salvatore DeLuca, who with all his riches, wanted nothing more than what he could not have.

This. Time with a group of friends and loved ones hanging out beside the sea.

"We can go for just a few minutes." Maris leans over from her chair and whispers, "Everyone here would understand."

"No, sweetheart. Because right now?" Jason asks,

motioning to their friends. "This is where we all need to be."

Yes, for Sal, Jason does it.

He holds onto this moment of happiness like he held onto that shiny brass carousel ring. If only for today.

The beach friends' journey continues in

CASTAWAY COTTAGE

The next novel in The Seaside Saga from

New York Times Bestselling Author

JOANNE DEMAIO

Also by Joanne DeMaio

The Seaside Saga

(In order)

1) Blue Jeans and Coffee Beans

2) The Denim Blue Sea

3) Beach Blues

4) Beach Breeze

5) The Beach Inn

6) Beach Bliss

7) Castaway Cottage

8) Night Beach

9) Little Beach Bungalow

10) Every Summer

–And More Seaside Saga Books–

Summer Standalone Novels

True Blend

Whole Latte Life

Winter Novels

Eighteen Winters

First Flurries

Cardinal Cabin

Snow Deer and Cocoa Cheer

Snowflakes and Coffee Cakes

For a complete list of books by *New York Times* bestselling author Joanne DeMaio, visit:

Joannedemaio.com

About the Author

JOANNE DEMAIO is a *New York Times* and *USA Today* bestselling author of contemporary fiction. The novels of her ongoing and groundbreaking Seaside Saga journey with a group of beach friends, much the way a TV series does, continuing with the same cast of characters from book-to-book. In addition, she writes winter novels set in a quaint New England town. Joanne lives with her family in Connecticut.

For a complete list of books and for news on upcoming releases, please visit Joanne's website. She also enjoys hearing from readers on Facebook.

Author Website:
Joannedemaio.com

Facebook:
Facebook.com/JoanneDeMaioAuthor

Made in the USA
Las Vegas, NV
02 May 2025

21636946R00215